THE LAST RESORT

COMING BACK TO MEXICO

THE LAST RESORT

COMING BACK TO MEXICO

A Novel

JAMES R. DAVIS

Santa Fe

Sunstone books may be purchased for educational, business, or sales promotional use. For information please write: Special Markets Department, Sunstone Press, P.O. Box 2321, Santa Fe, New Mexico 87504-2321.

eBook 978-1-63293-462-8

Library of Congress Cataloging-in-Publication Data

Names: Davis, James R., 1936- author.
Title: The last resort : a novel / James R. Davis.
Description: Santa Fe : Sunstone Press, [2023] | Summary: "Angry about losing his dream, Marquito returns to Mexico and takes a job at a five star resort where he meets elderly time-share owners, Vera and Ollie, who discover new life in old age as they help him escape the influence of a runaway, red-haired, radical and find his better self and true love"-- Provided by publisher.
Identifiers: LCCN 2022056807 | ISBN 9781632934628 (paperback) | ISBN 9781611396928 (epub)
Subjects: LCGFT: Novels.
Classification: LCC PS3604.A9587 L37 2023 | DDC 813.6--dc23/eng/2022127
LC record available at https://lccn.loc.gov/2022056807

WWW.SUNSTONEPRESS.COM
SUNSTONE PRESS / POST OFFICE BOX 2321 / SANTA FE, NM 87504-2321 /USA
(505) 988-4418

The Last Resort is dedicated to my wife, Adelaide Bouchardet Davis, who died several months before the publication of this novel in its revised form. Her assistance with the story, with technology, photography, and language is deeply respected and very much appreciated. In addition, I also dedicate this book to the many hard-working waiters, bellhops, maids, spa attendants, gardeners, front desk clerks, and scheduling coordinators who became our friends and taught us about the Mexico we came to love. Bless the dreamers who have lost their dreams and found new ones.

1

MARCO'S LOST DREAM

Marco awakens to the blast of the boat's horn. Then another. Passengers are scurrying around like rats, packing up their stuff, making preparations to disembark. He gets up from where he has been sitting and lurches over to a window to look out at the harbor, but he can't tell where he is. He just knows it's time to get off.

He lugs his stuff down a narrow passageway of steep stairs, enters the cavernous hull, and searches for the exit onto the pier. He joins the mass of passengers walking along beside the slow-motion string of cars creeping cautiously off the ferry. He follows a crowd of poor Mexicans, resisting the idea that he is one of them. As he nears the ticket office, he notices the parked cars and line of passengers waiting to board the ferry for the return voyage. Looks like everyone wants to be somewhere besides where they are. He can't imagine going back to the place he just came from, but then, he has no assurance that where he is going will be any better. The truth is, he doesn't know exactly where he is and has no idea where he is going. Finally, he spots a sign at the harbor that identifies the place as La Paz. Yeah, still Mexico, that's for sure.

He took the car ferry as a walk-on passenger from Mazatlán across the Sea of Cortéz without knowing its exact destination. He just knew he wanted to get the hell out of where he was and start over. He sucks in a deep breath of fresh air and enjoys the breeze from the sea blowing on his face. On the busy street corner at the entrance to the ferry dock, he spots a little kiosk and asks for a map of Baja. He opens it up and finds La Paz on the east coast of the Baja Península. The city is marked with a little star so it must be the capital of something. He learned the U. S. states and capitals in school back in Albuquerque. His parents tried to teach him the ones in Mexico, too, but he could only remember two states, the dog, Chihuahua, and the hot sauce, Tabasco.

La Paz is not where he wants to be. The fine resorts with the job postings are in Cabo San Lucas and San Jose del Cabo. He folds up the map and returns it to the guy working the kiosk. Marco asks about the bus station and the guy motions across the street with a single nod of his head, as if raising his arm to point might use up the last bit of his energy for the day.

Marco looks like an overgrown abandoned child standing alone in the run-down bus station lobby with the sum total of his worldly possessions stuffed into a beat-up backpack and shabby duffel bag.

"You need help," a man says in Spanish.

For God's sake, yes, he needs help. The guy has the look of a comedian, a perpetual joker, waiting for the right opportunity to tease. But then Marco suddenly realizes that he is the one who must look comical—tall and half-starved like a scarecrow, a gaunt worried look on his face, unshaven, disheveled. Not a good first impression. Not his true self.

The man asks him, "Where are you going?"

Marco says, "I don't know for sure. I'm looking for work at a resort."

"You need good English to be a waiter at a resort."

So, he introduces himself in English as Marco González and tells him, "I washed a lot of dishes in Mazatlán. I think I could be a waiter."

"Very nice English, man. I'm Omar."

"I lived in the U. S. for ten years."

"I'll try not to hold that against you. Just kidding, man." He shrugs. "Okay, what you need to do is get this big blue bus right here for Cabo San Lucas. Takes about three hours."

"What about you? Where are you going?" Marco asks.

"Oh, I've been visiting my grandmother here in La Paz for the weekend. She makes the best tamales in Mexico, and—no offense quierda abuela—but it's worth the price of the bus ticket just for her food. But now I'm going back to my parents' place in Cabo."

They buy their tickets, board the bus, and sit together. Slipping in and out of Spanish, they talk for a while, and then Marco asks Omar where he works.

"Sunset Point Resort. Come to think of it, one of the waiters there just got fired two days ago. Totally slipped my mind. Not the guy's fault really. He just got into a nasty confrontation with El Greco—that's what we call the captain, his name's actually Constantino—so now the waiter is history and there's an opening."

"Really? You think I might have a chance?"

"As much as anyone else if you don't mind working for an asshole."

"Oh, that sounds promising."

"Tell you what. You probably need a place to stay, right?"

"Well, yeah, but I don't want to be a problem."

"I stay with my parents. They have an old sofa where you can spend the night if you don't mind sharing it with my ugly sister. Just kidding, amigo. Don't look so shocked. Mexican hospitality."

"Well, I am kind of desperate."

"So is my sister," Omar says laughing, putting Marco at ease. "No, here's the thing. You can come out to Sunset Point with me in the morning and look the place over. You like it, I introduce you to the manager, not El Greco, the one who does the hiring."

"Awesome."

Marco's first impression of Sunset Point Resort is that it is the nicest place he's seen since he left the U.S. Maybe even nicer. Massive tan and brown trim buildings are arranged in a big horseshoe, rows and rows of rooms stacked one floor over the next, little balconies with what must be fantastic ocean views. It's nicely landscaped with native plants and palm trees and spotlessly clean because workers can be seen constantly sweeping and mopping and painting the place. Everything shines, nothing broken or run down. The food and beverage manager shows him the room for indoor dining when it is a little too chilly or hot for the guests and takes him down the steps to the busy outdoor dining space overlooking the beach and the sea. The ocean has a beautiful shade of aqua in the bright morning sun. Too bad about the huge cruise ships blocking the view of the mountain range sinking into the sea, but as the supervisor points out, those liners keep downtown Cabo prosperous. He takes Marco up a curvy walkway to meet the "ladies of the lobby," as he calls them, the concierge staff and front desk clerks, and then on over to Human Resources where Marco has to fill out the paper work to apply. He and the manager come back past the swimming pools, each one flowing into the next with a waterfall effect. His eyes can't help drifting over the tan legs of the good-looking American girls in their bikinis, lying leisurely on lounge chairs carefully arranged around the pools. He has to remind himself that most of the guests are older, I mean, they would have to have a shitload of money to afford this place. Besides he's sure the young girls are off limits to waiters.

The manager recognizes immediately how fluent Marco's English is, and he seems to be equally impressed with his good high school education in the U.S. Anyway, the guy is nice and seems to like him. So, after a brief interview, Marco finds out he has the job. Not only the job, but a free breakfast. He thanks the manager, who takes him back down to the open-air part of the restaurant to meet the captain of the wait staff, an unfriendly Greek guy, who speaks poor English and no Spanish. So, this is Constantino. When Marco is free of him, he finds Omar to thank him and tell him his good news.

Omar is all smiles. "Congratulations, amigo. Maybe you told them you were Slim's nephew?"

"Who?"

"The richest man in Mexico. Maybe the world."

"Oh, that Slim. No, I told the guy I had worked for El Chucky. Just kidding. I would never say that," Marco tries to joke back. He's just relieved to have a job and a free breakfast. Omar takes him downstairs through the tunneled hallways to the windowless cafeteria where the staff can sit down to eat.

"Enjoy. Just watch out for El Greco. He can be a real jerk. Just say, yes, sir, and yes, ma'am, and do what he says."

And "yes, sir," and "yes, ma'am" is what Marco has been saying ever since, not only to El Greco, but to everyone, mainly the guests. He can hardly believe the whole month of September has already passed. Back in the U.S. he would have started at the university. He would be studying for midterm exams. Shit, no chance of that now. At first, he was glad to have his job at Sunset Point, actually any job that wasn't selling shoes or washing dishes, and to have decent food and an apartment. But after a few days, when the newness of being a waiter wore off and the mindless boredom set in, he realized once again that he was going nowhere, and the old frustration and anger roared back to life inside him.

Sitting in his one room hell hole of an apartment, he tries to write to his parents. He has no desk or table, just a chair. The computer he had when he was in high school barely functions and there is no internet access in this desolate dump, anyway. On some days there isn't even running water. So, he will mail them a note in his own handwriting. He bends a long leg over one knee—the portable fold-up human writing desk—to support the pad of yellow lined paper he is writing on, but so far, he hasn't written anything. He just chews his mechanical pencil. How can he possibly explain why he hasn't written? He's been here for over four weeks now. Away from home for three months.

Queridos Madre y Padre,

He starts out in Spanish, but his written Spanish sucks. Whatever he writes will be loaded with mistakes. Better to write in English. After so many years in the United States, his mother and father learned to read English well enough to get along, and besides, his older sister Dolores can help. They will understand if he keeps it simple. But will they understand what he has to say? That's just the problem; he can't say what he would really like to say, what he's really feeling.

I just want to let you know that I am safe here in Cabo San Lucas. I am working in the restaurant of a big resort as a breakfast waiter. Sorry I haven't written.

At least he can say that he has a job. That will make them happy. He just hasn't had the chance to write or phone. That's not true. He could have contacted them long before now, almost anytime, to let them know where he is. But he hasn't done so because he has been so totally disappointed and frustrated. And he wants to tell them that in a nice calm way, but he doesn't know how to do it without being disrespectful and ungrateful all over again. He could just send what he has written so far, but it seems rude to be so abrupt after so long. They won't like that. He needs to add a few more sentences. Try to tell them what he is feeling but without attacking them.

As you know, I had my heart set on going to college. Coming back to Mexico just as I graduated from high school made that impossible, and I need to tell you that I've had a hard time dealing with that.

Marco realizes that his letter sounds kind of formal, like he's writing to his high school guidance counselor. Even though his words are carefully chosen, they will only make his parents feel guilty. Well, they are responsible, even though his dad had no choice but to return. No work, no food, illegal, go home. He gets that, but it ruined his whole damn life.

Why can't he just tell them that? A hard time dealing with it? Come on. It's been horrible. He hasn't dealt with it, and the anger just keeps roaring around and around inside him, churning his stomach to nausea one day and his guts to diarrhea the next. Is that what he's supposed to tell them? Do they really need those details to understand how he feels? No. Like a good son, he needs to reassure them that he is safe, that he has a job, and that he is in good health. Leave it at that.

He gets up and retrieves a bottle of water from the mini-fridge. He takes two empty bottles to work each day and refills them with the pure water they serve to the guests. God knows what his sensitive Americanized gut would pick up from drinking Mexican water. Oh, man, it is so awful here in so many ways. It's hard to believe that a country can be so poor, its people so desperate. What is the famous saying? "Poor Mexico, so far from God and so close to the United States." Jesus, Dad, why did we have to come back?

Marco stares out of his only window. He tries not to look out there very often because the view is so depressing. The sun is setting, and it's growing dark inside. He flips the switch that turns on the single bulb hanging from the ceiling and the room turns from grimy gray to yellow beige. He needs to get a reading lamp. He can hardly see to read or write at night and that's when he has the most time. He sits down in the chair and picks up the yellow pad of paper. He should write something more.

> *I know you said that I could go to a university here in Mexico, but once we got back and I saw the cost and learned about the written entrance exams—in Spanish of course—I was sure it wouldn't work out. I knew I had to get a job, but the size and fast pace of Guadalajara overwhelmed me. That's why I left.*

A little better, but still not the truth. That's not why he left. He left after the big blowup. He wasn't sure he could control his rage after that mess. How could a pleasant family dinner turn into such a horrible yelling, screaming, crying session, full of accusations and recriminations that never should have been voiced? How could he have gone off like that? He'd never unloaded his frustrations on his parents like that before. It was shameful. And as if he wasn't feeling bad enough, his older sister, Dolores, kept edging him down with harsh words about what an ungrateful little shit he was. There was nothing else for him to do but leave, embarrassed and disgraced the way he was. Sorry wouldn't fix that.

He had so much going for himself in the U.S. People said he was handsome like his father. Girls found his tall frame attractive. He had a sweet, gorgeous girlfriend. English came easy to him and he was a good student. He was even a track star in his senior year. Popular. A leader. But what good was all of that U.S. high school crap in Guadalajara? What was he supposed to do? Become a bilingual interpreter for a drug cartel? He had to get out.

I am sorry I disappeared so suddenly and without even saying good bye. With the money from my last paycheck from the shoe store—I wasn't very good at selling shoes—I hopped a bus for Mazatlán to try to get a job in a restaurant there. You won't believe the stacks and stacks of dishes I washed.

In Mazatlán he lived in a room worse than this, hard as that may be to imagine. He looks around. This room has become like a frickin' prison to him. He hates to come here after work, but he's got to sleep somewhere and sleeping on the beach is not all that romantic when you are alone. He has nowhere else to go.

That's his problem: he has nowhere to go and no way to get there. He had a future in the U.S., a bright future actually, a shot at the American dream, such as it is, but it was snatched away before he could even attend his first college class. He'd filled out the application forms, he'd been admitted, and he had a scholarship. Now he has nothing.

From Mazatlán I came to Cabo and here I am. At least I have pleasant working conditions, and I even have my own apartment.

He reads over what he has written so far—"pleasant working conditions" and "my own apartment"—and hurls the pad of paper across the room like a Frisbee. It lands in the kitchen sink. He can't send his parents that bullshit. He's trapped. He wants to tell them what he feels, but he can't. He'd like to explain himself, but that's impossible. Especially not that blow-up. Does he think they don't remember the awful stuff he said? Has anything changed? No, he feels the same way he did when he left: hopeless, angry, and confused.

He rescues his pad of paper from the sink, rips off the two pages he has written and tosses them in the wastebasket. He crosses the room with his writing pad in hand, sits back down in the chair, and slides his mechanical pencil between his teeth. But he can't write any more tonight. Maybe tomorrow. Quizás mañana. He thinks about having to get up and go to work, having to wear that damn uniform, bowing and scraping to the guests, doing whatever the boss wants, no matter how ridiculous. And having to keep that silly smile on his face through it all. Don't forget to smile. El Greco checks to see if all his monkeys are smiling.

What a wretched existence, sitting here alone night after gloomy night, locked up with his angry feelings. The room is not the prison, he is the prison. What has come over him? This is not the cheerful, fun-loving guy he was in the United States. He misses his high school friends. And Michelle. He has no real friends here. Not yet, anyway, except for Omar. Omar has been really good to him. But he's just another smiling waiter with no future.

2

VERA AND OLLIE MEET MARCO

"Are you...a...bathing suit?"

From his study, Oliver can tell by the inflection that Vera is calling out a question, but he can't hear what she's actually saying. Why does she do this? Now he has to put his book down and get up from his comfortable recliner to go find her. Rain is pelting the windows and splattering the driveway. At least there is no snow yet. He locates her in the bedroom where she is packing her suitcase. "What are you asking?"

"I asked if you were taking a bathing suit."

"Honey, we always take our bathing suits. The resort has three pools, four hot tubs, a sea, and an ocean. Why do you ask?"

"Because I look so completely frumpy now in this old maillot."

"Do you need a new one?"

"No, I need a new body. Look at this loose skin from my thighs drooping over my knees. And my hideous blue veins. Wrinkles on my forehead like a plowed field."

Oliver smiles at his wife. "My grandmother used to tell my mother to never look in a mirror and to hold her head so high she wouldn't see what was below her shoulders."

"Wonderful advice, Ollie. Get serious. I'm old."

"So was my grandmother. But you are lovely, dear. Each year you look younger than I do, because I am aging more rapidly than you."

"Stop it."

"Besides, love, at our age it doesn't matter." He pulls up his trouser legs, both of them, to the knees. "Look at me. I have one leg that is hairy and the other one looks like a plucked chicken. You could entertain yourself all morning playing Connect the Dots with the brown spots on my back. Would you like to see my back?" She frowns. "But here's the good news:

no one notices us anymore. I don't think a woman has looked at me in ten years."

"That's not true, Ollie. Women still look at you. I know. I watch out for my interests."

"Well, I say that by now we've earned the right to wear what we want, and if people don't like what they see, they can look the other way. If you need to purchase a new bathing suit, for heaven's sake, dear, let's go get you one."

"Oh, Lord, I can't go through that torture and humiliation. Besides, we leave tomorrow. I'll just take this one."

"Good. May I go back to my reading?" he grumbles amiably.

Vera is packing for the two weeks stay in November at their time share in Cabo San Lucas, Mexico. Such a lovely place. Paradise. That's what she called it on their very first visit, and that's what they have been calling it ever since. She loves to recall how they bought their first unit. Oliver told his assistant at the law office that he wanted to surprise his wife with a vacation in Mexico. The next thing he knew, Sarah was on the internet, looking up resorts. "Where?" she asked. "Acapulco? Mazatlán? Get me started." Ollie told her Cabo San Lucas because he remembered seeing a huge picture in the airport of an immense rock with an arch in it. In no time at all, three of the staff were arguing about which place would be best for Oliver and Vera: a hotel closer to town, a villa on the Pacific side, or a five-star resort on the bay. They found a good promotional for three nights and four days—that was about all the time he could take away from the office in those days—and they ended up at the five-star, Sunset Point Resort. Naturally they both had to listen to the sales pitch for time shares in order to get such a good deal, and as the discussion progressed, she became more and more interested, asking questions about the privileges, the maintenance fees, and the financing. When the salesperson excused herself to go to the bathroom, Oliver nearly jumped across the table. "What are you doing? You're acting like we're going to buy this."

"We are," she replied calmly. "I have a job, too, you know. Have you forgotten that I have a small savings? A credit card? I'm buying it for you. You need a place to go to get away from the firm. Besides, what are you going to do when you retire?" When the salesperson returned, she found Vera's credit card on top of the paperwork. "The studio, if you please, as we discussed." And that was that. Seven years ago. My, how time flies, except in "paradise" where it nearly stands still.

Each time that Vera and Ollie visited Cabo in the next three years, they upgraded to a larger unit, added a week, or changed to a fixed week or unit. Eventually they became four-star elite members—she doesn't particularly like the term—and they use their membership four times a year now that Oliver is "semi-retired." She hopes they can continue to go there together for a few more years at least. He is so sweet, so understanding. Surely it is not true that he's aging faster than she is.

Now distracted by thoughts of Mexico and growing old, Ollie has a little trouble settling back into his reading. Vera is the enthusiastic one in this marriage, and he is glad to relinquish that responsibility to her, but every now and then he feels a little twinge of excitement, too, enough at least to disrupt his interest in his reading. He makes it a practice to block out an hour or so each day to concentrate on reading now that he is "semi-retired." He maintains a place in the practice but doesn't go to the office anymore. As a matter of fact, he doesn't have much of anything to do, and he could go downtown and see if his former colleagues have any need for him, but he's afraid they won't. He would just be a nuisance. So, he reads.

Three years ago, when he became "semi-retired"—he never tells anyone that he's actually retired—they sold their spacious old brick and sandstone house in Denver and moved into a small home on the northern edge of Golden, an old-west Colorado town nestled up against the foothills of the Rockies and best known as the home of Coors Beer. Easy access to the mountains, an authentic small town, not a suburb, and best of all, one of those maintenance-free deals like a condominium, so there's no snow shoveling or yard work. Actually, he misses the yard work and snow shoveling. Sometimes he dreams up things to attend to around the house just to keep occupied. It's a good place for them, though, especially for Vera if something should happen to him. He doesn't particularly care for the look-alike, fake New England design, but at least the place is new, one of six recently completed single dwelling homes arranged around a quiet cul-de-sac. The neighbors are nice enough but not the kind of people he or Vera would want to get to know better after meeting them at the first and only Home Owners Association picnic. At the back of the property there is a walk out basement covered by a little deck upstairs with a view of the foothills. The only problem with their new residence is that there's nothing to do but sit on that deck and contemplate the meaning of one's existence. Retirement is fine, he tells Vera, but there's way too much time for solipsistic navel-gazing.

He puts his book down on the antique curly maple desk and goes back to the bedroom to pester Vera. Vera always has trouble packing for Cabo because she takes along so many presents for the employees of the resort she has befriended over the years. He doesn't like the extra suitcases, but he prides himself on being good natured, so he doesn't object. "Once a social worker, always a social worker," he says, nodding his head slightly, showing Vera that he comprehends how important the gift-giving is to her. It's not her fault that she has a big heart. She can't help but care about the people she meets in Mexico, and she is moved by the stories they relate about their ordinary but difficult lives. She has laid out the clothing and toys on the bed in neat stacks.

"What is all this stuff?" he asks, trying to sound a little grumpy.

"You know very well what it is, dear."

"No, I mean who is it for?"

"Well, the pants and tops are for Daniella's children, Cenia and Blanca. These are the toys for Rosita's children, a Lego set for Fernando and remote-control helicopter for the older boy, Solomón."

"I believe the helicopter was my idea," he says, floating around the room examining all of the stuff. What's this?"

"The pocket flashlight is for the evening waiter, Lino, and the three children's books are for the towel attendant, Ernesto."

"The one who gets up at five in the morning to attend his English class before work?"

"And stop scowling, Ollie. You know I wish I could take more."

He is not sure how she came to be assigned all of these cases or by whom, but he knows it has taken several years and he regards it as a more or less inevitable outgrowth of her former profession.

Vera awakens Ollie at four o'clock the next morning so that he can shave before they drive to DIA, Denver's international airport. By the time they park the car in an outlying lot, take the shuttle to the terminal, check in, go through security, grab a cup of cocoa, and get to the gate, Ollie looks exhausted. As soon as they are settled on the plane, he is asleep, even before they are airborne. Not Vera. She's too excited.

She rehearses in her mind what happens next: checking in through immigration, going to the baggage claim, snagging the guy with the big cart, loading on all of the suitcases, clearing customs, navigating the gauntlet of buzzards trying to sell time share deals, and finally getting outside into the sunshine. Cape Travel has their last name, Webster, on the list of transportation reservations, and from there it is an easy ride in the van to Cabo San Lucas along the new highway. Vera enjoys looking out at the five-pronged desert cactus native to the region and the colorful hillside gardens planted and watered by the resorts, and she cranes her neck for an occasional glimpse of the distant ocean. She finds a way to make conversation with the other passengers by asking them if it is their first visit to the region, while the motion of the van cradles Ollie in what looks to be a half-asleep and half-awake ecstasy.

Sunset Point Resort is within walking distance of town via the paved road that leads up to the resort's gated main entrance. Several resorts line the beach that curves eastward from the town marina, and Sunset Point is the last resort in that group before a long open stretch of beach along a broad bay. After that there is nothing bordering the shore but cactus, scrub brush, and arroyos, dried up riverbeds kept open by law for occasional floods known to be sudden and dangerous in an otherwise arid desert.

The van passes through the gate, revealing the inclined drive lined with hedges of pink and burgundy bougainvillea, and finally pulls into the big cobblestone circle in front of the lobby. Vera feels a surge of excitement, like an actress about to come on stage. She knows that as soon as the bellmen recognize them, there will be a flurry of "welcome-backs," and "bienvenidos," and "como-estás," and "how-have-you-been." Sure enough, the commotion commences. Sebastián opens the door and takes her hand to help her out. He hugs her and embraces Ollie. "Welcome, Señor Oily." Ollie never corrects the pronunciation of the staff. Óscar is already unloading the luggage and stacking it on a cart by the entry. Verónica, the Elite Concierge, suddenly appears to greet the new arrivals. Her face reminds Vera of the beauty of Salma Hayek, and she has the peppy personality and trim body that the management seems to require for the job. Her high heels click as she leads them inside through the automatic sliding glass doors. Vera loves the immense domed lobby with its prints of Frieda Kahlo paintings and copies of Diego Rivera murals. Hand-painted, brightly colored ceramic vases, like tall ginger jars, stand on the sparkling clean marble floor. A huge arrangement of fresh cut flowers on a glass top table invites inspection.

Ollie starts the registration process which has been all pre-arranged for their two fixed weeks in the assigned unit where they always stay on the seventh floor. When he has finished signing the discount cards and gathering up the slips for the Wi-fi and towels, Verónica leads them outside for a glimpse of the pools and palm trees and a breath of warm, sea-soaked fresh air. Ollie glances around. It is a huge engineering feat, the three huge wings of rooms arranged around the curvilinear swimming pools. Broad decks, meandering walkways, and almost every room with an ocean view. The owners had some smart architects and engineers for this project. It was built to withstand strong hurricanes and earthquakes.

"Look, Señor," Verónica points with pride to the new lounge chairs. "Much more comfortable." Her low alto voice seems misplaced in such a petite young woman.

"Good. The old ones used to kill my back." They do look new and fresh, a good addition.

"Everything is so lovely." Vera cups a pale-yellow hibiscus blossom in her hand. "I see that the palm trees have grown into adults now." She stretches back to see their tops and shades her eyes. Then she glances at Verónica, frowns, and whispers to Ollie that there is still no engagement ring on Verónica's finger.

"What's that?" Verónica asks in her low voice.

"I was just saying that everything looks freshly watered,"

"Yes, it's been very dry."

"Such a beautiful oasis," Ollie observes.

And Vera adds, "Paradise, indeed."

Óscar arrives at their room with their luggage shortly after they do, and Ollie gives him a good tip. He gives everyone a good tip. It's the least he can do. The suite is so familiar now it seems like a second home. They don't use the kitchen much, but everything is there just in case he has an overwhelming urge to whip up some fried chicken, but that's unlikely because the restaurants at the resort serve such delectable dishes. Not to mention the traditional Mexican fare in town. No need to cook. The large dining table in the living area, unused for dining, becomes their shared office, although they don't have much to do. A place for Vera's laptop and his Kindle. Not a real office. As they move into the bedroom, Vera throws open the drapes to let the sun shine through the gauzy white curtains onto the huge king bed. A sizable Jacuzzi adjoining the spacious bathroom goes to waste on old folks. The tile floors are gleaming and the beige walls with dark wood trim are unblemished. The art, trying to be both traditional and modern, doesn't quite work out, but who is he to say? When the suitcases are unpacked, and their sparse wardrobe is divided between the closet and top drawers of the chest, Ollie slides open the patio door, and they sit for a moment around the table out on the balcony to take in the view of the azure sky, the turquoise ocean, and the jagged mountain range that plunges into the sea out by the arch. They sip glasses of wine poured from the bottle that came in their welcome package, a tradition now upon arrival.

After a moment, Ollie asks, in a solemn voice, "Why do they dote on us like that? It seems like a bit much. I can't remember how it all got started. Is it because we have that Elite membership status?

"No, no. We treat them like human beings," Vera says in a soft, humble, matter-of-fact tone. "We are interested in other people, dear."

"Well, yes, presumably that's true. But why such a fuss over us?"

"Maybe it's because we don't think of them only as bellmen, waiters, and maids. We go beyond the social roles and remember their names. We want to know about their families. We ask how their day is going."

"Well, yes, but I should think that the other guests are doing that, too."

"Oh, they are polite and appreciative, I am sure, but most of them simply lack the knack for caring, for breaking through to the person behind the job."

"Seems odd. Maybe it's your background in social work, dear. You're a trained listener."

"Oh, Lord, Ollie, you don't need a master's degree in social work to let people know you care about them."

"As a lawyer I was trained to argue in public and represent adversaries as they bicker with one another. You're trained to draw people out, to listen for their feelings, and you're damn good at it."

"Well, Señor Oily, I think you're good at it, too."

"Perhaps. But it's not a natural thing with me. I have to work at it. Seriously, it's not." Ollie runs a hand through what's left of his thinning white hair. It's baffling to him that something so simple as caring should be so difficult.

Vera made sure that their fixed unit would be on the top floor, so there would be no noise above them or anything dripping on them. Once, before they had their own unit, they awoke suddenly in the wee hours of the morning to a veritable cascade, the unfortunate result of a stone drunk couple having left the water running in their Jacuzzi, before, during, or after their little orgy, who knows. When the maintenance service men were unable to rouse them, they entered with their master key and found them passed out and naked. Water everywhere. Still running. Ah, those pleasure-seeking American Puritans. Damn lucky they didn't drown.

At night, the sound of waves rolling up on the beach carries up to their seventh-floor room and wafts through the open patio door on a cool breeze that tosses the curtains. After a day of travel and busy week of preparation, their sleep is deep and uninterrupted. The next morning Vera wakens Ollie, as he likes her to do, to tell him to get up and shave, and then she snoozes for an extra half hour. Is this why women have a longer life expectancy, because they sleep longer? They don't shave every day? They both take a brisk walk around the entire resort—three separate hotels, same ownership—before stopping into the restaurant for breakfast.

"Good morning, María." Vera greets the hostess by name. "I'm glad you're still here."

"Oh, yes. I'm here. It's good to have you back. Outside as usual?"

"Yes, thank you for remembering."

"I will seat you with Marquito. He's the handsome one over there. I'm sure Marquito will take good care of you."

Vera and Ollie are seated at one of Marquito's tables under the massive awning that covers the outdoor dining area overlooking the sea at La Casona, the restaurant where they take their breakfast and dinner. Lunch consists of salted peanuts from a can and squares of dark chocolate eaten at the table on their balcony, but only if they get growly stomachs. Although they have just been seated, Ollie invites Vera to join him at the iron railing next to their table to take a look at the waterfront. Standing arm and arm like two honeymooners, they gaze silently across the beach toward the spot out by the arch where the Sea of Cortéz touches the Pacific Ocean. On the beach, the relentless hawkers, clad in white, are already trudging along in the loose sand, carrying their blankets, black cases of silver jewelry, and brightly painted bowls of various shapes and sizes. One guy has a pile of different kinds of sombreros stacked on his head. The sea is filled with water taxis, jet skis, paddle boards, and kayaks. Two boats some distance apart trailing colorful parachutes offer para-sailing to early morning adventurers. Joggers and walkers make their way at their own speed. Two children are playing in the sand, toy pails and shovels in hand. Gulls float effortlessly on the updrafts, a pelican cruises inches from the surface of the sea, and fluttering sparrows seek table crumbs at the restaurant, each species sustaining and enjoying life in its own way. An annoying cruise liner is just pulling in to anchor in the harbor for the day. In the distance, the luminous mountains rise up from the ocean to touch a cloudless sky.

Vera and Ollie return to their cushioned wrought iron chairs and sit quietly enjoying each other's presence, waiting for Marquito to appear. Sometimes Vera wonders if strangers think them to be unhappily married because they have so little to say to each other. But what is there, really, left to say after all of these years? Even so, she's glad when Ollie puts an arm around her as he did just then when they were standing at the railing enjoying the view together.

Vera spots a tall young man making his way toward their table, the one María identified as Marquito. He stands a short distance from them now, broad shouldered and trim, exchanging a few friendly words in Spanish with another waiter. His sharp jaw is clean shaven, his neatly trimmed black hair glistens and his eyes—such fine eyes—sparkle with intelligence. His skin is a lovely tone of light brown. Surely there is nothing wrong with a little eye candy for an old lady.

When Marquito is free to attend to them, he comes to their table, and Vera greets him with "Buenos días. ¿Como estás?"

"Mui bien. ¿Ustedes?" He bows slightly and repeats mechanically the mandatory mantra in English: "My name is Marco, and I will be your waiter this morning."

Vera enjoys the customary exchange of greetings in Spanish, but she can see that there is no need for it because Marco's English is without accent. Why does the hostess, María, call him Marquito? He's not short. Maybe because he's so cute. "It's nice to meet you, Marco," Vera says, using what seems to be his preferred name. "I'm Vera and this is my husband Ollie."

Marco looks surprised at the formal introductions. "May I bring you something to drink while you examine the menu?"

"Oh, we don't need the menu," Vera says. "But yes, please, decaf and orange juice. Ollie, what about you?"

"Decaf and cranberry, please."

Marco looks surprised again at their politeness.

Vera asks, "Are you new here? I don't recall..."

"I've been here about three months now. You come here often?"

"Well, we have fixed weeks in late November and February. Then we use our summer weeks at various times. It's a little complicated."

Marco hustles off to get their drinks, leaving Vera and Ollie to speculate. "With that flawless English," Vera says, "he must have lived in the U.S., wouldn't you say, dear?"

"You could ask him."

"I wonder why he came back to Mexico?"

"Returning would be difficult, wouldn't it?"

"He seems bright."

"There's that social worker's eagerness to spot promise," he grins.

Marco returns quickly with their drinks and asks what he can get for them. "Are you having the buffet or something from the menu?"

"Actually," Vera says, "we always order the same thing and it's not exactly on the menu."

"Whatever you like, ma'am. I'm sure I can get it for you."

"Well, we get a large plate of mixed fruits: melons, papaya, pineapple, whatever you have for today." It looks like Marco doesn't need to write anything down. He just listens intently.

"And then," Ollie adds, "we each like to have a granola and a small container of plain yogurt, please."

"No problem. I'll remember. Tomorrow, too, if you sit at my table."

"Thank you," they both say in unison.

When Marco comes back with their food, he asks, "Where are you two from?"

"Golden, Colorado, near Denver," Ollie replies.

"Oh, I know where that is. Straight north from Albuquerque on Interstate 25."

Vera pauses to clear her throat and then says, "I'm guessing that you lived for a while in the U.S. Your English is perfect."

"Thank you," he replies. "Actually, I lived there for ten years."

"And you have returned just recently?" Vera asks.

Marco gives a double nod. His smile is gone.

"Oh." Ollie shakes his head from side to side with raised eyebrows. "Some adjustment, I'll bet."

Marco nods again. Vera rescues the silence by saying, "We'd like to hear more about where you lived and what your experience was like in the U. S."

"Albuquerque," he says, but nothing more except, "Enjoy your breakfast."

3

FROM DREAM TO NIGHTMARE

When Marco has cleared and set up his tables, he goes to the cafeteria in the basement for lunch. He gets one free meal a day from the resort—breakfast, lunch, or dinner—but just one. For a windowless underground bunker, the staff dining room is actually quite pleasant. Well lighted and brightly painted in orange and yellow, it is spacious enough for eight tables with orange tablecloths and padded white chairs. Two flat-screen TVs hang from the walls, but nobody seems to be watching because the room is filled with the din of laughter and chatter. The staff from the whole resort is welcome there: maids, bellmen, carpenters, painters, waiters, and office workers. Everyone seems innocently happy except for one, Marco González, who sits alone.

Marco leaves Sunset Point a little after two o'clock. He's tired. He's been there since seven, but he can't tolerate going back to his shabby apartment. Not yet. He needs to relax. In the past few weeks, he's made a conscious effort to relax. He's made up his own do-it-yourself anger management class, complete with an invented list of mottos. Now Marco—he has to talk to himself—"Cultivate the Calm," "Cool is the Rule," and "The Goal is Control." And some of the time it works, but usually he slips right back into anger mode again and his insides start to roar.

He walks into town and crosses over to the Paraíso Mall. It has become his second home. Out front a gurgling fountain, like a huge overflowing birdbath, anchors the center of a circular drive landscaped with pointed gray-green cactus and rock. When a taxi pulls into the palm-lined drive, one of the mall attendants helps the occupants in or out by providing a small wooden stool to assist the ladies stepping up into or down out of the green van. Now there's a job: checking out ankles all day. At least, better than selling shoes. The revolving door at the entryway allows empty-handed patrons to enter while package-laden shoppers exit simultaneously, a perfect symbol of commercial enterprise. Paraíso is always busy because it's filled with Americans and Mexicans both and the price is right.

Once inside, Marco checks out the movies being advertised on the tall square kiosk with its colorful posters, mostly American films with titles of dubious translation. He wanders past the drugstore and laughs at the over-the-counter, specially-priced, supposedly-a-bargain sale on Viagra. He lingers for a second at the store next door to study the off-color English messages on the t-shirts. Then he is tempted to have a latte at the coffee shop, but decides against it. A left turn at the escalator to the second floor would take him by a bunch of gift shops and galleries, and he certainly doesn't need that, so he keeps going on past the indoor cactus garden, the benches with weary old ladies and nursing mothers, and makes his way to the Harley-Davidson store—the popular shortcut to the marina—where he stops to admire the elegant chrome beasts before stepping out into the blinding sunshine.

He loves the marina because the wide walkways bordering the bobbing boats are so clean and everything smells fresh, cleansed by an ocean breeze surprisingly free of the smell of fish. He wonders where all those boats have traveled and what stories their captains have to tell about their adventures, but mostly he wonders how the hell anyone gets enough money to own a boat. And there are hundreds of them tied up there, floating on the murky water, all jammed in together with their fishing rods fixed in place and jutting out at an angle. He walks along the east side of the Marina and climbs the wide stairway up to the Luxury Avenue Mall, which is hardly a mall compared to Paraíso, actually just a huge building full of ritzy shops catering to the Americans from the cruises. Lots of tourists today. Literally a boat load from the Princess Cruise Line anchored out in the harbor. They are swarming through the mall. Is that why people take a cruise, to go to a mall? Shopping at the Luxury Avenue Mall is out of the question for him and for most Mexicans who live in Cabo. Who can afford those overpriced designer boutiques: Sunglass Hut, Coach, Carolina Herrera, Cartier, Salvatore Ferragamo? All he can do is look, so he looks for a while at polo shirts, sunglasses, and watches before going back outside. He saunters along the wharf, past the nearly empty restaurants that require their waiters to stand out front and reel in tourists for a late lunch or early dinner. Red, white, and green signs, echoing the colors of the Mexican flag, name each restaurant, and as he walks past he glances at the posted menus, some in Spanish, most in English, a little Spanglish thrown in. Eventually he sits down at an outdoor table at the Mango Cantina to have a Corona. Nice spot in the shade on the south edge of the marina near the channel that leads out to the harbor.

While he's waiting for his beer, he recalls Vera and Ollie sitting across from each other at their table this morning like two cute geckos, she with that straight gray hair trimmed short and he looking over the tops of his black plastic reading glasses with blue eyes, combing his wavy white hair with outstretched fingers. They seem like a nice old couple, different from the rest, really polite and good tippers, but, hey, they're Americans, rich and privileged. He remembers Omar saying that Ollie was a lawyer. He has to have made some big bucks in that profession. Vera, she's the kind of person who looks like maybe she understands. Or at least wants to. Very few people understand—Mexicans or Americans—they just take the situation at face value and carry on. Five-star resort, everybody smiling and doing their job. Good service. What is there to understand, to question?

Marco looks up and sees a young American couple about his own age standing near his table. Both of them blonds with blue eyes. Dressed in sharp casual outfits. They're probably just off the cruise. She looks like she is trying to muster enough courage to say something to him in Spanish. "Por favor," she finally asks, with Midwestern r's that suggest that these may be the only two words she knows how to mispronounce in Spanish.

"How may I help you?" Marco responds.

"We're looking for an inexpensive restaurant that serves fish tacos," she says, smiling in clear relief that she doesn't have to blunder through in Spanish.

"You've come to the right place. Sit down."

The guy hesitates. She shrugs why not. "You're sure it's okay?" she asks.

"I'd be happy to talk with you for a while, and seriously, this is a good place for fish tacos." Jesus, she looks like Michelle. Beautiful blond hair, straight nose, perfect teeth. He smells like Polo aftershave. Rich Americans.

After they order and exchange names—we're Tom and Terri—Marco asks them where they are from and they say "Utah."

"Mormons?"

"Yep."

"Skiers?"

"Downhill."

"Utah Jazz fans?"

"Not really."

"How do you know so much about the United States?" Terri asks.

"I lived there since I was seven until a year ago when my parents decided to come back to Mexico."

"So that's why your English is so good."

"Well, yeah, I spoke English at school with my friends and Spanish at home. What about you?"

"Oh, we both took Spanish in high school, but . . ."

"No, I meant what are you guys doing? Are you still in school?"

"We're both first years at Brigham Young," Tom replies.

"Nice. Good school." A spark of envy settles on him and he knows he needs to brush it away. "Must be Thanksgiving break?"

They nod. In the silence that settles in, Marco looks them over and concludes that even though they are dripping with privilege, they seem pleasant and friendly. But they are definitely fish out of water. "First time in Mexico?" he asks.

"Yes, in fact, it's our first stop," Tom admits.

"Oh, wow. Okay, so when you are finished eating, I'll show you around a little."

"Oh, we don't want to bother you," Terri protests.

"No problem. I miss my friends from the U.S." When Tom and Terri are finished, Marco shows them how to ask for la cuenta. They examine their bill and pick up his bar tab. He helps them put down the right pesos and count their change. "Let's go."

He takes them all the way back around the marina and down the west side past the yachts and catamarans poised for fishing trips and sunset dinner cruises. They visit the Dolphin Center, a big tourist attraction for the kids, and actually catch a glimpse of a dolphin through the pool viewing window. Terri waves at the Dolphin and it swims away and then comes back for another look at her. She's thrilled. Marco is tempted to explain to them how dolphins are one of the few mammals, besides humans, that can recognize themselves in a mirror, but he sees Tom checking the time. They've got a half hour. Marco cuts over three blocks and takes them up to the Iglesia San Lucas. He doesn't know if Mormons are interested in other people's religions or not with all that missionary work they do, but it's a little gem of a building, the pride of San Lucas, light beige with pastel pink trim around semi-circular arched windows and doors. The church sits alone at a quiet spot up from the street, perched high above a gray stone wall that borders the sidewalk. The black iron gate is open and they go through a side door to peek inside. It's an old mission church, he tells them, one of the first in Cabo San Lucas. No, he doesn't go to church there.

Marco asks them what they are majoring in, and when they tell him, they ask if he is in college.

"There's not a real college in Cabo. I was going to go in the U.S. but when my parents came back that finished that. I had to go to work. Came to Cabo and found a job at a resort."

What do you do?"

"I'm a waiter." Silence. Not much to talk about after that, a true conversation stopper. What's to discuss: the napkins, the number of glasses, the types of silverware? Is the orange juice frozen or fresh squeezed? The silence is not their fault.

There's a blast from the cruise ship horn, and Tom and Terri check their thin stylish watches simultaneously, nervously. They thank him and shove off to catch the boat back to their liner. Terri manages a hasta luego. Marco tells them he has enjoyed their company, which he has, but he doesn't say how much she reminds him of his ex-girlfriend, Michelle.

He saunters back around the marina and sits alone on the broad steps of the long stairway leading up to the Luxury Avenue Mall. Moving back to Mexico was even harder because things were going so great with Michelle. He pulls out the picture of her that he carries around in his wallet. He almost never looks at it, but he still carries it even though he knows it's over. Just like he still carries around his acceptance letter to the university. Today he looks at the picture of Michelle to compare her looks to that Mormon girl. Michelle was blond, so sweet, so American. He goes into a kind of trance when he remembers her. He knows this because people ask him "Where are you, Marquito?" Not fully there. He can't help it.

When he thinks about her, it's like he's with her again. At school, the final bell rings and he's standing beside her at her locker. He's sitting at a football game watching her do her bouncy cheer leading thing: back flips, the splits, and climbing up to the top of the human pyramid. She was head cheerleader, so she got to be on the top. He remembers being with her on that breezy summer day when her parents invited him to go along to the hot air balloon festival. The day was so beautiful, and she was so gorgeous, and her parents were so nice to him. Overlooked that he was Mexican. He could tell they liked him. How could he have lost all of that?

Actually, he and Michelle were getting serious. Her parents took her back east to visit private colleges because she was a good student and had a good chance of getting in, but after seeing what she saw, she said she wanted to go to the University of New Mexico. They had a pact to go off to college together.

Then his brain replays the day he told her he had to leave the U.S. Instead of freaking out and thinking of herself first, she said, "Doesn't that make you just sick." Those very words. He had to blink back tears and turn away. It still makes him sad, just recalling how understanding she was. That was just the beginning of a lot of tears for both of them.

The next day when she met him at school, she said, "Can't you just stay here by yourself?" And he said "Are you kidding? I wasn't born here. I'm just as illegal as my parents. She had understood about his illegal status all along, but it was kind of an abstract thing to her until then. She knew he had a driver's license, which was legal, and a social security number that wasn't, so that he could work. But stay here? Alone? And worry every day about deportation or prison?

They agreed that it would be best not to see each other anymore. If it had to end, better to end it now. But then they kept seeing each other anyway. Things were really heating up between them and it was hard for them to control themselves. But she drew the line and he respected that. Then one day, it was suddenly over. She went to Vassar and he went to Mexico.

He's in his trance now watching colorful hot air balloons floating across an endless blue sky, maybe in Mexico, maybe in New Mexico—same sky, right? He needs to get his butt up off of this hard step and go home.

Marco makes his way over to the bus station and boards Transporte Público, the bus that he takes to get to his apartment. The locals call it the Pecera, because everyone is all jammed in and staring out like fish in an aquarium. Besides losing Michelle, he lost his chance to go to the university. He had worked his butt off in high school to get straight A's in the International Baccalaureate Program at Sandia High. The state had recently decided to give college scholarships to qualifying students who were sons or daughters of illegals. That plus in-state tuition. It was a big breakthrough. He wanted to major in history, minor in business, and go on to get an MBA. Follow his dream. By that time, maybe there would be a path to citizenship for him. Then the economy crashed, the housing industry tanked, and new construction dried up. After three months without a job, his father called the family together, he, his older sister, and his mom, and said they needed to go back to Mexico. Be with family. So that's what they did. Had to do it. But it exploded his dream and wrecked his whole life. He can't seem to let go of it. The details keep playing over and over again like an annoying song stuck his head, as if his brain is searching for some option they all overlooked. He starts to feel the anger churning in his stomach again.

The bus stops at the Pemex station near his apartment. He gets off and begins the half kilometer walk on the unpaved street to get to his apartment. The road is dusty, bumpy, and full of potholes, a poor excuse for a road, even a dirt road. Not like the U.S. where all of the streets are paved, not in gold, but at least paved, and the improved gravel roads are considered quaint and rustic. He remembers their house in Albuquerque, a one-story brick rental, nothing to speak of actually, but it seems fancy now. It was on a pleasant safe street, not far from the MacDonald's and the mall with the BestBuy and OfficeMax.

He trudges along past the rickety shops with barred windows, their wares set outside on racks gathering dust. The smell of fried onions and grilled chicken, mixed with an occasional whiff of garbage, drifts out from the taquerías and small cantinas. Skinny, scrawny dogs and starving, prowling cats scrounge for any morsel that drops. Marco hears music booming from a vehicle coming up behind him and veers instinctively to his right as a huge black pickup going way too fast bounces by. An old man in tattered trousers ambles toward him pushing a stainless food cart with a small sign advertising homemade burritos. He overtakes a young mother wheeling a stroller that nearly shakes her kid to pieces on the bumpy road. Her other child, a young barefoot boy, is trying to navigate his small blue scooter along any smooth place he can find. The mother wears a bright pink t-shirt stretched tight over baby number three. What was she, maybe fifteen when she had the first one? Looks like they are on their way to the park, an uninviting treeless rectangle of dirt and plastic play equipment just ahead on the left. Qué park?

He notices an ATV stuck at the side of the road away from everything. Out of gas? Maybe abandoned? Why so many old worn-out tires thrown around everywhere? He's always impressed by how many building projects go uncompleted in Mexico. Someone builds a few cement block walls and then they run out of money and that's it. You can't have capitalism without capital. Duh. Just relentless poverty. People seem to be living on the first floor of the house he is passing—at least there is laundry flapping in the breeze—but the second floor still stands unfinished. Quizás mañana. Mañana, hell. More like next year. Maybe never. He likes the bright yellow flowers on that shrub and the big spreading green tree with orange-colored blossoms, but they seem totally out of place on this barren, brown desert of a street, like they belong back in that forlorn park. He longs for the beautiful park near his home back in Albuquerque, the track around the green football field at his school, and the little patch of green grass in front of their home. Everything finished off neat and tidy.

Marco arrives at his apartment and climbs the stairs to the outside balcony hallway, lined with doors, the way in and way out of the rented rooms. The cheap motels in the U.S. where people go for an hour of undisturbed pleasure look better than this shabby place. He unlocks the door to his unit and plops down in the chair facing the window. "Don't get all excited about the ocean view," he says out loud, as if still talking to his Mormon friends from the boat. He sure as hell wouldn't bring them or anyone else he considered a real friend up here. The spectacular view is of a car repair shop surrounded by old junkers, and beyond that there's another glimpse of those perpetually unfinished block buildings. He unlaces his shoes, slips them off, and sprawls on the bed. ¡Puta madre! How did he end up here?

He knows exactly how he ended up here. He got in a fight with his family and left home. He got a job. He got a room. This room. He glances around at the grimy sink, the grungy two-burner gas stove, and the pathetic mini-fridge. Nothing to write home about, but a room. His room, which he can pay for with his own wages and tips. At least he's not living off his parents. Too little money and too much pride, that's his problem. The dim overhead light bulb is supplemented by a reading lamp next to the chair. He bought an actual 75-watt bulb for it. He found the lamp at a bargain price at Walmart and brought it home on the bus, lugging his new lamp awkwardly over his shoulder across the stretch of dirt road. Now when it gets dark, he reads. Books, newspapers, anything he can find and afford. Especially history.

God, how he loved history in high school. His junior year American history teacher, Mr. O'Reilly, was completely awesome. He remembers clear as anything the day O'Reilly told the students to take out a pen or pencil and follow along with him and write notes in the margin of their textbook. "It's okay, you guys, you need to make some corrections. Listen up. The people who settled in present day Texas were white, slave-holding Americans, mostly from the southern states. They settled in a Mexican state called Coahuilla y Tejas. The spelling's on the board. Write it in. They were called Texians, not Texans. They just moved in and settled on land that belonged to Mexico, which had generous immigration policies and made land available for growing cotton. Okay, you got that? "So, Mexico collected taxes, because it was their land, right, and they prohibited slavery. So, the Texians got all upset and picked a fight and they got one." O'Reilly was amazing. He wanted his students to know the truth.

O'Reilly was also the track coach, so when he asked Marco to come out for track, how could he refuse? It turned out that he could run fast, so O'Reilly made him into a sprinter and low hurdles man. In his senior year, he was team captain and won a bunch of medals. He liked track until one day he overheard some dude say, "It's always good for Mexicans to know how to run fast because that way they won't get caught when they're stealing." He did not find that amusing, but O'Reilly told him to shake it off.

Now, Marco studies as if he were still in school. He gets paperbacks at Walmart, City Club, and Chedraui, or he special orders at Publicaciónes Ghandi. He doesn't just read, he devours. He picks out things he wants to know about and finds out all he can on that topic. Economic development. Social justice. Mexican history and culture. He takes notes. Writes little summaries that he can come back to later on. Maybe he can't go to the university, but he can at least study. No one can take that away from him. He studies late into the night. He doesn't get to run much anymore, but to tell the truth, that's one thing he doesn't miss.

The next morning, when the alarm goes off, as it does six days out of seven, Marco gets up, grooms, dons his waiter's outfit, and meets the morning bus from the Sunset Point Resort out by the Pemex station. It takes him to work free so he can be on time for the breakfast shift at La Casona. Super name: the Big House. American slang for a prison.

As the bus bounces along he examines his state of mind—will he ever stop doing this?—and he realizes that no amount of managing his anger will make it go away. Some people say that everything is attitude, and all you need to do is think positively. That sounds like horseshit. Feelings grow out of experience, and until his circumstances change, how can he be positive?

The bad scene with his parents flashes across his mind. Okay, so he was overcome with panic—a panic attack where he did the attacking—but really, he had no idea how to survive in Mexico. He not only lost his dream, he was scared it would turn into a nightmare, and that's exactly what happened. But the yelling and screaming? That was inexcusable.

The bus arrives at the end of the road. He walks through the main gate, checks in at the fingerprint time clock, and makes his way through the dimly lit underground passage that takes him past the cafeteria and over to the restaurant. He can tell that he has a dark scowl on his face, and he knows that when he arrives at the top of the stairs and walks out into the sunshine, he is supposed to smile. That won't be easy this morning.

4

MATCHMAKER

Sometimes Ollie will venture away from yogurt and granola to order something daring like French toast and a side of bacon. Today is that day. He stands in line at the buffet grill where the special-order breakfast cook whips up pancakes, scrambled eggs, and omelets. Her name is Maribel, at least that's what it says on her badge, and she is cute as a button with that tall chef's hat and deep dimples when she smiles, which seems to be most of the time. She looks like she's enjoying every minute of it, keeping orders straight, moving the line along, and chatting amiably with anyone who wants a little conversation with their eggs.

When Ollie gets to the front of the line, he tells Maribel "pancakes, please," and introduces himself. "I'm Ollie."

"Yes, and that's your dear little wife Vera right over there." She points with the spatula in her hand. "Am I correct?"

Perfect English again, like Marco's, only with a delightful little accent that adds to her charm. "How do you know about us?" he asks.

"Everyone knows about you two, and besides I've been here for two years watching you, just waiting for you to ditch your granola and order pancakes. By the way, my apologies, Señor Ollie, for the way the people in the lobby mispronounce your name. My English is not perfect, but I know you are not oily." She cocks her head to one side and the dimples spring into place. She glances around and beyond Ollie to catch a glimpse of Marquito talking to Vera seated at the table by the railing.

"You seem to like what you do," Ollie observes.

"It's an art, and I come from a family of artists—well, my grandparents are artists anyway."

"If you let yourself go, you could do a Jackson Pollock with that pancake batter."

She laughs outright, a vigorous, hearty laugh. "You mean that dribble artist?" She makes a dribbling motion with the spatula, cutting swirly curves in the air. "Only one problema, Señor. In Mexico we do murals, so I don't know how that would work out exactly, but I guess I could throw some of this batter on that hot wall," she turns around and pantomimes with the spatula, "and see what sticks." She laughs again. If only he were fifty years younger. Oh, my god, is that what it would take? Fifty years?

"They call you Marquito," Vera observes.

"Oh, yes, everybody here calls me Marquito."

"But you are so tall," Ollie remarks as he sits down at his place with his plate of pancakes.

"Compared to the others, yes. It's like in the U.S. when people sometimes say bad but it really means good."

"So, with Marquito they are really calling you tall." Ollie observes. "Interesting."

Vera asks him, "Doesn't the ito in Marquito also make it a term of endearment?"

"It could be, but in my case I don't think so. Nobody here knows me that well, and if they did, I doubt they'd call me Marquito for that reason."

Noticing his scowl, Vera asks him, "What about Maribel over here. What does she call you? She certainly has her eye on you."

"Who? Where?" He appears a little flustered.

"The special-order breakfast chef at the grill. Right over there." Vera nods in Maribel's direction. "Look how cute she looks in that tall white chef's hat. Have you noticed the dimples?" Ollie smiles to himself at Vera's meddling.

"Well, yes, she's cute but..."

"And she watches your every move, Marco." Vera adds. "I've seen her rubberize scrambled eggs and burn toast while she's watching you."

Marco looks pleased but embarrassed. "I need to get your order, ma'am. The boss is watching me, too, you know, and not because he thinks I'm cute. What will it be for you? The usual?"

Vera nods while Ollie points to his pancakes. Marquito dashes off up the stairs to the indoor dining room and kitchen. Vera looks out at the sea. In a moment, Ollie lifts his eyes from his copy of the Los Cabos Daily News, the morning paper that he always picks up at the front desk in the lobby to read at breakfast. Looking over the top of his reading glasses, he says, "I think you embarrassed him, dear."

"A small price to pay to get him to notice Maribel's languishing affection for him. We women need to stick together since it is not we who do the asking. Besides did you see his face light up? It will give him something to think about this morning while he tends his tables."

"You're sweet." Ollie takes her hand. "Always match making."

Vera starts to fiddle with her napkin. Her attention has gone off to someone else. "We need to set a time to meet with Daniella and the two girls. I have many surprises for them."

"Let me see now. She's the evening hostess, right, and the kids?"

"Surely you remember Daniella?"

"Yes, of course, just not the names of the two girls."

"Blanca and Cenia."

"Yes, Yes. They must be growing up now." Ollie returns to his newspaper.

Vera remembers how they first came to meet Daniella. Almost three years ago now. She was the evening hostess then as well. Only she was pregnant. The baby was due the next month right after Ollie and she were to return home, so she promised to bring Daniella some baby clothes when they came back the next time. Vera remembers vividly the scene in front of the ice cream store up at the Palmita Market: how she was pleased to see such a darling baby but surprised to find out that Cenia had an older sister Blanca sitting right next to her. So Cenia had all of these new baby clothes and Blanca had nothing. If she was jealous, she didn't show it. Later that week at the mall Ollie spotted a toy calculator for children. They left it with Daniella who told them it really wasn't necessary, but that Blanca was thrilled.

Ollie looks up from his newspaper. "How old are those kids now?" he asks.

"Almost three and maybe seven or eight."

"Didn't her husband leave her?"

"Now your memory is working."

"It's just the names, Vera. Proper nouns and names."

"Yes, he left her. Such a pretty young woman she is. Quiet. Serene. Maybe not lively enough for him. Not a good match. Who knows? That's why I brought so much this time. She needs clothes for those kids. And money. You could give them some pesos, Ollie."

"So, her mother lives with them?"

"No, she lives with her mother. In her mother's house. Her sister and her husband are there and her children, too. Remember? We visited there last year."

"Oh, yeah, that tiny place with the linoleum floor. Small kitchen. But her mother served great tamales. Isn't her sister ill?"

"Yes, cancer is what I recall." Vera winces.

Marquito brings her breakfast. "I'll be back right away with your juices." He sails off and returns quickly with an orange juice for Vera and cranberry for Ollie, but no smile.

"Okay, so there is Daniella and the two girls. Who else?" Ollie asks. "Who else do we need to see?"

"Well, surely we need to get together with Rosita and the boys."

"Of course, we always see Rosita. We never would have figured out how to use our membership if it hadn't been for Rosita helping us with the booking. By the way, we need to check with her to see if everything is set for our visit in February."

"One of the boys—I think it's Fernando—has a birthday while we are here. In her last email, Rosita invited us to his party," Vera tells him.

"Oh, a little fiesta. That should be fun." She knows that he means it. Ollie actually loves these little cross-cultural exposures. "Yes, let's get that on the schedule."

Vera pulls out a small pocket calendar from her purse. She has never become accustomed to keeping her calendar on her phone. "Oh, look at this. Thursday is Thanksgiving," she notes.

"And you know what that means – they think they have to make that special turkey dinner for the Americans. I liked that last year." Ollie nods.

"I'll ask Daniella to make us a reservation. You are saying that you want to go, right?"

"As long as we don't have to cook and clean up afterward. Remember how we did that all those years?"

Vera doesn't answer but she does remember. It seems that the children always fought. It was pleasant enough when the children were little, but after they had grown up and become successful and unsuccessful each in their own way, there were tense and unpleasant incidents. Ellen and her husband Damon would fly up from Dallas, and Peter would drive down in his old jalopy from Boulder. Damon had made so much money in the oil business that Ellen couldn't possibly keep on top of spending it all, though she tried her best. There was nothing their overflowing life lacked except children, but they never disclosed why they had none. After about a half hour of his sister's shallow chatter, Peter would give up even the pretense of conversation. It's then that Ellen would ask him about his employment, pretending that she was drawing him out. "Like what are you doing now, Peter?" What Peter resented was her tone and the assumption that he was doing something different from what he was doing the previous year, which he usually was. But still, it vexed him. It was usually right after that question that the verbal battles broke out, and Ollie with all of his conflict resolution skills, and she with her social work background couldn't manage to prevent, quell, or resolve the conflicts that sprang from the smoldering dislike that their children had for each other, so there was always a conflagration. One year, exercising their parental prerogative, Vera and Ollie decided to book the time-share over the Thanksgiving holiday, and they have been doing so ever since, converting it into a fixed week. The children have not objected.

Ollie waits patiently through Vera's silence. He can see that she is thinking about something troubling from the furrows on her brow. Finally, he asks, "Who else?"

"Who else what?" Oh, yes, the schedule. "Well, there's Isabella, who does my nails, but I can see her on my own."

"Isabella? Let me see. Oh, my, yes, the baby must be born by now."

"Your memory is really improving, Ollie. Can that be at such an advanced stage of old-timers disease?"

"Don't joke about such a serious matter." Ollie gives her a rare frown. He's sensitive about his memory because he knows it's failing. "But how could I forget Isabella? Last time we brought all that stuff for the soon-to-be-born, and Isabella was so overwhelmed with gratitude that she invited us to a barbeque that we didn't know how to refuse. The next thing we know we're riding off in her husband's pickup to God knows where."

"Remember that pathetic little house with just one bedroom scarcely bigger than a bed?" Vera squints like it is hard work to visualize that tiny bedroom. "No place for a baby. They were going to put the poor thing in one drawer of a chest."

"And I asked her if she was nervous or excited and she said a little of both."

Ollie loves it when he and Vera can retell their favorite stories to each other like this. "And then I asked him the same thing, and before he could reply Isabella glanced at me and said in her flat-voiced broken English that this was not his first. It turns out he has two other children, one in Kansas and another in Arizona."

"You tried not to look shocked." Vera grins.

"Holy Jesus! I have to tell you I was shocked. What the hell was the poor girl thinking?" Ollie runs a hand through his hair, shocked again in the retelling. "So, then I went outside with him to help with the barbeque, but there's nothing to do but watch him and dodge the smoke. We're in the most God-forsaken dirt yard you can imagine except for that mango tree in one corner, the only green thing anywhere around. They worshipped that tree and ate its fruit."

"Apparently without knowledge of good and evil," Vera adds.

This makes Ollie laugh before he continues. "The grill is improvised from a steel drum cut top to bottom, one half lying on cement blocks and filled with charcoal." He gestures to indicate the shape of the drum and the surface of the grill. "Ah, but the steak and grilled onions wrapped in flour tortillas were more than delicious. Remember?"

"Unforgettable. And while you were outside, she told me that he had promised to marry her."

"Promised. Yeah, right after he gets two divorces."

"I doubt he married the others, dear."

"So, he wasn't a bigamist after all. Is there such a thing as a trigamist?"

"I think that would be polygamist, dear, but who's counting. He just had other girlfriends."

"And other babies." Ollie shakes his head. "And what about the ride back to the resort after the barbeque?" Ollie reminds Vera that the story isn't finished yet.

"The truck was running out of gas and you noticed and offered to buy. That was generous."

"Not really. I didn't want to spend the night pulled up alongside the road in that damn truck." Ollie has three fears when he is in Mexico and that's one of them, being stuck along the road. The other two? Spending a night in a Mexican jail or needing medical attention in a Mexican hospital. He's not sure if he's being prejudiced or prudent, but that's the way it is.

"So, the next day," Vera continues, "I made you take me over to Walmart so I could purchase a stroller for Isabella"

"A little expensive when it showed up on the credit card, but nothing we couldn't handle. Of course, completely beyond reach for both of them."

"Isabella cried, Ollie, when I gave her that stroller." They are both silent, disconcerted, on the edge of tears themselves, remembering Isabella's situation, the poverty, the boyfriend, his babies. Eventually Ollie says, "I'll go with you to see the baby. They might need something."

Breakfast has been over for quite some time. They have just been sitting there telling each other what they remember. Ollie is tired of shooing the damn twittering sparrows. "Well, let's begin our day," he says.

"What did you have in mind?"

"Taking a little snooze by the pool," he replies, in an expressionless voice.

"But, dear, we just got up."

"I know. How did I get so depressed by ten in the morning?"

On Thursday morning, Vera suggests to Ollie that they walk into town to the mall, not to the Luxury Avenue Mall, but the other one, the Puerto Paraíso Mall, where ordinary people from town shop and actually buy things.

"We need to walk fast to work up an appetite for Thanksgiving dinner," Ollie states emphatically. "That's always what I did growing up as a kid in Vermont. My brother and I would pick out a hill to climb. At first it was just the hill behind our house, but as we got older the hills got bigger and more challenging, and we argued more about which hill would be best. It became a tradition. We'd go on a long hike that morning so we could come in starving for that turkey dinner."

"I don't think they even serve seconds at La Casona."

"And I don't think we'll be starving. It's just the idea of the thing, dear. The tradition."

"I understand."

"I miss my brother. It's strange how you miss all the deceased family members at the holidays."

"And argue with the living," Vera adds.

They have put on old clothes and sneakers because the road into town is dusty and the sidewalks are uneven. As soon as they leave the pavement and irrigated bougainvillea hedges of the resort, the going gets tough. One misstep can mean a painful lower back muscle spasm, or even worse a fall, so they keep their heads down and eyes on where they are stepping. They pass two cheaper hotels, one with a fake waterfall cascading out of control over an outside wall, making so much spray they have to step out into the street to get past it. Back on the sidewalk again, they pass carefully around cables that anchor wooden electrical poles and jagged wire fences. Oddly, the sidewalk stops, just plain runs out, on the left, so they need to cross over to the one on the right, and when that sidewalk disappears, cross back to the left again. It might be better just to walk in the street if it weren't for the taxis zooming by on what seems to be their preferred route to town. They walk past an uninviting hovel of a shop nestled under a shady grove of palms trees where an old man—same old man getting older year after year—is selling activities: golf and fishing excursions, motor scooter rentals, as well as half-day trips up the Pacific coast to ride on an all-terrain vehicle, ATVs their called. The old man has a border collie who always yaps at those who pass. Ollie thinks the old man has trained the beast to herd potential customers over to his side of the road. It is warm today and a little sweat breaks out on Vera's forehead, and Ollie takes off his jacket and carries it over his shoulder hooked on an index finger.

As they stroll along, Vera wonders what Ollie is thinking about. Probably something more about his idyllic childhood in Vermont. She pictures his home town, the white clapboard Congregational Church with the tall steeple hovering at one end of the village green, where maple syrup, cheddar cheese, and fresh-baked bread are sold at the farmers market on Saturday mornings. She has heard about it so often she is nearly convinced that she grew up in Vermont, too. Hardly. A northern Ohio steel town, that's where she grew up. Lucky for her she got a scholarship to Middlebury and looked up from her studies in the library one night to see Oliver Webster—was he descended from a dictionary?—sitting across from her. Luckier still that he said hello, asked her to go with him for a milkshake, and escorted her back to the dormitory before ten o'clock, which was her curfew. When he went to law school at the University of Michigan, she followed him there to study social work, cutting her teeth on difficult cases in an internship in downtown Detroit. Such rich educational opportunities they both had. After she earned her master's degree in social work and he finished law school, they got married and moved to Denver, where he worked for a law firm that specialized in corporate cases and he made a pile of money on the big settlements. Funny how her aging mind goes on and on in such detail over things so familiar.

Ollie catches up with her and falls into step so they can talk. "We certainly have been privileged, haven't we?" he says out of the blue.

Good grief, has he been reading her mind as they walk along step by step through their lives. Is that what he's been thinking about, too? When you get old, you hardly need to talk because you know so much of what is in the other person's mind, bundled together like you are for a lifetime.

"I mean, consider where we went to school and the help we had from scholarships and the opportunity to earn our way so we didn't come out with a hundred thousand dollars of debt like students do now. Those days are gone forever."

Okay. They were both thinking about their past, nearly the same thoughts, but this is almost too much. Downright spooky. She still doesn't say anything. Does she need to?

"We had some good times in grad school, but we were both so serious. It made us nothing but serious for the rest of our lives. I think I worked too hard in my career. I don't know how much good I did, either, but I made a good living."

Vera nods. Talking and walking seem to go together for Ollie. He doesn't always have all that much to say, but once you get him walkin', he never stops talkin'. It's like his mouth is connected to his feet. It's time for her to say something so she uses that moment to change the subject. "I was thinking," she begins, "that we might look in the mall for a pair of earrings."

"For whom?"

"For me, silly."

"Funny you mention it. I was just thinking the same thing. I said to myself, she's always doing so much for other people, I wonder if I could get her something."

"Seriously? You thought that?"

"Am I a mind-reader, or what?"

"You're so sweet."

They arrive at the Paraíso Mall and congratulate themselves, as they always do, on still being able to walk into town. They saunter past several shops until they come to an authentic Mexican silver jewelry store, but after looking a bit, Vera concludes she would prefer a ring although she doesn't find a ring she likes either. They are all so expensive. "Really, Ollie, they are." She hatches a plan. She will ask Marquito if he will give them some help on his day off. What she has in mind is a small shop a few blocks from the marina area, somewhere that a young Mexican man might shop for something for his sweetheart.

The next morning, the day after Thanksgiving, when Ollie and Vera pause in the lobby to pick up Ollie's copy of the Los Cabos Daily News, he notices a clamorous commotion around a huge natural pine tree lying on its side, stuck in the sliding door at the entry like a beached whale. "It's the Christmas tree for the lobby, Señor Oily, shipped all the way from Oregon," Sebastián the bellman tells them in a merry voice. At least ten men are pulling and tugging on ropes wrapped around that poor tree, toppled in some distant forest and hauled down to Mexico against its wishes. Two of the men are sawing away at the lower branches, but it's still stuck. In no time at all, Ollie is right in the middle of things telling the workers that they should be coming in bottom first, not top first as they are, so that the pressure from the doors will push the branches up, not pull them down. As it is, the bigger branches at the bottom keep spreading outward and getting stuck against the doors. He knows he's right, of course; how many oversized Christmas trees has he slipped through the front door of the old family homestead in Vermont bottom first? But no amount of his shouting and pointing and demonstrating gets through to the workers, so they saw off a few more lovely branches and look up at him and smile. Because he can't bear to watch, he clasps Vera by the hand and they march off to breakfast. "Why do they think we need that huge tree anyway?"

"It is a lovely tree."

"Was," Ollie growls. "All they needed to do was turn the damn thing around. Common sense."

When Marco brings their glasses of juice, Vera notices that he still seems to be in a blue funk, wearing that horrible scowl that he's had each morning this week. She decides that it is time to intervene and ventures an observation. "You look a little sad this morning, Marco."

"Do you think so?" He flashes his smile but it fades quickly.

Vera has a sense about Marco. His sadness worries her. She wants to know him better, but she's not sure how much to push. "Sometimes people are sad when they have lost something important from their past. Or sometimes it's when they think they have no future."

'Would you believe both?" he snaps, frowning at her.

"And so young. I'm sorry to hear it, but I won't pry." He doesn't appear to be ready to say more. She waits for a moment, hoping he will, and then says, "I need some help with a minor matter. Ollie here wants to buy me a piece of jewelry. We looked in the mall yesterday, but without success. I'm hoping you can help us find a little shop off on one of the side streets. Something more authentically Mexican. Perhaps..."

"To tell the truth, I don't know anything about jewelry."

"I understand, but perhaps you could ask someone who does. The young ladies usually know about such things."

He jerks his head to stare at her straight on, as if he suspects she's trying to match him up with Maribel, which of course she is. Casamentera. "Maybe you should ask one of them," he says. The tone is sarcastic and disgruntled. He leaves to get the rest of their breakfast.

Vera frowns, running a hand down the back of her neck. Now what has she done? But her suspicions are confirmed. Behind his professional façade, this young man is very angry about something.

When Marco arrives back with their food, he says, "I'm sorry. That was very rude of me. I apologize. I'm a little down this morning. Some days I just don't have very good control of myself. Please don't say anything to my supervisor. I have a day off on Monday. I'd be glad to help you."

"How about we meet for chocolate malts at Johnny Rockets?" Ollie asks. He realizes that the place is a corny retro of an American diner, but he can't help suggesting it because he started loving milkshakes as a kid at the soda fountain in the country store, and he's never stopped. To this day, chocolate malts are one of his greatest joys in life. He hopes Marco won't think it's a dumb idea.

"A milkshake? I haven't had a milkshake since I left the U.S."

"Maybe that's one of the things from your past that you lost? Milkshakes?" Vera widens her eyes and cocks her head to the side. Marco is smiling at her.

"Monday at noon. I'll get a suggestion about where to shop."

"It will be good to talk with you."

5

THE LITTLE SILVER RING

When Marco finishes his lunch in the cafeteria, he gets up and goes over to sit in a vacant space next to Maribel. He's never paid much attention to her, but he considers he knows her a little from working on the breakfast shift together. And Vera was right: Maribel has been watching him. He's noticed that. In running track, even if you're first, there's always someone trying to catch you. It develops the peripheral vision. He's never really talked to Maribel before. I guess you could say she's only an acquaintance.

"Necesito tu ayuda." He starts out in Spanish, because he's not sure how much English vocabulary she has once she gets beyond omelets, pancakes, and crepes, which he reminds himself is a French word.

"Help? At your service, Señor Marquito, she answers in English. What's the problem?"

Better English than he had imagined. A cute little melodious accent. "Some guests, an old lady and her husband, have asked for some help in locating a neighborhood jewelry store, something not too expensive, away from the mall and the tourists."

"Let me think." She bites her lower lip and switches over to Spanish. "The best place might be that little store over on Morelos that sells jewelry, but also other things like scarves and purses. Melody it's called. You know where I mean? Not a very big selection, but everything they show is very stylish. Hand-crafted. Authentic. I could be happy with anything from Melody."

"Yeah, if you had the money or the boyfriend, which is about the same thing."

"Ouch, Marquito. Why would you say that? You know that's not what I meant. Something bothering you?"

"Well, to begin with, people calling me Marquito. I'm tired of it."

"Sorry." She stacks her dishes and silverware preparing to leave.

"No, no, stay. I'm the one who should say sorry. I know people don't mean anything by it, but Marquito is so Mexican. They called me Mark or Marcus in the States."

"Oh, really now. Do I detect that you don't know whether you are Mexican or American? I hear that if you stay there long enough, they give you that little hyphen and call you Mexican-American."

"Yeah. Which is only half as insulting as Mexican."

"I know that's probably true, but you're here now, so maybe you need to accept that."

"True. But I don't need to accept Mexico. Mexico is mierda." Her eyes widen, her lips purse in disapproval. "I'm sorry, Maribel, but it is."

"Well, if you're going to fix it, you need to get started in the next hour because it's going to take a lifetime." He offers to carry her dishes, but she refuses. They stand to leave.

"Melody on Morelos, right?" He double checks.

"Two blocks west of Lázaro Cárdenas. Hope things work out there with Vera and Ollie and if you ever..."

"How do you know their names?"

"Everybody knows Vera and Ollie. I was saying, you don't need to panic about going shopping with me. I'll bring my own money. No problema." Even when she smirks the dimples appear. Nice eyes, too. Jeez. Why was he so rude? He wishes he could play that scene again.

Even though he is on time, Vera and Ollie are already seated at a table on the outdoor veranda at Johnny Rockets waiting for him. Well landscaped with shrubs, flowers, a waterfall and small ponds, it is perched up on a knoll overlooking the marina, like a little piece of the U.S.A. from the 1950s. "It feels like I should be bringing you orange juice or decaf or something."

"No, this is your day off, remember?"

"Right."

"Sit down, so we can order those milkshakes," Ollie suggests.

"Sometimes Ollie is like an impatient little kid when he's waiting for his milkshake," Vera says apologetically.

"Chocolate Malt? Fries?"

"Perfecto."

When Ollie places the order, Marco reports that he has a good shopping tip, although he doesn't admit where he got his advice. Ollie's lips form a barely perceptible smile. He knows Vera's meddling has started something.

Vera asks Marco, "What do you usually do on your day off? What's typical?"

"Typical? Hard to say. Sometimes I just have stuff that needs to get done, like the laundry or getting a haircut, but I try to take care of those things after work, you know. I can tell you what I like to do. I like to go to Médano Beach."

"Ah, yes, right around the corner here." Ollie gestures beyond the Luxury Avenue Mall toward the harbor. "Every beach a public beach in Mexico. To swim?" he asks.

"To read."

"You like to read. That's good." Ollie nods his approval, being careful not to be patronizing. Good god, he reminds himself, it's not odd that a Mexican should like to read.

"Ollie reads everything. The children used to say that he would even read the milk carton."

"Are you like that, really?" Marquito asks, smiling at the thought.

"I'm afraid so. Yes, I spend a lot of time at home in my study reading."

"He always brings three or four books to Cabo, too, but lately I've been encouraging him to download on his Kindle. It saves room for my presents."

Marco has heard about these presents. The ladies of the lobby say she brings clothes for kids, toys, and stuff like that. He doesn't quite know what to make of this unusual couple. They seem to be old but young at heart, well informed but still curious, rich Americans but generous. "What do you like to read, sir?" he asks.

"History. That's first on my list, but also science. I love astronomy, the ocean, human origins. But sometimes I read novels, too, just not those legal thrillers. I had enough actual legal thrills in my career."

It's true then that he was a lawyer. "I like history, too, sir. American history. I had an awesome history teacher in high school."

"Where did you live?" Ollie asks.

"Well, we came across the border in Arizona. My parents with two little kids. Nearly got killed and then we almost starved to death for a few weeks in Tucson. So they tell me. My family eventually moved to Albuquerque."

"Ah, New Mexico. It was originally part of old Mexico, you know," Ollie points out.

"It was surprising to my family how many Mexicans were there. And my mom and dad both found work. That was the main thing. Work." He has a fleeting memory of his dad coming home grimy and sweaty, his clothes dirty, his boots spattered, after a day's work on construction.

When the shakes and fries arrive, Ollie says, "Sorry, Vera. I didn't mean to dominate the conversation." Marco notes how she gives her husband a half smile. They are easy people to talk to.

"But you eventually left New Mexico and your family came back. That must have been difficult," Vera says.

Does she mean the trip back? Of course it was difficult. He has horrible memories of that trip. He hesitates, then plunges in. "Crossing the border was scary but not so difficult actually. We decided as a family to return. We made a big deal about it being a decision and all, but actually there was no choice. In the downturn, as they called it, my dad couldn't find any more work, and we couldn't live on what my mom earned as a maid."

"You had to come back?" Ollie affirms.

"Sí, sir. Return home. Of course, it was never really my home. But at the border, they pulled us over to check our documents, and we had none, because we were illegal in the first place. But what could they do? Deport us? 'This is a voluntary,' the guy said. Not the first they'd seen that month, or week, or day, so they motioned us on through." Why is he telling them all of this? They don't need to know this. It's none of their business. But he continues on. "My dad was smart enough to send back most of our money well in advance. But just because we didn't have much on us didn't mean people didn't try to rob us. U.S plates on a nice car. Our clothes kind of gave us away, too. What little money we had was well concealed, so we managed to get through. After we got further south, things went better for us. We ate out of bags and drank out of cans until we got to my dad's family in Tonala, near Guadalajara. The trip was a pretty sorry welcome back, but when we arrived, naturally our families were glad to see us. Good Mexican family. They never forget you. It had been more than ten years."

Vera and Ollie are still listening even though he has stopped talking. He can tell that. Good listeners. Marco suddenly feels agitated. He notices his knee jouncing up and down. He hasn't told this story to anyone before, and he doesn't know why he is telling it now. This is the first time he has had an extended conversation about himself with Americans since leaving the States.

"My goodness, that's quite a story. Frightening. What I meant, when I asked about whether it was difficult," Vera continues, "was how it was for you personally. The adjustment."

Oh shit, he told them that whole story and that isn't even what she wanted to know. Adjustment? Hell, he hasn't adjusted. If he goes into that he might stand up on the table and start screaming and cursing. "I had a scholarship to go to the university." He pauses to decide if he should say more. "Yes, it was difficult." But he leaves it at that. He needs to compose himself.

"You say that so calmly," Vera notes, "but you must have been really pissed."

Now why is this dignified old lady using a word like that? But he admits it's exactly how he felt. Still feels. He notices that gurgling starting up in his gut again as he revisits his rage. He makes an ugly noise sucking up the last of his milkshake through his straw. It wouldn't be so bad if he hadn't had to give up his girl and his dream. That's what sucks. "Yeah, I was pretty upset." He nods his head several times, clenching his teeth.

"And still are."

"There's no future now. Just this dead-end job." Marco gestures with empty hands. "I'm sorry, ma'am, I shouldn't have said that."

"Smiling at all the rich Americans," Vera goes right on, "and saying yes, sir, yes, ma'am. By the way you do have a great smile. Doesn't he, Ollie? It must be hard to keep smiling after all you've been through."

She understands. Ollie, too. Not everything necessarily, but they at least understand it has been difficult for him. They seem to care about him. But why? She looks like she's working up another question. What the hell is she going to ask this time? He reminds himself that he doesn't need to answer. He's never discussed stuff like this with anyone, surely not resort guests.

"It's like you have to lead two completely different lives. How do you reconcile these two lives?" His first thought is that this is not something he ever realized he needed to do. He just has these two lives. That's it. One serving the guests in a fancy resort hotel, earning enough to pay the rent; the other living out the remaining hours of the day in town, on the beach, in the library, or in that hole of a room. But what the hell, nearly everyone who works at Sunset Point is in the same boat. What's to reconcile? It's a job.

He hasn't responded, so Vera says, "I'm sorry. Maybe I shouldn't have asked."

"No, it's just a hard question." He strokes his square jaw. Since he doesn't have an answer, he decides to make an observation. "Maybe it's not two lives, but two worlds. I mean, it's not like those of us who work at the resort are privileged in the daytime and poor at night. We still have the same life: poor all the time. But I know what you mean. Being exposed to the two worlds isn't easy for us."

Ollie says, "You're a very perceptive young man. That's an important distinction. Two worlds, not two lives."

Vera nods. "Indeed." Then she continues, "As we have become acquainted with some of the people who work at the resort, we realize they live in another world. Now no matter whom we meet, we can't help but wonder about their life. We see them in a completely different way. We picture them in street clothes, without their uniforms, not just the people we know, but everyone. They live in one world and we live in another. We are trying to understand that. The resort looks completely different to us now. Really American. But real people work here. They are Mexicans."

"I don't think that most people who work here think about that stuff very much, if at all."

"I am sure that you are right about what you call most people. But you aren't most people."

"I don't know what you mean," he tells her. He's getting perturbed. Won't this lady ever shut up? Is she feeling guilty because they're so wealthy? What's she driving at?

"You've lived in both worlds. You have the additional perspective that comes from having lived in the U.S. for ten years. You were brought up there. Went to school there."

Marco notices that her voice is strong and firm. She's trying to make a point, but he's not sure what it is. He can't tell where Vera and Ollie are going with all of these questions, but they seem genuinely interested in this business of reconciling all these lives and worlds. "Can you tell me more about what you mean by the word reconcile?" he asks. Why is he going deeper into this discussion when what he needs to do is bail? My God, El Greco would be hysterical if he knew that he was having a conversation like this with guests.

"It is about the contrasts," Vera replies. "Differences in wealth, in opportunity, in power. The lives of the guests, most of them anyway, are so different from the lives of those who wait upon them—the waiters, yes, but also the maids, the people who check the towels in and out, the groundskeepers, the painters and plumbers—all of these people lead lives that contrast sharply with the comfortable lives of those they serve. I don't need to tell you this, Marco. You can tell me much more about this than I can even imagine. But it bothers me. Even at our advanced age—Ollie and I talk about this a lot—we still ask why. Not just why, but what can be done."

A long silence is interrupted only by the shrill screeching of gulls, the uncontrolled laughter of boisterous customers seated nearby, and an unhappy child's crying in the distance. Marco doesn't know what to say. In fact, he has no idea what to say because he knows that a reply would take more than a few words and he doesn't want to make a long speech or lose control or anything like that. Vera seems to have a way of stirring him up.

Finally, Ollie says, "I am afraid we have touched upon a very sensitive topic. Maybe that's enough for today. What about a little shopping? You said you had an idea for us."

"Yes, shopping." Marco nods, greatly relieved. "I know where to go." He stands up. "¿Vámonos?"

Ollie pays the bill, leaving some pesos for his usual good tip, and the three of them, Marco in the lead, wend their way over to the simple little shop called Melody. Only two blocks off the main drag, Morelos is already a back street of cobblestones and narrow sidewalks. Stores are all crammed in close, some with steel security gates to be pulled down at night. Electric wires zigzag overhead like a huge spider web. He's never been on this street before. Definitely not like the mall. The shop has a wood sign with Melody carved in script and painted yellow. A small front window contains a smart display, and the bright blue front door is welcoming. In no time at all Vera is exclaiming over the beauty of all of the things she is seeing. She narrows down the choice to a pair of stylish hand-crafted silver earrings, a very modern ring with lots of interesting planes and angles, and a soft cotton scarf. But finally, she settles on something completely different, a wonderful hand-woven, naturally dyed, handbag from Oaxaca. As they go to pay, Vera points at a ring and says to Marquito, "Why don't you let us buy this little silver ring here for you to use as a gift someday when the right young lady comes along?"

"Oh, I couldn't permit that. Besides I don't have a girlfriend. The only real girlfriend I had was in Albuquerque, and that's finished."

"But you will have a girlfriend someday, maybe sooner than you think. Look at the beautiful turquoise stone. It would make a lovely friendship ring."

"Oh, but I couldn't."

"Maybe the young lady who recommended this marvelous shop would like something from it."

"She said she liked everything they have here," Marco concedes.

"See."

"But, no, it would be awkward. She would take it to mean something I don't intend. I'm not ready for anything like that with her or anyone else."

"Then save it. Here. We'll ring it up and you can keep it. And when the right moment comes, you'll know who should receive it. Done deal."

"But I..."

"Here. Slip this in your pocket."

They stroll back to Paraíso Mall so that Vera and Ollie can catch a cab back to Sunset Point. On the way, Ollie asks Marquito, "If I wanted to send you a book, where would I send it?"

For sure he's not going to give them the address of his shabby little apartment. Besides, he's not sure how long he'll be staying there. He'd move out tomorrow if he could afford it. "Just send it to the front desk at the resort. Verónica will see that I get it."

Vera and Ollie, now looking a little wilted from the bright sun, catch their cab back to the resort. Marco thanks Ollie twice, once for the milkshake and again for the ring, and they say goodbye. Marco decides to wander down to Médano Beach. He takes the short-cut through the Harley-Davidson store at Paraíso Mall, strolls along the east side of the marina, and slips through a narrow back street past Fisherman's Bar that takes him down to the shore.

The day is bright and clear, but the beach is never crowded on weekdays, at least not like it is on weekends. He has no towel, no gear, not even a book, just a head buzzing with perplexing questions and a stomach churning with familiar emotions. He finds a quiet and secluded spot where he can be by himself for a while, away from the screaming little children and far enough back from the sea to avoid the smell of exhaust from the outboard motors of the water taxis. He takes off his shirt, slips out of his sandals, and sits cross-legged on the sand in his jeans, hoping not to be taken for some sort of dorky yogi.

Vera and Ollie. Now there's a pair. She must be a psychologist or something. His high school guidance counselor was like her, always asking probing, unanswerable questions. He remembers his counselor saying that it's important to be in touch with your feelings. Well fine, unless your feelings are so strong or confused or outrageous that it's dangerous to be in touch with them. Even worse, he might act on them and who knows where that would take him. No, no, the last thing in the world he needs is to be in touch with his feelings.

Until today, Vera and Ollie were just a nice old couple who came to take their simple breakfast at his table each morning. But this afternoon she just walked right into his life like a CSI investigator. Snooping in his business. And he allowed her to do it, even encouraged her. Ollie's a little more laid-back, careful about intruding. But, Vera. Jesus.

Marco picks up a handful of sand and lets it trickle through his outstretched fingers until it's all gone. He picks up another handful and repeats this ritual unconsciously while he tries to sort out his thoughts. Two lives? Of course he lives two lives, work and all the rest, like everybody who holds a job. He doesn't really have a life at the resort, just a job. Vera and Ollie have their life at the resort, being waited on, having their room cleaned, basking in the sun, like all the other rich people who come to Mexico to be waited on. He knows he'll never have that life. But Vera's right about one thing: in the portion of his life that is lived at the resort he observes the life-style of the rich, he's exposed to it, at least enough to resent it, especially now, knowing he will never live like that. Two worlds, one that is definitely not his.

Not all of the guests are Americans. Some are from Canada, from India, and there are even a few ultra-rich Mexicans. He needs to keep that in mind. But what Vera is driving at, he thinks, is that the guests are all privileged and his job is to serve them in their state of privilege. That's what she wants to know about: how he feels about waiting on the privileged. How does he feel about it? Well, he hates it. Anyone with half a brain would hate it. Oh, you get to meet some interesting people, but most don't intend to get to know you in return like Vera and Ollie. Most people at the resort could care less about getting to know their waiter. Give me a break. They want their coffee cup to stay full, their empty plates cleared immediately, and the bill to arrive before they have to ask for it. What they really want is service with a smile. They don't picture the employees as having real lives. Some mornings he would like to scream, break some dishes, and snap somebody in the ass with their napkin. I'm not just this piece-of-shit Mexican who's supposed to bend over and pick up the fork you just dropped—you clumsy jerk—and run get you a clean one. I'm a human being.

The late afternoon sun, hovering just above the craggy mountain range, is still hot. Marco brushes little droplets of sweat from his forehead, being careful not to get any grains of sand on his face. He burrows both feet deep into the sand and covers them deeper by piling on more sand with a sweeping motion of his arms. Sometimes at the resort he sees little kids burying each other in the sand, their whole body up to their head. He wonders what it would feel like to be buried alive, to suffocate there, the pressure on the lungs so great as to make breathing impossible. Is that the problem with his life? Is he slowly suffocating here in Cabo, without his family, without his girlfriend, without purpose or hope? Is that what they mean when they call the tip of this barren peninsula land's end? What the hell kind of paradise is this?

He hears some girls giggling down by the water's edge, their high-pitched voices carrying above the sound of the surf. Why do girls always have to hang together like that? If guys do that, they're called a gang, and everyone gets all shook up about their being dangerous. People assume girls are harmless. Ha!

He goes back to picking up sand and letting it slip through his fingers. He needs to calm down, but he can't. Adjustment? Vera wanted to know if it was a difficult adjustment. Such sanitary words. Honestly, he hopes he has not adjusted. To that miserable little apartment? Why would he want to adjust to that? To a future snatched away? To a dream turned into a nightmare? Maybe he can find a way out of his hopeless situation, but right now he doesn't see how. It was really funny hearing that little old lady say pissed, but she was right, that's how he feels. That deep gnawing anger that persists day after day just won't go away. And the more he thinks about it, the angrier he gets. He read about that somewhere: anger feeds anger. So, it's best not to think about it.

His mind goes blank for a few seconds and then Vera's point suddenly becomes clear. He thinks he understands now what she was driving at. He was raised in the U.S. Being brought up there, going to school there, has made him different. Maybe this is why he is so confused. He's part

American and part Mexican, but not really either one. He's not sure who he is. When he was in the U.S., it was pretty clear that he was Mexican, but now that he's in Mexico he seems more American. He's like an American tourist in his own country, but it doesn't feel like his country. He doesn't feel at home here.

He throws a handful of sand downwind. Enough ruminating. Such a pity party he's having here all by himself on the beach. All because of that nosy old lady and her unrelenting barrage of frickin' questions.

He stands up, dusts off his feet and shoulders with his shirt, slips it back on, and picks up his sandals. He heads on down to the water's edge to catch a gentle breaker to wash off his feet. He's standing there balancing on one foot, trying to slip one sandal on to a clean foot, when Maribel's voice floats in like an uninvited ghost. Was she with those girls?

"So how was the shopping trip, Marco?" He notices that she is careful not to call him Marquito.

Maribel has taken him by surprise and he feels awkward standing there on one leg like a pink flamingo. Then a big wave washes in and nearly knocks him over. He barely catches his balance. He knows he will have to start all over again with the feet. "It was fine. Vera ended up buying a wool purse from Oaxaca." He feels in his pocket to make sure he still has the ring. "That lady sure can ask a lot of questions. She's got my brain all stirred up like she ran it through a blender."

"Yuk. Terrible image, Marco. Can't you come up with something else?" She smiles.

The dimples are definitely cute. So are the brown eyes, playful but sad, like the look of a puppy. "I've just been sitting over there," he motions with his sandals, "thinking about everything."

"I know. I saw you. I was over there," she motions toward the girls with a nod, "entertaining my friends. For some reason they think I'm funny."

She looks good in the turquoise bikini. She has a Mexican butt. Chula. That was Michelle's only short-coming, she had no butt. He doesn't say anything. He just looks out at the ocean, trying not to stare.

She asks, "What's bothering you?"

"It's . . . it's really complicated. I don't know. Sometimes I have these feelings, this resentment about serving all those privileged rich people up at the resort."

"Well, yeah, who doesn't? I think about that every morning when I go to work. But at least I'm making pancakes and scrambling eggs and not washing toilets. I get to joke around with people and be of service."

"Service? Oh, yes, Mexicans have always been someone's slaves, so we turn that into the virtue of service."

"Wow! You are angry." She nods her head back and forth and then shrugs. "For me, I'm glad I'm alive and that every two weeks I can take some money home to my mom and help out."

"You live with your mom?"

"Right now, it's the only way we all make it."

Marco has given up on having clean feet to slip into his sandals, so he just puts them on while Maribel holds out a hand to steady him. "Thanks for the tip about the store."

"Melody?"

"Like you said, it's got nice stuff. Good jewelry." The lingering sun has just dropped over the horizon and a cool breeze delivers a chill that makes him shiver. The beach is quiet except for the swish of the waves. "I need to go. Nice talking to you." He regrets being so angry with her, so unpleasant, so edgy. Why does he do that? "Really. I mean it. I feel better talking to you." They exchange smiles.

Marco heads back up the narrow street to the marina, through the mall, and on over toward the bus station. He trudges along feeling just a tiny bit happy, as much as he can allow himself just now, but he's still carrying a small tornado in his gut. He's had nothing to eat since the fries and milkshake, and his hunger only makes the torment worse. Yes, Sunset Point provides steady employment, not just for him, but for Maribel and many others like her. He gets that, but that shouldn't stop him from being critical of the set-up, the two worlds, the bowing and scraping to the privileged. And this whole damn thing about the United States and Mexico—the history, the border crossings, the wall, unaccompanied little children being sent there all alone, not to mention the cocaine wars—it's unjust to the point of being grotesque.

It's a funny thing about history: You can't go back, but you can change the future. Yeah, sure, what hope is there for that?

6

FRIENDS AND FIESTAS

Vera and Ollie are stretched out on lounge chairs beside the pool having a Vitamin D moment with the sun. By late morning the clouds have either evaporated or blown over the mountains leaving the resort with such a clear atmosphere that every plant, person, and object stands out in sharp definition. Ever since his cataract surgery, Ollie has developed a new appreciation of clarity and true color and he especially enjoys his improved vision in the dry air of Cabo.

Overhead the palm trees flutter gently in a breeze that disguises the sun's heat, creating just the right temperature to warm the bones. Ollie's oddly matched legs, one hairy and one hairless, stick out from his navy-blue bathing suit. Vera slips on a jaunty rose-colored hat to complement her old black maillot and rubs on a little sunscreen to keep her face from looking like that plowed field she dreads. She is eager to make a schedule and has her calendar in hand. "We are already beginning our second week, love. Can you believe that?"

Ollie sets aside his Los Cabos Daily News and folds up his reading glasses ready to give her his attention. "So, what's on the agenda?" he asks.

"Today is the birthday party for Fernando."

"What time?"

"Rosita will pick us up in front of the lobby at one o'clock."

"What else?"

"We need to see Isabella's baby. That's Tuesday at three o'clock at the Palmita Market."

"What about Daniella?"

"Yes, of course, I have the clothes for Blanca and Cenia. We'll ask Daniella tonight about a time to meet when she seats us for dinner."

Ollie scratches his head, sits up, and flings his legs over the edge of the lounge chair to face Vera. He scoots forward and says to her, almost in a whisper, "I've been thinking a lot about Marquito."

"Yes, I have, too. Maybe I shouldn't have asked him so many questions. You know me, professional voyeur. Insisting that people expose their naked soul."

"No, no, you were fine. It's just that . . . well, maybe that question about reconciling the two worlds, the two lives, maybe that's our issue, not his."

"Meaning?"

"I think you and I have become deeply troubled by the difference between our own comfortable way of life in retirement, here and at home, and the poverty and struggle we see in the lives of so many people we have come to know in Mexico."

"God, Ollie, that legal mind of yours. You hit it right on the head. Yes, exactly. It's our two worlds, that's the problem."

"It's like, what do you do when you discover that paradise has slums? That's our question."

"So, do you think I am projecting our problem onto Marquito?" Vera asks, worried that she is.

"Could be."

"But from his point of view..." Vera hesitates.

"What makes his point of view different," Ollie suggests, "is that he grew up in the U.S. As you suggested, he was Americanized in the schools. He almost had the good life in his grasp. Then it was snatched away from him."

"Instead of strolling through a lovely university campus, he is running his butt off here taking care of all of these overstuffed Americans." She gestures toward the pool where there is indeed a flock of supine resort guests with their bellies protruding up into the atmosphere like they are twelve months pregnant, some reading, others listening to music, and a few snoring, oblivious to the impression they might be making.

"Well, first of all," Ollie responds, "not everyone at this resort is privileged. Some people swipe out their credit cards for just a three or four day once-in-a-lifetime vacation. We met those working women from San Francisco, that black couple from Maryland both employed by the federal government, and the two nurses from Alaska. Not everyone owns time shares like we do. But that's not the point."

"What is the point, dear?"

"Marco had his identity ripped away. That's the unspoken problem of the illegals in the U.S. We want to raise them up like good little Americans, insist that they speak English, and we do a fairly good job of that, but then at the first chance we get, we send them home, with no regard for the fact that they no longer know how to live in Mexico. Aliens in their own country."

"Wow, Ollie, when you put it that way, it makes me even more concerned about Marco. He really needs someone to look out for him, some surrogate parents."

"I don't mean to minimize the economic issues," Ollie continues, "because he's also poor twenty-four seven."

"So, do you think that the people who live here in Cabo—I don't mean those working at the resort—do you think they are angry about their economic situation being Mexican and so often poor?" Vera asks.

From what I can tell, there are a lot of different responses that people make to being poor, not just here but in the U.S. and elsewhere. You're talking about people in the know, with cell phones, with access to social media. People who see the differences and resent what they see. Sure, some of them are upset, but not everybody's angry. Remember, it's been like this in Mexico for generations. Some people just accept that this is the way life is."

"Qué será, será." Vera gestures, palms up. She remembers the old song, and the melody kind of gets going in her head.

"Exactly. Others think life is better now but are impatient for more change. And don't forget, there is enough blame to go around for Mexico to share some, too, with regime after regime of corrupt politicians. A revolution that was more like a long civil war. Many people are disillusioned about progress through politics. Some, it seems, have an amazing capacity for happiness despite their poverty."

"Now you are really getting at it, dear. What makes people happy? That's the sixty-four-thousand-dollar question." Vera loves it when Ollie gets involved in a discussion like this. He's wise and she respects him for that.

"Maybe they don't require all the material things we think they need to be happy. Perhaps they have other ways of being happy," he says.

"But they don't have to be so damn poor either." Vera insists.

"Well, that's true, too. In Marco's case he is both poor and unhappy. Is it any wonder he's angry?"

As they enter the lobby to wait for Rosita, Ollie notices that brightly decorated faux packages have been stacked high under the Christmas tree to compensate for the missing branches.

"Look at the presents, Ollie," Vera says.

"Don't make me think about that damned tree. I dreamed about it off and on all night, you know, trying to figure out how to wire those branches back on, or glue them, or just have people standing there holding them."

"Oh, my, dear, just let it go."

They will always be thankful to Rosita who helped them with their booking in their first years of their membership. Now she's become a good friend. She picks them up in front of the lobby at one o'clock sharp. They pile into her old car—Ollie notes the cracked windshield—and she takes them into town and drives north a few blocks through a "residential" area of boxy rental properties on unpaved streets—no grass no flowers, not even cactus, just kids and dogs playing by the front door of the place they call home. Rosita maneuvers in and out among parked cars across those bumpy side streets, apologizing each time her friends go bouncing up into the air. They finally arrive at a brightly colored little restaurant where the fiesta appears to be already underway.

The open-air cantina has a roof of thatched palm leaves suspended above a slab of concrete where tables with bright red and white checked cloths are set up with matching red paper napkins and white plastic knives and forks. Vera and Ollie are introduced around to various friends, grandparents, aunts, uncles, cousins, and godparents, an extended family indeed. They are all very welcoming and those who know some English try to speak a few words. Some of the older women are dressed in traditional costumes of wide white skirts and colorful aprons. Fernando and Alfredo swoop in to say hello and then hustle back to play with their friends, comfortable in their jeans and t-shirts. They all play together happily, the older children looking out for the younger ones. When a baby gets cranky, it gets passed off to another pair of loving arms. The children don't seem to get into fights over toys; maybe, Ollie observes, because there aren't many toys.

To the children's delight, a brown turtle about the size of a salad plate has slowly made its way into the party. The children hover around close enough to get a glimpse of this odd visitor without impeding its progress across the cement floor. They are motioning to each other to "back off" or "make way." Eventually, someone who appears to be the owner picks up the mobile shell propelled on sturdy stubby legs and carries it back to the small plastic swimming pool that serves as its home. Some children follow the turtle, others resume their play.

Fernando's parents have decorated the cantina with red and blue crepe paper and matching balloons bundled in clusters at the ceiling in keeping with the Spiderman theme of the fiesta. Fernando wears his Spiderman shirt, and the heart-shaped piñata, with its multi-layered encasement of candies, has Spiderman pictures on both sides. Of course, Ollie has read about piñatas, but he wasn't aware of how the game actually works. "Look at this, dear," Ollie exclaims, "the rope goes through a pulley attached to one of the beams in the ceiling, so Fernando's father can pull on the rope to raise or lower the piñata, making it just out of reach of the stick that the children use to try to bat it down. How clever." The children wait patiently in line to take their turn to make a few swats with the stick. The older children try it blindfolded. Fernando's father makes sure that no one does any serious damage before Fernando gets his turn. When he finally takes up the stick, the guests begin to cheer him on. "¡Vá, Fernando! Vámonos!" His father raises and lowers the piñata, teasing poor Fernando by keeping it just out of reach, but Fernando keeps batting away with the stick, missing but persisting. "My God, Vera, that has to be frustrating. An American kid would have already hit his father over the head with the stick." Fernando doesn't give up, swatting away with all his might, pacing back and forth like a tormented little bull. Finally, his father lowers the piñata to within reach and Fernando connects with two swift swats, one after the other, blam, blam, and the candies go flying all over the place. The children rush in to grab up what they can from the floor. Fernando picks up some pieces to give to his mother and brother. Then he scoops up a few more and brings them over to Vera and Ollie. Looking a little tuckered out, he goes over to give a candy to his dad, who pulls him onto his knee to embrace him and congratulate him for being a year older.

A trio of guitar, bass, and concertina starts playing lively Mexican music, and the guests are soon bobbing back and forth and tapping their feet. Besides the food the owner provided, friends and family have brought in an abundant supply of burritos, tamales, tacos, and empanadas. The smell of fried onions, chili peppers, and browned meat drifts up from the tables along with the subtle scent of fresh-squeezed lime that seems to go on everything. For dessert there is an assortment of cupcakes, puddings, and cookies. Alfredo brings over two small dishes of rice pudding with raisins and cinnamon, always one of Ollie's favorite Mexican desserts. Rosita is bustling from table to table to make sure that everyone finds their favorite food. "Ah, what a grand fiesta," Ollie exclaims. "And as usual your boys are delightful. So polite and nicely dressed."

Vera adds, "It is certainly a lovely party. Thanks for including us."

"My pleasure," Rosita responds, full of smiles. "Have something more to eat."

When the party winds down, and they have said many good-byes over and over, Rosita is able to slip away and take them back to the resort. Rosita says good-bye again with hugs and soft kisses on the cheek and Vera and Ollie head for their room, their other life. Alone in the elevator, lifting slowly toward the seventh floor, Ollie says, "I feel like I'm part of the family. How do they do that?"

Vera says, "I don't know. They open their arms, feed us, and the rest is magic."

Ollie adds, "For me, being with people like that is one of the best parts of coming to Mexico now."

After breakfast the next morning, after the rush is over and Marquito has a little free time, Vera motions to him to come over to their table.

"More decaf, more juice?" he asks, flashing his wonderful smile.

"No, we're fine," Ollie replies.

"Oh, Marquito," Vera begins. "I want to apologize for asking so many questions that day we went for milkshakes. I can see how you might have thought me to be somewhat intrusive, or just downright nosy. I'm sorry."

"Oh, not at all, ma'am. It was good for me. Really got me thinking." He shifts his weight nervously from side to side, first on one foot, then the other and runs a tan hand through his wavy black hair. Then he stops talking and presses his lips together, as if to keep his mouth under control.

"I especially want to tell you that those questions about the two lives and reconciling the differences between the two worlds, those seem to be questions that Ollie and I have about our own lives, and it was thoughtless of me to lay all of that on you."

"No problem. Mainly, I guess that I'm angry about moving back to Mexico, you know, and all that I lost, but I know what you are saying about the two worlds. Well, I better not say much more. Not here."

Vera nods several times. "Let us know if we can help."

"I really don't know how," Marquito says holding a shrug in place.

"At the moment, I don't know how either," Vera agrees. She wishes she did. It's in her social worker soul to want to help.

Vera and Ollie go back up to the room to change into their bathing suits and pick up some books and magazines. It is usually a quick trip up the elevator and back down again, but Vera meets up with Carmelita in the outside corridor that connects all of the rooms for that floor to the elevator. Carmelita wears her hair pulled back tight and wrapped into a bun covered with a hairnet. Her oblong glasses have decorative, dull stainless frames, and when she smiles, she holds her lips together as if she's trying to hide her teeth. Her square face is deeply creased with wrinkles from the sun and it is hard to tell whether she is an older person who moves in a youthful way, or if she is younger person who just looks older because of her weather-beaten face. Vera imagines her as a reincarnation from Aztec times.

Carmelita sweeps the outside hallways all day long, keeping them immaculate so that no room service trays are left behind, nothing dropped is lost, and no crumpled leaf or cigarette butt is left to give the impression of untidiness. Carmelita does this in all three wings, all seven floors, and when she is done, she starts again, keeping all of the corridors spotless. Carmelita is a special challenge for Vera because Carmelita speaks no English at all. Vera's Spanish must be good enough for Carmelita to believe that Vera speaks Spanish, so when Carmelita speaks to her, the words come tripping off her tongue without hesitation, and Vera has to admit later to Ollie that she had almost no comprehension of what Carmelita was saying to her. Despite the language barrier, Vera and Carmelita have become good friends, and always on the day before they leave, Carmelita brings Vera a bouquet of yellow, pink, and orange, hand-made paper flowers. It's her hobby, making those flowers.

When Vera and Ollie finally get back down to the pool level, they stop to pick up towels from the towel boy, Ernesto, and Vera gives him the elementary level children's books she brought to help him practice his reading in English. "Oh, you didn't forget me," he says, barely five feet tall, but his whole body full of delight.

"No, Ernesto," Vera says, "How could I forget you when you are working so hard on your English."

"Someday you will be having me for dinner as your waiter," he promises. "Just being a little patient."

For the rest of the morning Vera and Ollie lounge by the pool, but Vera is quiet, a little out of sorts with herself. She lets Ollie snooze. She's worried that she has set something in motion with Marquito that could get out of control. With her former clients she was always certain that she would see them again, usually on a regular basis. There was structure. With Marquito she has no way to follow up, no opportunity to guide him as he works through his issues. It's like he's one of those wind-up toys: you wind them up and set them down, but you have no idea where they're going to go, or even whether they will stand or fall over. Marquito is definitely wound up tight. Could his emotional spring snap? Would she be responsible? She fears she may have lifted the lid on a Pandora's box.

That afternoon, Ollie and Vera stroll over to the Palmita Market to meet Isabella, the manicurist, and her "not-really-husband," Solomón. It is a lovely walk down through the hedges of pink and burgundy bougainvillea, and then back up along the road that serves the two other hotels, the familiar route of their morning walk. Palm trees rise majestically from the neatly-trimmed grass. The new parents are already seated at an outdoor table at the market and the baby is nestled in Solomón's strong brown arms.

"What name did you give this precious little bundle?" Vera asks, sounding like a minister at a baptism.

"Suzette," Isabella replies.

"She's adorable."

Ollie gathers up the orders of flavors so that he can get the ice cream cones for everyone: chocolate, cherry vanilla, butter pecan. The ice cream here is almost as good as Ben & Jerry's before it was sold off. He's back in a jiffy with his hands full.

The baby, sporting a big pink bow on a stretch band that encircles her head, is not only precious, but has the most expressive face imaginable for one so young. It's as if she is already talking, but without words, at least she has all of the facial expressions that go with talking. Somehow, she has already learned to do the most amazing things with her eyebrows, her little mouth, even her tan nose; and she keeps everyone entranced, especially her father, who won't stop looking down at her.

Suzette doesn't seem to favor either parent, and that starts Ollie to thinking about how babies combine the looks of the father and the mother. Sometimes, though rarely, attractive parents have ugly children; but at other times, perhaps even more rarely, parents who are themselves not particularly attractive have a beautiful baby. It has always been a puzzle to him how this can be. In this case, mother and father both have faces of the poor, of the countryside, but the baby seems to have picked off the best features of each parent—a straight nose, a delicately curved upper lip, tiny ears, arched eyebrows—and put them all together to make that beautiful, animated little face. It's the face of a little princess. Ollie wonders if Isabella and Solomón, with their royal names, somehow know this because they seem to be unable to conceal their own astonishment at how they have produced such a beautiful little creature. There is nothing else in their world at this moment but their little Suzette. Suddenly Isabella begins to tear-up like she's going to cry.

"Forevermore, Isabella, what's wrong?" Vera asks.

"Suzette almost died," Solomón explains. "She was in the hospital for two weeks with a serious respiratory infection. At first the doctors didn't know what it was. We almost lost her. Now we call her our miracle baby."

Isabella wipes her eyes, stands up, and places Suzette carefully in Vera's arms. The cascade of Suzette's talkative facial expressions continues, but she doesn't make a peep, not the hint of a whimper. Vera adjusts the sweet little pink bow and continues to rock her as Ollie sends his wife a subtle signal that he would like a turn to hold the little precious, too.

Isabella asks Solomón to tell them about his promotion. "Oh," he reports proudly, "I'm chief of evening security now at the power company. Now Isabella doesn't have to work so many hours doing nails, just three days a week, and she can spend more time with Suzette."

"Oh, my Gosh," Vera exclaims abruptly, "I almost forgot the presents. Where's the bag, Ollie?" He pulls it from under the table with a flourish and then takes Suzette. He can't remember when he started to love holding babies so much. Long after his own children graduated from infancy, that's for sure. Maybe he should run for office now. Soon the blouses and pants and jackets and sleepers are being held up against Suzette to check for size and color. Isabella is so overwhelmed with joy that she starts to cry again.

When Ollie opens the door to their room with the electronic card key, Vera can see that he is making a bee-line through the sheer curtains to the sliding patio doors that open onto the balcony so that he can soak up the angled rays of the late afternoon sun, one of the advantages of being on the seventh floor. He's eager for a snooze and settles into one of the lounge chairs. This gives Vera an opportunity to ring up the children on Skype. They are hardly children, of course, but she still thinks of them that way. Ellen, the daughter in Dallas, has traded up her car to a new model Lexus, and she's all excited about the cool electronic gadgets it has. A GPS, a rear-view camera, and an amazing sound system that really rocks. Ellen hardly sees Damon—he's so busy—so she just about lives in her car, hopping from mall to mall. She needed a new car, no doubt about it. So much for Ellen.

Vera tries Peter in Boulder. He answers immediately on his cell phone, like he's just sitting there waiting for incoming calls. Peter has changed jobs again. He's working on software for video games and loves it although the pay is really low. "Really demeaning, Mom." But he's all upbeat because Colorado has legalized marijuana, both for medical and recreational uses. Recreational? My how the meaning of that word has changed. Peter says he had Thanksgiving dinner at KFC with a new friend. Vera wonders if the original tastes extra crispy if you're stoned. Neither of the kids appeared to be missing their parents, leastwise not for Thanksgiving dinner. She wonders who the friend is, but doesn't ask. Somehow the children have never outgrown those patterns of non-communication that started in adolescence. Is that their fault or hers? Whatever went wrong with their kids anyway? Probably a much too permissive upbringing. She and Ollie let them become whatever they would become and that's what happened.

Vera and Ollie always bring a few fine clothes so they can dress for dinner, he in his blue and white pin-striped trousers and a button-down short-sleeve shirt, she in a print dress with simple costume jewelry, the cheaper the better because she hates to waste money on bling. La Casona becomes a different place at night, contrasting sharply with the bustling breakfast hours. The light canvas overhead awnings have been pulled back to open the restaurant to a canopy of stars and a moon of many phases that may show up when least expected. White tablecloths and crystal glassware add a touch of elegance. Above the front railing, strings of small lights run between brightly burning torches with flames that leap into the dark sky. Out on the ocean, bright white lights outline the mast and sails of a small private boat, and the cruise ship of the day, like a brightly lit floating hotel, sounds its horn for stragglers so that it can get underway for a night of travel to its next destination. The restaurant is quiet enough for serious conversation because the noisy younger children at the resort have been left behind in their rooms to enjoy room service pizza and watch downloaded videos.

That evening after Daniella has seated them, she stops by to arrange a place and time when Vera and Ollie can meet with her and the two girls. "Well, they always think it's special to go to MacDonald's, so if you don't mind."

"Yes, that's fine, Ollie says. "What time?"

"It's my day off, but Blanca has school. Maybe three-thirty?"

"That's good." Ollie taps Daniella on the shoulder. "My dear, you have two couples looking for a table."

"Oh, you're right. Talk to you later."

Vera and Ollie decide to make a dinner that night out of soup, salad and appetizers. Ollie loves the corn soup with just a hint of green chile, and Vera enjoys the sliced tomatoes with mozzarella cheese. They order an appetizer portion of coconut shrimp to share. Lino is waiting on them that night, and Vera reaches into her purse and pulls out the small flashlight she brought for him. He says he is delighted because it is just the right size to shine on the bills his customers struggle to read at night. He is so happy, and it's really nothing at all. They sit in silence waiting for their food.

"Listen to the waves, dear. Do you hear that?" Vera asks.

"Hear what? The waves, sure. Pretty calm tonight."

"No, I mean really listen, you get the sound of the wave rolling in, and then you get the sound of the wave rolling out again, but just for an instant, between the rolling in and the rolling out, there's a little interval of silence. Listen." She moves one hand as if she is conducting the sound of the waves like an orchestra.

Ollie listens not just dutifully but with what appears to be genuine curiosity. "Well, gosh, dear, you're right."

"Do you hear that silence?"

"Well, if it's silence, I'm not quite sure I hear it, but I know what you mean. Just for a split second, there's nothing."

"Exactly. Well, now, I think that's where Marquito is. He's right in the middle of that little silence where there's nothing."

"In that little moment between waves where he doesn't know whether he's coming or going, so to speak."

Vera rubs the back of her neck. "Who will come into that space and time, the silence between the waves, and how will they influence him? He is remarkably vulnerable, Ollie, that's what I worry about."

"The right person could make a big difference."

"And conversely, the wrong person with the wrong message at just the right moment could fuck up his life forever. Excuse me. Ruin. I meant to say ruin."

"No, no, you're the social worker with the cool street talk. It's okay. I see what you are saying. But what can we do?"

"Not much. That's what's bothering me."

"Maybe warn him?"

"That's a good idea, dear. Warn him about what could happen. I'll warn him."

Vera is glad to see Daniella coming toward them and is even happier to see that she is carrying a plate of small round sugar cookies. "These are not on the menu," she says. "They're from the cafeteria. They're for the staff, but everybody loves them. Mexican cookies. I thought they would go well with your decaf. We'll just call them Daniella's galletas. Just between us."

The next day, on Daniella's day off, Ollie and Vera go to meet her and the children, Cenia and Blanca, at MacDonald's. They catch a cab in front of the lobby because they have too many presents to carry for walking. They leave early and arrive early, so they have a little time on their hands. Vera starts to list off all of the MacDonald's they have been in all over the world: Hong Kong, Vienna, Riyadh, Stockholm, São Paulo, New York City. Ollie is amazed at how many she can recall and pretty much describe the location. "I think the fanciest was the one in Saudi Arabia, the one with two stories and all of that gold glitz. Remember?" He doesn't, but that's okay because he leaves it to Vera to remember things like that. "Did you ever think," Vera asks him, "that when we were young college students at Middlebury, we would travel to so many places in the world?"

"Well, I didn't know I'd be working for an international law firm with offices strung out from the Halls of Montezuma to the shores of Tripoli."

"Better than being in the marines, I should think. And you were so sweet; you always let me tag along when I could use my vacation days and get unpaid leave."

"Tag along, nothing. I needed you. Without you I'd be confused, I'd get lost, I'd misplace things."

"God, Ollie, you make me sound like your nanny."

"No, no, much more than a nanny. When I got frustrated, you'd listen to me. When I couldn't think about how to resolve a dispute, you'd suggest a strategy for getting agreement. You were indispensable."

"A small job for such rich compensation, getting to see so much of the world."

"Good thing we were young then. Travel's hard now. It's about all I can do to get on the plane in Denver and get off in Cabo." He lets out a long sigh. "At least we have our memories, eh?"

"We do. And we enjoy them. But it can be dangerous."

Ollie is puzzled. "How's that?"

"A lot of older people only have memories. They've given up on having a future, and they have nothing to do in the present, so they live in the past."

"We wouldn't want to be like that, would we? Or are you implying that we already are?"

"I'm just saying we could get like that. Maybe we need a project."

Just then, Daniella, Cenia, and Blanca come bursting through the door, so Ollie doesn't get to ask Vera what she means by project. He struggles to his feet for the greetings and hugs. The children, with big smiles of anticipation on their faces, slide into the booth next to their mother. Ollie asks them in his best Spanish what they want to drink and eat, and they speak back that rat-a-tat-tat machine gun Español at him just as if he understood, so he has to ask Daniella to translate. That will teach him: never show off in front of a little kid. He returns quickly with the soft drinks and French fries and has to be careful not to step on Cenia, who is now waddling around with the confidence of a duck out in the aisle. He notices that Cenia's previously pudgy little face has thinned out so that she shows the potential of becoming quite pretty, maybe prettier than Blanca someday, who is struggling a bit just now with missing front teeth. Soon the table is stacked with an abundance of blouses and pants and skirts. Daniella thanks them again and again for the clothes, but what the children like most, of course, are the toys. Not much money for toys in that family. Blanca is captivated by anything that poses a cognitive challenge: a mechanical game, a small piano keyboard, a toy computer. She could become a genuine nerd if she had the equipment.

When all of the presents are opened and all of the toys tested out and then packed up again, Ollie slips a few pesos into one of the plastic bags.

Vera asks Daniella about her sister. There is no response. Daniella makes a valiant effort to gain control of her emotions before large tears come splashing down her cheeks. She is scarcely able to get out the two words, she died.

"Oh, I'm so sorry," Vera says in a whisper, the fingers of her right hand shooting up to cover her mouth at this alarming news.

Vera is seldom blind-sided. She's seen everything, but Ollie can see that this has taken her completely by surprise. He just shakes his head.

"Last month," Daniella says, brushing the tears from her face with a small white handkerchief she has retrieved from the sleeve of her blouse. Turning to Blanca, she asks her to take Cenia over to the corner with the play equipment.

"What about her children?" Vera asks "Where are they?"

"They live with us. Her husband is very nice. Sends us what money he can, but he doesn't earn much. He didn't want to live with a house full of women, so he left. He visits."

Ollie is counting heads – Daniella, her mother, Cenia and Blanca and now two more in that little house, which he remembers vividly now: the worn-out linoleum floors, the dimly-lit kitchen, kids crowded together in a small bedroom. Some things he remembers too well.

"How do you manage?" Vera asks.

"Barely, just barely. But my mother is wonderful. She still finds time . . . oh, I almost forgot. She made you tamales." Daniella finds a little container in her big purse and hands it to Vera.

"Now she didn't need to do that," Ollie says graciously.

"She wanted to. She's a saint."

Vera and Ollie, freed of all of their packages, decide to walk back to the resort. Vera walks ahead of him in silence. She glances back every now and then to see him following in her steps on the narrow, irregular sidewalk that switches from one side of the street to the other. When they have almost reached the gate, Vera says, "I was so embarrassed."

Ollie takes her hand. "You didn't know."

"I knew it was cancer. I should have been more sensitive."

"I doubt that any amount of sensitivity can soften such stark news," he says.

"Daniella is really grieving. I remember she told me how close she was to her sister. Such a tragedy. My God, Ollie, how are they going to make it?"

"Hard to say," he responds, but with no answer. Vera can tell that Ollie is worried about them, too. He's chewing the side of his cheek and he hasn't done that in years.

Passing through the gate, they trudge up the driveway among the bougainvillea, greet the bellmen, and catch the elevator to the seventh floor. No more visits, no more friends to meet; now they can just enjoy their remaining days before they go home on Saturday. Enjoy? Vera wonders how she can enjoy anything with so many people on her mind. She and Ollie must find a way to help. Not just a few presents toted down in suitcases. Something bigger, something that will have more impact. They've got all those investments. Why is their wealth just sitting there? What's to become of it? Just let it go to their children? She promises herself to have a serious talk with Ollie when they get home.

Vera and Ollie are spending an evening in their room. The heavy drapes have been pulled shut over the sheer curtains by the evening maid who turns down the bed and leaves two little chocolates on the pillows. Ollie hears only the sound of the refrigerator turning on and off as he reads on the living room couch. Vera surfs the bedroom TV without finding much of interest. Finally, she pokes her head into the living room and says, "What about tonight?"

"Tonight?" Ollie asks, a little surprised, though he knows perfectly well what this coded question means. "Well, sure I'm always interested." He puts down his book. "I better go take my pill."

They brush their teeth, which has become a prolonged evening ritual now because their meticulous care has been well rewarded with minimal dental problems. They prop themselves up side by side on the bed to watch some TV. The news on CNN is so depressing it makes them nervous. "Can we switch channels?" he asks. "Is there a movie?"

A movie in English is not easy to locate, but Vera eventually finds a promising French film with English subtitles and an R rating for nudity. Ollie gets so engrossed that he doesn't notice that Vera has fallen asleep. When it is over, he glances over and doesn't know whether to wake her or not, but he hates to let the medication go to waste. Finally, he says, "Vera, honey. Sweetheart. You fell asleep."

"Oh, so I did. Thank you for waking me."

Ollie says, "Let's use the Jacuzzi. There it sits and we never use it."

"You must be kidding. We could get seriously injured getting in and out of that thing. Break a hip, smash a knee."

"We can be careful. I could help you." Actually, he is not so sure he can maneuver the damn thing either.

"Have you been fantasizing about having a hot time in the old tub tonight? Well, keep fantasizing." Vera stands up, fluffs up the pillows, and pulls back the covers. "I think this might be best. In the dark. Like we always do."

The next morning Vera asks, as she often does, "And what about last night?"

"Marvelous," Ollie replies. It never ceases to amaze me how a couple of old dudes like us can still wring a little pleasure out of these rickety bodies of ours."

"But we completely forgot to pack. Now we will have to hustle."

"Not a problem. We have so little. We could probably give away the rest of our clothes if they weren't dirty."

When they have packed their things, Vera surveys the empty suitcases, and says, "It was a good visit."

"You made many people happy and I know that makes you happy." Ollie gives her a hug. "Let's get some breakfast and say good-bye to Marquito."

Of course, Marquito is there. "The usual?" he asks.

"Yes," Vera replies.

"Not for me," Ollie responds. "I'm going to do the buffet. Hard to tell when we'll get real food again today."

"No problem, Señor. I'll be right back with your juice and decaf." He dashes off.

Vera leans over to Ollie, who is enjoying his last edition of the Los Cabos Daily News for a while. "I want to say something to him, but I don't want to make matters worse."

"I'm sure you won't." Ollie looks up at her over the top of his reading glasses. "Just let him know that you are concerned about him."

Vera thinks about what she will say. She listens to the sound of the waves coming in and going out and to the magical silence between the swooshing sounds.

When Marquito returns, he says, "You must be leaving today. Am I right?"

"Yes, it's a pity," Vera says.

"It's especially a pity, when you consider what you are returning home to. Have you heard?"

"No, what?" Ollie asks.

"A foot of snow and a temperature of three degrees. I keep track of what's going on in the U.S."

"Yes, you do. Would you like to go back?"

"Well, not to a foot of snow, but in any case, there's no chance of that now. That's finished."

"Look, Marquito," Vera lays a hand on his forearm, "I'm worried about you. You are in a difficult time in your life, and I know you are upset. Promise me something. Don't rush into anything. And be careful who you associate with. I know I sound like a mother, but listen to me. Something very good could happen to you. Really it could. Be patient."

Marquito frowns, not knowing what to say. He shifts from one foot to the other. Finally, he says, "Something very good? I don't know how that could happen to me."

7

ASHLEY MOVES IN

La Casona has been non-stop busy all morning. The holiday season has arrived and so have the guests. The "all-inclusive" mostly take the buffet, but it seems like the "a la carte" are different for each person at each table. Now it is winding down. The steamer trays from the buffet are returned to the kitchen mostly empty and the remaining dirty dishes are bussed from the tables. Maribel's grill is scraped clean and the left-over ingredients she uses have been returned to the storage refrigerator. Marco unfolds a small note placed in his hand by Maribel. "Here. It's from Verónica."

"What's this about?"

"I don't read other people's notes, Señor, so I guess you will need to read it yourself. Perhaps an invitation to a ball?"

"Well, thanks. Yeah, gracias." But he doesn't know what else to say.

He strolls up to the lobby and finds Verónica at the concierge desk working with an arriving couple with two cute blue-eyed kids. She interrupts her conversation long enough to hand him a package. Oh, yes, Marquito, this came for you. I don't know why it was sent here, but no problema."

He smiles and thanks her. Outside the sliding doors, he greets Óscar and Sebastián, the bellmen working the arrivals. He goes down the hill toward the main gate and detours into the underground parking area to record his check out time. At the main road leading out of the resort, he catches a bus to the Paraíso Mall. On the bus he opens the package. He can see that it is from Vera and Oliver Webster in Colorado, and he knows that it is a book. He wiggles it out of its cardboard container. A hardback. He reads the title, A Wicked War, then glances at the back of the dust jacket. La hostia! A history of the Mexican War. How nice of Ollie to send him such a perfect book.

He goes through the revolving door at the Paraíso Mall, finds a vacant spot on a bench, and sits down gently next to a dozing, gray-haired Mexican lady. The author of the book is a woman, Amy Greenburg, a professor at Penn State University, and right up front she identifies the major players, at least the Americans. For the title she has borrowed a phrase from Ulysses S. Grant, a U.S. President and Civil War general, who called it America's "most wicked war." Interesting. Marco starts to read it right then and there. In a few minutes he is completely absorbed in it, transported back to the U.S. in the 1840s, back in time and across a vast space, traveling by book.

He reads his new book every afternoon at Médano Beach and every night in his apartment in the light of his lamp. He can't put it down. When he has finished it, he is sorry because he knows that he won't be able to travel there anymore. Of course he will reread sections of it to learn the names, dates, places, and events. Except for a few details, Mr. O'Reilly, his high school history teacher, got it all damn straight. A war of territorial expansion provoked by the Texians. Manifest Destiny. God's will that America should spread from sea to shining sea.

At breakfast this morning, Marco waits on the family with the two little blue-eyed kids who Verónica was working with in the lobby. He remembers them because of the blond mom and the Asian dad, maybe a grown up Korean or Vietnamese love child from one of those U.S. foreign wars. But the kids, the next generation, have these unbelievably blue sloping eyes. Asian eyes, but a spooky, infinite azure like the sky itself. As soon as their plates are cleared, the restless kids jump out of their chairs and gain permission to go play in the sand on the beach. They scurry off as their parents yell after them to stay out of the ocean. The parents are lingering over coffee now at the same table where Vera and Ollie sat every morning. Nice enough people, but quiet.

Marco misses Vera and Ollie. They knew how to liven things up a little with all of those questions. It gets boring beyond words being a waiter, every morning the same thing – handing out menus, taking orders, running for juice, and refilling coffee cups. He notices that his mind goes flitting off in every direction like a butterfly. Sometimes to think about butterflies. Does a butterfly have any purpose? Do they exist just so humans can say, oh, what a beautiful yellow butterfly? Can something exist without purpose? But that's absurd. Just pure being? Stuff like this gets spinning round and around in his head, and he's glad for these mental meanderings because they break up the monotony; but it's also annoying because he can't always keep those weird thoughts under control, and sometimes it causes him to mix up the orders or bring stuff to the wrong table. But then again, maybe it's okay for a butterfly to exist without a purpose. Maybe its purpose is just to be bonita.

Holy shit! He is jarred back to reality by what he sees at the water's edge. He slams down his tray and starts running across the restaurant, darting in and out through the tables and down the steps toward the beach. He knows he has stripped off his waiter's jacket and somehow freed himself of his shoes, socks and pants because he feels the warm sand on his bare feet. He bounds across the beach in the broad leaps of a gazelle, hurdling over sunbathing bodies. Never having taken his eyes off of the spot, he races past the screaming little sister, dives in, and comes up on the first try with the blue-eyed older brother, who is nearly strangling him in a headlock as he swims a few strokes back to the shore. He flips the boy upside down and starts shaking him, and when he turns him upright, he starts coughing and gasping for breath. No mouth to mouth necessary. Finally, the eyelids open and those infinite blue eyes stare at him. A blue so blue it's as if this little guy's soul has been to the edge of the universe and back. Then the kid lets out a shrill cry for his mother.

By then his breathless parents, frantic to get to their boy, are stumbling across the sand, barely able to keep from falling with each step. When they arrive on the scene, the mother grabs her son and starts kissing him all over. Now the younger sister starts screeching. She needs kisses, too. The father thanks Marquito profusely, many times, graciously, and apologizes for the inconvenience. Inconvenience? Jesus, your kid almost died. When Marquito is sure the blue-eyed wonder is okay, he retreats from the crowd that is gathering around the family, and stoops down for a second to catch his breath, let his pounding heart recover, and gather his wits. He feels a gentle hand on his shoulder.

"Are you okay?" Maribel asks softly. "I didn't know if you could swim."

He looks up and smiles. "That would have made it a lot more difficult, huh." She doesn't even smile at his little joke, she just stares at him, looking worried and mystified.

"No but really, how did you know what to do?"

"Oh, I took this Red Cross lifesaving course when I was in school in the U.S. I never used it, but like they told us, you never know when you might need it."

"Looks like today was the day. You're shivering. Let's get you back up to the restaurant."

As he walks back, awestruck guests hand him his pants, his shoes, his socks, his jacket, apparently in the reverse order of his taking them off. He can't remember, it all happened so fast. When he enters the restaurant, all eyes are on him—maybe because he is standing there soaking wet in his underwear? He gives the onlookers a smile of embarrassment and a shrug. His tray. What happened to his tray? It looks like the food has been served. Of course Omar and the other waiters are all over it. "Take a break, Marquito," Omar says. "Go dry off. We've got it. That was fantastic."

It's then that he hears the gruff voice of the captain, El Greco, in his face. "Oh, hero. Go change yourself. Get back to work. We've got many works to do here, Marquito. And Maribel, you've got a long lining up of many peoples waiting. This is not your business. Your business is om-el-ettes."

¡Aayyyyyy Dios mio! Marco really has to talk to himself fast to control his anger—don't do it, Marco, the goal is control—to keep from decking the guy right on the spot. So sarcastic. Hero? Glory? He wasn't trying to be a hero. He just did what he was trained to do. Instinctively. And did the jerk have to say that to Maribel? ¡Hijo de la chingada! He notices that his hands are in fists. He wants to tell him to leave Maribel out of this, but he doesn't; he just grabs a clean uniform and goes to the employees' restroom. Without a word. Without a look. In five minutes, he's back at his tables. More coffee? More orange juice? Yes, sir. Yes, ma'am.

At the end of his shift, Marco heads down to the mall on his usual route home. But he doesn't go home. He can't shake the sarcastic tone of El Greco. He's still pissed. He walks three sides of the wide walkway around the marina, past the boats and restaurants and then back again, hoping that maybe he can walk it off. He weaves in and out among throngs of tourists—two boatloads today—and finds them annoying. Suddenly tired out, Marco decides to go back toward the Mango Cantina.

He is almost there when he becomes aware of someone walking beside him. He slows his pace, but the person doesn't pass him. He speeds up, she's still there. He's pretty sure it's a she. So, he stops. She stops. He turns to her. "Who are you?"

"My name is Ashley."

Her confidence catches him by surprise.

"May I help you?" Marco sounds a little curt, but all he wants is some time alone and to have a beer and calm down.

"I'd like something to drink."

Marco is once again taken aback by this American boldness; a Mexican girl would never do that. "Okay, just up ahead here, there's a little place I like." She's walking in step with him now. He steals a sidewise glance at her. She's in shorts and a revealing tank top. ¡Guapa! Red hair. Orange actually. Short on the far side but long strands plunging across her right eye, blowing in the breeze like flames from a fire. He looks at her more directly. The arm nearest him has an elaborate tattoo, kind of a paisley print dotted with her freckles. She has a nose piercing. Another one in her navel. Only God knows where else.

When they reach the Mango Cantina, the waiter starts to seat them outside and she asks for a spot further in. He seats them inside, as she suggests, at the back in a corner.

Marco feels her green eyes drilling holes in him. He looks away and asks, "Are you on a cruise ship?"

"Yes."

"Which one? There are two today."

"Disney."

"Oh, with Mickey Mouse and Donald Duck?" She smiles. She's actually quite attractive when she smiles. "And your parents?"

She nods and smiles again. "Them, too."

"No, I mean, where are they?"

"We split up."

She orders a Corona and the waiter suggests a shrimp ceviche. Marco shrugs and she says bueno. He hopes she's paying.

"You're in school?" he asks.

"Berkeley."

"U.C. Berkeley? You must be a genius."

"I was until I hit the university. At least my parents thought I was. Now their grown-up gifted child is struggling."

"Majoring in?"

"I have absolutely no fucking idea," she says, shaking her downcast head. She looks up at him with those piercing green eyes again and asks, "You lived in the U.S.?"

"Ten years. More than half my life."

"You miss it?"

"Yeah, a lot."

They are quiet. There's something about her he likes. Ella es muy buena onda. Seems independent. Takes charge of things. Free spirit. And she's been to the university. Wow. That's impressive. "So, tell me about Berkeley."

"Berkeley is irrelevant," she states emphatically.

"Ah, okay. That's a pretty strong word for a university with such a good reputation." He would have given anything to go to a place like Berkeley.

"Universities, in case you didn't know, amigo, are run by and for professors. Professors become hugely self-preoccupied with their scholarship, you know, on such topics as 14th century love songs for the mandolin, or their research on the sex life of mites and ticks or whatever."

"Mites could be relevant from what I understand about the trouble they are causing the bees."

"A remote possibility. But you know what I mean. There's all this shit going on in the world today; well, actually it's the same old shit that's always been going on."

"My dad used to say misma mierda, diferentes mosquitos. Same shit, different flies." She looks like she gets the Spanish. Not just a smile, but a laugh this time. They both laugh.

Then she turns serious again. "I mean, come on, endless wars, deadlocked revolutions, chemical warfare, corporate greed, political corruption. Cops shooting defenseless black people. Not to mention the U.S. and Mexico: thousands of people dying in the fight to control the drug routes to supply our cocaine habit. And the fucking idiots in Congress can't seem to figure out what to do with 12 million undocumented Mexicans living in the U.S. Doesn't it piss you off?"

"Well, yes, me especially. And I live here now, after all those years there, with no hope of ever returning. But you're right about all that stuff." It feels good to meet a person his age who gets it. And from the States, too.

"Hey, maybe you're better off here," she says, touching his forearm. "I know it's probably no picnic making a living in Mexico, but the U.S. is really fucked up now, believe me. And the students at Berkeley, all they can imagine to protest about today is higher tuition, sports teams with tribal names, and Confederate statues, blah, blah, blah." The food arrives. She asks, "How did you end up back here?"

If she's interested, why not tell her? She's angry and indignant. She'll understand how he feels. He will tell her everything except about Michelle. Women usually don't want to hear about other women, and he's pretty sure this one's not going to be impressed that his girlfriend was a cheerleader. So, he leans forward and with an intimate voice, while she devours the ceviche and downs her cerveza, he gives her the whole sad story of how he had to come back to Mexico. She nods her head up and down and shakes her fork like to make exclamation points at key places while he tells her what happened. He notices his leg bouncing up and down and knows he's all stirred up again.

Just then he hears the horn from one of the boats. She looks at her watch: thin, stylish, green. "I think that's the other boat," she says.

He continues on, telling her about the trip back to Mexico, his brief stint selling shoes, how he took the ferry over to La Paz. She doesn't flinch when he tells her he's a waiter.

"Oh shit," she mumbles, "I think that was my boat." She makes no move to get up.

"Don't you want to see if you can still..."

"Forget it. It's too late. There's no point in running my ass off with a bladder full of beer to try to catch some goddam tourist boat. Besides, I'd like to eat another ceviche. I love Mexican food."

He jerks his head back and stares at her. He is sure he is frowning, but her face is without expression, the strand of bright orange hair hanging over one eye. She's certainly not worried, so why should he care? Then it dawns on him. Maybe she never meant to get back on that boat. That was just her ride to Mexico. She orders a ceviche for him and another for herself along with a pitcher of beer. He doesn't want to be nosy, but he asks her anyway, "Won't your parents be hysterical?"

"You mean more hysterical than they always are about me all the time anyway? Yes, of course, but they're not actually on that boat."

"So, you were on that boat alone?"

"What do you want me to say, I was jilted on my honeymoon? Hell, can't a college student take a little vacation break on her own?"

"Well, yeah, why not? But...are you running away from..."

"Poor word choice. I'm just sitting here. Do I look like I'm running? Away, the boat is pulling away without me. I did actually run away once when I was fourteen. But they found me and hauled my ass back to California. Locked me up in a snooty ding farm for intensive therapy for a month. Like a frickin' castle with these broad green lawns and spreading trees. You can see how much good it did," she snickers.

A fresh supply of food and beer arrives. Confused about what he should say or do, Marco just chews and watches her chew, trying to take in this strange girl who sits before him like an exotic animal in a zoo. You can learn a lot about a person from the way they chew. Like, she's really impatient for the next bite. He tries to think. He knows he should probably butt out, and he could of course just stand up and give her a "nice-to-meet-you" and walk away. He remembers his father telling him: Walk away from trouble, son. But something about her is very intriguing. Not just her muscular little body, but her brain. She knows what's going on. Smart and angry. A little messed up maybe, but, hey, he's not exactly going to win an award in the emotional intelligence department right now either. Not after almost decking El Greco this morning. God, was that just this morning? Finally, he asks, "Have you been in Mexico before?"

"Several times."

"With your parents?"

"Yes, but also as a one-term exchange student in high school. My parents delighted in immersing their gifted daughter in broadening experiences," she says sarcastically. "So, I speak a little Spanish, but your English is way better than my Spanish. I love it here, actually."

Marco smiles to himself. They seem to have something in common. She hates the U.S. and loves Mexico, and he loves the U.S. and hates Mexico. That should make for an interesting conversation. She just sits there chewing and drinking as if she didn't have a care in the world, the epitome of self-centered mindfulness, when in fact the sun will soon be going down over the jagged cliffs and she doesn't have a place to stay. He feels a little sorry for her, but wonders why. He asks, "Do you have any thoughts about where you are going to stay tonight?"

"I was hoping you would be gentleman enough to ask. No. I thought you might have an idea."

Coy. Extremely coy. Is she asking for a suggestion or inviting herself to his place? He decides to describe where he lives, knowing how inadequate it is. That should scare her off. "I have a very small apartment. Well, it's actually not an apartment. Just one room. I don't even have a couch, just a chair. And you have to walk a horrible dirt road to get there. It's really an embarrassment."

"Sounds great. I'll take it."

"You must be kidding. Really, it's just a hole of a place in a bad neighborhood."

"I didn't come to Mexico to stay in one of those fancy resorts. Oops, sorry, I guess that's where you work."

"They might actually have a vacancy at Sunset Point."

"Not for me. Walking in off the street the way I look?"

"Well, my place might be kind of a last resort, no pun intended, for a night until you can find something else."

"Thanks. I really have no choice."

But he is sure she does. Somewhere in that oversized lime green canvas tote there is a purse, and in that purse, there is a driver's license, a passport, a phone, a few credit cards, her ATM pin, and maybe even a stash of pesos. Hopefully also a change of underwear. She doesn't need to stay with him. But now she has taken his description as an invitation.

Ashley rides with him to the bus stop at the Pemex station. They trudge along the dusty dirt road to his apartment. She doesn't seem put off by the pathetic road and the poverty bordering it. In fact, when he asks her if she's ever seen such a terrible road, she comments that this is nothing new for her in a been-there-done-that tone of voice. They climb the stairs to his apartment and he opens the door. "I warned you."

"I wasn't expecting an ocean view, you know," she says, stepping inside, her sharp eyes quickly moving across the meagre surroundings, the sink, the fridge, the lone chair, and the double bed. She nods. "It has possibilities."

"Yeah, of collapsing in an earthquake."

"You'll see."

It sounds like she is planning to stay.

She pokes her head into the bathroom. "Running water. A shower. All the comforts of home."

"Ha! Not the comforts of your home, I'm sure."

"Well, we won't go there."

"Not legally anyway." He sees her smile. She got his bad joke.

"The basic human necessities are here, amigo. I see you have a small library."

"Oh, not much. Just a little stack of books. You like to read?" he asks.

"Naturally, as long as it's not assigned."

"I read at night, sometimes 'til one or two o'clock. In fact, I was thinking, we might take turns with the bed, and you can sleep while I read, and then you…"

"You are so respectful, Marco. Maybe we could pick up a two by six back there in the road and put it down the middle of the bed here, like the Quakers used to do, you know, instead of a log. Come on, amigo, I'm not going to molest you. We can each have our side. You can share. Remember, like pre-school."

"I missed pre-school. I was still in Mexico then. No pre-school here; never learned sharing." He's made her laugh again. Great smile. Fantastic body. And she will be right next to him. Hmmm. How about that? She flips her hair back.

That night, having forgotten the discussion of sharing, Marco sits up in his chair to study A Wicked War, while Ashley lounges on her side of the bed in her skimpy pajamas. She's traveling light but well prepared: toothbrush, lip gloss, underwear, pajamas, paperbacks, iPhone, and a ripstop nylon windbreaker. She knew exactly what she was doing. He hopes she knows she's going to have to keep swiping those credit cards.

Marco notices that Ashley is tossing and turning. She reads a little, dozes, then sleeps. He watches her. It's kind of nice to have a woman in his room. Michelle always had a really nice smell. He misses that. Ashley has nice perfume, too, and she actually looks quite beautiful when she sleeps, like she's more relaxed. Maybe they can help each other relax. He gets so relaxed watching her that his book falls on the floor. It wakes her up and she rubs one eye like a little kid. She asks him, "What are you reading?"

"A history of the Mexican War. Actually, I've already read it. I'm studying it now, taking notes, trying to learn the names, the dates."

"Like you got a fucking exam in the morning?"

"No, because I want to learn."

"Well, yeah, me too, but what I want to learn is never what they want to teach. So, there you are. Now you know why I'm flunking out of Berkeley."

"That's a shame. I wanted so bad to go to college. I was already admitted to the University of New Mexico." For sure he wouldn't be flunking out.

"Like I say, it's mostly irrelevant." She nods her head a little and looks straight at him. "Hey, why don't you come over here and tell me what you learned about the war." She flicks her head to shake the hair back from her eye.

Is this an invitation? Or maybe she really wants to learn about the war. "Yeah, like a bedtime story," he says, opting for the war. "Okay, but don't expect Winnie the Pooh or Mary Poppins. This stuff is ugly." He sits on the bed and pulls his feet up under his thighs. "Okay this is good for me because I can test how much I can remember."

"Remember the Alamo. That's all I can remember. Fight to the last man. Have you ever heard of anything more ridiculous?" She flicks her head to shake the hair back from her eye.

"So, you already know this stuff?"

"A little, but that's all I remember." She shrugs.

"At least you remembered the Alamo."

"Hey, don't play with me, you slug," she teases.

"Okay so the Americans were settling on Mexican lands in a Mexican state in a big area south and to the west of present-day San Antonio. They complained that the Mexicans were against slavery and were taking away their freedom by levying taxes."

"Their freedom. That's ironic." Her eyes bug out.

"Really. So, the Americans, instead of leaving to settle somewhere else, started to push the Mexicans back toward the Rio Grande. But the Mexicans fought back. It was their land!"

"That's where the Alamo comes in?" she asks.

"Not only killing every last man at the Alamo, but the town of Gilead, too. Santa Anna took out three hundred Americans one night and had them shot."

"So now we've got to remember Gilead, too. But, hey, I think they had it coming." She purses her lips and shakes her head up and down.

"This motivates Sam Houston to organize the rebels and he beats the shit out of the Mexicans at San Jacinto: fourteen hundred Mexican casualties in eighteen minutes, with only seven of Houston's men dead. So, at the battle of San Jacinto, they capture Santa Anna, and..."

"Oh, my God. When was all this?" she asks.

"In eighteen thirty-six. And they forced him to sign a treaty acknowledging Texas independence with a border at the Nueces River—this is important—considerably north of the Rio Grande. So, the Texians, as they were called, announced their self-proclaimed republic on land they had taken from Mexico in a Mexican state. Andrew Jackson offered diplomatic recognition to the country of Texas, not state, but country, and the Texans turned to the U.S. for annexation."

"Jesus, that really makes me proud of my country. You know, sometimes when I hear the truth, like this, I just get so fucking angry and depressed, I have to go sleep. Escape. She turns away from him suddenly, pulling the blanket up around her face and shutting her eyes.

With this abrupt shift in Ashley's behavior, Marco goes back to the chair and tries to study. But her anger has rekindled his own. The book lays open on his lap late into the night while he relives his return to Mexico, fighting his own war all over again and sparking the familiar rumblings inside him. And of course, he thinks about Michelle and the plans they made together.

The next day, Marco wakes up at his usual early hour and notices Ashley beside him, sleeping like a tired child, belly down, one leg hanging out from the covers. He slips out quietly so as not to awaken her. He can't stop thinking about her at work, wondering if she will even be there when he returns. How did this happen to him? He remembers Vera telling him to be careful.

When he comes back to the apartment that afternoon, he finds a card table with a yellow checkered tablecloth, two folding chairs, some plastic dishes, and a small bouquet of flowers in a pottery vase. He looks around. An additional pillow on her side of the bed, and a soft lavender bedspread. She's placed a small cushion on the chair and put the books in a two-shelf bookcase. Damn, she's definitely been swiping those credit cards. "Where did you get all of this?" he asks.

"Went shopping. Stuff's so cheap here I didn't even need to nick anything."

He searches her for a sign of a faint smile, but her wooden face tells him she's serious.

"How do you like it?" she asks.

"Well, it really transforms the place. You have great taste, but..."

"But what? You're worried I'll stay? If you can put up with me a few more days, you can keep it when I leave. Everything but the vase. I like that vase."

"Won't your parents cut off your credit cards?"

"Those are my cards, amigo. They don't watch the bills very close. It will take them a while to even know I'm gone. Besides, they're in France for a month."

"But won't they eventually track you down when..."

"I don't see your parents trying to track you down."

"That's true." He's never thought about himself as running away, so why does he think of her that way? But won't her parents want to find their missing daughter?

When the sun goes down and the tired old droopy drapes are yanked across the front window, Ashley opens the refrigerator and pulls out two chicken burritos.

"Where did you get these?" Marco is astonished.

"From a sweet little old guy pushing an aluminum cart."

She warms the burritos in a pan and when she serves them, she says "listo," and they sit down to eat them in the folding chairs at the new table. As he thanks her, she is all smiles, the most he's seen her smile. When they are seated, he looks up at her face, still smiling, and he feels a tinge of worry. An image of Vera and Ollie pops into his head. Is this how it starts? The next thing you know you're sitting across from this same person for every meal for the rest of your whole damn life.

After dinner, he finds his book on the Mexican War on the new bookshelf. She's messing with her Galaxy, so he starts to study again.

"You got another quiz tomorrow?" she asks without looking up.

"Nope. Just studying up for the bedtime story."

"There's more? Let me know when you are ready. It's interesting."

His eyes catch her from time to time as he glances out over the top of his book. She reads for a while, but falls asleep. Then she wakes up and she's on her phone again. She gets up and brushes her teeth. She tries on some lightweight exercise pants—must have bought them today, too—and she's modeling them and asking him what he thinks. Then she's reading again. What do they call that? Attention Deficit Disorder. Maybe that's another reason she's flunking out, besides motivation. But her grades must have been good enough for her to get in. She's a sketchy little case, that's for sure, but he finds there's a part of him that likes having her around. It's not so lonely. He likes her self-confident independence, her intelligence, and even the feminine touches she brings to the apartment. In spite of Ashley's distractions, he wraps his mind around the rest of the war. When he thinks he's got it, he says, "once upon a time." He sits next to her on the bed as before.

"Let's go." She sits up, lays down her book, and puts her phone away.

"Okay, for almost ten years the Texans maintain their independent little country, and they keep petitioning for annexation, but there's resistance in Congress to adding another slave state. But the more general issue is territorial expansion."

"Oh, oh, here we go again." She throws her head back and rolls her eyes.

"The Whigs want to emphasize internal improvement of what the U.S. already has."

"Like the Louisiana purchase," she observes.

"Yes. Good for you. See, you know your history. The Democrats, the opposing party, are pushing expansion and Manifest Destiny."

"Hold on. Remind me about this Manifest Destiny thing again."

"Expansion is inevitable. It's simply the destiny of the U.S. to occupy the whole continent, and besides, it is God's will."

"Oh, bullshit," she roars. She crosses her legs, faces him, and leans toward him. "Okay, I've got it."

"So, Clay is supposed to get the Whig nomination and win, only he kind of cooks his own goose by speaking out so strongly against expansion, and the convention nominates a dark horse named Polk."

"An unknown. And he won?" she asks.

"Barely. By five thousand votes. This is bad news for Mexico because he's an expansionist. He even wants to snatch some of Canada, too, but he backs down because he doesn't want a war with Britain. But Mexico? Mexico's another matter because Mexico is weak."

"Why weak?" She looks puzzled.

"They just got their independence from Spain in eighteen twenty-one and they're trying to get rid of the old colonial ways, deal with the Church, and build a strong country, but it's going really slow."

"So, let's pick on poor Mexico," she says, a little more outrage in her voice each time she speaks.

"Then Polk gets Texas made the twenty-eighth state in eighteen forty-five. He sends an envoy to Mexico to negotiate extending the border of Texas south to the Rio Grande, to double its size. Oh, by the way, he tells them, perhaps you could sell us the rest of the area north of the Rio Grande, present day Arizona, New Mexico, and California."

"Hey, that's a big chunk of property. And Mexico refused? How inconsiderate," she says sarcastically.

"So, Polk sends Zachary Taylor to lead a military expedition to the Rio Grande, hoping to provoke an incident."

"Let me guess. It works?" she asks.

"A Mexican commander on the south bank sends troops across the river and kills eleven men in an American patrol."

"Just what Polk wanted."

"A reason to invade Mexico. American blood shed on American soil," he says and pauses to look up at her. He's having fun with her, just like when he and Michelle would quiz each other before an exam and throw in a trick question.

"Hold on a sec." She frowns. "It wasn't American soil, not yet. It was Mexican soil."

"Wow, you are really paying attention, amiga." She got it. She's really smart. "It was a lie to the people."

"So, what's next? Do I have to wait until tomorrow night?" she asks impatiently. "This is so shameful."

"No, I think I remember the rest. I'll make it quick. There were two big invasions by U.S. troops, one from the north across the Rio Grande, and there was a big battle at Buena Vista in—let me think—eighteen forty-seven. Lots of casualties on both sides, including many from disease. Then there was a southern invasion assisted by the navy landing at Vera Cruz and a march over to Mexico City."

"And more casualties," she observes.

"By now over thirteen thousand American dead, and the anti-war sentiment is growing. So, Polk sends this ambassador named Nicholas Trist to negotiate. Polk actually wants all of Mexico, and they are still making offers to buy. If the boundary is set at the Rio Grande, twenty million dollars. Throw in Baja California, thirty million."

"Baja? Right here where we are now in Cabo San Lucas?" she asks.

"Exactly. Trist turns out to be the hero of the story, because he defies Polk and settles on just half of Mexico."

"Just half? How fucking generous is that?"

"A lot of illegals in the Southwest today say they are just resettling what rightfully belongs to Mexico. I told you it was an ugly story."

"Jesus." She sits there shaking her head, her nose ring bouncing back and forth, the strands of orange hair flapping over her right eye. "Doesn't it just make you want to burn something down or blow something up? I mean that sad, sad history alone is justification for some act of terror," she states unequivocally, slashing the air with her right index finger.

She's right. It makes him angry, too, saying it out loud like that. But whoa, an act of terror? He decides to let that remark just sit there while he gets up to replace the history book in its place on the new bookshelf. Apparently, Ashley is ready to sleep, devastated and depressed by the truth again, so she rolls over, pulls the new pillow over her head, and sprawls out on her side of the bed. So far, at least, the sleeping arrangements have been working out okay.

Marco sits in the chair for a while, enjoying the new cushion, but his insides are roaring. It can't just be his anger. Maybe the burritos were a little off? He starts thinking about Ashley. She just falls into his life and then he starts to like her. Is that the way it works? He probably should encourage her to get her own place, but for now, he's kind of enjoying her. For some reason—actually quite a few reasons—he's attracted to her. She's a Berkeley student and he can hang right in there on his favorite subject. They have a lot in common in the way they look at things. She has that built in crap detector that Hemingway talked about. No doubt about it, Ashley knows the scoop, and once you do, you're going to be angry because there's just so much crap in this world. He admits he may be a little embarrassed about her appearance—she's really different from Michelle—but for now, that's okay. And for sure she's attractive in other ways, too. So, let's just see where this goes.

On Marco's day off, three days later, they go to Médano Beach, not really his first choice—not out in public with Ashley—but she's going stir crazy staying in the apartment while he's at work, or just wandering the back streets shopping and taking photos. She's been tracking her parents' activity on her phone. They keep calling her, trying to reach her, and when they call, she can tell where the call is coming from, but she never answers. They're still in France.

At the Pemex station they hop a bus to the mall. She springs for a couple of beach towels, some sunscreen, and buys herself a new green and white polka dot bikini, plus a long diaphanous blouse, both of which she wears out of the store. He remembers that word diaphanous from a vocab test in AP English. The outline of her body shows as she walks along and the waiters around the marina stare and call out guapa. She doesn't notice, or if she does, she doesn't seem to care. He likes that.

Together Marco and Ashley make their way past the Fisherman's Bar and down the narrow street to the beach. He's not keen on bumping into employees from the resort, so he leads her over to the same secluded spot where he had his pity party after those milkshakes with Vera and Ollie. Jeez, was that just a couple of weeks ago? "I thought you might like something more out of the way," he tells her.

"Yeah, yeah, this is good."

"In case the cops are looking for you," he teases.

"Why would they be looking for me?" She glares at him.

"Or your parents. Would I be an accessory for hiding you from your parents?" He means it as a joke.

"Jesus, you worry about everything. It's not a crime to help someone. I'm just here because I happen to like Mexico. So, relax."

They do relax, sprawled out on the new beach towels, and Ashley tells him about the life she detests back in California. She and her mom and dad live in a huge house on the edge of a redwood forest in Marin County. The house is way too big. Her father is working or commuting for ten hours a day. Her mother flits from client to client, making calls associated with her interior design studio. Ashely is the only child. Her father's work is so technical she can't even begin to describe it. Her hovering helicopter of a mother enrolled her in private schools for gifted children. Not just one, but serially over the years, constantly searching for the perfect school worthy of her talented daughter. Is it any wonder this gifted child never made any friends?

Marco knows it's his turn at show and tell. He strokes his chin a little, and then he tells her about his parents, simple working-class people, always wanting what was best for him. His father is strong and has a way with tools. He's really smart in solving mechanical problems. His older sister got a job as a store clerk right out of high school, and the last he heard she was working in a shop in Guadalajara. He tells Ashley he misses them, and in the telling realizes how much he actually does. How odd that two people who hardly know each other, he says to her, can babble on so much just lying there side by side gazing up at the blue sky. Then they grow silent. He wants to tell her how angry he is, how much he hates his job serving all of those wealthy Americans, and about El Greco, his nasty boss. He hesitates. Maybe he's not ready. Why not just to enjoy a peaceful afternoon with Ashley and a quiet stomach.

That night they are both wiped out from a long afternoon in the sun, so they flop on the bed and are asleep by ten o'clock. Marco wakes up because everything is shaking. The illuminated numbers on his digital alarm clock read 2:24. His first thought is an earthquake, but he is fairly certain that the quakes that created the Sea of Cortéz were much further north. The shaking continues and as his eyes become accustomed to the dim light, he sees that it is not the room that is shaking, but the bed. He glances over. Ashley is pleasuring herself, or at least trying. That's kind of sad when he's right here.

He stretches out an arm and his hand accidently comes to rest on her breast. That's all she needs. She starts kissing his forearm, then his neck, his chest, and then back up to his mouth. He does not resist. He feels her hand reach into his underwear, and with a few deft strokes, she makes him ready. The next thing he knows, her underwear and then his, go flying across the room. She rolls on top of him and begins moving like a tormented wildcat. She starts breathing hard, then making little noises, shouting out yes, yes, and finally producing several long, low howls.

She rolls onto her back spread eagle, a flaming fire of fuzz inviting him to take his turn.

8

ALONE TOGETHER AT OLLIE'S HOLIDAY PARTY

Ollie and Vera are back in Golden, Colorado, trying to adjust to single-digit, near-zero temperatures and a foot of snow. "A one-mile gain in altitude and a seventy degree drop in temperature," Ollie says.

"I think we got a couple more inches last night." Vera gazes out the front window, her hands on her hips.

"More like six." Ollie is zipping up his hooded parka and putting on his Gore-Tex gloves, like he is headed for the Arctic.

"You know you don't need to shovel it, dear. They'll come by and take care of that," she reminds him.

"Yeah, by three o'clock in the afternoon if we're lucky. I hate to drive over it with the car. Packs it down. Besides, shoveling is good exercise and takes me back to my Vermont boyhood. If only I wasn't so sore the next day."

Vera putters around the nest doing laundry, changing the bath towels, and emptying waste baskets while Ollie is shoveling. When he comes in, she serves him hot cocoa and an oatmeal cookie. He says he wants to make a cherry pie. Vera does the lion's share of the daily cooking for meals. When the spirit moves him, Ollie makes a tasty beef stew, scrumptious fried chicken, or healthful whole wheat pancakes. He also fancies himself an expert pie baker from having watched his mother closely as a kid.

Vera is holding down and then rotating the round, plastic, zippered contrivance that contains the pie dough while Ollie wields the rolling pin. "It's good to be home, but on a day like this I can't help but dream about sitting in the sun beside the pool in Cabo," she says.

"There you go with our two lives again."

"Sometimes I wonder just how many lives we have."

"I guess that depends on how you count. Could you turn that crust container around a little for me, dear?"

"Oh, I'm sorry. My mind wandered."

"More than two?" Ollie asks.

"Two what? Oh, lives? Well, yes, you see we have our infancy and childhood, our adolescence and college years, our work lives and careers, our family life, and now our retirement, with our lives here and in Mexico. Who could ask for more incarnations than that? The good thing is that we don't need to die before each new life."

"That's as many lives as I can handle right there. I surely don't need any more," Ollie grumbles, banging down the roller and reaching for the Pyrex pie plate. "The way I see it," he continues, "is that we are the same person stretched over a long period of time, but we are also several different people, too, living out the paradox of our many lives. Could you hand me the filling, dear?"

"That's profound, dear. You really are good with words." She scratches a particular spot on the crown of her head and then fetches the bowl with the pie filling. "Lately," she continues, "I feel like I'm in a movie, and I'm not only in the movie but I'm watching it, too, like both actress and audience, as if I'm having some out of body experience."

"In a movie? That's a good comparison," Ollie points out, "like life, movies are mostly illusion." He is rolling out the top crust now.

"Remember when we went on that Sound of Music Tour in Salzburg?" Vera asks.

"How can I forget it?"

"They just filmed the front of that big house at one place and snatched a view of the back from a completely different site. The road where the kids were hanging from the trees was actually some distance away, not near either of the houses at all."

"And the gazebo was in still another place. The church for the wedding was in the next town over, if I recall." Ollie says.

"The inside of the house, we were told, was a sound stage in Hollywood. It's like you say, dear, everything to create the illusion of something real."

Ollie wets the top edge of the lower crust with cooking oil to ensure a good seal, puts on the top crust, trims it, presses it down with the tines of a fork, spreads melted butter and sugar on it, and cuts a few decorative slits to let out the steam. "So, we go through life portraying different characters in scene after scene, living out our illusions, and then we try to convince ourselves they are real."

"Is it really that pointless?" Vera asks, frowning.

"It's all pointless until you taste a piece of this cherry pie with a chunk of Vermont cheddar cheese, and then you say, aha, at last something real."

"Now you sound like a Zen monk."

On Saturday mornings, Ollie and Vera drive downtown, park at the handy public parking garage, and take their breakfast at the award-winning Golden Diner. They arrive early to avoid having to stand in line. Ollie is not sure why they keep coming on Saturday when retirement is, as they say, seven days of Saturdays. Maybe to give some structure to their otherwise formless week. When he retired, Vera ordered a special clock from eBay marked out with seven vectors with a single hand pointing to the name for that day. He remembers asking her what the hell that was for, and she told him, quite bemused with the unconventional clock, that he had better wait and see how often he would use it before condemning it. Now he checks that darn clock regularly, and if the hand is pointing to Saturday, he knows they need to hustle down to the Golden Diner for his peppery sausage gravy over biscuits and Vera's one egg easy over with wheat toast. Their two decafs are filled every time the waitress passes.

"Look at all that has to be done to run a restaurant." Ollie loves to observe and analyze everything. "Getting people seated, orders taken when folks are ready, food cooked and delivered quickly to the right tables, checks issued, money collected, tables cleaned, and then it starts all over again. Quite a merry-go-round."

"I'm not sure many people notice all that, dear, but you sure have a knack for enlivening the commonplace."

"It keeps people occupied, I guess." Ollie nods several times, like he's not sure this is a very good reason.

"It's like La Casona here, a smooth operation but without the formality and finesse."

"That's funny," Ollie responds. "I was just thinking of La Casona. I miss the fresh fruit plate."

"I was missing Marquito as our waiter. I wonder if anything exciting is happening in his life."

Ollie says, "Let's hope not until we know what it might be."

"Not just Marquito. I miss the others, too. I wonder how they're doing."

"Well, it's Mexico, you know. A hard life."

"I've been thinking, Ollie."

"Oh, oh," he teases.

"No, seriously. I'm wondering how we could have a bigger impact. Something more than a suitcase full of clothes and toys."

"What did you have in mind?" he asks.

"Money. Significant sums of money."

"Do you think money will solve their problems? Make them happy?"

"Not alone, but it can help. It would be up to them to decide how to use it, but it could actually turn some lives around. I mean, big time."

"Like block grants? So, you think we should give our Mexican friends money? Our money?"

"Yes, why not? What do we need it for?"

Ollie nods his head, raises his eyebrows, and runs a hand through his disheveled gray hair. "You have a point, but I'm going to need some time to think about that."

"I knew you would."

There is a brief silence and then out of the blue Ollie says, "This is the last Saturday for the Christmas Market up in Georgetown."

"We used to enjoy that so much."

"Let's go then," Ollie says, with the excited voice of a child before Christmas.

"You mean now? We didn't plan to go to Georgetown today." He can see that Vera has been taken by surprise.

"When you're retired you can do whatever you dang please whenever you want. Do you need anything? We can run home," he suggests.

"No, I'm good to go. It's just so spontaneous of you."

"Spontaneous people live longer."

"Now where did you read that?" she asks.

"I didn't. I made it up." He smiles to himself. "Gotcha that time, huh?"

In forty minutes, their SUV exits Interstate 70 and pulls into historic Georgetown, nestled into a deep valley among several steep, rocky mountains, with cliffs sometimes adorned with Bighorn Sheep. The roads coming up were plowed and dry, but there is enough snow in the streets to make Georgetown into the picture-perfect greeting card. Old-fashioned street lamps decorated with swags of pine and red ribbon set off the cowboy-movie facades of the business district. An old mining town, indeed. Ollie parks the SUV, Vera takes his arm, and they wend their way on foot up the main street, crossing from side to side to make sure they don't miss any of the cute shops. The Shoppe International sells Christmas tree ornaments from all over the world, but also placemats, candles, and hand-crafted wooden toys from Sweden. The Western store seems to specialize in cowboy hats and boots. Of course, Ollie has to go in the hardware store to nose around a little. Run by the same folks for generations. At the end of the street is the ice cream parlor, End of the Line, and in addition to fantastic ice cream, they sell sweatshirts and fleece-lined jackets.

"Want an ice cream cone? Ollie asks. "You know it's the best butter pecan in the world."

"Are you crazy? On a cold day like this?"

"Okay, I have a better offer. I've always wanted to go on that hayride."

"Now I know you've lost your mind, not just your memory, but the whole kit and caboodle."

"Then you will just need to live with my caducity."

"Good, God, dear, where did you get that word? A person needs a pocket dictionary just to carry on a simple conversation with you."

"Then you're agreed. Here comes the wagon now. Look at those magnificent horses. Have you ever seen such beauties?"

"Seen, no. Smell is another matter. To me, every horse smells the same and it's not eau de Cologne."

"It's a delicious barnyard fragrance," he says, taking a deep breath. "You must develop an appreciation for it. Here, let me give you a hand into the wagon."

Before Vera knows what has happened, he has her in the wagon and all cuddled up like a puppy beside him on a bale of hay. The driver hands them a thick, wool horse blanket and makes sure they are comfortable. It has started to snow, big white flakes coming down so slowly you can pick one out and trace its journey to the ground. "I hope you're happy," she says.

"It's the closest I'll ever get to Christmas in Vermont out here in Colorado, and that's the closest I'll ever get to heaven. Smell the air." He takes another deep breath.

"I'd rather not," she says, staring at the rumps of the two horses.

"I suppose you'd prefer the smoke from the steel mills in Ohio?"

"They're gone. At least the smoke is."

Wagon wheels crunch in the snow and sleigh bells jingle to the gait of the horses. The ride through town, in front of the Presbyterian and Catholic churches, down to the park, past the bandstand, across the river, and back up the main drag again, turns out to be quite pleasant. How can Vera not think this is romantic? When the horses come to rest, Ollie tips the driver, and says to Vera, "Now we can go get what I came for."

"And what might that be?" she asks. "My God, you're like a little kid today."

"The bratwurst with sauerkraut and German mustard."

"You're hungry already? You have the appetite of a teenager."

"Well, to tell the truth I'm not really starving after that fine breakfast, but I can't miss the bratwurst."

"Well, have one then. At least get the one with the whole wheat bun."

The line is short and Ollie is soon chomping away on his bratwurst. As he pushes a little stray sauerkraut up into the corner of his mouth, he says, "You know, I didn't mean to sound like I was rejecting your idea about the money at breakfast. It's a good idea. I just need to think about it. Figure out how we could do that." He finishes the last bit of bratwurst and throws the paper plate in the trash container. "We are really a long way from Cabo San Lucas this morning, aren't we?" he says.

"In distance, yes, weather, yes, but in spirit, no. Isn't it odd how the mind can keep you close to the people you care about even when you are so far away?"

Before they leave, Vera asks for a bag of roasted chestnuts, and Ollie buys them for her because they are, after all, roasting on an open fire, and she is humming the song. Back in the SUV, heading home, they pass the frozen lake stretched out in front of Georgetown, frozen so solid that two jeeps have driven out onto it. "Now there's a cold sport," he says. "Ice fishing."

"Sport? For whom? The fish? It must be cold for those little fishes. How do they survive?"

"By staying on the bottom," he says.

"Folks at the bottom know how to survive."

On Wednesday morning, Ollie and Vera have rare plans to be apart, a luncheon for her and shopping at Safeway and a haircut for him. "When they arrive back home that afternoon, they are both agitated and eager to talk. "Ladies first," Ollie insists.

"Well, you won't believe what my old friend Muriel said."

"About what?"

"I'm about to tell you. I shared with her a couple of my so-called cases from Mexico."

"Which ones?"

"Daniella and the girls. And Isabella, Solomón, and Susette. And I told her a little about my idea of making some grants."

"Like Bill Gates only much smaller."

Vera ignores him. "And she was quite negative about it. She said that she didn't think the money would do much good because it would probably just be squandered on cars and fiestas and tequila. When I asked her why she felt that way, she said she remembered some cases at the child welfare agency where we used to work together for those years, and that whenever Mexicans came into money, it always got squandered like that. When I asked her if poor Americans acted the same way, she surmised they did, but usually it was the blacks. For God's sake, Ollie, this is a social worker who's supposed to have a little multi-cultural savvy." Vera's hands are shaking like a quaking aspen tree when she gestures. "And what do I hear instead? Pure, unadulterated prejudice."

"I know, I know."

"Then Muriel said that the problem with the Mexicans is cultural, that they are never on time and they're lazy. I could have slapped her face right then and there."

"But you didn't."

"Well, not and be arrested for assault."

"And you probably didn't say anything. But I didn't say anything either. Listen to this. I'm sitting in Del's Tonsorial Parlor waiting for the barber who cuts my hair to say 'next,' and three guys are sitting there, talking their talk, and sure enough the conversation comes around to Mexicans. They want to build the wall along the border even higher and finish it off with barbed wire and then post snipers. They have no idea, of course, how the number of Mexicans wanting to come across the border has dwindled since the time of the recession, nor do they have a clue that we already have six hundred fifty miles of eighteen-foot fence, forty thousand border patrol agents, and a bunch of drones. I was reading up on this last week, Vera, in a book called *The Dangerous Divide*. Did you know that there are two thousand miles of so-called border? It's mostly open space, not settled, and it absolutely cannot be secured. That was the considered judgment of the author. And listen to this: We taxpayers paid Boeing over a billion dollars to build a virtual fence, the electronic eyes and ears of the Customs and Border Patrol Agency. Only you know what happened? After five years they had secured only fifty-eight miles and then gave up, concluding that it was not a feasible project. Nonetheless, these jokers, sitting in the barber shop, ignorant of all of this, want to secure the border before anything else is done. They are completely opposed to immigration reform and what they call amnesty because, they say, those Mexicans who came in illegal need to be sent home. Never mind assimilation, they need to be expelled. And that includes their kids who will just grow up and commit more crimes and take more of our jobs."

"Ouch. That's harsh. Kind of breaks your heart, doesn't it?"

"And you know what, dear, I knew all of what I just told you and didn't say a word. Either."

"It's hard to speak up in a situation like that," she says.

"We say that it's none of our business. We hide behind that."

"But, of course, it is our business. But then again, what can you say? Jesus, Ollie, how did all this prejudice get going about Mexicans?"

"It has deeper roots than you might think. In the book about the war, you know, the one I sent to Marquito, the soldiers who invaded Mexico found Catholics—there were strong anti-Catholic sentiments in the country at the time—and they found foreigners who spoke Spanish, and they discovered that a lot of these people had brown skin, kind of a mixture between the Indians who they had already massacred and the Negroes who they were using for slaves. This didn't keep them from raping their women, of course, but in general, they didn't like these people because they were different from themselves and they'd been taught that they were the enemy. They disliked them so much that they weren't sure what the heck they were going to do with them once the war was over. It comes as no surprise that large numbers of Mexicans were living on the land we took from them." Ollie provides an ironic smile.

"So, it goes way, way back."

"And continues on and on."

"It just doesn't fit with the lovely people we have come to know in Mexico," Vera says, shaking her head from side to side. "Our friends."

Ollie runs a hand through what's left of his freshly-cut hair. "Next time I've got to find a way to speak up. I'm embarrassed. Ashamed. Disgraced."

As Christmas nears—a modest wreath with a red bow has already been attached to the front door—Vera and Ollie are scheduled to go to Ollie's staff party at the firm. Neither one of them is very enthusiastic about going, but because they are still being invited, they feel obliged to attend. The weather is fair and the evening promises to be unseasonably warm. Ollie suggests that they drive over to the courthouse and catch the light-rail to Union Station and hop on the free bus that traverses the 16th Street Mall to Stout Street, where the firm is located. It is much easier than trying to fight the holiday traffic and find a place to park.

Red poinsettias adorn the entry area, a tree decorated all in gold stands in one corner, and the reception desk has morphed into an open bar. The Websters are greeted by the senior partner, and two of Oliver's old colleagues say hello then drift away. It is already crowded and noisy, hard to hear well enough to carry on a serious conversation. Ollie notices that most of the men have detached themselves from their wives and are gathered at one end to talk shop. Lawyers seem never to tire of talking about the law. Do they know anything else? The other end of the room is populated by forlorn and abandoned women casting furtive glances at one another. Ollie has always refused to play the separate-the-sexes game. He calls it social bifurcation by gender and Vera calls it the bowling league. Where are the female attorneys? Surely there must be more of them by now. "So many young people," Ollie leans over and whispers into Vera's ear. "We stick out like two old sequoias in the middle of a Christmas tree farm."

Vera and Ollie wander over to an ill-at-ease young couple, new arrivals at the party like themselves, to say hello. It turns out that she is the attorney and he is a demographer who works for the State of Colorado on employment data. Ollie is delighted to find that she graduated from his alma mater, the University of Michigan, but when he asks her about his old professors, she doesn't know any of them. "Of course not, silly," Vera reminds him, "they would all be dead by now." The demographer smiles. He gets it. Ollie wonders how he might strike up a conversation with a demographer, but he can't think of a single question to ask. He remembers having had that problem only once before—with an actuary. The young couple moves away.

A young woman with a white apron over a dark uniform politely offers hors d'oeuvres made of mostly unrecognizable ingredients: something black (maybe seaweed?) wrapped around something orange (maybe salmon eggs?) on an elliptical, emaciated rice cracker. Ollie and Vera have learned long ago to avoid such proffered delicacies, dreading solitary confinement to the toilet for the next twenty-four hours.

They are about to leave when Sarah Schwartz, Ollie's former administrative assistant, appears to wish them happy holidays. "So nice to see you. You're still here?" Ollie asks, being her straight man, knowing how funny she is.

"Like a tattered law book sitting on a remote shelf. Twenty-four years this year."

"Almost long enough for one of those engraved silver bowls," Ollie observes.

"Don't knock it. I was in charge of ordering them, you know. We used to call them the toilet bowls."

"At least you know what to do with a toilet bowl."

"Oliver!" Vera reprimands him.

"I see your sense of humor hasn't changed," Sarah says, not laughing. "Where do you have your bowl, smarty?"

"Packed away." Ollie replies.

"They tarnish," Vera observes, politely.

"Don't we all." Ollie observes. "What about here, Sarah, have things changed for you at the firm?"

"Oh, yes. Not much need for me anymore. Sometimes I feel quite useless. The young ones all want to do their own work. Hardly anyone knows how to use a good administrative assistant these days. Not like you, Oliver."

"We were quite a team, weren't we?"

"Yes," Vera chimes in, "and not knowing how to use you is their loss I should say."

"And the firm's," Oliver adds.

Sarah shrugs. "Are you guys still going to Cabo San Lucas?"

"Yes, we are," Vera replies, "and we shall be forever grateful to you for your making that very first booking."

"It's funny how things work out, isn't it? So much left to chance. I just spotted this nice resort and said to myself, like playing God, let's just put them here." She points to the floor with an index finger. "Life is an out-of-control casino, right?"

"With high stakes," Ollie confirms. "And the older you get, looking back, it seems even more dicey. Like everything is chance. Somebody else's choice. I don't even know why I chose to go to law school."

"My husband Abe would say that it's just God sneezing, but it's awfully hard to believe in God and work in a law firm, wouldn't you say, Oliver?"

They all have a good laugh at that and then say their good-byes. Ollie is silent most of the way home, but eventually he says, "I won't ask you to go to that party anymore, dear, and I surely won't go alone." He looks out the train window, but he mostly sees his own wobbling reflection against vague shapes drifting by. "I feel so detached, so alienated, like that bug we read about in college." Vera frowns. What the hell is he talking about? "Remember that story, Vera, we read it together at Middlebury in Comparative Literature."

"That was a long time ago, Ollie. How do you expect me to remember something like that?"

"I don't. I'm talking about that short story by Franz Kafka. This guy awakens one morning and finds himself transformed into a gigantic insect, you know, like a six-foot-long beetle lying on his back in his bed. And the rest of the story is about how his family reacts to him and how he feels about himself."

"The image of the insect is coming back slowly now, but why tonight, dear, on the train, in the dead of winter?"

"The professor called it a parable of alienation. But really, dear, how is a twenty-year-old kid supposed to understand anything like that? I'm sure I didn't. I was rereading it the other day, and now I get it. That's what I felt like down there tonight: a goddam out-of-place bug. Totally alienated. It took more than fifty years, but now I understand Kafka."

He smiles, but then notices Vera staring at him, looking worried, concerned about what's happening to her husband. He has upset her. He didn't mean to do that. They are both aging, and at the same rate naturally, but maybe he's taking it harder than she is. Not adjusting.

9

A DOSE OF MEANING

At the beginning of the week of Christmas, Ellen and her husband Damon arrive from Dallas to spend two days before driving up to Vail for a ski holiday between Christmas and the New Year.

"What a nice surprise, you two," Vera greets them as they arrive. Damon wears a cell phone over his ear. Nice Ivy League haircut, but he looks a little buttoned-down, kind of preppy for someone on vacation. Vera notices that Ellen has a new hair style with highlighted strands of her natural auburn hair just touching her shoulders. "We're glad to see you."

"Where are you staying in Beaver Creek?" Ollie asks.

"Ah, at the Ritz Carlton," Damon says, trying to sound nonchalant. "We got a nice package deal."

Vera and Ollie exchange hidden smiles. "You won't mind our little guest room?" Vera asks. "It's not the Ritz."

That night Ollie cooks up a beef stew and serves it over biscuits made from trusty Bisquick. Tonight, the pie is apple, full of cinnamon and nutmeg, and served as usual with Vermont cheddar cheese.

"And where do you get Vermont cheese out here?" Damon asks.

"From the Vermont Country Store shipped direct by U.S. mail. It's best to order it in the winter months."

"I would never think to put pie and cheese together, but every time you serve it, it's good," Damon says, staring at the cheese in his hand. "But then, there are a lot of things I would never imagine."

"For instance?" Vera picks up immediately on Damon's tiny hint of self-disclosure."

"Well, to tell the truth, I never thought I could be this rich and so unhappy."

Vera and Ollie exchange quick glances. Could this be why Ellen and

Damon have stopped by, to announce their separation? Ellen looks up at her husband with a barely perceptible frown. Finally, Vera manages to say, "Really?"

"Oh, sorry. I didn't mean to alarm anyone." Damon laughs nervously. "I guess that was a conversation stopper. What I meant to say was that I work so hard and the work is so stressful, I just don't enjoy it anymore. I never thought I'd hear myself say that."

"He works such long hours, you wouldn't believe it," Ellen adds.

"Always someone bugging me about something," Damon says. "That's the problem. I get calls all the time and a bunch of emails, people seeking advice or approvals on this or that. It's like I'm tied to a tree and the hounds are coming. I can hear them barking before they arrive. Everyone wants a piece of my flesh. Maybe it's time for me to do something else."

"Remind me how old are you, Damon." Vera says, in her best social worker's voice.

"Forty-three." He looks surprised at the question.

"Excuse my asking, but now I can tell you that you are right on schedule."

"For what, a nervous breakdown?"

"No, for the very typical and quite normal midlife crisis."

"And I can tell you that once it starts it's hard to finish it," Ollie says.

"Midlife crisis?" Damon shrugs.

"Well, you just come to a point in your life when it's natural to ask a lot of tough questions," Vera says.

"And it's not just about work and family, it's bigger than that." Ollie nods.

"This is pretty big the way it is," Damon says.

"No, I mean the spiritual issues. Like, what is the purpose of life? Why are we even here? What does it all mean?"

Now it's Vera's turn to look perplexed, and she feels the furrows wrinkling her forehead. Hopefully, Ollie won't give his lecture on the bug.

"I do, of course, think of those things," Damon says. But what do you mean that it's hard to finish?"

Ollie takes a deep breath and says, "Well, you make some provisional decisions. You have to. You change jobs or keep the one you have, but if you keep the one you have, you change the way you approach it. You decide to stay married to the same person, but you alter a lot of things in the relationship. But now, you're always second guessing everything, asking if it was the right decision. So, you never stop playing Monday morning quarterback to your life."

"Really?" Damon's face loses all expression and he sits motionless.

"Take me for instance," Ollie goes on, "now that I'm retired, I have no idea whether my life, as I lived it, had any meaning at all, you know, working at the law firm all those years. What good did I do? Help some big companies get bigger, some rich companies get richer? And now what? Surely, I won't be remembered for my beef stew, and don't want to be. But my life now, going to the bank, getting a haircut, shopping at Safeway, it's totally meaningless."

Vera and Ellen stare at each other, each quickly sneaking a look at her husband, and then looking back, too puzzled to comment. As Vera raises the teapot, her eyebrows come up. "More tea anyone?" Has Ollie told her how useless he feels? Maybe she hasn't been listening.

On Christmas day, Ollie and Vera are alone again, and they treat themselves to dinner at their favorite German restaurant, Westfalenhhof, near the top of Coal Creek Canyon. Ollie orders the special, traditional roast goose, while Vera has her usual, Wienerschnitzel. The cozy restaurant is decorated for the holidays with toy houses placed in each of the windows along with wreaths and candles. German folk music, with its oom-pah, oom-pah rhythms, plays softly to create the continental ambiance. It works. It's like stepping off the plane in Bavaria without having to pay an arm and a leg for a ten-hour ride in a flying sardine can.

Not having much to say that day, they just enjoy the food. Vera feels like she can no longer read Ollie's thoughts. She is always respectful of his silence, but lately, ever since that bug-on-its-back episode and his confession to Damon, Ollie has appeared to be a little gloomy, like a loon on a glassy New Hampshire lake, diving down, and then coming up somewhere totally unpredictable to make its eerie cry. It's hard to tell what the hell he's going to say next. If anything.

The days between Christmas and New Years are uneventful as always. Fresh snow has arrived, but Ollie lets it sit there on the driveway, not in the mood to bundle up and go wrestle with snow. He tries to read, but falls asleep. It's a welcome distraction when Peter calls to ask if they will be home that afternoon because he wants to drive down from Boulder for a little visit. He says he has a surprise for them. They tell him yes, of course, that they'll look forward to seeing him and hearing the surprise. Luckily his sister has come and gone so there will be no close encounters with the aliens from Texas, but they don't need to tell him that.

When they open the front door, they see Peter and a woman that appears somewhat younger than he, holding a child that looks to be not quite two. "Come in," Vera says.

"What have we here?" Ollie asks.

"Amanda, these are my parents, Oliver and Vera."

"And this is Katie," Amanda says.

Vera peers at Amanda. She is plain, but then Peter is no prize.

Snowy shoes are left at the door, and jackets are hung on the coat rack in the vestibule. As Peter and Amanda settle awkwardly onto the living room couch, Vera makes crows-feet frowns at the little girl and glances up at Ollie who replies with a half shrug. Who are these people? Katie is let down to the floor and immediately starts planting tiny fingerprints around the edges of the glass coffee table. Ollie pulls up an antique chair as Vera scurries off to the kitchen to put the kettle on for tea. She scrounges in the fridge for something to serve, finding only some leftover fruitcake that the firm has sent to Oliver from Georgia. But fruitcake for a two-year-old? What the hell does a little kid eat? She can't remember. Then she thinks of Ollie's Cheerios. Yes, that will work. And those green grapes. Her kids always liked grapes.

When Vera returns to the living room, she can tell they've been talking about the weather: what it's been, what it is now, and what it's going to be like for the next five days. Gloomy like Ollie? What is this ridiculous male preoccupation with the weather? But the roads are good, she hears Peter say, well plowed, salted in the places where it's needed. She's sure they have squeezed all they can out of the weather, wrung it dry, so to speak. She decides to ask Amanda how she met Peter, guessing that she will probably get a fuller report from her than Peter.

"Oh, we work together." Amanda says, but does not elaborate.

That's it? Guessed wrong about that one. "Making games?" Vera asks, not sure what that means.

"Yes, mother, at the place I told you about, that same place."

Silence. It's a little difficult to go on from there, and Ollie looks completely stumped, so Vera asks, "When did you meet?"

And Amanda responds, "My first day on the job."

Single syllable words, Vera notes. Six in a row. "And you've become friends."

"Yes, Mom, good friends."

Ollie is keeping an eye on little what's-her-name, to make sure she doesn't crash into anything breakable. He gets up and reaches down a long arm and Katie latches onto his index finger. She walks around the room attached to him like that.

Vera wants to do her child welfare interview on Amanda. Were you married? Do you have other children? Is the father known? Educational background? Food stamps? But she restrains herself. The whistle on the teakettle is singing, giving Vera an excuse to go to the kitchen and get herself under control. People who don't speak make her nervous.

In the dining room, when the fruitcake and tea are served, Ollie picks up Katie and curls her onto his lap and wraps a big arm around her. He likes the way that feels and she doesn't seem to mind. She picks out the Cheerios one by one from the cereal bowl, carefully practicing the use of her index finger and opposing thumb, supposedly the characteristic that distinguishes humans from apes, although it's hard to tell at this age. After each Cheerio she looks up at him and grins. A little charmer.

Vera knows from experience that the best way to get Peter to talk is to avoid asking him questions—just sit there and wait him out until he's ready, a talent his sister never developed. Finally, the moment arrives. "We've been looking at a house." He glances at Amanda and she nods, encouraging him to go ahead. "We've been living some at her apartment and some at mine for a while now, but we've been thinking it would be nice to have just one place, something a little bigger." Peter is silent. He used a lot of words in that last sentence; maybe he has run out. Amanda nods at him to get him started again. "With our two salaries we think we could make the monthly on a house, but we don't have enough saved for the down payment."

"So, whose house would it be?" Vera asks, still wanting to learn what Peter's relationship is to Amanda.

"Good question, Mom. We don't plan to get married."

"Not just yet anyway," Amanda adds.

The silence is long this time. Finally, Ollie asks, "How much cash would you need? Ten thousand, twenty, twenty-five?"

Vera is shocked. Doesn't he need to think it over?

"Twenty thousand would be great, Dad."

"As a loan," Amanda adds.

"No need for that. I'll get you fourteen tomorrow and six next year. That would be early next week, in January, you know." Ollie smiles at his own joke. "That way we won't have tax problems."

"My gosh, that would be wonderful, Dad." Now it's Peter's turn to look shocked.

Vera notices that everyone is smiling. Even Katie. She can feel a big smile on her own face, too. To be honest and truthful with herself, she has never quite been sure whether Peter actually liked women or not, and she had doubts that this moment would ever come. She doesn't know much about Amanda, but she can see she is built like a real woman. And Katie, only God knows where she came from, but she's sure cute. So now Peter has a family. Maybe this also explains why Ollie is so quick to respond with an offer, not needing to think it over. Just take care of them.

Katie picks up one grape and eats it, then she picks up another with her thumb and forefinger, leans over the edge of Ollie's lap, and drops it to the floor. "Look at this, Vera, she understands about gravity." Ollie doesn't seem to be troubled by the little pile of green grapes accumulating on the carpet. He looks too happy to be annoyed by something like that. It seems like this is the first time she has seen him smile all week. Vera catches herself smiling again, but for a different reason. Look at how that little tyke has taken to Ollie. He has always wanted a grandchild, but why must the means of acquiring one be so unconventional?

On New Year's Day—once again they have slept in front of the TV through the dropping of the ball—Ollie makes his healthful buttermilk whole wheat pancakes with blueberries, healthful, that is, until you drown them in butter and Vermont maple syrup. After breakfast, while Vera makes the kitchen tidy, Ollie retreats to his study. It never takes her long, even with Ollie as the boisterous cook; and when she has finished, she decides to enter Ollie's intellectual man cave and initiate a little live conversation. She plops down in the desk chair by the computer, next to his recliner where he sits slumped, reading intently, surrounded by books stacked and spread out open on the floor around him. "What in the world are you studying?" she asks.

"Life," he says, not looking up.

"Seriously," she asks again.

"Yes, very seriously. It's an urgent matter, and I need to find the answer.

"Ollie. Look at me. Stop. What's going on with you? You seem so tense. So gloomy. What's bothering you?" she asks, a little desperation creeping into her voice.

The tone catches his attention. He removes his reading glasses and looks up. "Well, first of all, the numbers. There are too many of us. Seven billion going on nine. The population has quadrupled in the last one hundred years. We have almost five million right here in Colorado. Five million, and I can't even begin to imagine what a billion is. How can one individual life have any meaning? We are utterly insignificant."

"Can you draw that conclusion just from the numbers?" she asks.

"Yes, of course. And those seven billion are the ones still living today. Look how many have lived and died already, on back through human history, across the generations to our origins in Africa."

"And the sheer numbers make you feel insignificant?"

"Yes, of course, but then when I read in the field of astronomy," he points at a big blue book speckled with stars lying at his feet, "it just makes matters worse. Our sun is just one of many suns in our galaxy, and now they are talking about billions of galaxies and universes, plural, not just one universe."

"It does seem a bit overwhelming."

"Our nothingness is quite apparent, my love. Let's face it," he sighs.

"Even more apparent when you are retired, wouldn't you say, dear?"

Ollie ponders that last remark before he replies. "You are suggesting perhaps that I am more aware of my nothingness because I have no work, no way to be useful? Well, yes, of course, that makes it even worse."

"To be without the meaning you derived all of those years from your work."

"Work which I now see as mostly meaningless?" He runs a hand through his hair. "But retirement does not make the philosophical question of our meaninglessness any less important. I wish I had asked such questions more urgently when I was young."

"True, but why is it consuming you so just now?"

"Because I need to know. I can't go to my grave like a bison led over a bluff."

For a split second, Vera wonders if he's suicidal, but she shakes that off fast. She listens through his pause until he begins again.

"Sometimes when we are flying in from Cabo, I look down at all those twinkling lights, which most people think are so beautiful, and it gives me the creeps that the land is crawling down there with homo sapiens all trying to cope with their nothingness."

"I guess that's what we have to do, dear."

"Ah, but all we do is build illusions."

"Like the Sound of Music tour."

"Worse. Illusions of our significance. I mean look at the absurd things people do, dear, to cope with their nothingness. Groping for a little meaning." He closes his eyes and reaches out into the air like a blind person. "Take our neighbor Donald next door, refinishing antique cars."

"Well, maybe he just happens to like cars."

"True, but they have become his life. His day job is his leisure and his real job, the thing that gives his life meaning, is working on those damn cars all weekend long."

Vera raises her eyebrows, perplexed, but she doesn't say anything.

"Across the street is Charlie, the ultimate sports fan, running around in those ridiculous long shorts and orange jerseys with the big numbers on the back, falling into a blue funk when his beloved Broncos crash. And not just Broncos, but Nuggets, Avalanche, and Rockies as well, not to mention his college teams."

"And Tricia is forever in that van running those kids to soccer practice, softball games, and swim meets," Vera adds.

"And that's how they build the illusion of meaning in their lives." Ollie throws his hands up over his head.

"And the lives of their children. I'm beginning to see what you mean, dear."

"Can there be anything shakier than to build a life on sports?" Ollie asks.

"Well, it is dubious, I guess."

"And don't even get me started on the Swansons."

"The hoarders?"

"Their basement is so full and their garage so loaded up to the ceiling that they can't even get their cars in it."

"Well, yes, agreed. But tell me dear, is it all illusion? Aren't some things a little less illusory than others?"

"That's what I'm working on. That's why my study is so serious."

"And urgent." She crosses her legs and adjusts her position in that uncomfortable desk chair, waiting for more.

"That's why I'm reading Sartre." He points to a stack of books at his side.

"Sartre? The existentialist? Oh, my God, Ollie, you are in deep."

"But it's helpful. He says that the riddle of our existence is solved by choosing."

"Oh, I remember this stuff. We took that philosophy course together our senior year. I recall something about not choosing is still a choice, but at that time I was just worried about whether you were going to choose me."

"More precisely, 'If I do not choose, I am still choosing.' But Sartre says it so well." Ollie fumbles to put on his reading glasses and pick up the right book. "Let me find it for you. I was just reading this yesterday. Here. 'Man is nothing else but what he makes of himself.' And here, a few pages later. 'Life has no meaning a priori, and it's up to you to give it meaning.' But there is a heavy ethical responsibility in our choices, dear. Here, listen to this: 'man being condemned to be free carries the weight of the whole world and for himself as a way of being.'"

Which is exactly the way Ollie has looked to her for the last few weeks, like he was staggering under the weight of the world. What is she to do with her aging Atlas? He puts Sartre on the floor beside his chair, and picks up another book off to his left. "And who is this?" she asks.

"Camus," he replies with even more enthusiasm. "Albert Camus."

"Oh, God, Ollie, the prophet of the Absurd?"

"Yes, we were reading him together in that same class along with Kafka."

"I recall something about a very strange guy who shoots an Arab on the beach on this sweltering hot day."

"Good memory, dear. *The Stranger*. And it was absurd for him to do this because he had no motive, didn't even know the guy."

"So why not shoot him, right?" Vera shrugs. But her worry about where this is going is mounting.

"If life is pointless."

"And absurd. Ollie, you aren't thinking of killing somebody, are you?"

"But that's just the point, dear. It is hard to know what you will do if life is pointless and absurd." She must look so shocked that Ollie tries to reassure her. "No, I would never kill someone else."

Startled, she loses control and shouts, "Just yourself?" She is on the verge of tears.

"Oh, no nothing like that. You know me better than that, dear." He reaches over and pats her on the knee. "Besides, after floundering for days, I think I've found the answer."

"Well, let's hear it before I have a stroke. I can't imagine what my blood pressure must be." She rubs one hand down the back of her neck.

"Camus wrote another novel called The Plague. No one knows exactly what this plague is. Maybe disease, or more generally, human suffering. Maybe it's the Nazis. Camus was a resistance fighter, you know. But the critics suggested, even back then, that the plague is a symbol for the Absurd. The central character, this Doctor Rieux, goes on fighting the plague, risking his own life, though it seems hopeless. I wrote a term paper on The Plague."

"I'm waiting for the answer, dear."

"The answer is to resist. To find some contribution to make wherever you are stationed in life."

"To fight the plague. It is a good metaphor," Vera agrees, scratching that tiny spot on the top of her head, but she wants something more specific.

"Resist in our own way, through our own resources, in our own time," Ollie insists.

"And that makes you feel better?" Vera asks cautiously, staring at him.

"It does." Ollie tips back in his chair, a distant gaze in his eyes, and breathes out a long sigh, followed by two deep breaths. Vera waits. Finally, he sits forward and says jubilantly, "Let's do it."

"Do what?" She's sure it's not sex.

"Give the money, like you suggested."

A smile instantly spreads across her face and her eyes open wide. "That's fantastic! Do we need to change our wills?"

"No. Wills deal with what's left. Both kids will have what they need no matter what. This is about the here and now while we are still alive. We need to spend our money now while we can still do some good with it. Resist the absurd. Fight the plague." He shakes a fist in the air.

"Give money to our poor friends in Mexico," she shouts and jumps up from her chair to join him in shaking a feeble fist fervently. She holds his face in her two hands and plants a kiss on his forehead. "I am so excited. Thank you, dear." Then looking him straight in the eye, she rattles off her questions. "How much? How many people? Who?"

"That's for us to choose."

10

THE DANGEROUS YOUNG RADICAL

The past holiday season was booked to nearly full occupancy at Sunset Point Resort, and Marco was busy with work and occupied with trying to keep Ashley happy through the holidays. What is a holiday to a waiter—just more work, not even the day off. Ashley said she never missed her parents, but he wonders about that because he missed his family a lot. The holidays intensified his memories of the U.S., particularly how the music was always playing in the malls and the houses were all decorated with elaborate light displays. He remembers his mother shopping with coupons for the best bargains and wrapping the presents in red and green paper, and then her insisting on their going as a family to the Christmas Eve mass at the Spanish-speaking church even if it was only twice a year counting Easter. He and Michelle exchanged gifts that last year, a heart on a gold chain for her and an engraved ID bracelet for him, which he appreciated for the sentiment but seldom wore because it drove him a little nuts having something loose on his wrist like that. One thing he knows for sure after the holiday season at the resort is that he would be happy never again to hear "Feliz Navidad."

He has been so busy that he hasn't even had time to get a haircut. It's been four weeks now—right before he met Ashley—and he knows that long hair can get him in trouble with El Greco, so he promises himself that he will get a haircut today. He doesn't mind spending a few pesos for a good haircut, short on the sides and a little longer on top, and he always goes to La Tijera Veloz and the same stylist, a short woman of Mayan descent. She loves to chatter on with him in Spanish, and she knows everything that's going on in Cabo. If she hears it, she tells it.

To pass the time as he waits for her, Marco picks up one of those beauty magazines with pictures of the latest hairstyles for women, and as he's glancing through, there on page forty-two is a picture popping out at him of this beauty with a hairdo like Ashley's. Same red hair and everything. He looks closer to make sure it isn't Ashley because to him she has the face and body of a fashion model. She's turned out to be an okay girlfriend and having someone to be with is definitely better than being alone. She knows how to talk about stuff, and that's important. What's best is she understands his anger because she's got anger herself, just different issues. She knows the world is really fucked up and she can describe exactly how and why. Ah, but he especially likes it when she crawls up on top of him in the middle of the night to make earthquakes.

He reads a few lines to see if this odd coiffure has a name, and sure enough, there are the words in English, *asymmetrical bob*. His principal at Sandia High had a haircut like that, but they called it a comb-over.

Marco is laughing to himself about how they could have named him Asymmetrical Bob, when he notices the chatty little stylist standing at his side asking him what he is so happy about this afternoon. He holds up the picture and tells her that he knew a guy back in the States who wore his hair that way. Un hombre, a guy. She laughs. Then she tells him she's seen some red-haired gringa running around Cabo with that style and it looks like hell. He decides to change the subject to the films currently playing at the Paraíso Mall. She cuts and chatters, more chattering than cutting, and then she asks if he knows who it was that saved the drowning child at Sunset Point. He admits that he is the one, but then, suspecting she already knew, he wonders if she has connected him to Ashley.

Lately, Ashley has been floating out across the city with the confidence and abandon of a bold seagull. Then he pictures a seagull with an asymmetrical bob and it cracks him up. He can't figure out why Ashley was keeping such a low profile when she first arrived. Now he is wondering, as they are seen more frequently together, what people think and are saying about them. After all, her appearance kind of stands out in Mexico. Has the word begun to spread among his co-workers that Marquito has a new friend, an American girl with red hair? Is she living with him or what? Suspecting that people might be gossiping about them makes him uncomfortable. Ashley wouldn't give a damn. Why does he care what they think? But he does.

On Marco's day off, he and Ashley have started a tradition of taking two big bottles of chilled Corona and some empanadas down to Médano Beach. They sit in the same spot as before. Something is crazy about that spot on the beach. It's like they are sitting at the mouth of a volcano, on the crater's edge, and instead of molten lava, it's their own feelings about the hypocritical world they live in that come bubbling up and gushing forth, first hers, then his, alternating, until they are both boiling over with rage.

He tells her more about what it's like to be a waiter, running his ass off to serve a bunch of self-satisfied rich people, bowing and scraping, all the while having to smile.

"It's all about wealth and privilege," she says, tossing the lock of hair from her eye, even though it falls right back in the same place where it was. "People at a resort aren't even aware that they are privileged, and if they were, they sure as hell wouldn't admit it. They think they've earned it and they expect outstanding service because they're paying for it. What they forget," she waves an index finger, "is that they actually had a lot of people investing in them, giving them a start in life, providing a good education and teaching them the personal skills needed for success. It's called social capital, and most people are totally oblivious to how they've been somebody else's investment."

"But what about you, Ashley," Marco asks, knowing he's venturing into a sensitive subject.

"Hell, yes," Ashley says. "You're damn right I'm privileged, but there's a difference. I know it, and I'm trying to do something about it. Just because I grew up in that stuffy family doesn't mean I have to live like they live."

"Do they expect you to do that?"

"Of course they do. Not to live like they live is a real slap in the face, right? You can't imagine how oppressive it is living in that over-privileged family. That's why I had to get out."

"That's why you're here?" Marco asks.

"Partly. Yeah, partly." She clams up. Sips her beer. Swishes her hair. Then she switches the subject. "Hey, you were going to tell me about El Greco."

"Okay, but first I have to tell you about the drowning."

"You drowned someone?"

"No, I saved someone." So, he tells her the whole story about how he rescued the little blue-eyed Asian kid. "And the boss called me 'hero,' real sarcastic like and told me to get back to work."

"Such a jerk."

"He doesn't always fire people. If he doesn't like someone, he makes their life so miserable, they just leave. This week I saw him torment this one guy all morning long, following him around everywhere, humiliating him in front of guests. So, he left."

"What a pain in the ass."

"For sure. We only have a few women, the hostess, special order cook, and a couple of waitresses, but they suffer the most because he's constantly criticizing them and the next minute, he's got his hands all over them and they're afraid to say anything."

"What an asshole. Hey, he really deserves some attention. I mean, there ought to be some consequences for that kind of crap."

"Consequences? I'll drink to that, but what?" Marco asks.

"We just need to kick his ass some way."

"Well, yeah, but I need my job."

"He doesn't need to know who did it. You can still enjoy the revenge. Let me think about this."

They fall into a long silence, sprawled out on their towels enjoying the sun for a while. Ashley is covered from her asymmetrical bob to her painted green toenails in sunscreen and she looks like an albino Raggedy Ann among all of the Mexicans. She has a great body, but for her to get a tan without burning is a challenge. They doze off. She sleeps for a short time and then Marco hears her sit up to take another gulp of beer. She finishes one bottle and opens the next. She fidgets, but Marco doesn't say anything. He's half awake and half asleep, soaking up sunshine. She lies down next to him and he feels her head bump up against his and he opens his eyes in time to see her long, tattooed arm extended to take a selfie on her cell phone. It all happens so fast he doesn't know what to think. She starts ranting again.

"The differences between countries like the U.S. and Mexico," she says, "that's about privilege, too."

"But there are some really rich, privileged people in Mexico, too," he says.

"Of course there are. And many poor in the U.S. But in general," she asks, "which is the rich country and which is the poor? We both know the answer to that."

"So, you're saying the same thing applies, that the U.S. is privileged without being aware of how it became so. And the people there can't understand why Mexico is poor?"

"Exactly," she replies. "No concept of history, not to mention economics or social structure. I mean, we know that one reason Mexico is poor is because of the so-called wicked war, right? But what about Mexico's long and oppressive colonial history under Spain, the rape of her natural resources, the embedded privileges of the landowners after independence, and the long and painful Mexican revolution. How many Americans have a clue about any of that?"

"Wow! You know a lot about Mexican history. I'm impressed."

"Well, don't be 'cause I just read the stuff this week," she says, a faint smile curling her lips.

"So, to explain to themselves why Mexico is poor," Marco builds on what Ashley is saying, "Americans have to invent all that shit about us Mexicans, like we're lazy, we're backward, we have a so-called culture of poverty, and we're a bunch of superstitious Indians who sacrifice virgins, blah, blah, blah. I heard a lot of that crap when I lived there."

"But people in the U.S. ignore what we know now about the incredible civilizations that were here before Cortéz and his exotic diseases wiped them out: ninety percent of the population dead, defenseless against those European microbes. Can you believe that? Come on," Ashley yells, "these are the people who invented a frickin' 365-day calendar."

"Yeah, inherently dumb and backward people, right?" Marco's anger jerks him to his feet. Besides, he has to shake the sand out of his swimsuit. Ashley is so agitated she looks like she's going to puke. Maybe the beer. She's been drinking most of it. He helps her stand up. She looks a little woozy.

Ashley reaches out her tattooed arm to grab his shoulder, partly to steady herself, it seems, but also to make sure she has his full attention. She stares at him with those intense, unwavering green eyes and says, "We need to do something about all this shit, Marco. We need to wake a few people up. Bring off something dramatic. Agreed?"

Marco and Ashley stop at the public restroom at the beach and then catch the bus to the Pemex station. Marco picks up carnitas from a taquería. When they mount the stairs to the apartment and go through the door, Ashley pulls back the brightly patterned drapes, new ones that go well with the lavender bedspread. He sets out the cheap dinnerware and fake silverware she picked up at the shop by the bus stop. So domestic he has become. At least the place looks livable now.

Every now and then Ashley makes these wild comments, like 'something dramatic!' But he doubts she has ever done anything. Mostly talk. But he doesn't think she's telling the truth about leaving Berkeley, and that bothers him. He has an idea to test out. Without looking directly into her face he says, "You are awfully smart, amiga, you know that? I won't use the word gifted, because I know what that does to you, but you learn things really quickly."

"What do you mean? Like that Mexican history? Those were some Wikipedia articles I read on the computer at the library."

"Well, yeah, but you remembered the essentials," he says, and then pauses. "So, I'm finding it difficult to believe that you're flunking out of the university." He looks up at her and she looks away.

She starts to say something and then stops. "So, you don't believe me?"

"I didn't say that." But his suspicions are being confirmed.

Then she says, "I was suspended." She fiddles with her paper napkin.

"So, you are going back to school, then."

"Screw them. I'm never going back there."

On the third day of the third week of January Marco wakes up and finds a note on the table reminding him that today is the six-week anniversary of the day they met. Ashley must have put the note there in the middle of the night. The note has a row of X's and O's. Six weeks, and he didn't expect her to stay more than one night. But she's such a sexy little animal. She'll want to celebrate. So, what's the problem?

At breakfast that morning at Sunset Point, he's bringing out orders and thinking about butterflies, but not just butterflies. Also seagulls, how they can fly with so little effort, and turtles, why they are so slow. He needs stuff like that to occupy his mind while he's looking out for drowning kids. All of a sudden, he notices this bright orange asymmetrical bob bouncing by down on the beach. Damn. Is she coming to visit him at work? He hopes not. He sees her nick a black towel from a lounge chair and throw it over her arm. He puts his tray down and sets out the plates of food, all the time trying to keep an eye on her as she comes up the steps from the beach to the deck around the pools. The security guard doesn't stop her, though he looks at her kind of funny, then smiles to himself, like he thinks she's weird. As Marco refills coffee cups, he loses her. She disappears like mist in the cool morning air. Shit. Where did she go?

La Casona is busy and the guests just keep coming like a flash flood until one o'clock. Marco is running all over the place, trying to keep his mind on the orders, but now instead of butterflies, his head is filled with that image of Ashley walking right up those steps like she's a Five Star Elite member with that black towel over her arm. When the deluge of guests ceases, he goes downstairs to the cafeteria to eat and sit for a few minutes to rest his feet and cool off. Maribel passes by, but there's no hello, no dimpled smile. When he is finished eating, he checks out and goes through the main gate to the road that leads back into town. He sees Ashley sitting there waiting for him on a flat rock in the stone wall amidst the bougainvillea. She has picked a cluster of some of the salmon-colored blossoms that grow wild down there and stuck it over her ear. He's not very happy about her being there, but he's curious about what she's been doing. Like a good Mexican, he puts on a smiling mask to cover what's inside. "What's up?" he says to her. "I thought I saw you here this morning down on the beach."

"Yes, I saw you, too, running your ass off and smiling at everybody. Fucking hopeless job you've got, man."

He's pooped, but they can talk more privately out in the open—better than in the bus— as they walk along together.

"First of all," she begins, "the resort is wide open. If it was a bank, it would be robbed every day including Sunday. The security at the beach is almost non-existent. Hell, anyone with a towel can pass for a guest. I wandered all over the pool area. Even took in a little sun. As long as you keep saying hola to everybody, you're fine. I found a couple of doors at the lower levels that enter the tunnel system. Or you can just ride the elevator down to the basement, and there you are."

Whoa. She really found her way around. For sure she's smart and assertive. "But there are security cameras all over those tunnels," he warns.

"Not all over. They aren't positioned well. There are coverage gaps. Anyway, there's a lot a person could do without too much trouble. So, what do you want to do?"

He's surprised at the blunt question. "Look, Ashley, I'm not sure I want to do anything. I sure as hell don't want to spend time in a Mexican jail."

"Jail is jail. The goal is to stay out. Don't get caught. So, what are your goals besides staying out of jail?

"Goals for what?"

"Hey, dude, you got amnesia or something? I may have been drunk, but I think we agreed to do something dramatic."

Marco is confused. Did he agree because he didn't object? He doesn't remember agreeing to anything. He stares at his feet. He'd like to run. Dash over a few low hurdles. She seems serious, or at least serious about making plans. He doesn't know how to respond.

Ashley continues on, flapping her arms and twittering like a sparrow, "Okay, the goal is to get people's attention. To let them know that there are people out here, like us, who will terrorize their privileged lives. So, we need to disrupt the normal functioning of the resort, ultimately to shut it down, at least for a while. It would cost big bucks to shut this place down even for a few days."

"What do you mean, shut it down?"

"If something dramatic happens, the guests will flee. Grab the first flight back to the U.S. or Canada. Panic spreads like Skippy peanut butter in a situation like this and it only takes a few things to happen for people to say I'm outta here."

Wow! She's really hyped up and speaking way too loud. "Like what?" he says softly. I told you I don't want to go to jail."

"Some people need to die." Her arm is extended like a rapier, slashing back and forth. "Terrorists call them demonstration killings. I mean, if a few people at this resort died over, say, three or four days, guests who are already here would flee, and those with reservations to come would cancel. It's not something you can keep quiet."

"Died? Did you say, if a few people died?"

"Well, they don't have to die. They could just get very sick and it would have the same effect. Especially in Mexico where Americans still panic over Montezuma's revenge."

"But how will they get sick?"

"I knew you were going to ask that. Could you do a little bit of the thinking here, too, so I don't have to do it all? You're in the kitchen, right? It would be easy to slip a little poison into a few dishes. Nothing fancy. Rat poison would do."

"I'm sure I couldn't do that."

"It could be random. You don't need to know who's going to get the dishes. Five very sick people would close this place down."

"But they would trace it to the kitchen."

"To the kitchen, yes; but to you, not at all. We just need to be careful."

"I don't like this idea of poison."

"Okay. What about the water. The desalinization system looks like it would be easy to disable. No water, no guests. Same effect. They go home, others cancel. People start to panic."

"Are there other options?" he asks, not really wanting to know them.

"The swimming pools. The three pools at this place are all connected. I could have dropped stuff in the north pool by the lobby this morning—or you could do it at night—and people would start getting sick or scratching themselves to death. Same effect. The panic would spread and people would leave. What good is a resort without swimming pools?"

Marco is exhausted. He's sweating. His intestines are making gurgling noises and he is a long way from a bathroom. He can hardly put one foot in front of the other. He doesn't ask any more questions because he doesn't want to hear any more answers. She actually used the word terrorist.

When they get into town, Ashley wants to go to the Biblioteca Pública to use a computer. "But that's in a completely different part of town," Marco complains.

"I know where it is. I go there a lot."

"Maybe another day," he suggests.

"Come on, I have things to show you."

Wow! She's completely manic. There's no stopping her now, so they go.

The library is a small single-story adobe-looking building with bars on the windows. "Are they afraid someone is going to steal some knowledge?" she asks. "No, just kidding. I know it's the computers that would be stolen, but it does look odd—bars on the windows of a library. Quite symbolic."

The library is also the smallest building in the area of La Delegación, which has a fútbol field, a covered stage for cultural entertainment, and the mayor's office. Not like the libraries in the U.S., Marco observes. Not very functional. Not well located. Does it even have books? He signs in and they list their purpose as browsing. The little room to the left of the entry houses the computers. In no time at all Ashley is doing a Google search. Marco pulls up a chair and sits beside her. She types in P-O-I-S-O-N-S and presses Search.

"What are you doing?" he asks.

"Look at all of the different kinds of poisons. It gives the brand names, generic names, and dosage information." Is this what she wants to show him? Poisons? She writes down information in a small notebook that she retrieves from the hip pocket of her shorts. Ashley always appears to be prepared. Marco is aware that he is squinting, that his nose is wrinkled up, and that his stomach is really roaring. He finally realizes that she is serious, and it is making him very nervous. She closes that search and begins another on water contamination. He asks her to stop. But then she opens another one on automatic weapons. "Look at these. Aren't they beautiful? We probably don't need these, though. They are too cumbersome and expensive. Besides they can get you into a lot of trouble if you get caught."

"Are you aware that they start watching you when you visit sites like this?"

"No worries, amigo, nobody even knows I'm in Mexico. Besides, I used your password to sign in. Just because you don't use that no good, useless laptop anymore doesn't mean you can be careless about your password."

"Ashley, for God's sake, turn the damn thing off."

"No, I want to check out Barbie Dolls. That'll throw 'em off. Just trust me. I know what I'm doing." She smiles one of her half smiles.

Such a sardonic little smile. Yes, she does know what she's doing. That's the problem. And who knows what she has already done? Or will do next? Finally, he says, "I'm outa here. You are crazy, woman, completely crazy."

"I thought you were up for this." Her voice assumes a whiny, disputatious tone as she trails after him. "It seems you have no nerve. It takes guts to be a rebel, you know. You need to commit."

Marco insists that they get the next bus home. He turns and looks at her hard. Same red hair, same green eyes, but now he sees a completely different person. He suddenly realizes what she is and that he may be in serious danger hanging out with her. His whole life could be ruined—yeah, way more ruined than it is already. He's no longer confused, he's terrified. Will she poison him for not celebrating their anniversary?

Marco doesn't need to ask himself philosophical questions about butterflies and turtles to fill the empty spaces of his mind while he is serving orange juice and coffee to the privileged guests at his tables this morning. His mind has no empty spaces. Instead, it seems jammed to overflowing with images of Ashley poisoning people, or contaminating swimming pools, or maybe even setting buildings on fire or blowing stuff up. He imagines her standing ready with an AK-47 and a bandoleer slung across her chest. ¡Ay Dios mio! He doesn't want to be involved in that violent stuff. That's not who he is. He may be pissed, but he's not stupid.

It is all he can do to focus his attention on his work. He finds himself offering coffee refills to people who are drinking cocoa and bringing take-away boxes to tables where the people have already eaten everything. He drops a plate, but his quick reflexes enable him to catch it on the end of his toe, but then it goes careening off and starts rolling around and around until it settles into a noisy spin that brings a frown from El Greco, first at the plate and then at him. He's got to talk to someone sane before he blows up.

He finishes his shift and goes below to the cafeteria and finds Maribel. Does he have the courage to sit down next to her, to talk to her after so long, to say what's bothering him? Probably not everything, but at least something to get a little conversation started.

"Hi, Maribel."

"Well, Señor Marco. I don't believe I've talked to you for a while." She doesn't look up from her food. He just stands there. "Perhaps you have been too busy now that you are so famous."

"Yes, I've been busy, but no, not actually too busy to talk. I'm sorry. It's just that..."

"You've been preoccupied. You must have a lot on your mind trying to keep that girl happy."

"Don't tease me, Maribel. I need to talk. Seriously. I'm really confused."

"Still?" Maribel doesn't look directly at him until the word seriously registers with her, and when she glances up into his face and sees his horrified expression, she says, "Oh, my, Marco, what's wrong. You look like you've seen a ghost. Sit down."

"What my imagination sees is worse than a ghost. But first, tell me, are people talking about me and that girl? How did you know?"

"You need to understand, Señor, that you are not Marco the waiter around here anymore. You are Marquito the guy who saved the little boy from drowning. You are a celebrity. You are the Brad Pitt of Sunset Point, you know, like when they were filming Troy. Everyone knows about you: the maids, the bellmen, the men who cut the grass and care for the pools. And they all want to know more about you because you are famous."

"But do they connect me to the American girl? Tell me."

"Of course they do. Someone sees you together at Médano beach, another spots you at the Mango Cantina, others notice while you are at the bus or going to the library."

"The library?"

"Different people, of course, see you in different places. It's kind of a game they play, like whale watching. Oh, there he is. Then he flips his tail and dives down deep and you don't see him for a while until he surfaces again and spouts. And they all talk, Señor, blah, blah, blah. What do you think people do in this cafeteria?"

Marquito holds his head with his hands over his ears. He should have known better. He wasn't aware that he was famous. But the talk, yes, he suspected they were talking. "Geez, what do they say?"

"Well, you have to admit she is an easy target with that hairdo. The place was really buzzing when she was out here yesterday. Everyone enjoyed getting a closer look."

"Mierda." He pounds his fists in the air. "I'm sorry. Excuse me. I didn't know she was coming out here."

"It sounds like you don't want to be associated with her."

"I think she may be running away. Not just from home, but from something serious. I'm worried now that she might be dangerous."

"Dangerous? Really?" A hand flies up to cover her mouth. "Then I can see how you don't want to be linked to...Okay, so you're in a mess, and you need to talk to someone." Maribel stacks her dishes hastily, takes them over to the counter, and returns. "Let me make a suggestion. I will arrange my next day off to match yours. I'm inviting you as a friend—just as a friend, you understand—to come with me on the bus up to Todos Santos for the day. I want you to see the other Mexico and meet a real Mexican woman."

"That's all I need, another woman in my life."

"It's my grandmother. Besides we can talk, you and I."

"What will I do with Ashley?" he asks.

"Anything but bring her along. If she's old enough to run away, she's old enough to stay home alone."

11

WITH MARIBEL IN THE OTHER MEXICO

On their next day off, Maribel and Marco meet at the Tranporte Águila bus station to catch the early morning bus to Todos Santos, a small town to the north just inland from the Pacific coast, an artist community and home to the Hotel California, coincidently the same name as a song made famous in 1976 by the Eagles. Maribel and Marco begin to chatter excitedly and he asks her where she learned English. Only then does he discover that she was a one semester exchange student in high school. So, she lived in the US, too. California. She knows the situation.

As soon as they settle into their seats, Marco begins to lay out the problem, how it all began with his feelings of loss and anger, his being upset about being back in Mexico, and his having lost his girlfriend and his grip on the future. He mentions Vera and Ollie, whom Maribel says she remembers well, and how Vera's questions about his two lives stirred up his resentments. She listens sympathetically until he tells how Ashley missed her boat and just picked him up, but that story sounds so contrived that he has to reassure Maribel that it's true. He was vulnerable—Vera sensed this—and this red-haired rebel came into his life, like he was just waiting for her. He admits he enjoyed her company, but now he can't figure out how to get rid of her. She says she's been suspended from the university. Her parents have no idea where she is. It seems like she might be some kind of terrorist, seriously, a dangerous person who could do some real damage. This is what's been making him so nervous lately. That story, with all of the details and questions from Maribel, takes the full hour for the bus to get to Todos Santos.

"Okay," Maribel says as they pull off of the main road and start toward the town, "maybe we can figure out what to do with Ashley on the way back, but for now let's focus on you. We need to get you calmed down, get rid of that worry and anger, and find the real Marco, who I'm sure is not a terrorist and probably not even a rebel, just a person who gets upset and confused, when he isn't saving little boys from drowning. Turn off all the noise in your head, take some deep breaths of the cool air you will find here when you get off the bus, and prepare to discover the real Mexico. Got that?"

"Got it. At least I'll try." For the first few minutes, what he sees looks like the same old Mexico he's seen elsewhere: brick streets, rickety buildings, and never-ending cactus. They turn the corner at Benito Juárez Street and start to climb the hill, past a striking little building painted in bright pink and blue, shops with hand-painted wooden bowls, and a store with wool rugs from Oaxaca displayed on the exterior walls. Eventually, on their left, they pass the bright orange Hotel California, well stocked with tourists, but nothing special. As they walk along, Marco begins to sense the serenity of the quaint old rural town where everything is historic and the pace is slow, as if one foot is stuck in the past.

"Breathe," Maribel tells him, "and look at the blue sky and feel the sun. See if you can understand why our ancestors worshipped the sun."

They cross the street and walk up to the church, another mission church like the one in Cabo, only older and bigger, called Misión de Santa Rosa de Todos Santos.

"I want to go inside," Maribel tells him. At the door she points out a nearly life-size sculpture of Mary and Joseph and Jesus as a young boy. Joseph is holding a mallet and Jesus has a carpenter's square. "Artisans," she points out. "Remember this. I'll tell you about it later." She enters the sanctuary, crosses herself, and dips down on a bent knee as she was taught as a child. He can see that she's religious. She slips onto a bench and then kneels down on both knees as she begins to pray. Marco just stands in the back, knowing what he is supposed to do—his parents did teach him—but feeling awkward because it's been so long since he's done any of that. Besides, he has some pretty negative views of the Catholic Church from what he's read. So, he just looks at the simple straight lines of the sanctuary and the bright sunlight pouring in through the clear windows. It is peaceful. He sits down on a bench for a moment, trying to calm himself, as Maribel suggested, and enjoys the tranquility until he feels her tap him on the arm, ready to go.

They leave the church, cross the street, and step up onto the plaza, an open area paved in brick, with black metal benches in rows on two sides under the shade of gently waving palm trees. From the plaza, the

Pacific Ocean is just barely in view, and it adds to the serenity of the scene having the ocean there off in the distance. They sit for a while and Maribel doesn't say anything to disturb the peace and quiet. Finally, she stands, and says, "Let's go meet grandma and grandpa." They pass the ornate little bandstand at the end of the plaza—everything here seems to have an artistic touch—and walk two blocks up Constitución Street to the gallery. Her grandparents, known affectionately as Abuela and Abuelo, turn out to be artists, working together in their studio, she as a painter and he as a sculptor. They live across the street upstairs over a restaurant. "I have a short commute," Abuelo jokes. Marco can tell they are educated. A small radio is playing classical music. "Bach?" Maribel asks and Abuela tells her it is one of the Brandenburg Concertos. When they finally get around to introductions, Maribel presents Marco as a friend from the resort where she works.

Her grandmother, known more formally as Doña Conchita, is a tall thin woman with gray hair pinned up in back with shell combs. Her glasses are on a chain around her neck. Don Pedro has a full gray and white beard that rests comfortably on his chest and long silver hair tied neatly in a ponytail at the back of his neck. His alert eyes radiate earnestness and curiosity as he talks and listens. His wife has just finished a new etching that hangs in the gallery for sale. Marco is drawn to it because it is filled with butterflies. It has a prominent face, the face of a troubled but serene woman with hair that seems to turn into the shape of a butterfly body and wings. The head is surrounded by smaller butterflies scattered through the rest of the picture, and they stand out in blue against the squiggly etched lines of the background. "Does the butterfly mean anything in particular, Doña Conchita?" he asks.

"Well, they say that today it has become the symbol of the liberated woman. But I've always liked butterflies and drew them and painted them long before women were liberated or butterflies were appropriated for their symbol." She smiles a quiet little smile to herself, and Marco thinks he sees the familial resemblance of Maribel's deep dimples.

Marco looks more closely at the bottom left of the print at an inscription in Spanish: tu tiempo es ahora una mariposa. "Something like, our time is as short as a butterfly's life?" he asks Doña Conchita.

"Yes, that's good. That's the point anyway. So short. So precious. We trade a day of our life for each day's activities. When that day is gone, a piece of our life is gone. It happens every day, but it all adds up fast. Then it's gone. Butterflies live very short lives, you know. Maybe you need to be a little old to understand a butterfly's life."

Don Pedro is finishing a piece of sculpture made from a plum tree branch. It stands straight up about a half meter tall. The lines follow the natural twists and curves of the branch, but he has chiseled out faces in the branch, some more obvious than others. The more you look, the more faces you see: larger ones, smaller ones, the face of an ancient Indian, a Spanish ancestor, a young woman with her hands over her breasts, and at the bottom at the side, the face of an angel. Painstaking detail. "Tell me about it, Abuelo," Maribel asks. "This is something new."

"Well, yes, and it still needs some sanding and polishing, but it is just the faces of various people, our human faces all growing out of this one branch. I'm suggesting that we are all different but all joined together, the faces from the past and present, the young and the old. There is a kind of energy that encircles it and holds the faces together. When I add the wax, it will bring out the grain of the wood and make the whole piece more unified."

"It's already beautiful, Abuelo, and I can't wait to see it finished."

"You may not. It's already sold. They're coming for it next week."

"What a pity," Marco exclaims, "It will disappear? Doesn't it make you sad to part with it?"

"That's how I earn my living, son. But if it makes someone happy and enriches their life, that pleases me."

"And what is this?" Marco has drifted into another room of the gallery and is pointing to a large boat-like structure with a tall female figure sweeping up from the prow and holding a lantern. She seems to be guiding a boat filled with three small children.

"Yes, this is a commissioned piece for a university. The woman is searching, holding the lamp that brings light and truth through poetry and philosophy."

"And what is this little figure clinging to the side of the boat?" Marco asks. "His bottom half looks like a sea urchin, but he has wings."

"He is a protector of the children, the next generation. So important. You see how he is looking out for danger. And he is equipped to handle anything coming up out of the sea or from the air."

"A kind of guardian angel?" Maribel asks.

"Yes, but not an angel. Another image of the protector, the benign force in life."

Marco walks all the way around the boat, looking at each figure separately. He especially likes the alert gaze of the protector.

"Wouldn't you kids like some lunch?" Doña Conchita asks. "I believe they are waiting for us across the street."

The restaurant itself is a work of art, but it is all quite simple and natural. Tables and chairs are scattered about, inside and out, but Abuelo leads the way through to the back to a veranda covered with a burnt orange tile roof. He takes a few steps down from the veranda to a more secluded area below, where they are seated at a wooden table for four under a palm-thatched umbrella. Hand painted blue tiles form a square around the base of a palm tree that provides additional shade to other tables. A cut-out log that serves as a small garden for several varieties of miniature cactus is nestled onto a ledge. The red brick wall behind them is overhung with vines covered with bright yellow flowers. The wooden table is a soft red and the top surface has a border of a repeated design of small light blue fish. Marco's eyes drift up to the upper wall of the veranda where they entered, and he notices a painted ceramic Saint Francis in a pointed-arch alcove. Another wall has two small wooden shelves held up by angels, and on the shelves, two battered tin lanterns rest. He doesn't remember ever seeing a place so beautifully decorated and so cozy and peaceful as this. A place of harmony and enchantment. It is like another Mexico, surely not the one he knows.

The grandparents chatter with Maribel to catch up on her life with her mother, who is their daughter, and the other children. They ask her several times if she is all right, and then they ask her again if she is sure she is all right. Marco notices and wonders if she had been ill earlier in her life. He knows that he understands very little about art, but he is curious and can't resist playing the good student that he was in school, so when the right moment arrives, he asks, "Your art, both of you, seems so Mexican, but I'm not sure I know what that means. What is Mexican about it?"

"That is a wonderful question," Don Pedro replies, "but very difficult to answer. Every culture has its art. I think it is what you have grown up with, something that has become a part of you, the colors that surround you, the shapes and textures you see frequently."

"And then there are certain themes and motifs," Doña Conchita adds. "You see moons a lot, Toltec and Mayan design elements, and a lot of elongations and contractions. Nothing is portrayed as it actually is. Figures grow in and out of animals and physical objects."

"Like a woman growing out of the front of a boat," Don Pedro suggests.

"Or a boat growing out of the behind of a woman, depending on your point of view," Doña Conchita is shaking one hand back and forth. "And there is a magical quality about a lot of it. Not surrealistic, but the mystery beyond the physical. Things that can't be, but are."

"And where do you get the inspiration for your art?" Marco asks. "Where does it come from?"

"Art comes from the soul," Ortega answers confidently, "from somewhere deep in our being. I know that people would disagree, perhaps even laugh at me, but I believe we are all deeply connected with each other, not only our contemporaries but also with our ancestors, with those who lived and struggled before us. Not just genetically connected, but spiritually. For me there is an energy that comes from that, and I simply release that energy through the pieces I create."

"For me it is the endless possibilities that exist in butterflies," Doña Conchita adds, "their shapes and colors, their short lives, the meaning that comes through their meaninglessness. I can't stop thinking about them. Because their lives are so short, I try to capture them in my art, give them a little longevity there, a place in time that stretches out their short lives." She rubs her hands together, as if to soothe her arthritis. "Then again, there is suffering. That's a strong theme in Mexican art. We are never without our suffering."

Don Pedro glances at Maribel and then says to Marco, "I don't know if any of this makes any sense to you—may I call you Marquito?—but if you try to create a work yourself, something we have just been calling art, you will begin to feel what happens."

They get up to leave, and as they meander up the steps and outside to the front of the restaurant, Marquito asks Don Pedro, "What about Mexican politics? Are we making any progress as a nation, or will things be as they have always been?"

Don Pedro replies, "Most politicians only serve themselves, not the people. They are probably not our hope. But, yes, we are making progress in the private sector and in our cultural life. The art scene in Mexico City is quite lively again with new museums and galleries opening. I never give up hope."

Maribel and Marquito say their good-byes with hugs and kisses and retrace their steps back through the plaza to the church. They stop inside, and Maribel asks, "Now who do you think did this sculpture of the Holy Family?"

Marco looks at it with awe as he says, "It has to be your grandfather."

"Let's call that A+ on your first quiz. Now let's go down to the Hotel California."

They find one whole room there next to the lobby dedicated to an exhibit of sculpture of Don Pedro and the painting and prints of Doña Conchita. "Wow, Maribel, they are famous."

"Not all over Mexico, but in the Baja, yes. But you would never know it to talk to them, right? They are humble people, but also very productive."

They walk back down Benito Juárez Street and turn left to return to the park across from the bus station. It is a clean, well-equipped park, not like the one by his apartment, and they sit on a bench in the shade to wait for the bus. Children are playing on the bright yellow, red, and blue slides. The girls are dressed in ruffled dresses, the boys in denim shorts, and their parents are encouraging the timid ones to have a go at the slides. A dark-eyed little girl chases her puppy, a black schnauzer, and when she catches it, she picks it up awkwardly and totters over to her mother to get her to hold it while she takes another turn on the slide. Marco wonders if he will ever be a father, and he would like to ask Maribel what she thinks about having children, but doesn't. He can see that she likes these children, though. As they leave to get on the bus, the little girl waves and throws Maribel a kiss.

On the bus ride back to Cabo San Lucas, they talk about Ashley. He tells Maribel how Ashley was just a friend at first, sort of an accidental acquaintance, but that now he doesn't trust what she says about anything. He's sure she's hiding something. It's painful for him to recount how he has dug himself into such a deep hole with this relationship. Maribel listens patiently, though he can tell from her expression that she must think he is a complete idiot not knowing what he was getting into. Finally, she says, "Well, the first rule of holes, is that when you find yourself in one, you should stop digging."

"Don't make matters worse?"

"Exactly. Stop encouraging her. Stop playing in her game with her rules, like this arrangement is going to go on forever."

That makes sense," he admits.

"The second rule of holes is to figure out how to crawl out."

"This is more difficult."

"I don't see why it should be, unless you are reluctant to let her go."

"It's just that each day I let her stay on it makes it more difficult to find a reason to send her away. I need a good reason. I don't want to start a big brawl."

"Qué reason?"

"A reason that's understandable and acceptable to her."

"To her? Good grief, Marco, what about a reason that makes sense to you? Don't you have a lot of good reasons? The one that's at the top of my list has to do with your hiding her. If she's already running from the law, and the police find her with you, you can be implicated in her concealment. It doesn't matter whether she told you or not. And what if she does something violent like you described, kills somebody or poisons someone? As her closest friend, you could be in deep trouble. End up in jail. It will take expensive lawyers to get you out. You don't want that, do you?"

Maribel and Marco are quiet for the rest of the trip, bounding along together side by side on the bus. Just before they get off, Marco thanks her for the day and she says, "I did this today just as a friend, just as someone who cares about other people. Today you saw where I learned that. I've had my problems, too, and it really changed my life. I just want you to see that there is an alternative to the life you are living and whatever plans you might be making. An alternative, that's all. There are many lives that a person can live here in Mexico, some good, some very bad." They step down from the bus, and he gives her a long hug. She looks up at him and her serious face is worried with concern, dimples gone. "I'm not one for giving advice or even making suggestions," she says, "but based on what you told me today, mi querido amigo, I'd say it's time for you to take care of numero uno."

When Marco returns to the dark and desolate apartment that night, Ashley is not there. Her absence surprises him, but he is even more surprised at how delighted he is about the prospect of her being gone, not just out for the night, but gone permanently from his life. As he turns on the lights and looks around, he finds, to his disappointment, that her belongings, except for what she must have stuffed into her lime green canvas tote, are still there. She has put some yellow flowers like daisies in the vase on the table. He sits in the chair and pulls a book from the small bookcase. He tries to read the new book Ollie has sent him on Mexican culture by Octavio Paz, but he is too distracted by what Maribel said about numero uno to concentrate. She's right. Much as he has enjoyed having this little fling with Ashley, he definitely must end it now and tell her to leave.

At just after midnight, like a goblin coming from a grave, Ashley arrives home. She struggles with the key at the door, and then bursts into the room with a curse. "This fucking key is so impossible." She wobbles, then hobbles across the room.

"Maybe it would help if you had someone to hold the door still for you."

"I'm not drunk."

"What then?"

"Never mind." She sets her tote on the table and tries to let herself down gently into one of the chairs, but she nearly collapses and slams in hard anyway, the metal chair scraping on the floor. She is silent. It looks like she is trying to regain enough control of herself to talk. Finally, she says, "I had a good day." Her speech is slow and slurred. She's definitely wigged out.

"That's nice," he replies, "I did, too."

"I was tailing El Greco."

"My boss?"

"I know his habits now. He's easy to track.

"Did he see you?" he asks, putting his book aside.

"We wouldn't want that, would we? That would spoil the plan."

"What plan, Ashley? What did you do?" Marco asks with undisguised trepidation in his voice.

"Relax, I have a great plan. You'll love it."

Marco just stares at her. She's like a frickin' octopus. If one arm doesn't strangle you, one of the others will. He has to get rid of her. He senses the potential disaster looming up before him now. It's like Maribel said. "I've been meaning to tell you," he begins.

"Don't you want to hear the plan? Since you don't have much courage for the big plans, I thought we could start out with a little plan for El Greco. It will be really easy to bring off."

Marco doesn't really want to know about this plan, but it looks like he's going to hear it whether he wants to or not.

"After El Greco finishes his supervision of the morning shift, he goes to a bar down on the marina for a couple of beers. He just sits and drinks until sundown. When it gets dark, look out, he really cuts loose."

"Where does he go?"

"He always goes to a jumping bar called La Divina, over on Lázaro Cárdenas, where the local locos go. A loud outdoor band plays music of the north, how do you say, Norteña. He likes to watch the hot Mexican girls."

"How do you know he always goes there?"

"You can tell from the way people greet him. It's like they're waiting for him. Hey, Constantino. Bienvenido. You're late. But later in the evening he goes into a corner away from the band and drinks alone. Every now and then he gets up to go to the bathroom. That's when we get our chance."

"Our chance for what?" Marco is frowning.

"To play bartender."

"You're not thinking of poisoning him, are you?"

"Thinking of it, yes, but, no, I wouldn't plan that because I know you wouldn't have the guts to do it."

"Me?"

"You're going to put the pills in his drink. You're the one who wants to get even with the asshole, not me. I found this great stuff I bought before I left Berkeley. Can you believe I've been carrying those pills around all this time? I must have forgot about them. So, I had to test one out to see how strong it is. I couldn't remember."

"That's what you've been doing tonight? Drugs?"

"That plus watching El Greco. I just took one. I'd say about three would really fuck him up good."

"Three?"

"It's like prunes. The dose depends on the results you want to get. And if you really want results, mix prunes with Ex-Lax. So what do you say?" She twists the chair around and sits in it backwards, her pale, muscular legs spread along the sides.

"To tell the truth, I think it's very dangerous, both for El Greco and for us. If anyone sees us, they'll make the connection that's he's my boss, assign a motive, and there you are. And what if something goes wrong?"

"Oh, amigo, I'm really disappointed in you. You aren't worth shit. I go to all this trouble today tailing El Greco, I make a good plan, provide the stuff, and you back out like a little pussy cat before you even give it a try."

Marco doesn't reply to her harsh accusation. He just stares at her.

He can't even recall how all of this damn rebel talk got started, maybe just a fantasy, but now he knows he can't go through with it. "Look," he says softly, "we need to talk. There's something I've been meaning to tell you."

"What's that?" she asks, her drooping eyes dazed.

She looks like she's starting to fade fast. Oh, hell. Maybe this isn't the best time to tell her. Maybe she won't understand or even remember what was said if he tells her now when she's so wasted. He blurts it out anyway. "I need you to leave."

"Now? Like this? In the condition I'm in?" Her droopy eyes suddenly bug out. "Where the hell do you think I'm supposed to go?" She can barely control her wild gestures, her arms flapping like a Pelican's wings.

"Well, maybe not tonight," he agrees. She knows how to make him feel sorry for her.

"Hell, no. And not tomorrow either. I can't rent an apartment on a credit card, for shit's sake. I don't even have a job." Her voice is shrill and desperate.

"Maybe you need to get one if you plan to stay in Mexico. We hire illegals here, too, you know."

"I can't believe what I'm hearing. I thought we were together. I mean, look at all I did to fix this place up." Her eyes track around the room and come to rest with a strong nod on the flowers. "Now you want to pitch me out in the street?"

"Not in the street," he says.

"Well, where?" Now her voice is trembling, strained.

She's crushed. That's exactly what he didn't want to do, hurt her. He feels sorry for her all of a sudden. She's so mixed up. Hell, she needs help. But the time has come and he has to finish what he has started. "I just think it would be best..."

"Best for who?" she shouts. She struggles to get up to her feet, but it's hard for her, rising from that spread out, awkward position. She fumbles for her equilibrium and tries to take a step toward him but has to hold on to the back of the chair for support. Suddenly, she whirls around to the table, picks up the pottery vase with its impromptu bouquet, and heaves it at him. Marco ducks. The vase makes a terrible clatter as it shatters on the wall behind him, and the water that was in it starts to drip down the wall.

"What the hell are you doing? I thought you liked that vase."

"I thought you liked me," she screams. She turns toward him and starts to advance, dragging the chair, scrapping it along the floor, the tattooed arm suddenly outstretched with a flourish, her index finger shaking at him.

She draws up close to him and they stand face to face, toe to toe, but he doesn't budge. He's ready to give her a shove, but thinks better of that, and instead says calmly, but in a strong voice, "Look, Ashley, it's over. Finished. You can't stay here anymore. Got it?"

"I'm really disappointed in you, you son-of-a-bitch," she shouts. Then she turns away and switches to a more sinister, foreboding tone. "Well, okay, if you haven't got the guts to go through with any of this, I guess as a last resort, I'll just have to do it on my own."

12

ASHLEY APPREHENDED

The typical joyous welcome back for Vera and Señor Oily in February appears even more filled with clamor and excitement than usual. The bellmen and ladies of the lobby seem eager to tell them something. Verónica, the concierge, is the first to burst forth with the news. "Have you heard about Marquito, our hero?" she asks.

"Why, no. Some good news, I hope?" Vera replies.

"He saved a boy from drowning in the ocean, the beautiful, blue-eyed child of one of the guests."

"Really? Tell us about it," Ollie requests.

Everyone huddles around Verónica—the bellmen, the other concierge staff, two of the front desk clerks—as Verónica relates in her low voice what has become the legend of how Marquito's quick thinking and fast action saved the drowning boy. "He is a real celebrity now." But the smiles fade abruptly, erased from each face one by one. Verónica looks away. The bellmen contemplate their feet. Others go back to work. There is silence.

"What is it?" Vera asks. "Is something wrong?" She squints and rubs the back of her neck.

"Well," Verónica begins and then turns to the bellman Óscar. "You tell them."

"Me? Why me?"

"Well, tell us, please someone tell us," Vera begs.

"There is an American girl—they say she is a runaway who came off the Disney boat—and she's, well, not exactly Snow White. Actually, she's not a good influence at all," Óscar begins.

"She's got orange hair," Verónica recovers her confidence to speak, "and she wears it kind of funny." She makes a face and holds a hand over her right eye while she sticks the fingers of the other hand up from the opposite ear.

"But what disturbs us," Óscar continues, "is that Marquito seems so upset. He goes around frowning, with this worried look now, like something is really bothering him."

"Some people think she is dangerous," the bellman Sebastián continues with a worried look himself. "A real menace. She sneaks around out here like she is up to no good."

"I'm telling you; we are all on high alert when she is around here," Óscar says, shaking his head from side to side.

Ollie is puzzled. "What does this girl have to do with Marquito?"

Their eyes go back to the feet again. No one speaks until finally Verónica says in a low whisper, "They are seen together a lot."

"And?" Vera asks.

"Well, we don't know for sure, but we think she is living with him, which, of course," Verónica adds quickly, "would not be our business except that we all love him, you know?" She keeps gesturing with her hands even after she has stopped speaking, and then she looks up with her expressive brown eyes, and adds, "And we hate to see him so worried."

Ollie turns to Vera and mutters, "Looks like he ignored your warning, dear."

"Can't something be done?" Vera asks.

"That's why we are so glad you are here, Señora. Perhaps you could speak to him." The raven-haired heads are all nodding in concurrence now. "He listens to you," Verónica adds.

Vera is not so sure about that.

At breakfast the next morning, Ollie makes it a point to get up from the table and go order pancakes as an excuse to talk to Maribel, hoping she might know something more about Marquito. "Oh, yes, Señor, I know quite a lot about Marquito. He has confided in me and for this reason, I can't say very much."

"Do you think he would talk to Vera? I don't know if she and I can help, but even if it's only to listen, that might be good."

"Listening is fine but he definitely needs more than listening. Maybe a few swats with a piñata stick. But, yes, I'm sure your help will be welcomed. We talked. He's just waking up to what a mess he is in. Actually, we talked very seriously when I took him to meet my grandparents in Todos Santos. But I think he is still under the influence of the wicked witch." She waves the spatula back and forth and around as if to cast a spell. "He says he doesn't know how to get rid of her, though he insists he's tried." She glances down at his pancakes and bites her lower lip. "Oh, my god, Señor Ollie, look at how dark they are. Burnt. You can't eat these. My mother is right. She says I can't boil water without burning it, so how can I be a cook? Let me make you another order."

Ollie smiles fondly at her. "It's okay. I'll just eat cereal this morning. Besides, you have a line waiting now, dear. See if Marquito will talk to us."

When Ollie returns to the table, Marquito is there to pull out his chair and hand him his napkin. He says he is happy to see them, but they can tell he is not really happy about anything. He is nervous and he hardly smiles. He brings them the usual, and afterward when the bill is signed to the room, he says, "Of course I would like to talk to you. But no difficult philosophical questions, please. I need answers."

They meet at six o'clock that night at María Corona, a small restaurant in town, not too expensive, with traditional Mexican food and superb guacamole, made fresh at the table in a small stone bowl that reminds Ollie of a druggist's mortar and pestle. Tiny lights fit for a Christmas tree are wrapped around the trunks and lower branches of the two mimosa trees in the outdoor serving area. Colorful lanterns hang at the entryway. The place is quiet enough to speak and be heard, but noisy enough to not be overheard. Marco is shy, nervous, and embarrassed, without eye contact as he crunches on the chips and guacamole. Vera doesn't remember seeing him like this before. He begins slowly, but gradually his listeners draw him out.

Finally, Marco tells them everything, including his worries about Ashley's dangerous plans and about her maybe being some kind of terrorist. Vera says that he has no choice but to get rid of her, and the best way to do that is to go to the police. Her parents might be starting to look for her now, so the police don't need to be told all of the details, just that he has a tip about a runaway. After all, she hasn't committed a crime yet, not that they know of anyway. Ollie agrees to go with him to the police, just as a friend for now, but to stand by him as legal counsel if he needs it. He must report Ashley as a runaway immediately. Just that, nothing more. He can give the police her favorite haunts, places she is likely to be found, but not his address.

Meanwhile, in case Ashley decides to act on her own, Ollie and Vera will be on the alert to any possible irregularities at Sunset Point, and

Marquito must be ready to act if they notice anything suspicious. He needs to review who is in charge of each operation around the resort and be ready to notify them. The goal is to get this young lady out of Mexico before she does serious damage to the people at the resort. If she starts to implement any aspect of her plan, her efforts must be contained by expert damage control.

"And for now, stop looking like a criminal," Vera tells him. "Let's get rid of those crow's-feet."

"Really?" He frowns even worse. "I'm giving myself away?"

"From now on," Vera says, "only smiles. Enjoy the flan."

The next day, after breakfast, Ollie and Vera sit by the pool while Ollie finishes reading the Los Cabos Daily News. As he looks up over the top of his reading glasses to see if there is a reason why the young children next to him are crying, he notices them scratching, like they had been bitten by a swarm of Vermont mosquitos, the big ones that come out in August to turn everyone in the Green Mountains into agitated, swatting zombies. But there are no mosquitos in this part of Mexico. The children look like maybe they have an outbreak of hives, but that's not it either. As Ollie glances around the pool, he alerts Vera, and together they notice that all of the children are out of the water, which is quite unusual, scratching, jumping from foot to foot, and doing something Ollie calls a Mayan rain dance.

"Ollie," Vera says in a stage whisper, "this was one of Ashley's plans, remember, to disable the swimming pools. Run and tell Marquito."

Well, Ollie doesn't run anywhere these days; he gave that up five years ago, but he can still walk fast with those long legs of his. Vera watches him going to fetch Marquito at a pretty fast clip, a little bent over, but speedy, weaving across the deck like he is chasing a greased pig at the Vermont State Fair. He slips out of sight and doesn't return.

Within the minute, Vera notices that the upper pool is not emptying across its waterfall into the middle pool anymore. Then she notices the pool maintenance personnel are kneeling beside the pool with their test kits. They test the upper pool and then the two lower pools. Everything seems fine below, so they return to the upper pool and begin laying out big white plastic hoses to drain it. Meanwhile, the little kids are standing around whining and scratching themselves like monkeys in a zoo, so Vera decides to alert Verónica in the lobby. Vera still runs, but it is questionable whether it is one bit faster than when she walks, and when she arrives at the lobby, Marquito is already there talking to Verónica. They agree to share with the parents of the children, calmly and without alarm, their hypothesis that some substance may have entered the pool unintentionally, and that the best thing to do would be to take the children to the spa, get them showered down with a soothing soap, and then see that they are well covered with an aloe vera cream sold at the spa, but provided free in this case. Marco dashes to the spa, finds Isabella, alerts her and her co-workers to the plan, and from there he sprints up the hill to the on-call doctor's office behind the Palmita Market to get the Doc on board to come down for a little consultation and to calm down any hysterical parents. Vera returns to poolside and finds Ollie talking with the pool maintenance people. She catches him up on the damage mitigation plan. Damn, they've got to find that orange-haired girl and get her ass outta here.

The upper pool is drained and scrubbed and within a half hour the children are showered off and playing video games in the shade of their parents' beach umbrellas, not particularly missing the pool while it is being "fixed." In fifteen minutes Marquito is back on the job at La Casona explaining to El Greco that he had an attack of flu. "Okay for this time, hero, as long as your tables are covering." El Greco appears a little unsteady on his feet this morning, maybe a little hung over. Oh, my god, will Ashley try to carry out that plan for El Greco? Is that next?

After the shift ends, Marco scans the beach and searches the labyrinth of tunnels for Ashley to make sure she isn't up to something else. He can't let this go on. After checking with Ollie and Vera and thanking the folks in the lobby and spa, he walks into town with Maribel.

"So, we had a lot of excitement today." Maribel says. "I wonder what's next." Her voice has a little sarcastic tone to it, unusual for her, but she also sounds worried.

"More excitement than I wanted, that's for sure."

"You had the response well organized."

"Did anyone see Ashley out here?"

"Not that I've heard of, but I'm sure she..."

"She's clever. Do you think people perceive that I'm part of it, that I know things?" He strokes his square jaw impatiently.

"Not yet. They just think you are a good leader because you are their hero. Now they expect it of you. You were like Spiderman, bouncing around out there today. If only you could fly. I'm just teasing. Actually, you handled it really well. But..."

"For sure we've got to get her out of here before something tragic happens."

"Now you're thinking straight. Get her into the hands of the police."

"That's what Vera says. Ollie and I are going to have a little talk with them this afternoon." He blows his cheeks out and exhales slowly. "I don't look forward to that."

"Just don't say much."

"I think her parents might be looking for her now."

"Really? You think they might be here?"

Marco shrugs. "Could be."

"Where does she hang out, besides your place?" Maribel asks.

"I think she takes some lunch each day at Mango Cantina. She loves their fish ceviche."

"That's it? Fish ceviche?"

"Well, there's also a busy little bar she enjoys at night called La Michelada. But I've heard her mention Squid Roe and Cabo Wabo, too. Do you know those places?"

Maribel nods. "I know about them."

"Other than that, I guess it's Médano Beach. Maybe she will pick up some other guy there and make his life miserable."

"But we can't wait for that. First get her out of your apartment, then out of Mexico."

"I know, I know." Now his voice is strong with resolve.

Marquito and Maribel part at the bus station where they take their separate buses home. "I hate to go to the apartment," Marquito tells her.

"There's always the remote chance that you will discover that she's gone." Maribel twists her head and gives him her dimpled smile as she steps onto her bus. "Good luck."

Before going home, there is this matter of the police. Marco meets Ollie, who has taken a taxi to the police station. They go over their strategy before going inside, but it all turns out not to be worth the worry. The officers are very businesslike and thank them for their concern, but say that they are already on the alert for Ashley. They can't say much, but her parents are now actively looking for her and so is the State of California. No further questions. Kind of abrupt. No way to pull any pesos out of anyone's pocket this time. It was still good, though, to have Ollie standing at his side. Who knows what the police will do in Mexico?

Marco spends the evening alone in his apartment. He's relieved about the visit to the police and glad that Ashley is not there. It would be hard to face her tonight. He tries to read a little Octavio Paz, and it's interesting, but he can't concentrate. It's been five days now since he told her to leave. He gets up and opens the window and looks around the apartment, checks out the kitchen, the bathroom. She must have packed most of her stuff in the lime green tote, because there's nothing left, just her toothbrush. Maybe tonight will be the night she doesn't come home.

Shortly after midnight, he hears the key rattle in the door. Shit! She's still here. He can tell from her footsteps that she's relatively sober. She goes straight to the bathroom and when she comes back into the room, she doesn't speak, doesn't even look at him. He puts his book aside and marches over to her. As he lifts her chin, to make her acknowledge him, she backs away, the first time he has seen her look frightened, like maybe she thought he was going to hit her or something. "That was very serious this morning," he tells her. "Some of those kids had a bad rash."

"Nothing more. They'll get over it." She seems to have quickly regained her confidence.

"We had to shut down one of the pools. Drain it."

"I thought that's what you wanted. Close the place down."

"Look, Ashley, I told you what I want. I want you to get the hell out of here. Now."

"Well, I can't leave quite yet."

"Why not?"

"Because I want to see your reaction to what happens tomorrow. I think you'll like it," she snickers.

"For God's sake, what are you doing tomorrow? You're going to get yourself into some serious trouble."

"I'm already in serious trouble. Haven't you figured that out, amigo? You think I'm on vacation?"

"After today I don't want to have anything to do with you or the stuff you're planning. Just get out and leave me alone."

"So maybe tomorrow..." she begins.

"Not tomorrow. Tonight. Now." He goes to the door and opens it.

"Fine!" She raises her eyebrows and slings her tote bag over her shoulder. "What about my toothbrush?" she asks like a child searching for one last excuse.

"Buy one." She must know that she has pushed him past the limit. He doesn't want to hurt her and wouldn't, but she must know he could. "And hand over the key," he adds in a stern voice.

As she walks through the doorway, she turns and hurls the key at him. Marco slams the door and locks it behind her.

"You lousy, mother-fucking asshole." A string of American profanities—he thought he knew them all—reverberates down the steps from the apartment and echoes out into the dark night. Marco breaths a deep sigh of relief.

At breakfast that morning at La Casona, Marquito helps to organize the work, making sure that all of the other waiters have their assigned tables and that the juice dispensers are filled and the pastries set out because El Greco has not shown up yet. He asks Omar what's going on, but Omar only shrugs, but then he points to the sea and says, with a sad face, "Maybe Zorba Pequeño has drowned. I mean, really, who would save him?" By nine o'clock, Marco starts to worry about him. He can hardly believe he is actually worrying about El Greco, but he can't help but be afraid that Ashley might have carried out the plan for El Greco on her own. Oh, shit, what if she killed the poor son-of-a-bitch?

At nine thirty, during the busiest time of the breakfast shift, the restaurant is packed. Waiters are running up and down the stairs to go back and forth to the kitchen, carrying trays of food, dirty dishes, coffee carafes, and individual juice glasses, sometimes gripping three in each hand. There at the busy intersection at the top of the stairs, El Greco suddenly appears poised as if he is about to sing an opera aria. Does he think it's a stage? He pulls a white handkerchief from his pocket and holds it over his head as if breaking into a little Greek folk dance. He slides his feet from side to side without taking them from the floor; but it's definitely a challenge for him just to stand upright there let alone dance and wave that hanky over his head. He suddenly seems to realize that his brain can't make his feet dance. Marco wonders if he has any idea what he is doing or even where he is? He's way beyond hammered, more like jack-hammered. His eyes are glazed over pretty bad. How many pills did Ashley put in his tequila?

El Greco has apparently decided that he needs to come down the stairs. By now he has unwittingly gained the full attention of the guests and the staff, including Vera and Ollie, and a hush has fallen over the open-air restaurant. Forkfuls of pancakes are suspended in mid-air and cups of coffee are held immobile just below hushed lips. Maribel is watching from the grill, one eye on El Greco, the other on Marco. As El Greco steps off the first step, he teeters back and forth like he's going to lose his balance. In a flash, perhaps because Marco can anticipate disaster better than anyone else in the room, he bounds through the tables on his long legs, weaving in and out, appearing at El Greco's side just in time to catch him. The weight of the inert body nearly crushes Marco, but at least he keeps the jerk from hitting the floor. He stands him up like a clothing store mannequin, making sure he doesn't topple, and suggests that he go back up the stairs toward the kitchen. But El Greco has his own mind. He manages to stand without falling, waves off any further need for assistance, and shuffles over to the railing that bounds the ocean-view tables.

He stands there at the rail, no doubt trying to get a grip, as everyone listens to the mesmerizing roll of waves and watches to see what will happen next. Marco knows intuitively what could happen next, and taking no chances, he sprints through the tables—how many times does he have to do this?—dashes across the beach hurdling lounge chairs, and with a surge of energy hastily assembles several lounge chair cushions right below the spot where El Greco is standing. He hustles back to his tables. The guests watch and whisper as El Greco sways forward and back very slowly, toe to heel and heel to toe, all the way up on his toes and all the way back on his heels, back and forward, back and forward, like a child's swing, until he leans forward just a little too far and folds over the railing like a gymnast on a high bar, executing a perfect summersault onto the cushions ten feet below. The guests all stand at once, like sports fans rising together to cheer the scoring of a goal, and then they rush to crane over the railing to see what happened to the poor fellow who went tumbling over. There lies El Greco, all spread out motionless on the cushions. Maribel has already called Verónica in the lobby. Help is on the way. Marquito calmly refills coffee cups.

At two o'clock that afternoon, at the close of the shift, the general manager of food and beverage services gathers the waiters in the kitchen to get their input on who might be able to fill in for El Greco on a temporary basis until a new captain is found. The employees are afraid to speak up at first, but their eyes all shift to Marquito, and finally Omar asks, "What about Marquito?" The others join in saying one by one, "Marquito,

Marquito, yes, Marquito." It is a groundswell of support for someone who is once again their hero. Jeez. He's surprised, but pleased. Wow! But does he really want to be the captain of the waiters? He promises himself: not like El Greco.

Finally, Omar asks, trying to sound innocent, failing to conceal a grin, "What happened to Señor Constantino?"

The manager replies, "Must I explain? He crashed and burned. He's gone and won't be back."

Funny. No one asks if he is okay.

The next day Marco arrives at Sunset Point ready to commence his new duties as temporary captain. He was supposed to have a day off with Maribel, and he realizes that he is missing her, not seeing her in her usual spot, wearing her hat, smiling her cute smile at the guests. He wonders what she will be doing today. The other waiters seem unusually cooperative this morning, especially Omar who is no doubt happy to have El Greco gone and Marquito in his place. This makes Marco feel good. He tells Vera and Ollie as modestly as he can about his new appointment—they only knew of the fall of Constantino, not the rise of Marquito—and they congratulate him enthusiastically. "Now you have a reason to smile," Vera says.

"Plus," Vera reminds Ollie, "we have some news, a kind of announcement we want to make to you and several others."

"Yes, that's true," Ollie adds, "so when we get that red-headed troublemaker packed up, and on her way back to California, we want to meet with you, Marquito, privately.

Now what could that be about?

At the end of the work shift on the following day, Marco meets with Maribel in the cafeteria where she has been waiting for him patiently while he makes sure everything is finished up right. Everyone has gone by now, so they are alone.

"What is it?" he asks. "I can't wait to hear."

"Well, you won't believe the good luck. I'm at Médano Beach, and I see this older couple walking along in the sand, each step a struggle."

"Like Vera and Ollie?"

"Not that old. More like my mother's age. But Americans for sure. Well dressed, in fact over-dressed for the beach, you know. She's got nice shoes and a skirt, and he's carrying his suit jacket over one arm. And the lady has this picture in her hand, and she's showing it to everyone she can, but they all just shake their head and walk on. So, I decide to go over to them and check it out. Well, you won't believe it, but it was a color photo of Ashley, different hairdo but the same red hair. Couldn't be anyone else."

"Oh, my god, her parents? What did you do?"

"Well, I told them that I recognized her, really casual like, and that I thought I'd seen her around. They said she was a runaway, so then I knew for sure it was Ashley."

"But come on, what did you do?" Marco asks again.

"I mentioned that she was often seen eating lunch in the Mango Cantina, back in a corner. Maybe between noon and two o'clock. But I suggested they better get the police to go with them so she wouldn't slip through their fingers again. They said they had already worked with the police, but they were completely useless, and that's why they had to come down here themselves with the picture."

"And what did you say to that?" Marco asks.

"I told her—the mother did most of the talking— that the police were like that when they didn't have much to go on, but with a lead, they could be very helpful, in fact, indispensable in apprehending her because it was unlikely that she would go willingly if she had run away. I told them that the police had handcuffs and other things that could be very persuasive. Besides, there might be issues now getting her out of Mexico and back into the U.S. again."

"Is that true?"

"Oh, I don't know, but they bought it. The father, especially. He said they needed to get the police involved, lay a trap for her at the Mango Cantina and take her forcibly into custody. I even showed them where it is. Wasn't that nice of me?" She raises one eyebrow—how does she do that?—and cocks her head to the side.

"I can't believe this. Ollie and I went to the police you know. They sounded like they were already on it."

"Well, they were scheduled to pick her up today, so if all went as planned, Ashley is in the hands of her parents and the police as we speak."

Marco feels an unusual lightness in his whole being, and he tells Maribel that he wants to jump up, and shout, and sing, and dance. "Hmm. Reminds me of El Greco." she says. "But do you have a handkerchief?"

Then she takes him by the forearm and says, "Look, if we don't see her around in the next few days, she's probably gone for good."

"I just hope she won't implicate me."

"And look at this." Maribel reaches down the front of her blouse into her bra and pulls out a one-hundred-dollar bill in U.S. currency. "They paid me a reward."

Maribel starts to giggle and that hesitant giggle grows and ends up in one of her deep laughs. They both start laughing uproariously, shaking their fists in the air. Marco jumps up and starts spinning around, clapping his hands and stomping his feet. When she stands to join him, he gives her an embrace that sweeps her off her feet. "Thank you, thank you," he says as he puts her down. But then his mood changes. "What are her parents like?" he asks.

"Nice enough to me. Privileged. Self-assured. A little arrogant. But sad. Worried sick as parents would be about a daughter like that. I could tell they were really weary from searching for her."

"I feel sorry for them," he says.

"Well, if you have to feel sorry for someone, better them than her."

"Well, yeah, but she's really screwed up and needs help. But I'm just so happy, so relieved. How can I ever thank you enough?"

"You can help me spend the hundred bucks!"

13

OPENING THE HEART

Vera and Ollie are seated that night by the hostess Daniella at a reserved table in La Casona, and of course they ask about the children, Blanca and Cenia. Daniella is holding for them a table with a view of the sea, outside by the railing—Constantino's acrobatics bar—and tells them that they are sitting down at just about the right time to see the full moon come up out of the sea. "Right about there," she points. "It's at a slightly different place and time each night, so you will need to watch for it, but it's a wonderful experience." Ollie knows about the changing appearance and positions of the moon, and he has tried over and over to explain this to Vera, first with oranges, then apples, salt and pepper shakers, bowls, anything he can get his hands on to create a model, but she never seems to get it. Could it be his explanation?

Later, when Daniella is caught up on seating guests, she comes back to the table and asks them if they have heard the latest about Marquito.

"The latest?" Vera asks. "I don't know. He's a little difficult to keep up with."

Daniella tells them that Ashley, that American girl he's been seen with a lot, has finally been reunited with her parents with the help of the municipal police. "So, it looks like she's on her way home."

Vera and Ollie exchange knowing glances. Daniella does not reveal, and may not know, many of the details, but those can wait until tomorrow morning, Ollie says, when they can get the story straight from the horse's mouth. Daniella frowns, apparently confused by the idiom.

Tonight, they have only to finalize their plans for making the gifts. Ollie had made arrangements weeks ago to transfer a considerable sum of cash, just over three hundred thousand U.S. dollars, to the Scotia Bank in the Paraíso Mall. They intend to meet each of the recipients, one by one, to give them the number of their individual account at the bank and reassure them that no repayment is expected—it is a gift outright, not a loan—and that there are no strings attached, no expectation, except to use the money to enrich their lives and the lives of their children, if they have them, and to do so in thoughtful and creative ways. Vera has written out these instructions in Spanish painstakingly with the dictionary before leaving Golden, and she will give print copies to the recipients to prevent any unintended misunderstanding. She and Ollie also want to make sure that the recipients will not worry about why they were selected and someone else was not, and for that reason the donors ask that the recipients not talk to anyone else about the gift, except for one person, who will be their representative here in Mexico, and that is Marquito.

Ollie has worked out the business, financial, and legal arrangements as well as the proper language over the past several weeks, and tonight at dinner they will need only to go over the list of names, account numbers, and sums of money to double check and make sure that everything is correct before they begin to meet the recipients. They place their order of soup, salad, and appetizers, check everything over in their carefully worked out plans, and sit in silence as they wait for their food. They watch for the moon to come up.

Although the evening is cool and a gentle breeze is surfing in on a restless sea, Ollie's forehead is covered with tiny beads of perspiration that Vera can't help but notice.

"Are you alright?" Vera asks.

"I'm fine," Ollie replies, then admits, "I just have a sensation in my chest, like a little indigestion."

"But we haven't eaten since breakfast."

"It's just a way of describing the sensation. Like I would like to burp. Everything would be fine if I could just burp."

Vera remembers this as one of those items on lists of dangerous symptoms, but she can't remember if it is heart attack or stroke.

"Oh, look," Ollie says, "over there. You can just see the top of the moon. It looks a little flat, the way the light plays on the sea."

Is he trying to distract her or himself? She is observing him carefully.

"Look how fast it comes up," he exclaims. "And the color is quite unusual, not the typical moon color, a deep orange. I think they call that a blood moon."

He looks okay, but he's still sweating. He starts to rub his left shoulder. Is he having some pain? Pain is on the heart attack list. So is the left shoulder. She asks him, "Is the pain going down your arm?"

"Look at that moon. It's almost up and the reflection is already glittering across the water in a straight path to us. So beautiful."

"Ollie, for god's sake, forget the damn moon. Look at me. Are you having pain? Chest pain? Pain in that arm?"

"All of the above, but it's not all that bad. It'll go away."

She looks around for Daniella. She's standing at her hostess desk. Vera starts to panic. "Ollie, I think we need to get you to a hospital."

"I'm okay. Besides if I'm going to die, I'm lucky to be right here in paradise already. The bands of angels won't even have to swing low to carry me home." The pain turns his smile into a grimace. "You know, I think I will be okay, if I can just lie down for a few minutes." He pushes his chair back and goes down on one knee, then to his side, as he tries to stretch out on the still warm concrete floor. "That feels good," he says.

No time for dithering. Ollie needs help. Vera jumps to her feet and catches the attention of the waiter, Lino, who points to Ollie as he signals to Daniella, who gets on her cell phone. Then Daniella brings two wool blankets, one to go under him and the other to cover him. She gets down on her hands and knees to tuck him in like she would her children.

It seems like forever, but in a jiffy the first response paramedics are wheeling the gurney down past the swimming pools and up into the dining room. They put oxygen on him, start an IV, and hook him up to a portable EKG. They ask Vera whether he is diabetic and what medicines he takes, and she tells them as best she can recall, anxious as she is. Then she says to one of the paramedics, "I want to go with him. He doesn't like to be alone."

"You can go to the lobby now, Señora. They already have a taxi waiting for you. The driver will follow us."

The taxi arrives shortly after the ambulance at Centro Médico Cabo San Lucas, and the emergency team is already working on Ollie when Vera steps inside. She stands for a moment, a little disoriented. No one is paying attention to her because they are working on Ollie, as they should be. Finally, she locates him, lying on his back all hooked up to machines, and she goes up to him and squeezes his hand. He recognizes her and smiles a little hopeless smile. "Now I've done it," he says apologetically. Messed everything up."

"You're going to be fine, and we'll get back to our little project when you are feeling better." Then she has to tell him good-bye because they are taking him off for treatment. A nurse leads her to the waiting room outside of cardiology.

"We are going to do some work on him, Señora, a heart catheterization for sure, maybe a stent, we'll see. It may take some time, dear, so please be patient. We will talk to you as soon as we have anything to report."

As the medical personnel wheel Ollie away, he is filled with apprehension. Just what he had always hoped to avoid, a serious medical problem in Mexico. But what can he do now? He can do what he is told. He can be cooperative and cheerful. Cooperative is okay, cheerful is asking a lot. They take him down empty twisting hallways and through outer rooms that lead to inner rooms, but the little crowd of experts never leaves his side, wheeling along the equipment he is hooked up to. As they start connecting him up to various monitors and screens, he feels more secure. They won't let him die. What he feels mostly is regret. He and Vera were so close to making those gifts, putting the money in the hands of those who could really use it, and now he is concerned that he has messed that all up. He ponders what would happen if he died and Vera had to follow through on her own. Would that work? Are the signatures in the right places? Will her power of attorney cover this? He smiles a faint smile. Is this what he's going to do—worry right up until the very second before he dies? A nurse asks him if he would like to see the procedure and points to a screen with a thumping heart. Good God, it must be his. He says, not really, and that's the last thing he remembers.

Vera sits alone in the drab waiting room. There is nothing there but a ticking clock and a few magazines in Spanish. The room is clean, but it needs paint. The nurse was friendly but friendly is not the most important quality right now. The staff looked competent but a little frantic. So here lies Ollie in a Mexican hospital. Do they both, she and Ollie, still have latent prejudice about the competence of the medical personnel, or is it natural, even realistic, to believe that medical services in a poor country won't be as good as those in a more developed country? Then she reprimands herself for her qualms, for assuming that Ollie's treatment will be inferior. How shameful of her!

She tells herself to focus more positively on Ollie, on his generally good health, on the quick work of the first responders, and on the fact that he was conscious and smiling when she said good-bye at the ER. He will be fine. He won't need much. On the other hand, what if it is worse than they thought? What if he needs open heart surgery? What if they only need to put in a stent, but they goof it up and he has complications? An infection. How many disquieting "what-ifs" can she dream up? That's what comes from living with a lawyer; they're paid to foresee the worst.

Vera tries to calm herself, but only grows more agitated. Could she lose him? Right here in Mexico? Now? They both know, being the age they are, that they don't have too many years left, but die now? No, not now, and not Ollie first. They have talked many times about what they would do if the other one dies first. Of course, the wills are set up to deal with that, but emotionally how would one go on without the other? In growing so close, they have become dependent on each other, each in their own way, and now they can't picture living alone. She doesn't want to sit here alone in this waiting room even for a few minutes. Is that the price a person has to pay for a happy marriage, living on after a spouse's death in loneliness? Would it be better if they were not so happy, if they were constantly wrangling over trivialities and bickering about each other's shortcomings and failings, so that when one dies the other is not bereaved but relieved? No, no, no, she knows couples like that, and she would prefer to be happily married clear through to the end. Picturing her life alone without Ollie, she has worked herself into a little crying jag. She pulls out a handkerchief and blots her tears. Forevermore, why is she sitting here at land's end contemplating death? Surely Ollie is not going to die.

She needs to give herself a little pep talk. Come on, Vera, look on the bright side and hope for the best. Send some positive energy to him wherever he is behind those closed doors. Remember something nice about him. He is always so sweet in his eccentric ways. Anxious as she is for some word about Ollie, she nonetheless dozes off. Or must have. She knows she has been sleeping when the nurse touches her on the shoulder and says, "Señora Webster. Your husband is going to be just fine. One stent. Just one. Some plaque broke loose in one of his arteries and blocked things up pretty bad. Made a clot, which we had to dissolve, and then we put in the stent to be safe. We want to watch him tonight and all day tomorrow, but then he can probably go back to the resort and resume a normal life, with a little extra rest, of course."

"Oh, that's such good news. I'm relieved."

"Where are you staying, dear?" the nurse asks.

"Sunset Point."

"The place where the waiter saved the young boy from drowning."

"You know about that?"

"Oh, yes, we know about things like that. We're in the same business, you know: saving lives."

"Oliver and I know him. Everyone calls him Marquito. He's a fine young man," she says proudly, seeing no need to tell the nurse about the close call he just had with that troubled American girl, Ashley.

That night, alone in their seventh-floor room at the resort, Vera wraps herself in the terry cloth robe provided as an amenity to guests and steps out onto the balcony to sit for a moment in the lounge chair, Ollie's favorite spot for napping. The resort is wrapped up in a nocturnal hush, as if uninhabited, the children tucked in bed, the revelers tired out. Pool decks are hosed down and the music turned off. Sprinklers rustle in the gardens. The palm trees stand relaxed, as if resting after a windy day. That same full moon is now overhead in a clear sky, at the apex of its journey, casting its glow down onto the still surface of the swimming pools. Deck chairs are meticulously aligned in groups of three, umbrellas folded down. Vera listens to the waves rolling softly onto the beach. They provide the calming sound that produces the desired soothing, and soon she is ready to sleep. She crawls into bed alone. How huge that king-sized bed is without Ollie. She is sure now that if anything happened to him, she could never come back to Sunset Point Resort alone. She shivers.

Ollie is welcomed back by everyone who knows him. They tell him how glad they are that he is okay and that they were worried about him. He is tired, but he says he is good to go, in fact, he feels better, actually stronger now. But time is running out. He and Vera have only three days left before they need to leave to go back to Colorado.

They want to meet with Marquito first because he is their representative in Mexico and they want him to be the administrator of the gift accounts. He takes a half hour break—he's the boss now—and meets them in front of the lobby. From there, they slip over to the hospitality business lounge next to the spa, a quiet place where guests, mostly Americans, come to use the free computer services to catch up on their work while they are on vacation. Luckily, no one is there at the moment so they have the privacy they need.

First, they outline for Marquito what they would like him to do: straighten out any problems there might be at the bank, answer questions the participants might have, and serve as a communication line to them for the recipients so that they are not bombarded with a lot of emails. Vera shows him the instructions she has put together in Spanish and goes over them with him. When asked if he is willing, Marquito says bueno and that he is honored to be entrusted to do this for them.

"So, let's begin with you," Vera says.

"Me? I thought I was your representative."

"No, you are one of the recipients, too. You've read the instructions. You know the purpose. So, the first gift is to you Marquito. It's for fifty thousand dollars."

His head jerks back and his eyes bug out. He doesn't need a calculator to translate that into pesos; he knows what $50,000 can mean in Mexico. "But I don't understand," he says. "Why me? Why would you give that amount to me? You hardly know me. I've done nothing to deserve it. And I have to say, I haven't been very responsible lately. I'm not..."

"Stop," Vera says firmly, with both hands palms-up, beside her face. "Are you telling me you have no dreams?"

"Dreams? Of course, I have dreams, but they are just shattered dreams, completely out of reach."

"Sometimes dreams come true." Ollie says. "Look, we want to do some good before we die, and after what happened to me with my heart, now more than ever we want to make these gifts. We invested some money when we were younger, and it grew into an amount that is far more than we can spend in our remaining years. Now we would like to reinvest some of that money in a few people we know here at the resort. We don't know what they will do with it and we don't expect anything in particular of those who receive it. We are pretty sure we have chosen people who won't waste it."

"Oh, no, Señor, you can be sure I won't waste it. I'm just overwhelmed. It was only a few weeks ago that I was so angry, so depressed, and completely without hope. And now this. How can I ever thank you?"

"By using it in ways that make you happy. That will make us happy," Vera says, a broad smile already spreading across her face.

"And one thing more, Marquito," Ollie continues as if to conclude, "the gifts we are giving are all to Mexicans, so they are also a small gift to Mexico, a little repayment—not much you understand—but a little compensation for our ugly history. We have both read the same book, right? You know what I am talking about, but not only the land, but what we've done to the people, and what we continue to do to the people here, at the border, and in the U.S. If you look at it that way, this is really nothing. Spit in the ocean."

"But it is what we want to do and it is what we can do." Vera says.

Suddenly Marquito feels that lightness in his being again that makes him want to stand up and shout, sing, and dance, but instead he says, "When do I begin?"

Vera says, almost whispering "We will inform the others of their gifts tomorrow."

Vera and Ollie, with the help of Verónica and Marquito in locating the people involved, have set up a schedule for the next morning and afternoon, with a little siesta for Ollie from noon to two o'clock.

Rosita is the first to arrive, taking half an hour away from her office as the booking director. They chat about the boys, Fernando and Alfredo, how they are doing in school and how their latest interests are developing. Ollie thanks her again for her help in booking their time-share weeks at the resort, and then they hand her a copy of the instructions in Spanish, though her English is nearly perfect. As she reads, she begins to shake her head from side to side. "But I haven't done anything special," she says. "I was just doing my job." Then they tell her the amount, $50,000 and she bites her lip and looks away. "I can't do this," she says. "The company wouldn't approve."

"Your employer doesn't need to know and won't know." Ollie reassures her.

"This is between us," Vera adds, "and it's not about your job. It's about you."

Rosita is quiet for a while. She doesn't speak but her face is a kaleidoscope of changing emotions that Vera can't quite read. Finally, she says, "My husband is a very proud man. He doesn't like to accept help."

"Then maybe you can suggest to him," Vera says, "that this is for the boys. You can use it as you wish, of course, but maybe you will both continue to work hard at your jobs, as you do, and continue to live like you do, but with the idea that you can dream a little bigger for the boys."

Rosita's eyes can't hold back the tears after that and she whispers, "My god, you two, you are so generous. How can we ever thank you?"

Ollie says, "We are trying to thank you, Rosita, for letting us into your life, for inviting us to your home, for letting us be a part of the fiesta, for giving us a real taste of Mexico. Thank you."

Daniella, the evening hostess, makes a special trip into the resort that morning to meet with Ollie and Vera. Blanca is in school, but she leaves Cena with her grandmother, who has made a small plate of tamales for Daniella to bring to her friends. When she reads the instructions and learns that she is to receive $50,000, she just starts crying like a baby, uncontrollably, ending in sobs, as she tries to pull herself together, and then crying some more. Vera and Ollie know that she is also crying for her sister all over again, and they have to comfort her before she can regain her composure enough to speak.

"I just want to move to a better house," she sobs. Nothing fancy. Just a place with more space for us, for my sister's children, and for my mother who has been such a saint through all of this. It's so crowded there." And then she starts to cry again, clasping her hands together.

Solomón brings Isabella, the manicurist, and baby Suzette, who is dressed in one of the outfits that Vera brought in November. Suzette has a matching yellow bow on a band around her head, and she's making noises now that almost sound like words to fit her animated faces. When they read the instructions and hear the amount of $50,000, Isabella looks away as Solomón says, "But my job is good now. I'm a supervisor. You don't need to do this. We don't need help. We're planning to move to a new place next year."

"Don't think of it as help," Ollie suggests. "You can keep your pride and still have a little money in the bank for a rainy day. No one needs to know it is there or how you got it."

Isabella looks at Solomón, apparently sensing his reluctance. She touches his forearm, and whispers a few short sentences to him in Spanish. He nods several times as he listens.

"Thank you," he says to Ollie and Vera. "Thank you very much. It will be there in case something happens to Suzette again, like insurance. Thank you. I'm sorry. You two have done so much for us already, and now this. It's hard for me to understand." He pulls on his lower lip and then says, "Ever since I met Isabella, my life has been blessed. I don't know exactly what it is. Why me? You can be sure that we will spend this only as Isabella wants."

And so, it goes through the morning on into the afternoon. The bellmen, Sebastián and Óscar each get $10,000, and Óscar says he will always remember them because it is the biggest tip he has ever received. Verónica, the concierge in the lobby, who also receives $10,000, says that now she is so rich, maybe someone will marry her. Ernesto, the towel boy, says he knows what to do with part of his $5,000, because his car broke down that morning and he missed his English class. Now at least he can get his car fixed and pay for some more classes. Carmelita, the little gray-haired lady who sweeps the out-door corridors, floor after floor, day after day, points to her mouth and tells Vera in Spanish and pantomime that she has always wanted to get her teeth fixed, and that if there is money left over, she will get her aging mother's teeth fixed, too, maybe dentures.

At the end of the afternoon, Maribel arrives, full of curiosity and excitement, because Marquito has told her only that he is a personal representative for Vera and Ollie in Mexico, but that he can't say what that means until she talks to them herself. She's completely confused when she arrives, so they show her the instructions in Spanish. But then she is even more baffled about why she should be on the list, especially at $50,000. And when they ask her if she has any dreams, she talks about getting a studio where she could begin to draw and paint and make things like Abuela and Abuelo do. And when Vera asks if Marquito will be part of her dreams, she says she doesn't know because that will depend on Marquito once he finds out about her. She looks down and away and a single tear begins to run down her cheek, like it has come rolling out from some unhappy experience in her past. She thanks them for considering her separately, independently from Marquito, because she doesn't know where things will end up with him, not because of him, but because of her. "You see," she says, "I have a past, and he knows nothing of it. We've started to become good friends, I guess. Right now, he says he loves my smile and my dimples, but what about when he hears the rest?"

14

MARIBEL'S SECRET

Marco has been busier than a male whale in breeding season—which it is in March, for the whales, that is—and Sunset Point Resort has been at nearly full occupancy accommodating the migration of U.S. students on spring break. He enjoys his new role as captain of the breakfast shift, organizing the assignments of the wait staff, supporting them, and going around to all of the tables to ask if everything is alright. In his spare time, he flirts with Maribel. People must wonder why she needs so much supervision. She seems a little reserved around him and a bit distant, like she's embarrassed about something or maybe a little miffed about his behavior with Ashley. Which? Maybe he should ask her? It could be both.

But today at two o'clock, Maribel has agreed to meet him to go shopping for a laptop. That old computer that he had in high school in New Mexico is for sure defunct now, and he misses not having the internet, so he has decided that this is the first purchase he will make from his new account. He has fretted about even this small decision for several days because he has promised himself, as he did Ollie and Vera, that he will not waste their money even though they made it clear that it is his money now.

Marco and Maribel splurge on a taxi because it is the quickest and most direct way to get to Office Max. They look at many brands and sizes and the choice eventually comes down to two. Maribel has been reading all of the information and summarizes the advantages and disadvantages of each one so well that he asks her which one she favors.

"It's your computer," she says quite seriously, "but if you are asking me, I slightly favor this thinner one here. How is it those Americans say? More bang for the buck?"

"I think you are right," he says. "More punch for the peso." She laughs that deep laugh. Then they start looking at cell phones. "We have the computer, so we don't really need a smartphone."

"What's this we? You have the computer, but you are right about getting something simple, just to be able to talk to people.

"What's this people? I meant you and me. And for texting, too. That way I can keep track of you."

She turns away.

"What's wrong?" he asks. I was just teasing. Actually, I wasn't. I want you to be...my girlfriend now."

She is still looking away, but eventually she turns to him and says, "Okay, Marco, me, too, but first we need to talk."

She's right. How thoughtless of him. He has a boat load of explaining to do. "Yes, it's rude of me to think that I can just come back into your life after all that happened with Ashley. Like, oh, Ashley's gone, so let's find someone else. God, Maribel, I am so sorry. That's so insensitive of me. Rude. I'll slow down. I'll even butt out if that's what you want me to do, but I meant what I said."

"No, it's okay Marco, I feel the same way about you, but first there is something you need to know. You see, I have a past, and it's a long ugly story."

Marco looks astonished. He has a past, too, so recent, in fact, that it is barely past. How could Maribel have a past? She's so sweet. "Maybe on our next day off," he gingerly suggests, "we could spend some of that hundred bucks of yours and take the glass bottom water taxi over to Lovers Beach, you know over by the arch. Do you know I've never seen the arch? Just heard about it."

"I could prepare a little picnic. But I'm warning you, Marco, don't expect to have a pleasant little afternoon tryst at Lovers Beach. This is going to be tough for both of us."

Marco is asked by the manager of the food and beverage operations to stay after the morning shift to talk. Did he do something wrong? He's forgotten El Greco, but not the feelings that go with his reprimands. He needs to remind himself that his supervisor is un hombre simpático, not a jerk like Constantino. Actually, things seem to be going very well: the waiters are working much better as a team, and they seem more committed to high standards of service as the mission of the resort. They like him and he likes them, and Omar says everything is cool, so what could be the problem?

The manager invites him to sit at a table inside the now vacant restaurant and pours two coffees. He tells Marco, "I hope you know how pleased everyone is with your work. Nobody says much as long as things are going well, but we do notice. You have a talent for encouraging people to do better."

"That's good to know. I'm enjoying it more than I thought I would."

"I want to make your appointment permanent now, but I have a deal for you to consider. We have a vacancy for captain at the dinner shift."

"That's nice, but I kind of like mornings." He thinks about not seeing Maribel.

"That's good. We're not asking you to give that up."

"Whoa. Both jobs?"

"Before you say no, let's talk about hours and pay. What do you think it would take?"

Marco thinks it's best to talk about hours first. "Well, the times when supervision is most needed are from seven to eleven in the morning. I don't know about dinner. Maybe five until nine?"

"That makes eight hours, and you can run the staff meetings at seven and five."

Marco figures that will give him time in between for reading, for getting personal things done, maybe take some online classes. But they're asking him to do two jobs. Smart for them. "What about pay?"

"It's a consolidation, but the pay could be a lot more than what you make now."

Marco nods. "Sounds interesting."

"Then I will check with my boss and HR. It will be a good offer. Believe me, we don't want to lose you. Management is thinking about creating a new position down the road that includes coordination of breakfast, dinner, room service, poolside service and the bars. Maximize efficiency, increase profitability. Do you know anything about cost accounting?"

"No, but I can learn."

They shake hands and embrace. Nice! He phones Maribel immediately to share the good news, and that afternoon he goes to Publicacíones Ghandi to special order two books, one on general accounting and the other on cost accounting. It never occurs to him to question whether he can do the two jobs or understand those books.

Vera and Ollie are back in Golden adjusting to the unpredictable fluctuations in the Colorado spring weather: warm on Monday, cold on

Tuesday, bursting buds on the crabapple trees on Wednesday, covered with snow on Thursday. A sixty degree change in temperature is nothing. Some days, Ollie says, you can have winter, spring and summer all on the same day. He has found it a bit difficult returning to the higher altitude of the Mile High City and its environs, and the doctor at Kaiser Permanente has put him on a diuretic for a few days to get rid of the extra fluids he is retaining. When he told the doctor what happened in Mexico, he suggested that he see a cardiologist for some further testing just to eliminate the possibility of future problems, either at home or away. He doesn't procrastinate this time.

Vera is finishing her handful of daily chores. They returned to a spotless house because that's the way they left it, so she hasn't had much to occupy herself. Ollie knows that the Homeowners Association takes care of the landscaping, but it never reaches his standards, so he changes into his gardening clothes, goes out to buy a few perennials, and adds them to the rock garden he has created next to the lower-level patio. Hey, it's spring and what's an old geezer to do if he doesn't watch the NCAA basketball playoffs?

A few days later, Vera hears the beep announcing a new email, and when she checks to see who it can be, she is surprised to see something from Marco González.

Hi, Vera and Ollie:

I want to let you know that I used some of your funds to purchase a new computer. I hope that's okay. I am really happy having one again. I have the morning shift job permanently now and they made me the dinner captain as well. I was really surprised. We adjusted the hours and they are asking for a good raise for me.

Maribel and I are becoming better friends now, but she has been a little distant with me lately. She says she has something important to tell me, but then she doesn't. I don't know what to do. I can't believe I got so entangled with that Ashley. I guess I just felt sorry for her. At least she's gone.

Marquito

Vera decides to sit down right then and there to reply.

Hi, Marquito:

It was good to hear from you. I'm glad that you have a computer and that we can communicate like this now. Please don't hesitate to send us emails because we miss you.

Congratulations on your new appointment. We always believed in you and we are like proud parents hearing your good news.

As for Maribel, I am glad to know that you are deepening your friendship. You don't have your mother or sister close by to tell you, so I will give these free tips. Court her in an old-fashioned way. Hold her hand in public. Put an arm around her. Open doors for her. Surprise her with something romantic. When she is ready, she will tell you. When she does, listen patiently and don't tell her what to do. She just wants to be understood.

Ollie is looking over my shoulder reading what I have written and he is scolding me for my matchmaking again. But you know me, I can't help but play Cupid.

Please contact us at any time if you have questions or concerns or if you just want to share some good news. We love to hear from you. Ollie sends his regards.

Vera Webster

Vera's comment about being proud parents hits Marco over the head like a piano dropped in an animated cartoon. He hasn't talked to his own parents since he arrived in Cabo San Lucas. He wrote that letter to let them know where he was and that he was safe, but he never mailed it. What has he been thinking? How disrespectful. He needs to do something now. Immediately. The last he knew, his sister Dolores was still living at home with them. He hates to think about talking to that grouchy sister of his, but he calls her cell, anyway.

"Bueno," says the familiar voice of his sister.

"It's Marco."

"¿Marco, quién?" she asks.

"Marco, your brother." There is a long pause, and finally he says, "Marquito, your little brother."

"I know, I know. I just don't know what to say to you, you little snot. How could you do this to us? Your own sister, your parents. Do you know how much we have worried about you?"

"I'm sorry, I..."

"Sorry? For god's sake, Marquito, how could you treat them like this? Mother can hardly sleep at night and your father just keeps working, working, hoping he can save enough money to send you to college."

"I have some good news," Marco says, trying to deal with the lump in his throat while hoping to turn the ugly conversation with his sister onto a more positive path.

"Well, tell your mother and father. You don't need to go through me like I'm the Angel Gabriel or something to make your announcements. Here." She gives him their dad's cell phone number at work. "Call him. Tell him your news."

Marco feels ashamed. Though his sister's bossy, reprimanding tone always puts him on the defensive, he knows she is right this time. He promises to call his father and asks, "How have you been, Delores?" trying to put himself back in her good graces.

"Well, I'm married."

"Married?"

I would have invited you to the wedding if I had even a clue where you were, you creep. What about you, are you married?"

"No, but I have a good job."

"Is that your good news? A job?"

"No something more."

"Call your father at that number and let him tell our mother that Señor Lazarus has come back from the dead. If you call her, she will think it's a ghost. Maybe collapse. Then you won't be able to tell her nothing. Nada."

Marco and Maribel meet at the Paraíso Mall at ten o'clock and walk over to Médano Beach together. He carries the picnic basket she has prepared, she takes her tote with the towels and sunscreen and bottles of water, and they plod along together hand in hand across the loose sand to the metal fold-up table where the excursions are sold. They buy two round trips and she rubs sunscreen on her face and arms while they wait.

"I like you dark," he says.

"Yeah, well, I'm dark enough."

While they sit on the beach to wait for the next boat, Marco tells Maribel about the conversation with his sister, if that angry lecture could even be called a conversation. "More like a car wreck."

"No one dead, but everyone injured?"

"Exactly. My sister was really upset, to put it mildly. What should I do?"

"For the car? Go to the body shop and repair the damage. For the injured? That may take time. Attention. Love. You can begin by calling, like she said." She smiles and shrugs, but quickly becomes somber again. "Wait until you hear my story. It's more like a train wreck."

In a few minutes a boat is free and they go down to the shoreline and crawl up the little ladder on the side near the stern and find a place to sit. The boat is not actually glass-bottomed as advertised, but there is a transparent section in the middle where a keel would be on a sailboat, and the passengers can look down into the sea through it. So far, no fish. Maybe later.

The trip also provides a tour, a nice surprise that includes a view of some stinky sea lions and a bumpy, bouncy, splashy ride past the end of the cape—the real land's end—and magnificent views of the famous natural stone arch, both from the Sea of Cortéz and the Pacific side, looking through the arch both ways from different perspectives. Maribel shows him how to use his imagination to see a huge rabbit drinking water out of the ocean as he looks at the arch from the Sea of Cortéz, and then over on the Pacific side she shows him how to look into the space under the arch, not at the arch itself, to see a big hunched up turtle.

"I'm not so good at this," Marco says, but he loves her game.

"You're too literal. But to be honest, Abuelo and Abuela showed me how to see those shapes when I was a little girl."

"Of course, the artist's eye. Seeing things that we mere mortals never see." At that moment, Marco begins to see some things about Maribel that he's never noticed before. She has her hair in a ponytail, but today she has the tail in curly ringlets that bounce across her shoulders. Her hair shines in the sun and her shoulders are smooth and clear, as if inviting to be touched. Sure, the dimples are there, but now he notices the smile, too, and the curve of her upper lip. He needs to stop staring and say something. "Do you make stuff, too?"

"Me? I try to sketch and paint, but I don't have much time or space for it now. Maybe someday."

The boat takes them back around to Lovers Beach. The guide, who also pilots the boat, tells them that he will return several times, every hour on the hour, until four o'clock, and they can get any boat back they want up until four. Marco and Maribel climb back down the ladder and wade across the shore until they reach the dry sand. From there they trudge up a long broad sandy hill—this place is bigger than it looks from the boat—finally reaching the crest of a knoll which provides an open sweeping vista of the Pacific side. A perfect March day with a clear sky and bright sun, but not too hot.

"Wow! What a fantastic place this is," Marco says.

"How come you've never been here?" she asks.

"Maybe I was waiting for you to bring me," he says with a flirty smile.

"That's so sweet." She points. "Here, over here. See how one of the cliffs makes that little area of shade? Let's sit over there."

They spread out their towels and sit cross-legged opposite each other but then Maribel says, "You know, this might go better for me if you could just lie down and look up at the sky. I'm not sure I can face you while I tell you this."

"Okay, I can do that, but really it's okay. Just tell me."

She slides an index finger through the air horizontally and Marco knows better than a dog that he had better lie down.

So, Maribel begins her story. "I went to high school here in Cabo San Lucas, of course, and I had a lot of friends because the girls thought I was funny and the guys thought I was attractive. I was kind of early in my development if you know what I mean. When I was in grade ten, age fifteen, I was attracted to a guy in grade twelve who was very handsome, at least I thought so then, and very rich. I won't say what family he is from because I have agreed not to speak their name. He lived in one of those mansions up in Pedregal."

"Where?"

"That expensive housing up on the mountain overlooking the marina and the bay. Pedregal. As in rocky. High up, where the rich people live."

"Okay, I think I know where."

"Anyway, he kept flirting with me, throwing me compliments, and the little stupid one here thought she was in love."

"Yes, but normal for a girl of that age." Marco says, already defending her, wanting to sit up, but lying there as she asked, not looking at her but at the empty blue sky.

"His family had a boat, a yacht actually, docked in the marina, and one night he invited me to go for a ride with him, just a little ride, he told me, out into the bay. I knew my mother would disapprove, but I might never get a chance like that again, so I went anyway. My mother was very strict, maybe too strict. I will tell you more about my mother later when I need to, but for now, it is only important to remember that I went with him. It was my choice, and I knew better."

It is quiet for a while and Marco pictures her trying not to cry, but he doesn't look at her. He senses she is looking away. He waits patiently.

"Thank you. I think I can continue now. So, he powers up his father's yacht and navigates out into the bay, which I am sure he shouldn't have been doing with that boat, but he did. So, he stopped the yacht out in the bay on the Sea of Cortéz side, away from all of the other boats, and he dropped anchor. I asked him what he was doing. He said he wanted to show me around the boat. He took me below the main deck to a lovely little space for sleeping, and that's where it happened."

"He raped you." Marco has to fight with himself not to sit up. He clenches his fists.

"That's what everyone says, my grandmother, my grandfather, the priest, the prosecutor, but it has taken me a long time to admit that this is what happened. I liked him. I told him to stop, of course, and I resisted and yelled and screamed, but no one was anywhere nearby. He was strong and forced me, yes, but I thought it was my fault, and when I told my mother, she blamed me and told me it was my fault. It was only later, that my grandfather and the priest said that I was the victim of a horrible crime."

She stops and he wonders if she is crying. "But Maribel," he says softly, "why would you think this would affect our relationship? We are both damaged goods and hardly anyone marries a virgin these days. What's the problem?"

"The problem is that you have only heard the first part of the story. But if you don't mind, let's take a break for a minute."

"A little intermission?"

"You might call it that, and we better eat now because you may not have much appetite when you hear the rest."

He sits up and helps her lay out the picnic. On the plastic plates she has provided, she serves beer-battered shrimp with fried onions wrapped in flour tortillas. She pours glasses of homemade lemonade from a bottle. Everything is elegant, with stainless forks and cloth napkins. Marco says that the shrimp is the best he's ever tasted and thanks her for getting up so early on her day off to make them. They eat in silence, except for the chirping of the pesky little sparrows who want to be part of their picnic and the occasional screech of a soaring gull overhead. When they are finished, Maribel packs everything up and asks Marco if he is ready to hear more. He lies down again as a signal for her to continue.

"A month later—every young Mexican girl knows how to count to twenty-eight—I missed my period and soon after took the test that showed I was pregnant."

"What? No way. One time?"

"One time, but apparently the right time," she replies. "My mother was hysterical. She said it would bring shame on our family, including the reputation of my grandparents, and that we should deal with it ourselves. I wasn't to tell anyone. After a few days, I couldn't stand it any longer, carrying that burden all alone, so I went to confess to a priest up at El Santuario de Guadalupe, you know, the big modern looking church to the north of the city. The priest told me that the father of the baby needed to know. The priest reminded me of the evils of abortion and suggested that maybe our romance could end in marriage."

"See, that's the trouble with the Church," Marco says.

"Hush. Just listen. There's more. Not all priests are alike. So, I told the father of the baby and he responded with a wooden face without emotion."

"¡Puta madre! Oh, excuse me. I'm so sorry. Go on."

"He invited me to his house in Pedregal, and being the naïve little person I was, I thought it was an invitation to meet his parents. But when we got there, no one was at home. No parents, no brothers or sisters, just the two of us. He asked me what I was going to do about the baby, and I asked him what he was going to do. I'm sure it was those words that set off his anger. I only meant it as a question, but he flew into a rage. He started slapping me and slamming me around. He beat me with the handle of a broom; he went straight for my belly." Maribel's voice cracks, and Marco wants to sit up and comfort her. "Of course, I yelled and screamed, but up in that big, house at the top of the hill, the neighbors' houses were quite some distance away. He just kept flailing away at me." Maribel pauses before she says, "This next part is really awful, but I need to tell you because it is the part of my story you must know."

"I'm horrified. I can't believe what I'm hearing, but go on if you must. What happened?"

"There's no easy way to explain the rest, but he gave me the crudest most violent abortion anyone could imagine with that broom stick."

Marco sits up, his face covered with the horror of what he has just heard. He is speechless. Maribel searches his eyes for a moment, but then looks off into the distance to finish her story. "He got some towels and ordered me to clean up the mess. Can you believe that? It was so humiliating. When I eventually got home, I told my mother what happened, and she blamed me again, this time for my stupidity, and told me I would be all right. But when the bleeding wouldn't stop, she called her parents."

"Abuela and Abuelo?"

"Sí. They told her to forget about her pride and get me to a hospital. When the doctors said I needed surgery, my grandparents rushed me to La Paz, you know, the state capitol, a bigger city with better services. I had three surgeries and spent the rest of the summer in Todos Santos. It was there that I met Padre Carlos."

"Another priest?"

"Yes, but he was totally different. The doctors saved my life, He saved my soul. Yes, Padre Carlos helped me recover my senses and heal my spirit, and I will be forever grateful to him. As you might guess I was an emotional wreck."

"The train wreck we talked about."

"I spent many hours in the counsel of Padre Carlos to deal with my totally mixed-up feelings about what had happened and how I had been treated. Confused, humiliated, ashamed, bewildered, forsaken, and forlorn. There were days when life was so bleak, I just stared at him blankly, enveloped in a stupor of gloom. I told him I wanted to die. But he gave me hope and brought me back to life. He and the Virgin of Guadalupe. He taught me how to pray to her. To me, my recovery was a kind of miracle. I hope you can respect that," she says, finally looking up to meet his gaze.

He notices the honey-brown irises of her sad eyes and nods as she pauses before continuing.

"Abuela and Abuelo were patient and caring, too, and they nurtured me back to good health with their love and positive philosophy about life." She takes a deep breath before going on. "So, here's the point—and this is what I want you to know—I will never be able to have babies." She bursts into tears, trembling and sobbing.

"My god, Maribel, you had to go back through that horribly painful story to tell me you can't have babies?" His eyes are blinking to fight back the tears.

"I thought you should know why," she sobs.

He slides over beside her and holds her tight until the sobbing stops and she catches her breath. Finally, Marco asks, "Whatever happened to this repulsive criminal?"

"What always happens to the sons of the rich? His parents paid the investigators, the attorneys, the judge, and even my mother. Everyone was paid."

"Mexican ointment for a rapist and a murderer. He should have gone to jail."

"And where was the evidence to convict him? Just in the frivolous testimony of a silly, love-struck adolescent girl. No witnesses either time. He pleaded to a lesser charge and was given a suspended sentence of three years."

"Where is he now?"

"His father owns a lot of real estate and five restaurants along the coast. He works in his father's restaurant in San José del Cabo, the other Cabo, you know, and thank god I have never seen him since. He is never to come near me, and I am never to speak his family's name, but I worry because he is still on the streets. I have nightmares about meeting him."

"Wow! I can't believe what money can buy." He senses a touch of the old anger smoldering inside, but this time he knows it is the natural indignation that he feels over something so horribly wrong. And it happened to Maribel.

"After my daily sessions with Padre Carlos, Abuela and Abuelo helped me make the transition back to a normal life. I stayed with them, went to school in Todos Santos, and they found this lovely family for me to live with as an exchange student for one semester in California, a suburb of San Diego. Getting away was good for me, and I still write to the family, but I wanted to come back, finish high school, get a job, and go on. Eventually my mother said she was sorry about how she handled things and invited me back into the family."

A cool breeze coming in from the Pacific blows across the white sand. Marco is still so shocked he hardly knows what to say. He just wants to pull her close and tell her that it doesn't matter. Finally, he begins, "I just want you to know, Maribel..."

She holds up the palm of her hand. "Before you say anything at all, you need to take some time to gain perspective before you go any further with me. Not having babies is one thing, a serious issue in itself, but you need to understand that I still have some bad days. Sometimes I need comfort. Then at other times, I just need to be alone. Time to be with God. You need to think about all of that."

On the four o'clock boat back to Médano Beach, Maribel seems like a new person, relieved, unburdened, spirits lifted, and smiling again. She's humming some old ranchero song he doesn't recognize. They look through the transparent panels in the bottom of the boat and this time they see a lot of different kinds of fish: round yellow fish with black stripes, thin narrow fish colored light blue, and shimmering orange ones. The fish make Maribel so excited and happy that she can't stop pointing to them and exclaiming over them, so that Marco can share with her the beauty she sees in their different shapes and colors.

Marco knows that he should take time in the next few days to think things through, slow down a little, and consider all that Maribel has revealed to him, but he finds that difficult; his heart keeps telling his head that nothing she told him makes any difference. She was so young. Surely, she can't be held responsible for what happened. He did not grow up with traditional ideas of purity anyway, so that is certainly not an issue. God knows he is no saint himself. Perhaps someday he would like to have children, but he is hardly at the point in his life where he wants to be taking care of a little baby. Would he regret someday that he is married to a woman who can't have children? Maybe, but he would surely accept that, knowing the horrible circumstances that made Maribel's situation what it is. He smiles to himself. He knows he has fallen in love with her, so he can't give these concerns the rational consideration she would like. Nothing she said makes a difference. And if she needs a little extra love now and then, well, he has love to give.

Maybe the more important question is why she would want to have anything to do with him so soon after he has made such an ass of himself with Ashley. It seems like a long time ago now that Ashley was living in his apartment, but actually it has been only a few weeks. He came very close to the brink of a catastrophe with her—he recognizes that now—and he is relieved that Ashley is gone. Did he love her? Ashley was a fling, at best, and a horrible mistake, at worst. Does he have any lingering feelings for her? Not at all. Does he hope to see her again? Never. What he recognizes now is that she manipulated him, using his anger for her own purposes. What he needs to do is to toss that whole experience with Ashley into the dumpster of dumb decisions and move on with Maribel. In a very short time, she has brought him unexpected calm and serenity. He feels like a completely different person around her. He loves her and he knows that. The real question is not will he have her, but will she have him? She is probably having second thoughts, wondering why she told this unreliable guy her full story. She's probably preparing her good-bye speech or writing him a text message telling him it's over. No, if he has any romantic intentions at all with this beautiful girl, this work of art, he had better act on them fast before she changes her mind. Now.

Marco persuades Maribel to go parasailing with him on their next day off. She's a little hesitant at first, but then he tells her that they can go up together side by side at the same time, and she says that might make her feel a little more secure. She's never been before nor has he—too expensive—but they still have some change from that hundred bucks, and this looks like a good way to spend it. They watch for a while to see how it works before they buy their tickets. The boats are rigged with big, colorful parachutes that are let out slowly on a long line. "See, they strap you in together," Marco points out. "All you have to do is hold on and float around up there. When they reel you in, your feet come right back down onto the platform where you stood when they let you out. So, what's so hard about that?"

"Nothing," says Maribel. "I just wonder what it's going to feel like up there with nothing under you."

"Actually, we're just strapped to the chute, so there's no need to sit on anything."

"Okay, let's go up there and talk to God."

They buy their tickets and a water taxi takes them out to the parasail boat along with four boisterous kids and their nervous parents. Marco and Maribel wait their turn. Finally, when they are all strapped in—click, click—the motor roars, the boat accelerates, and they feel their feet leave the platform. Soon they are floating in the air out behind the boat climbing higher and higher as the line extends. She clings on tight at first, a little nervous. But then she shoots him one of her famous smiles that displays those special dimples. "What do you think?" he asks.

"Fantastic. Pure bliss. The most amazing thing I've ever done. Look at where we are. Oh, Marco, look at the arch from here."

"What's it look like to you now, a dragon maybe? Hey, listen to our voices. The only sound there is." They both listen for a second.

"It's so quiet," she whispers. "You can't even hear the boat. Let me just experience the silence." She closes her eyes.

While Maribel is enjoying her solitude, Marco takes from his little finger a ring that he has concealed there, the silver ring that Vera and Ollie bought for him, telling him that he would know whom to give it to someday. He pries Maribel's hand loose from the sail strap she is grasping like a falcon and slips it on her ring finger, quickly and deftly, almost before she knows what has happened.

"What's this?" she asks, eyes opening wide.

"A friendship ring, and if all goes well, I'll get you another one someday."

"Marco, I can't believe it. You're so romantic. Up here in the sky like this?" She looks at the ring on her finger. "Oh my gosh, I can't believe this is happening." She looks over at him and he kisses her on the cheek, and then touching her on the chin to turn her face, he kisses her on the lips. Then again.

The line from the boat has been let out as far as it will go—more than two hundred meters—and they hover almost motionless alone together in time and space under the colorful red and blue parachute. Finally, Marco says, "This is a good place to throw away the past, yours and mine both. Just let go of the bad memories. Let them drop where they will and sink to the bottom of the sea."

"Sounds like good advice, but the problem with that is that those memories aren't out there," she points ahead with an index finger and then releases her hand just long enough to point to her head, "they're up here. I learned from Padre Carlos that I can't get rid of my memories, I can only learn to live with them, and that's what I'm trying to do."

"I understand. I can see how that's best for you."

"And for you also, mi amor. You will have your memories, too. Maybe not as horrible as mine, but you will have them because we all have them."

"That's true," he agrees, nodding, noticing that they are quickly making their decent.

"And my guess is," Maribel continues, "that you are not finished with that little red-head yet. Even a snail leaves a trail. You think she is a memory, but she's not just a memory, she is a ghost, and she will come back to haunt you in ways you never imagined."

"I hope not," he shouts over the noise of the motor as they descend. He is shocked.

Their feet touch down on the platform at the back of the boat.

15

AN ANNOUNCEMENT FROM ASHLEY

April and spring at last. Crocuses first, followed by daffodils and tulips. Today Vera and Ollie are home, not quite alone, because they are babysitting their "granddaughter." It might be more accurate, Ollie points out, to admit that they are spoiling Katie while Peter and Amanda are out shopping for a new previously owned vehicle. As soon as Katie wakes up from her nap, her grandparents will take her into town so she can eat part of Ollie's ham and cheese sandwich from the D'Deli and sip some of his chocolate milkshake from Golden Sweets, without malt today because Katie makes faces when it has malt in it. She and Ollie have become good pals, and he never misses an opportunity to keep her for a day. While the children were growing up, Ollie was so busy with his lawyering that he wasn't a very engaged father, as they say so politely today to avoid that ugly word *neglect*. Now it seems he is trying to recover some of those precious moments he lost with his own children by giving his full attention to Katie whenever she is around. She seems to help him fill in some of the empty spaces in his life. Today Ollie is a little impatient for Katie to wake up from her nap. Lately, Vera has been noticing those empty spaces in her own life. She is missing her friends in Mexico and wishes Marco would email or call with some news, or maybe seek some advice.

Marco phones his father. He has been procrastinating for all these many weeks, knowing that his call is more than overdue, but dreading it after talking to his sister Dolores. Now he has even more good news to share: he has a girlfriend. He has learned how to use Skype, so it won't cost as much, and he is sitting in María Canela, a cybercafé he spotted right across the street from the restaurant, María Corona, and he is ready to go with his wi-fi connection. He tries the number his sister gave him. No answer, but the voice on the answering service is unmistakably his father's.

He's glad for the reprieve, but now that he is prepared with what he wants to say, he wants to get through, make the contact, and be finished with it. He orders an iced coffee and cinnamon pastry and calls again in fifteen minutes.

"Bueno."

"It's Marco."

"Oh, Marco, it is so good to hear from you. Dolores said you called her. I've been waiting for your call."

"I am so sorry. I want to apologize."

"Yes, you owe your mother some apologies, but I am just so glad you are calling now because I want to know if you are happy."

"Very happy, father, but only in the last few weeks. I went through some bad times. A little angry and lost, you know, but I'm okay now." He certainly doesn't want to try to explain about Ashley.

"As long as you are happy now. How are things for you? What are you doing?"

"I have some very good news. I'm the captain of the restaurant staff at a big resort in Cabo San Lucas."

"Captain? Already. Bueno."

"And I met this older couple at the resort and you won't believe this, dad, but they gave me fifty thousand dollars."

"It is hard to believe. Americans?"

"Yes."

"Even harder to believe. No, just kidding."

"And I have a girlfriend. A Mexican girl."

"She's beautiful, of course?"

"A beautiful smile, yes, beautiful in every way. Very kind to everyone and very positive. She's good for me."

"I'm happy for you."

"And one more thing. I saved a young boy from drowning in the ocean. Everyone around here treats me like a hero."

"You had that course while you were in high school."

"You remember?"

"Marquito, I remember everything about you as a boy, but I don't know your face anymore now that you are a man."

"I'm sure we will get together soon. Tell mom everything."

"Call on Sunday. After church. You can tell your mother all the details."

"What about your job?" Marco asks.

"At least I have one. It puts food on the table and we save a little. Actually, I like it. We're building some big impressive buildings."

"You are both well?" Marco asks.

"We are all well, gracias a Dios. Thank you for calling to let us know you are well, too. It's just so good to know that you are safe and happy. And rich, too. God bless you."

In the next few weeks, Marco calls his family on Sundays, making a special point to remember Easter. Maribel has introduced him to her mother and sisters, and he goes there for a meal sometimes: tamales, enchiladas, flautas. Her mother seems nicer than he had imagined her, but he can see how she was a pain for Maribel as a teenager, so strict about everything. He can't quite picture Maribel's mother as the daughter of Abuela and Abuelo but who says children need to be like their parents. Actually, he can't picture Maribel as her mother's daughter either. Nevertheless, he's starting to feel like a part of her family.

In early May, Marco suggests that he and Maribel catch the bus over to San José del Cabo to celebrate the long Labor Day weekend. He's heard they have a good celebration over there. Maribel freezes. She doesn't want to run into el monstruo, the name they have given to the jerk who nearly killed her. But when Marco reminds her of the low probability of that in all those crowds of people, she agrees. She really likes all of the cultural festivities and food for that holiday: gorditas, tostadas, flautas, pozole, and of course churros.

"I remember as a little boy—one of the few things I remember—how much I loved churros," he says, rolling the r's fiercely.

"And that's a good place to find them," she admits.

Maribel and Marco have both been managing their memories, but it is never easy, so they do whatever they can to avoid the reminders that set off uncomfortable feelings. Marco has rid his apartment of every trace of the furnishings that Ashley bought. He never goes to the Mango Cantina. He's actually thought of moving to another place to live, but he's dreaming that sometime soon he can move into a little house with Maribel, so he's willing to wait. As for Maribel, he notices that when they walk around the marina, she doesn't look at the boats. It takes real courage for her to agree to go over to San José del Cabo.

When they step off the bus, they find themselves in the middle of a lively celebration. Singing and laughter fill the air and the shrill sounds of the mariachi trumpets float above the din. Strands of green and yellow triangular flags mark off the pedestrian street with its small shops and places to eat the traditional foods and drink anything from tequila or sprite to that marvelous rice and cinnamon drink, horchata. They walk up and down that street, and then wander over to the adjacent park. A big stage has been set up there with rows and rows of white folding chairs in front, but a lot of people just stand and kind of mill around. He and Maribel watch a mime and then a couple of programs with young boys and girls in white costumes. Then the stage is occupied with the adult dancers, handsome young men and women in traditional costumes. Marco asks Maribel if she has ever learned to do the Veracruz dances like that where the women shake those big, colorful, lacy skirts from side to side, and she says she never learned, but always wished she had.

"Actually," he says, I'd like to learn how to stamp my feet and click my heels like that, and spin around with that big sombrero. She tells him it's never too late to learn to be a Mexican, and then she laughs that deep laugh.

"I'm sure we could find some group that would..." She breaks off in mid-sentence and an instant pallor comes to her face. She grabs his arm and he can feel her trembling. "Oh, my God," she says.

"What is it?" Marco asks.

"It's him."

"Where?" He doesn't have to ask who him is. He's already on red alert.

Maribel nods in the direction of a man walking along with great difficulty, heading past them toward the pedestrian street. She pulls Marco further into the crowd so as not to be seen, and then points. "Over there, the one with the limp, the guy with the cane, all hunched over like an old man. My God, he can barely walk. And his face, I hardly recognize him. I wonder what happened."

Marco watches as the man disappears into the thick crowd. "You're sure that's him?"

"Positive. But I can't imagine what happened to him." She is very agitated, and then suddenly she reaches into the rear pocket of her jeans for her cell phone. "I have to find out. I have an old high school friend in Cabo San Lucas who knows what happened to me, the only one I ever told." She dials and tells Marco, "She always knows stuff."

As near as he can tell from overhearing Maribel's end of the conversation, it sounds like the twerp was beat up, but Marco has to wait until she finishes up to get the details. "What happened?" he asks.

"He was messing with some guy's girlfriend, and the guy, not just the guy but three of his friends, too, nearly killed him. They broke his leg in two places, several ribs, and smashed his face every which way, so he had to get new front teeth. She thought I knew."

"So," Marco says, "what the law couldn't fix, the lawless did. Very Mexican." Maribel seems really shaken up, so he puts an arm around her and holds her tight.

She takes a deep breath and looks up at him. "I would never wish ill on anyone—Padre Carlos taught me that—but at least I know he won't be able to hurt me ever again. Don't you think that's good, Marquito? Oops. I forgot, I called you Marquito."

"I think you are finished with him now. And by the way you can call me Marquito. I like the sound of that name on your beautiful lips."

More weeks of courtship pass and June arrives, the wedding month, but there is no wedding. That's okay with Marquito as long as it happens someday. He and Maribel cherish their good times together, falling more in love, if that even seems possible, each day. The heat and humidity combined in June are making afternoons uncomfortable, so they spend as much time as possible in the mall and the air-conditioned shops. They go to María Canela's, but it is so crowded that they have to wait to get in the door. Finally, they purchase iced coffee and grab two chairs near an outlet. Maribel has brought a sketch pad she carries around with her now. She says she can't do butterflies like Abuela because that would not be original, so she has started a series with fish, amazingly creative abstractions of the various shapes suggested by the fins and tails and eyes and mouths of fish, done in bright watercolors of mostly yellow and blue with touches of ink for black lines here and there. Very Mexican, he thinks, but he still can't say exactly why. Today she is sketching, just playing with the shapes, and Marquito loves to watch her. That makes her happy. In fact, everything seems to make her happy these days, even making breakfast omelets at La Casona. She has been teaching Marco to be patient and calm, and although he is a slow learner in that department, he is catching on. Watching her sketch helps. It's soothing watching her hand glide across the paper, seeing nothing turn into something, blank space takes on form.

Today, Marco has brought his computer to María Canela's because he wants to check out online bachelor's degree programs in the U.S. But before he does that, he has something else on his mind. "Maribel, I hate to interrupt you, I mean I could watch you drawing all day, but I need to ask you a question."

"What's that?" she asks without looking up.

"Don't you think we should tell Vera and Ollie about our secret?"

"What? That we're in love?" She shoots him a coy smile.

"No. I mean, yes, but no. What you explained to me, you know, about not having babies."

"I did leave them with the impression that I had a past, and that once you heard about it you might ditch me. I don't know. It's really personal."

"Do you mind if I tell them? I won't go into any of the details. Just tell them that this was your secret and everything is really good with us now."

"Of course, tell them about our romance." She smiles but doesn't look up from her sketching. "They are our friends and our benefactors. Besides, you know how they are, especially Vera, the casamentera, always trying to match us up. She'll be delighted."

When Marco is finished with the email, he goes back to his Google search. He starts with the University of New Mexico, which is where he would have gone to college, but then he searches for other programs and finds one at Arizona State. But they are expensive and it looks like it will take forever for a degree. Maybe that's not so important right now. What's important is Maribel. She needs a place to work. With her natural talent and her grandparents close by, she may not need to study. Besides, he's got his hands full studying those two accounting books.

So, Marco and Maribel make their plans and dream their dreams. Study. Work. Get married someday. Pool their funds. Rent a little house so that she can have a studio. She likes the sound of that. He would get married tomorrow, but she wants to wait. Maybe she is still not sure about him yet, afraid he will want babies someday. He knows now that this will never change his mind about Maribel. He's too crazy about her. He desperately wants to make love to her, but she says no, not yet, not until they're married, and that's just the way it's going to be. Well, with Maribel's particular situation, maybe that's okay. Maybe this is her way of trying to forget, acting like it never happened. But how is he going to last? That bothers him.

The next afternoon, Marquito decides to go back down to María Canela's, but this time alone, to call Vera on Skype. He needs some advice. Surprisingly, he gets Ollie, who explains that Vera is visiting the neighbors across the street learning about a gluten-free diet. Marquito didn't know that Ollie even knew how to use Skype. Maybe he just knows how to answer.

"Something I can help you with?" Ollie offers.

Marquito is not so sure he wants to talk about his sex life, or lack thereof, to an old man in his seventies, but then again, maybe they have that in common. A better topic for Ollie than for Vera, that's for sure. Still, he decides to shift the topic slightly. "As Vera probably told you, Maribel and I are starting to get serious with this romance, and I feel like I really know her well now, but there's just one thing..."

"Religion?"

"Geez, Ollie, are you psychic or something? How did you guess?"

"It wasn't a guess, just a swift calculation of the probabilities. So, is there a problem?"

"Well, she's very religious, and I'm not. She's very Catholic, and I take a pretty dim view of all that's gone on with the Catholic Church over the centuries, especially here in Mexico."

"That seems perfectly reasonable to me. There are a lot of Catholics who are concerned about that, too."

"She had this one priest who helped her when she was going through some difficult times."

"Well, it's good to know that there's at least one priest left who is helpful."

"It's not just the priest, it's the Holy Mother and all the saints, and particularly here in Mexico that Virgin of Guadalupe."

"Sometimes we humans need all the help we can get," Ollie points out.

"But you don't believe in all that stuff, do you, Señor?"

"Oh, heavens no, that wouldn't work for me at all. I'm too skeptical."

"Me, too. That's a good word, skeptical." Marquito is trying to remember how he got that way. O'Reilly, his history teacher, for sure was an influence, but also his biology teacher. Maybe his dad had a little impact there, too. He remembers him rolling his eyes a lot.

Then Ollie tells him, "Skepticism is the foundation of science. Science exists because people question the prevailing assumptions. They want better explanations. Skepticism provides the prime motivation for knowledge. It's a positive thing."

"Yeah, for sure. That's cool. Way cool. Interesting how you and I see things alike on stuff like that. But it makes me kind of embarrassed and uncomfortable around Maribel, being the doubter I am."

"I doubt that you are a greater doubter than the King of Doubters, Oliver Webster."

Marco watches Ollie bouncing back and forth and side to side on the screen, waving his arms all around, and he wonders if Ollie even knows he's on camera. "But Señor, this doesn't help me to know what to do about Maribel. She's very religious."

"What do you believe?"

"I don't really know, but sometimes I look at all of the grains of sand on the beach, or I think about how big the ocean is, or I look up at the stars and I think, wow!

"Wow? That's it? Just wow?"

"Yeah, wow!"

There is a brief silence before Ollie says, "Maybe that's your way of being religious. Does she know about that?"

"I've never told her."

"Maybe you need to tell her." Marquito hears Ollie pausing to clear his throat.

"What does she think brought the two of you together?"

"For her, the Hand of God"

"And for you?"

"Blind fate, me being the blind part."

"Pretty mysterious either way, wouldn't you say?"

"I guess so. Kind of a miracle that we found each other and love each other."

"And did I just hear you say the word miracle? Tell me, is she a good person?"

"Oh, yes, way better than I am. She's almost a saint."

"And did I just hear you say the word saint? Maybe you two aren't so far apart on religion as you may think. Look, Marquito, perhaps you just need to talk to each other about it a little. Let her know what you doubt, but also what you believe. Tell her you can respect her beliefs if she can respect your doubts."

"Wow, that's awesome, sir." Marquito thanks Ollie for the fantastic advice, they say their good-byes, and sign off.

In five minutes, Vera has called him back. "Ollie says you two had a good talk about religion while I was across the street, but he had a hunch there was something else you wanted to talk about with me. Is that so?"

My God, that woman can be so direct. He can't tell her no, but he's fairly sure he doesn't want to talk to Vera about sex anymore. Maybe he could change the subject or just ease into it in a general way. "Well, yeah, ah, Maribel is really religious. And traditional, too, you know?"

"And?"

He knew she would say "and." He knows better than to start something like this with Vera. "And...she wants us to postpone...she wants us to wait..."

"No sex until you're married, right? That must be very difficult for you considering how attractive she is and how young you are. Ollie was like a young stallion at your age."

It's hard for Marquito to picture Ollie as a stallion at any age, but there goes Vera again, knowing the whole damn problem by experience and intuition and jumping right into the middle of it with both feet. "I don't know what to do."

"Well, it seems like you have two choices. You can make an issue of it, in which case you run the risk that the discussion turns into a quarrel, and the quarrel upsets her so badly that you lose her. She has her reasons, I'm sure, religious or not. So, there you are. Your other choice is to wait until you are married, but to hasten on the wedding. Do something to make that wedding happen sooner, so you don't have to wait so long. Set a date. Make it clear how long this wait is going to be. When you know how long, you can handle your passions better."

"Geez, Vera. How do you come up with such good advice?"

"Thanks, but you need to understand I'm not just playing cupid here. If you two are made for each other and if you're really serious, why not set a date?

For the next few days, Marquito tries to approach the subject with Maribel in the most subtle and not-so-subtle ways, like asking her what she thinks is the best wedding month, or asking her opinion about how long the perfect couple should wait to get married, but she doesn't take the hint. Then he asks her what she thinks about priests having to be celibate. Finally, he just drops it.

Two weeks later, already July, Marco goes to María Canela to google some accounting concepts. He's a little stuck on "present value" and "opportunity costs." He's been studying hard and needs to take a little break and refill his iced coffee. When he sits down again, he decides to check his old email address to see if his sister Dolores has written him. To his complete amazement, he finds an email from Ashley.

Hello Marquito:

I know you haven't heard from me since I got back to California. Excuse my quick exit, but someone tipped off my parents, I guess. Ruined my plans. I promised myself I wouldn't bother you anymore, but there is this matter I need to tell you about. Something I thought you ought to know. I am pregnant with your baby and he will be born in early September.

The news jolts his brain like an electric shock. He has to look away from the screen for a moment to recover his senses. ¡Hijole! He is learning through a frickin' email that he is about to become a father. How could this happen?

Although I'm definitely Pro Choice and I've demonstrated for them a lot; when it came right down to it, I just couldn't have an abortion even though that's what my parents wanted me to do. I always seem to be on the opposite side from them. Anyway, I thought you ought to know that I didn't kill your baby. To tell the truth, I don't know what I'm going to do with him. I'm still pretty confused and I'm in a bit of a mess here in California. I don't think I'll make a very good mother.

Please reply. It will be good to hear from you.

Ashley.

P.S. If we can name him Angel, you can call him Angelito.

Marquito is dumbfounded. How old is this email? Two days? That's not so bad. He needs to respond, but he has no idea what to say. He reads the email again before he sends a copy of it to his new email address to make sure he doesn't lose it. A father? A baby? Him? A son? How the hell is he going to keep his mind on his work tonight? He checks the time. Due back there in forty-five minutes. Should he tell Maribel? Not yet. Maybe never. He needs to think. He wishes he could talk to Vera and Ollie. He will email them tomorrow, but not now. His father will be pissed. He can't tell his family something like this. He knows he's hyperventilating. Maybe having a panic attack. He hurries back to the resort, stunned and dazed. Maribel was right: the ghost of Ashley has come back to haunt him.

Somehow, he gets through the evening shift, and when it is over and he has checked out, he cuts back through the lobby and the swimming pool area and goes straight to the beach. He needs to walk. Maybe run. Jump some hurdles. Damn, this is more than a low hurdle. The sea is choppy and the waves are crashing up on the shore. A crescent moon casts only a dim light. He heads up the long stretch of beach along the bay, walking in the dark, away from town, away from Sunset Point Resort, toward the empty undeveloped lots. Vast open stretches of sand are before him, everything quiet and peaceful except for his pounding heart. He is the only one he can see on the beach. The hawkers have gone home and the runners have disappeared until morning, their footsteps leaving behind shaded impressions in the sand. Only a fool would be on this part of the beach at ten o'clock at night. Yep, only a fool. He hears a popping noise, like a gunshot in the distance. When he looks back toward town, he sees fireworks bursting over the harbor, one after the other in shades of red, blue, green, and white. At least someone has a cause for celebration.

First of all, how did it happen? Ashley must not have been taking the pill. He just assumed that a sophisticated California woman like that would be on the pill. Assumed? That was his first mistake. He was so sure that he never bothered to ask her. It's not like he threw himself on her. She was always the one who initiated sex. He wishes he could talk to Vera. He pictures her trudging along beside him. He listens for her voice, for those questions she would ask. He hears that voice asking: Do you think it was intentional, Marquito?

All of a sudden, the light bulb comes on in his badly wired brain. Oh, my god, could Ashley have planned this all along? She found the right guy, fixed up the apartment, you know, built the nest, and then she crawled up on him in the middle of the night to make a baby she could raise with the love she never had. All of it calculated? He hates to think so, but looking back, everything appears to have been well planned. But at the time he had no idea. How could he have been so blind, so completely fucking stupid?

Everything was going so well with Maribel. Oh, yeah, like everything was going so well with Michelle back in New Mexico. Is he going to lose another girlfriend? Only this time he's really in love. He knows he's in love with Maribel and he thinks she loves him, too, but how can he tell her about the baby? It could ruin everything. Maybe she doesn't need to know. Maybe he doesn't even need to reply to Ashley. Just let the whole thing blow over. It'll go away. Or will it? Will Ashley keep bugging him? Will she fly down to Cabo San Lucas one day, just show up, to leave the baby on his doorstep like a frickin'stork?

He can't go home, not to that barren little apartment haunted by the ghost of Ashley. He will sleep on the beach. It's warm. Actually, still hot. All he needs is a lounge chair and a couple of dry towels to use for blankets to keep off the chill of the wind from the sea. He walks back toward the resort and finds what he needs. He has trouble getting settled, twisting around and around on the lounge chair. Never knew they were so small. He is exhausted, physically and emotionally, but his mind keeps leaping around from one thing to another like a fucking frog in a jumping contest. Like the one they read about in Honors English? Mark Twain? He gives up on sleep. He's just going to have to sit up all night and figure out what to do. The sound of the waves calms him down. Swish, swish, swish. He imagines Maribel's hand drawing fish.

He must have slept a little. It's bright, but what woke him up was not the sun but the exuberant chirping of the goddam birds. Such a racket they make. Never knew they could give so much advice: the blah, blah, blah of the babbling birds. He needs to email Vera today. He checks his watch. Good thing he's right here at Sunset Point because it's already time to begin the breakfast shift. Mierda.

When he appears on the steps of La Casona, he remembers El Greco coming into work that morning simultaneously hung over and pepped up from Ashley's pills. Marquito knows he has to pull himself together. Hopefully no drowning children to save this morning. Today he is the one who is drowning. His good friend Omar is there waiting for him. "Hey, Marquito, are you okay?" He taunts him a little. "You look like you slept on the beach, man. What's this with no shave, wrinkled uniform, bed head. Must have been some night, eh?" Marquito doesn't smile. Omar backs off. "Are you sure you're okay, man?" Marquito glances around at the tables, the buffet. Oh, God, there's Maribel. He races up the stairs, shoots through the dining room, and disappears into the kitchen.

He leaves at eleven o'clock, as soon as he can, picks up his computer from his locker, and gets permission from his boss to use the Wi-fi connection in the hospitality business lounge. Something urgent? Yeah, really important. Family matter.

He gets online and sends an email to tell Vera and Ollie what happened. Then he phones them. He can't wait. "Did you get my email?"

"Well, yes, dear, but just a few minutes ago," Vera replies.

"Vera, what should I do? Everything was going so well with Maribel. I thought I was finished with Ashley."

"Lady Ashley? It's hard to be finished with the past."

"That's what Maribel says. Oh, Vera, I need some advice. I'm totally bewildered. I'm terrified to tell Maribel. I love her so much. I'm afraid everything will blow up and our relationship will be finished."

"That's what she thought about telling you her secret. Right? But it didn't happen."

"That's true. In fact, that's when I figured out I was in love with her."

"Well, what do you conclude?" Vera asks.

"It's better to be honest?"

"Usually. In this case, yes, I think you can't hide something as big as this. Kind of like trying to hide an elephant in a bassinet."

"Maribel told me that Ashley's ghost would come back to haunt me."

"She has female intuition. Sometimes we see things that men have trouble seeing."

"Really?"

"So, tell her the truth. It may not go as badly as you think."

"But it's not just Maribel, what should I tell Ashley? What can she do with it? Him? My son? Tell me. You're a social worker."

"Let's think about that. She could give him up for adoption, but legally she needs your permission, too, if she knows where you are."

"Which she does."

"You have some rights in this too, Marquito."

"I guess that's true," he says, not having ever thought about rights to a baby before.

"Now listen carefully. I have a difficult question."

"Your questions are always difficult," he says, dreading what's coming.

"Would you ever want this baby?" she asks. "To raise it?"

"Well, I've thought about that a little. But I'm so young."

"Young is relative. Fifteen is young, but for most of human history, that's how old mothers and fathers were."

"Ashley says that she doesn't know what she will do with him. Besides she's in some kind of trouble up there. Says she wouldn't be a very good mother."

"In that case, the baby could be taken from her. In court. But that's the American way. Custody fights. Lawyers."

Marquito thinks he hears Ollie in the background saying, "I heard that."

"So, what's the alternative?" Marquito asks.

"Inquire in a very gentle way to see if she would like to consider giving the baby to you to raise here in Mexico. Tell her you feel some responsibility. But only if you want to do that. Only after you talk to Maribel."

"That's a big decision. Huge."

"Ollie says that this is how we build meaning in our lives, by the choices we make. And not to choose, is a choice in itself."

"Wow, that's deep. You are always so wise, you two. I would just like a little bit of your wisdom. Maybe I wouldn't make such a mess of things."

"It's easy to be wise about other people's problems, Marquito. You'll get your turn. For now, talk to Maribel, tell her the truth, discuss what she thinks about raising your son. If she can't have a baby, maybe she would like to raise yours. If, and only if, that's what you both want to do, then ask Ashley if she wants to give him to you to raise."

Now Marquito's mind is in a jumping frog contest again and that's way worse than fluttering butterflies. What will he say to Maribel? This is definitely not material for a text message. He has to face her in person. How should he begin? When? Where? Raise a baby? What about their plans? Her studio? His studies? Their jobs? Croak, croak, ribbit, ribbit.

He can't seem to calm down. By September he will have a son in California, soon to be raised by a manic/depressive mother who is barely competent to take care of herself, let alone a baby. His baby. He's not ready to be a father. Father? What a frightening word that is. Dripping with dedication and responsibility. Then it dawns on him how dedicated and responsible his own father has been, doing his best even in the toughest times.

At two o'clock that afternoon—he has no time to waste—he meets Maribel at the end of her morning shift, and they catch the local bus to the Paraíso Mall. He has told her only that they have something important to discuss. From the mall they cut through to the marina and walk clear around past the Dolphin Center to Iglesia San Lucas, the old mission church where he took the Mormons from Brigham Young that day. Luckily, the black iron gates are open. He's sweating profusely. Maribel looks cool. She always looks cool and fresh. She never even sweats at the grill when she's making pancakes.

The setting inside is peaceful, calm, and full of light, and Maribel tells him that she came here many times after the beating to pray and ask for God's guidance. Well, it looks like he picked the right place because if ever there was a time for God's guidance, it is now. They sit side by side in a pew in the back. At least it's cool. He is restless, conscious of his perspiration, but he composes himself, takes a deep breath, and begins, "I heard from Ashley."

Maribel looks away. She is sitting straight and still, head high, as if she's holding her breath. Maybe counting. "Go on," she says.

"I don't know how to say this so I'll just say it and get it out there. Ashley's pregnant. A baby boy will be born in September, and she says I'm the father."

Maribel keeps looking away, her eyes going from window to window, her head nodding. "And…" she says.

"That's all I know. I assumed…"

"Assumed? That she was on the pill?" She looks him straight in the face. "So, it's true. She wasn't just living with you. You slept together, too, like everyone was saying. Is that correct?" Anger resonates in her voice.

He's just starting to explain and he's already in deep shit. Her reaction is much worse than Vera predicted. What has happened to Maribel's thoughtful way of listening? Marco wavers, afraid he will lose her. "Correct. But I really never thought that…"

"Not just once, but many times?" Her unblinking eyes are boring a hole in him, and her voice has a tone he's never heard from her before.

"Yes."

"Well, it looks like she got what she wanted from you, Señor.

"A baby?"

"That's my guess. Part of her plan."

"Really? You believe that? A plan? That's what I think, too. I mean, now at least, looking back. At the time I had no idea. I really don't know how I could have been so completely stupid."

"I guess that makes two of us." Some tenderness appears in her voice for the first time. That's a relief. "Now what?"

"Ashley says she is in some kind of trouble, maybe something with the law, but I don't know for sure. She also says she doesn't think she will make a very good mother."

"So, she can put him up for adoption. At least she didn't have an abortion."

"That's what I thought she would do."

"You hoped for that?"

"No, that's not what I said. I would never want that."

"I'm sorry. I shouldn't have said that. Forgive me."

"Forgive you? I'm the one who needs forgiving. What a terrible mess I've made." His eyes are welling up; he can't help it.

She turns toward him and takes both of his hands. "Okay, what are the options? What are we going to do?"

"We? You're still willing to say we?" he asks, fighting a lump in his throat, surprised.

"Unless you want to crawl back to Ashley like a wounded iguana. She could probably get some immigration papers for you now, you know."

"No, no, no. That never even crossed my mind. I don't want to go back to the U.S. that way. Or any other way. I don't want anything to do with that crazy woman."

"Okay. Sorry again. My apologies. But she is the mother of your son."

"Solamente esto. Nothing more."

"So back to my question: What are we going to do?"

"I talked to Vera. She thinks Ashley could be proven unfit to keep the child. She says I have rights, too. But instead of a legal fight, Vera says I should inquire, very gently, to see if Ashley might be interested in giving up the child."

"To?"

"To me. Well, to us if you are still willing to have me, but only if you are willing to help me raise it."

"Him."

"Yes, of course, I meant him. She wants to name him Angelito."

"Wow, you're really asking a lot. I guess you know that, right? We're really young. Are you ready for this?"

"I know I am not ready. That's why I need your help. I think we could do it."

Maribel slips down on her knees, resting on the little bench provided for prayer. She looks back over her shoulder at him. "Don't just sit there staring at me, either go back out the way you came in or get down here with me. Because if it's we, that includes God. Got it? That's the only way I would know how to do it."

Marquito slips down onto his knees. He doesn't know what to say to God. It's been a while. But to tell the truth, he'd rather talk to God right now than to have to talk to Maribel about this baby. In moments like this, he decides, it's best to keep silent. Silence reigns. When Maribel gets back up off her knees, raises her downcast eyes, and makes the sign of the cross, he knows the silence is over, so he asks, "What do you think?"

"I think I'm in a tough spot. If I agree to help you raise your son, and I have to get up every morning to face someone who reminds me of Ashley—I mean nothing against green eyes and red hair, but if that's the deal—it's not going to be easy for me. But if he looks like you, and we can call him Angelito, it could be nice. I mean a huge challenge, but actually fun."

"He will remind us of Ashley, no matter what he looks like, and he will be bringing up painful memories we can't avoid. Like you said, there will be memories, but it's just how we deal with them."

"Did I say that? Sounds so simple, doesn't it?"

Maribel stands and slides out into the aisle. Marquito puts an arm on her shoulder and starts to hug her, but she pulls away. "One more thing," she says, biting her lower lip and pointing an index finger at him. "Ultimately, this has to be your decision."

"Why my decision? What happened to we?" he asks.

"Because one of the parties here, namely me, is too involved emotionally to make an objective, unbiased decision." Her eyes are big, sparkling.

"What do you mean?" he asks, a little confused and puzzled.

"This may be the only way we can have a baby. I think I want to do this. I want this baby."

16

A FAMILY WEDDING AND A LONG TRIP

The next day, Marco leaves a little early after a slow breakfast shift to slip over to the Hospitality Center again to use the Wi-fi connection. July, being hot and humid, is the beginning of low occupancy season at Sunset Point Resort so it is quiet and private in there today. He is eager for some air-conditioned relief after perspiring since sunup. Besides, he wants to get an email off to Ashley to determine if she will consider giving the baby to him instead of going through adoption procedures with some perfect strangers in the U.S., a process that she may have already begun. Time is passing quickly, and the baby, his baby, he reminds himself, will be born in just a couple of months.

It takes him longer than he wants to compose the email because he has to make a lot of changes in the wording before he gets it the way he wants it. He is surprised when he hears back from Ashley within a half hour.

Dear Marco:

I was really relieved to hear from you because I didn't know if you ever checked that old email address anymore. It is good to know that I haven't lost touch with you, amigo. I know how shocked you must have been with my news about the baby, and I appreciate your telling me what you are thinking.

Here's the deal. I was involved in some protests before I left Berkeley. I can't say much because I am in the final stages of a plea bargain, but in a nutshell, members of an evangelical right-to-life group shot a doctor on the steps of an abortion clinic near here, and some of my friends retaliated by burning down their church. Not a nice thing to do, to burn down a church, you know, but they had it coming. I was among the accused, so that's part of the reason I was trying to run away to Mexico although my parents didn't know about the church until they brought me back to California. To make a long story short, my father hired some high-priced lawyers to get my sentence for arson reduced to three years, which is a lot less than it could have been, but look where that leaves the baby: no mother or father. My parents won't help out because they said they would have no part in raising some black-haired, brown-eyed, dark-skinned Mexican. Can you believe that? They told me to tell that Mexican boy he can have his damn baby back.

That's why it didn't take me long to think over your offer to send the baby to Mexico and let you raise him as your own. That's really nice of you, and makes me feel like you don't completely hate me after my rude departure. I admit I got a little manic in those last few weeks. Anyway, the answer is yes.

Here's what I suggest. My parents are going to be so happy to get rid of this baby that they will drive down to Tijuana with him—I already checked this out with my father—and will bring his papers with him as well as the clothes and blankets I've been given by my friends. So if you can get a ride up somehow, you can meet at the restaurant in Parque Moreles and pick him up. Kind of sounds like a drug deal, but it's a baby, our baby, and it will be perfectly legal.

If this works out, it will make me very happy, and believe me, there hasn't been much for me to be happy about lately. To tell the truth, I've been very depressed. I never thought I would end up in prison. Not the life I had planned.

I'm glad that you met someone who likes you enough to take on the responsibility of raising a child you've had with another woman. I hope you can make a happy home together. It is what I have always wanted.

Fondly,
Ashley

Marco reads over Ashley's email three times. He finds a touching sadness in it. Wow! Going to prison? He could have been going with her. Who would not be depressed? He recalls how depressed she got when he was telling her about the Mexican War and she had to escape by going to sleep. Now he feels sorrier for her than ever. But the good news is that it's not going to take a lot of persuading to convince Ashley to let him have the baby. Thank God for her racist parents. Maribel would say that this is the grace of God bringing good out of bad. In any case, it's just a matter of working out the details now. He sends off a brief note to Vera and Ollie, texts Maribel, and then hurries back to Sunset Point to catch her when she gets off at two o'clock to share the details of the good news.

In the next few weeks, Marco and Maribel discover that they suddenly have a lot to do. In early August, they take the bus up to Todos Santos to tell Abuela and Abuelo their news. Maribel's grandparents offer to drive them up to Tijuana, a long, tedious journey up the full length of the Baja Península, but they are eager to be the first to see that baby.

Maribel tells Marco that they ought to get married if they are going to be parents. Well, it's not the first time a baby has hurried up a wedding. When he tells her that he worried she would just keep postponing, she smiles and says she always wanted to marry him, but she was afraid he would run off with another woman who could give him a baby. But now, no worries, that's already happened. Sometimes Maribel has a barbed wit, and he loves it when she skewers him like that.

In Todos Santos, she introduces him to Padre Carlos, who can't seem to stop telling Marco what a special person Maribel is, and Marco says he already knows that, but the priest insists that he is only beginning to grasp how special she is. The most resilient person he has ever known. Marco thanks him for all that he did for her, and Maribel asks if he could officiate at a very small wedding, as she and Marco have discussed, in the Misión de Santa Rosa de Todos Santos. He says he has always dreamed about such a wedding for her, and that he would be happy to do so. Marco wants to make sure that small is big enough to include his parents. They pick September 15 for the wedding date. Oh, my god, that could actually be Angelito's birthday. A baby born on their wedding day? That would be awkward to explain. Why does everything have to be so confused?

The next day, after returning to Cabo, and with wedding plans set, Marco and Maribel begin to look for a house to rent, with a bedroom for baby Angelito and some extra space for Maribel's studio. They are delighted when they find a partly-furnished, white stucco rental property with a red tile roof. It has a wall out front with pink bougainvillea growing over it and a black iron gate that opens onto a small veranda. Nothing fancy, but comfortable, near the bus line and not too far from her mother's place. It seems that everyone is volunteering to help care for that new baby.

Vera and Ollie are enjoying the warm, summer days of mid-August in Colorado. Katie scarcely needs Ollie's index finger when she walks now, but she hangs onto it anyway. Such simple joy she brings to that man's heart, tagging along with him everywhere he goes, the younger generation replacing the old, he says. Ollie has done a lot of landscaping around Peter and Amanda's house in Boulder, and it really looks quite lovely with its spreading maple trees and back yard of green grass. Katie has become a master gardener, unafraid of mud, slugs, or angle worms.

Today, Vera is checking through her calendar to see what is scheduled for the rest of August and on into the fall. Ellen and Damon are coming up during the third week of September to go "leaf-peeping," though no one in Colorado uses that archaic expression from Vermont. The aspen trees will be dressed to the nines in shimmering gold, so Ellen and Damon have invited the parents for a weekend at the Ritz in Beaver Creek to enjoy the leaves and the crisp fall air. They'll just have to see how Ollie does with the additional altitude.

Vera's computer makes a soft ping to alert her to a new incoming email from Marquito who is full of excitement about the wedding, the house, and the trip to pick up the baby.

"We've got to see that baby, Ollie."

"What baby?" he asks.

"Baby Angelito. Marquito's Little Angel."

"Oh, that baby. When are we due to go down there again?"

"We always go in November around Thanksgiving, remember? It's time to book the flight." She flips her calendar ahead to November and counts the weeks. "Angelito should be almost nine weeks old by then."

"November, eh? If I last that long."

She gives him a scowl. "Meaning what?"

"Well, that I'm really not very keen on going back to Mexico."

"Really? I think you'll do just fine."

"Like last time? Looking up at the moon from the floor of the restaurant? Getting all stented out in a Mexican hospital?"

"Looks like they did a good job."

"True, but I hate to push my luck. Maybe you could go by yourself."

"Which would be enough to give me a heart attack right there. I don't do alone anymore, dear. Besides, we need to check up on all of those people we gave the money to."

"I thought we weren't going to do that." Ollie rakes a hand through his white hair and produces one of his rare smiles. "You know, dear, that is just one of the best things we ever did, giving that money. So little to us, so much to them."

"I didn't really mean we'd be checking up on them; it's more a matter of curiosity. Besides, what about that baby? Aren't you curious about what that baby's going to look like?"

"What baby?"

"Jesus, Ollie, you're really losing your marbles."

Marco's parents travel across the Sea of Cortéz on the ferry to attend the wedding in September. His mother said she would rather meet the bride than see the baby. She can see the baby later. Right now, she wants to meet the girl who is gracious enough to marry her son after he got himself into such hot water. Just how hot the water was, Marco hasn't told her, and he assures Maribel that his mother doesn't need to know her whole sad story either unless she wants to tell it. Maribel agrees that for now she prefers to have her future mother-in-law think she is pure and perfect.

Maribel's grandparents and Marco pick up his parents at the ferry dock in La Paz and take them to Todos Santos. That evening they have a get-acquainted dinner at the little restaurant underneath the small apartment where Doña Conchita and Don Pedro live. The restaurant has been reserved for the wedding party and a long table has been set up out back on the veranda under the tile roof, in a cozy spot overlooking the wall with flowering vines, the palm tree, the cactus garden, and Saint Francis in his niche. The angels sit quietly on their shelves and the lanterns are illuminated. In addition to Doña Conchita and Don Pedro, there is Maribel's mother, Señora Alejandra, and Maribel's two sisters. Marco's mother and father, Señora Lupita and Señor Luis Miguel, are introduced to everyone, including a special high school friend that Maribel wanted to invite.

Marco sits quietly listening to the table talk, his mind adrift, his attention, flitting once again like a butterfly, from one conversation to the next. He hears his father talking to Don Pedro about how he produces the bronze castings for his larger sculptures. Maribel, her high school friends and her sisters seem to be deep into clothes and shoes. The mothers and the grandmother are bonding over the difficulties of raising children, remarking nonetheless on the loss they feel as parents when the children grow up. Marco notes how these groups seem to have formed almost automatically, and he wonders at the ease and natural flow of adult conversation, so polite and refined. Good god, is he an adult now, too? He is not really a part of any of these conversations, and his mind, when he is not listening, is free to worry, which seems to have become his main specialty lately. How will everyone handle that long trip up the Baja next week to pick up Angelito? Will the car hold up? What if Ashley changes her mind? She's that way. Unpredictable. She has a right to change her mind if she wants. What if her parents grow fond of that cute little Mexican baby and decide to keep him to raise him themselves? What if he's not a cute little Mexican baby at all? What if he has red hair combed already into an asymmetrical bob? Maribel stills his tapping fingers and asks, "Where are you, mi amor? Overwhelmed?"

"Someone has to do the worrying," he says.

"Not tonight. Just enjoy the party."

The next day is for sleeping in, wandering around town, exploring the gallery, holding private conversations on the benches at the plaza, and getting acquainted and reacquainted under clear blue sky. It's hot here, too, but agreeable. Nothing is rushed. Time stands still in Todos Santos. Marco glances at his watch, thinking it must surely be three o'clock, but he sees that it is barely past one. He has prepared lengthy apologies for neglecting his parents, but they brush them off, telling him how happy they are for him and how cute he and Maribel look together. His father admits that he did nearly the same thing himself years ago, neglecting his parents for weeks, when he went off to the U.S. with two small children. Maybe that was his own declaration of independence. His mother tells him how they agonized over the decision to come back to Mexico because they knew how upsetting and confusing it was going to be for him. She says that she never stopped praying for him and that she knew he would come through the storm, but that it was difficult for her not knowing where he was or what he was doing. Marco says that it's good that she didn't know too much about that storm, but that he is actually glad to be back in Mexico now and that he would never have met Maribel if they hadn't returned. He says he feels like his old self again around her and that in spite of spending those years in the US, he knows he's Mexican, especially when he is here in Todos Santos with Doña Conchita and Don Pedro. He says he's really in love with Maribel and his parents say they can tell.

On Saturday, the day of the wedding, Marco joins the families gathered outside at the front of the Misión de Santa Rosa de Todos Santos waiting for Maribel to walk across the Plaza with Doña Conchita and Don Pedro. A small crowd has gathered at the edge of the plaza. Apparently, everyone in Todos Santos knows Maribel, and they are all here to wish the beautiful bride well on her wedding day and take a look at the groom. As Marco stands there with his father, he overhears the muffled words of a young girl saying something about "a tall handsome hombre" as another says, "with the smile of a soap opera actor from Univision."

His father smiles fondly at him and says, "They're talking about you, son."

"Not me."

"Who else then? You are the center of their attention."

How does this happen? He wonders. People always talking about him. This time he doesn't mind.

Earlier that morning, a mysterious delivery arrived by car from someone who said they worked at Sunset Beach Resort in Cabo San Lucas. They left things for the bride and groom at the church. For Marquito there is a card of congratulations with a hand-written message addressed to "Our Hero" and saying: "We are happy for Maribel but sad that we are not in here place." It is from Verónica and nine other women from the concierge staff and front desk, who sign as "The Ladies of the Lobby." Another card, this one for Maribel from the breakfast waiters, in the handwriting of Omar, says: "Come back soon because we cannot survive long without your smile." Inside a small box, Maribel finds a floral crown of paper bougainvillea in a pink so natural and crafted so well that the flowers could be mistaken for real. A small card says simply "Felicitaciones" and is signed by Carmelita, the lady who sweeps the hallways. Maribel puts it on immediately, noting that it will complement her dress, as Abuela helps her adjust it for the right effect. Abuelo has crafted gold rings for Maribel and Marquito to exchange during the ceremony, and Abuela has created a small bridal bouquet of daisies with a cascade of pastel ribbons.

Everyone who enters the church passes Don Pedro's unusual sculpture of the Sagrada Família. When the service begins, and the bride and groom are standing before Padre Carlos, he reminds the two families of their own sacred vows, now intertwined even more closely in the marriage of Marco and Maribel. Marco glances fondly at Maribel in her simple lavender dress; no fancy wedding gown for her. Her long black hair is wound around and pinned up and the smooth, clear skin on the back of her neck is exposed.

The luster on her lips reflects the candlelight. Her whole being radiates a natural beauty of body and spirit. She gazes exclusively at Marco now with her sparkling brown eyes, and she seems to be wearing a perpetual smile reserved only for him. He catches her gaze and locks it into his own. Her calmness surrounds him and gives him peace and a quiet mind that he never imagined possible. But he is having trouble convincing himself that he is actually standing right here on this spot getting married to her in this moment of time. Still as he looks at her, he knows there is no other place he would rather be and no woman he would rather marry. The words of the priest are falling all around him like pattering rain, and he is so lost in the joy of the moment that Maribel has to nudge him to respond to the priest's question, which he has just barely heard, something about what he loves about Maribel. He doesn't need to think that over and says, "She is steady like a rock in a restless sea." The priest smiles, like he is surprised at such poetry coming from a waiter. And when the priest asks Maribel the same question, she says, "Marco is sweet and kind, the way a man should be." And when Padre Carlos asks them why they want to get married, Marco says, "I am my true self when I am with her," and Maribel says, "He's my gentle hero." They exchange the rings and repeat what Padre Carlos tells them to say, and then the priest does some magical thing that makes them married and showers them with blessings and benedictions and good wishes. They kiss and it's over.

When the celebrations begin to die down that evening, Marquito and Maribel slip away. Abuelo and Abuela have arranged for a room for them at none other than the famous Hotel California. They climb the stairs to their spacious, traditionally decorated room and collapse into each other's arms. As he begins to kiss her, Maribel says, "Wait." Wait? For god's sake he's been waiting for months. Enough of this old-fashioned romance, this illusion of two virgins going to bed together for the first time on their wedding night.

But before he can protest, Maribel takes her little traveling bag with her into the bathroom and throws him a smile over her shoulder as she closes the door. And so, he waits. He sits uncomfortably on the one small wooden chair. The second-floor room seems a little stuffy. Too hot. He goes over to the window and opens it for a few minutes. Then he closes it again. Too noisy. Besides, they need their privacy. He sits on the edge of the bed, bounces a few times, and then goes back to the chair. He wishes he had a book, but he didn't bring one because he didn't think he would be reading on his wedding night. Maybe a book on making love? Let's see, it says here on page twenty-three... He's sure it will be completely different with Maribel. He's making himself nervous. He slips off his clothes and sits in the chair in his tee shirt and briefs.

When she finally opens the bathroom door and steps out, he is stunned. She stands before him in a skimpy, soft pink shorty nightgown, smiling that one and only smile of hers. He is overwhelmed by her beauty. Her hair is done up different and she has a little blush on her cheeks. The sheen of the pink gown glimmers slightly against her brown skin. She's put on her floral crown again and has given it a jaunty tilt. Elegante. He had always thought she was cute, and naturally he has seen her a lot in her sexy little turquoise bikini, but this is different. She rotates around for a 360 view, faces him again, and then strikes a pose like a model. She's beautiful, drop-dead gorgeous, like an ancient goddess come to life, beckoning him to approach her. All he can say, as he rises from his chair, is "Maribel, mi corazón, I just want to look at you."

"That would be disappointing on our wedding night, mi amor, especially after waiting for so long. Thank you for the compliment, but I hope you will get over it."

"No, I mean linda, truly beautiful."

"I was dreaming about this night when I first saw you in your wet underwear, the day you saved the little boy from drowning. I never thought it would happen to us, but now here you are in your underwear again." She blushes and covers her grin with one hand. "Nothing could be more perfect."

He looks down at himself and they both laugh as they rush at each other to embrace. They fall onto the bed in each other's arms.

"I hate to remove this beautiful gown," he says.

"And you know how I love you in your underwear," she teases.

"But..."

"Yes, but..."

And when they are finally naked together, he is gentle and hesitant with her even though she tells him everything will be all right."

Marco abandons his hesitancy as he unleashes the stored-up passion of many months. They try a lot of things, actually, going right to the edge and then waiting so they can try something else. He should have known that Maribel would be a creative love artist, too. He feels sensations with her he has never felt before, knowing for sure now, as she has been saying all along, that there is supposed to be a difference between love and sex. Maribel has been right about a lot of things, and he hates to admit it, even about waiting. When they have finished, they lie still next to each other, satisfied and exhausted, happy beyond imagination.

"More?" she asks.

"I think I need a little intermission."

"To get ready for the second act?"

The honeymoon in La Paz, though brief, is blissful, with long walks along the waterfront on the broad mosaic-patterned malecón and delicious meals in quaint restaurants where they are the guests. When Marco gets back to Sunset Point, he is anxious to firm up the plans to pick up Angelito. His manager at work has been sympathetic to his need for time off to get married, but when he asks him in all seriousness for time the following week to drive to Tijuana to pick up his baby, Marco is sure he is having a credibility problem. When he tries to explain, the boss tells him that it is no one's business and that if he needs more time off, he should take it. "For sure you must know that everyone around the resort is happy for you and Maribel, and they're all hoping the baby will look like you."

The trip to Tijuana is long and tedious, as expected, no doubt about it, with minimal stops along the way to eat and to pull off the road to sleep. The car is filled with cases of bottled water and bags of healthful snacks, and several pillows and light blankets. Marco and Maribel have second thoughts about whether it was such a good idea to bring their grandparents on this long, difficult journey. Marco has brought along his US driver's license so he can help with the driving, but still, it is a long, arduous trip. The navigation is not difficult, though, because there is really only one road, Route 1, up through Loreto, Santa Rosália, Lázaro Cárdenas, and Ensenada, but that road seems endless, like a new definition of infinity. First Maribel asks, and then Abuela, "Will this road never end?" until the frivolous question grows serious as the answer seems to be no.

Finally, after two long days of driving, they arrive at Rosarito, the town nearest Tijuana, an easy morning's ride for tomorrow, and they pull into a shabby motel where they can rent one room with two queen beds and sleep stretched out instead of all curled up in the car along the road.

It will be a much-needed night of rest before they meet Ashley's parents at Parque Moreles the next day at noon.

On the following morning, they are at the park by eleven thirty, sitting at a table outdoors at the restaurant where Ashley told everybody to meet. It is a nice park with a zoo and a waterfall and equipment for kids. Don Pedro folds his arms across his chest and rests his beard there as he settles himself for a little nap, still weary from the long drive. Doña Conchita chats with Maribel who appears calm and prepared, the look of motherhood already on her face. Marco wonders how they will recognize Ashley's parents, and then he remembers that Maribel met them that day when they were wandering the beach with the photo. The dad sounds nice enough, but he wonders what that mother is going to be like.

He tries to picture himself being a father. He only has a few minutes left before that baby shows up to change his life forever. He's not sure he will know how to hold a baby. There weren't any babies in his family; he was the baby. Now he will be giving the bottle and changing diapers. He can't quite picture himself doing that. It's all happening too fast.

He starts to worry that Ashley has changed her mind. He hasn't been able to check his email for a few days. What if she's told him the deal is off? She's like that. He blurts out, "What if they don't show up?" Maribel frowns and resumes her conversation with Doña Conchita. He wonders what Ashley is doing today. How does she feel about giving up her baby? What do you pack to go to prison? He feels sorry for her.

So, they sit in silence for another fifteen minutes, each wearing a worried look of their own design, until finally Maribel spots Ashley's parents walking up to the restaurant looking a little lost. The father is carrying a baby blanket that to Marco looks way too small to have a baby in it. Maribel signals to Marco and her family to come up and greet them.

After cordial introductions, everyone huddles around as the blanket is unfolded and one by one they get their first glimpse of Angelito. He has medium brown skin, neither dark nor light, and his eyes are dark, not green. His hair is black, but as the rays of the noonday sun hit it, there is an unmistakable trace of orange. The glint of the color makes a highlight, nothing vibrant, in fact hardly noticeable, but a shading that makes his hair beautiful. Young as he is, he has a lot of hair, his most distinguishing feature. Marco glances over to see if Maribel is okay with the baby, and he sees maternal delight spreading across her face as she gently receives the tiny bundle from Ashley's sedate, well-dressed father. Everyone is smiling except Ashley's mother, a skinny, nervous, twitchy-looking woman, who has suddenly become very businesslike, apparently without even a pang of regret at giving up her grandson. She begins pulling papers out of a tan file folder and is reviewing them with Marco. He finds the birth certificate, the release for adoption, and the permission to take the baby across the border, all signed by Ashley. If nothing else, these parents are organized. No doubt the father's high-priced lawyers prepared everything. Ashley's mother also hands over, with unguarded disdain, a large plastic bag of baby clothes and blankets. As they exchange pleasantries, thanks, and best wishes for a safe journey home, Marco asks about Ashley. Her mother says that she is fine and in good physical health, but that she is struggling with postpartum depression, as so many young mothers seem to these days. This week has been especially difficult. They all shake hands—Ashley's family does not hug—and as her father is holding Maribel's hand he says, "Haven't we met?"

Taken aback, Maribel only manages to say "Perhaps," but when she smiles, the father knows who it is.

"I'll never forget those dimples," he says. "You helped us find our daughter." He reaches for his wallet. "You'll have some expenses now. May I help?" Maribel holds up both palms.

"No," Marco says firmly. We both have jobs. We can manage, but thank you for thinking about that." Absent-mindedly he shakes the father's hand again. "We don't want to keep you now. Thank you again for your trouble in bringing us Angelito." It's time to get out of here. The father looks like he could change his mind about the baby. But not that mother.

The trip home doesn't seem as long. Angelito sleeps most of the way, awakening only for a bottle and a diaper change. Maribel and Abuela came well prepared for that. He can't take his eyes off of Maribel holding that little baby. He notices the miniature-size fingernails, the little dark eyelashes. He suddenly realizes that a baby is a miracle. And Maribel a mother? How miraculous is that? Like she says: In Mexico, Marquito, things that can't happen still happen.

17

A FORGOTTEN NOTE

In October, Vera and Ollie are still debating whether to go to Sunset Point for their fixed week time share in November as they usually do. On the one hand, Vera would really like to see everybody and the new baby, and she wants to encourage Ollie to go if he is capable of doing so; on the other hand, she doesn't want to be the one responsible for having pushed him out of his comfort zone if something happens to him while he is there. It seems that in their old age they are constantly sitting on the horns of one dilemma after another, like riding a bull that doesn't know whether to go left or right. But in the end, it's not Vera who persuades Ollie to come to Cabo, it is Marco. When he learns that Vera and Ollie might not be returning, he emails Ollie directly and tells him that he is arranging for a fancy dinner party on the beach for them at which time all of the recipients of their gifts will stop by to greet them one by one. Also, Marco has invited them for dinner to his new house, the place he and Maribel are renting now, to spend some time with Angelito and to meet Maribel's grandparents. He can't spoil those plans. He needs to go. Ollie negotiates their stay down to one week instead of the usual two and Vera agrees that this might be best. She books the flight online that day, grabbing the last two seats together.

Ollie and Vera's arrival at Sunset Point in November is met with the usual clamor. Óscar and Sebastián take their luggage and Verónica has arranged their express check-in, so that in no time at all they are in their seventh floor one-bedroom paradise overlooking the resort, the beach, a section of the mountain range, and the Sea of Cortéz. Vera never tires of that view. Ollie seems fine and he usually does better at sea level anyway, at least when he's not having a heart attack. By the next morning they are settled into their routine: eating fresh fruit and granola at La Casona, reading the Los Cabos Daily News, and taking a little nap after breakfast by the pool. In the afternoon, they take a cab to the Paraíso Mall and go visit the little shop called Melody, where they bought Marco the silver ring he gave to Maribel. What a story that was. Marco was so excited the day he gave Maribel the ring that he had to phone them twice on Skype. They stay in town for an early dinner at María Corona and come back to the resort for decaf and dessert at La Casona.

Maribel brings Angelito out to the resort the next morning to meet Vera and Ollie because she can't wait for the night of the party. Ollie goes on and on about how cute he is with that brown skin, Marco's eyes, and that little tinge of red in his hair, which is still awaiting its first cutting. The week starts to go by fast, almost too fast. The special Thanksgiving dinner with turkey and dressing is served graciously on Thursday night for the appreciative Americans, and Marco makes all of the necessary arrangements for the dinner on the beach for Vera and Ollie on Friday.

And what a party it is. Ollie and Vera watch their step as they carefully make their way along the improvised walkway in the sand lighted by flickering candles protected in brown paper bags from the light breeze. Pink bougainvillea blossoms strewn along the walk lead them to folding chairs around a table set with a white cloth and legions of silverware and crystal. In the dark, the sea makes only a soft swish, interspersed with those precious moments of silence. When they have finished their coconut shrimp, corn soup, and tamarind salad, Vera and Ollie begin to receive their guests.

Rosita brings the two boys, Fernando and Alfredo, months older and inches taller, carrying their new laptops. Polite, scrubbed, and shined as usual, the boys share a few words of their expanded English vocabulary. Their mother says that the money, secure in savings accounts for their education, seems to have influenced their improved performance at school. Rosita got a promotion, and her husband has his own food truck business and is doing well serving workers near building sites.

Fifteen minutes later—Marquito surely has this thing organized—Daniella arrives with the girls, Cenia and Blanca, dressed in outfits that Vera remembers bringing on her last visit to Cabo in February, clothes almost too small now. Daniella has moved into a bigger and newer house, with only two girls to a room, bless their hearts. Greatly relieved, her mother sends her blessings. Her deceased sister's husband visits his daughters more frequently now, and he feels comfortable to let his new girlfriend join them. If that works out and they can settle into a place of their own, they may take the girls. Daniella has no immediate prospects for a husband and says she's in no hurry after the last one.

Solomón and Isabella bring baby Susette who has sprouted into a toddler walking everywhere now although currently out of her league in the loose sand. Solomón assures them he will marry Isabella soon, but they are so happy she says she hardly cares. They plan to start Suzette in a private preschool when she is three; meanwhile as soon as she actually starts talking, she's going to learn her numbers and colors in both Spanish and English. Solomón's job is steady and Isabella does nails only two days a week, but her schedule is full on those days. The joy of their lives, Suzette still makes those funny faces but now the sounds imitate words. No further health problems, gracias a Dios.

Sebastián the bellman has taken a trip to Mexico City to visit his parents, and his colleague Óscar bought an engagement ring for his girl. Verónica has two boyfriends now but she can't decide which one she likes best. She confesses in a low whisper that she spent some of her funds on clothes. Ernesto, the former towel boy, a waiter now, continues to study English, though seeming quite fluent. He says that if Marco gets promoted again, he wants his job. Carmelita has fixed her teeth, they look beautiful, but her mother passed away before they could do hers. Ollie tells Vera that he is surprised at how little of the money has been spent and she says she noticed that, too, but that many of the recipients seem happier and more confident just knowing they have it. Vera can tell from the smile on Ollie's face how happy he is.

On Saturday night, Marco is a little nervous as he greets the guests at the street outside. Maribel calms him down and asks him what could possibly go wrong and he agrees; she's right, what could happen? Such lovely people. Doña Conchita and Don Pedro, who have driven down from Todos Santos, have picked up Vera and Ollie at the resort and brought them to the house.

Although the house is modest and plain on the outside, when Vera and Ollie step through the black iron gate, cross the veranda, and enter through the carved wooden door, they are struck by how Maribel's cheery artistic touch is everywhere. A love seat and two wooden chairs painted blue are arranged to maximize open space, walls are freshly painted white, and in each room at least one wall has a bright color, orange, yellow, pink.

Maribel's portfolio of art work of fish-inspired abstractions is making its way up onto the walls, sometimes framed, but more often held in place at the four corners by architect's pins, so it can be easily rearranged for the addition of some new work. Doña Conchita has run a new series of the butterfly etching and has given a framed copy to the newlyweds, and Don Pedro has made a new casting of an older sculpture, a favorite of Maribel's with all sorts of benevolent fantasy creatures, that sits on a pedestal guarding the entryway.

"Sorry. It's beginning to look like a gallery," Maribel apologizes, but Marco is quick to say that he loves what she creates so much, that he has to have every piece up somewhere. Vera and Ollie keep wandering through each room asking Doña Conchita about the fish motif in Maribel's work and the butterflies in her own, and they are curious about the mingling of human and non-human figures in the work of Don Pedro. The older folks become instant friends, who act like they have known each other in some previous life and are merely four genial souls getting reacquainted. Maribel asks Vera and Ollie to pick out one of her drawings to take back home with them, and she fetches a mailing tube to keep it from getting crushed on the plane.

When Angelito wakes up from his nap, he is the star of the circus. He can't do a whole lot yet, but everyone just fixes their eyes on him like he is the most precious and amazing child in the whole world. Everyone has a comment. "Such a cute nose," Vera says. "Look at all of that hair," Ollie adds. "I can't believe those miraculous little finger nails," Abuela comments and Abuelo says, "I swear he has a little mustache. Sí, sí, maybe growing up to look like Pancho Villa." Angelito grasps the blue and yellow rattles that Maribel has made from household objects, but he can't quite shake them, at least not intentionally. It is not exactly Cirque de Soleil yet, but Ollie says that a young baby before an audience of loving eyes is still the greatest show on earth. "May I hold him?" he asks. Angelito quickly snuggles into a cozy spot hanging over Ollie's shoulder. He walks around with him like that, gently patting the baby's back, while the food is being set out on the table.

Dinner is a communal effort with guacamole and salsa prepared by Maribel as an appetizer, tamales and chili rellenos sent over by Maribel's mother, and rice pudding with raisins and cinnamon brought down in a cooler by the grandparents who also brought galletas, assorted traditional sugar cookies sent from the restaurant below their apartment. During the dinner, Ollie asks, "Can Vera and I be honorary great grandparents?" and Marco tells them, "You already are." It is a wonderful, festive time together, full of jubilation and the clinking of glasses in toasts to happiness. Angelito has cooperated by going back to sleep without a whimper.

Singing drifts in from the open front door. As the guests make their way onto the veranda, they find outside on the street a little band of musicians with guitars of various sizes, bongo drums, two violins, and a trumpet. "I believe we are being serenaded," Maribel says. "Listen, it's one of my old favorites, a ranchera." The sad song cascades through the cool evening air.

"Even if you don't know the Spanish," Ollie says, "that mournful melody by itself is enough to make you want to bawl."

"Marco," Maribel whispers to him, when the musicians have finished their third number and have grown silent, "you need to pay them."

"I already did."

"You hired them? To come by here tonight for our party?"

"Sí, mi amor, Marco replies. "¿Es un problema?"

"You are so romantic," she beams back at him.

The air is filled with repetitions of gracias and de nada as the musicians wander away down the street into the dark.

When the dishes are cleared and the guests are sipping their coffee and finishing up the last of the galletas, Maribel comes in from the bedroom with a small envelope in her hand, the shape of a thank-you note, with Marco's name on it. "I almost forgot," she says, giving the envelope to Marco. "I found this among the blankets that Ashley sent. I hadn't thought to unpack them until today, now that it is growing a little cooler at night."

Marco sets it down in front of his dessert plate, a little embarrassed and disturbed.

"No, read it, Marco," Maribel insists. "I'm sure it is a lovely little thank-you note for your agreeing to raise Angelito. I'm sorry I didn't remember it until now. Go on, open it, and read it to us all." She sits back down in her place beside him and puts one hand on his back as if to look over his shoulder.

Marco opens the envelope, takes out the note, and swallows the last of his cookie with a sip of coffee. He reads the first line to himself but then, quite suddenly, he spreads an open hand across his face and passes the note over to Vera. "I can't read this. I can't believe it's true."

Vera glances at the note and a look of shock registers even on the face of the old retired social worker. "What shall I do?" she asks, rubbing the back of her neck.

"Read it," Marco says, his voice cracking. "Everyone in this room is going to have to know about this note sooner or later. I just know I can't read it."

Vera clears her throat and reads.

Dear Marco,

By the time you receive this, I will be gone from this earth. The reality of spending three years in prison has knocked me down in the last few days, and I can't pull myself up.

I can't sleep at night and when I get up in the morning, I just stare out the window and cry. The slightest thing makes me cry. My parents are at wits end trying to take care of me and the baby, too. They will be free of the baby when they deliver him to you in Tijuana tomorrow, and when they return home, they will be free of me, too.

The only bright thing in my life is to know that you will be raising our son, Angelito.

Ashley

The guests are dazed and the shock has created an abrupt silence that no one knows how to break. Marco blinks back the hot tears that fill his eyes, tears of sadness, but also anger. How could she do this? Send such devastating news in a note buried in some baby blankets? Doesn't she ever care about what she's doing to other people? Maribel rests a hand on Marco's arm, Ollie wipes his lips with his napkin, Doña Conchita fumbles with the glasses hanging around her neck, and Vera folds the note up and puts it back in its envelope. Still, no one says anything. There is no eye contact, not even the dismayed shaking of heads. Frozen silence. The only sound is of breathing. Finally, Don Pedro, tugging absent-mindedly on his beard, says, "Maybe it would help if we all joined hands to remember Ashley." Each person takes the hand of the one next, and Marco soon feels himself encircled by their concern, their silent love. At least it helps him to calm down. Finally, he blurts out, "She always made me feel sorry for her. And I always did. I guess that's what she wants now." What he doesn't say is how annoyed he is by her relentless and reckless self-centeredness, even in her death. Everything always planned for maximum effect to play on someone else's emotions.

People begin to talk softly, trying to find their way back to some normal conversation, but it doesn't work. Like it or not, the party is over. Guests mill about taking the last of the dishes and cups from the table to the little kitchen. Vera and Ollie thank Maribel and Marco for their hospitality and assure them once again that they are delighted to see them married and happy in their own home. Vera whispers to them that it's going to be okay and that things will work out. Maribel remembers to thank Abuela for the rice pudding. Marquito hugs Vera and embraces Ollie with a thump on his back and tells them how grateful he is for their turning his life around. Maribel thanks them for being so generous to her and her husband, not quite comfortable yet, with that word *husband*. Marquito feels a lump expanding in his throat as he watches everyone saying good-bye. It's hard for him to swallow. He wonders what Vera and Ollie must be feeling, knowing that this is most likely the last time they will be in Cabo. They can't help but feel sad, saying good-bye. It wasn't supposed to end like this.

Doña Conchita and Don Pedro, as promised, will take Vera and Ollie back to Sunset Point Resort before they drive back to Todos Santos. There is one more round of hugs before the elders slide awkwardly into their places in the car that travelled the length of the Baja Península with that note. Marquito doesn't want them to go. He has a question he wants to ask Vera. He wants to rush out to the car and stop them, but it is too late. Ollie rolls down the back seat window and tries to smile as he waves, and Vera blows random kisses lovingly into the night as the car pulls away. Standing on the veranda waving good-bye, Marco puts one arm over Maribel's shoulder and finds himself speechless as he stares straight ahead at the space where the car was parked.

How odd it was that he should meet Vera and Ollie at all, traveling from so far away as they did to be seated at his breakfast table at La Casona, and then for no good reason at all, taking a liking to him. Such generous and good-hearted people, giving their money away like that. But it was the meaning behind the money that made the difference: helping some worthless Mexican waiter feel valued. Why did these beautiful old butterflies flutter into his life and why are they vanishing now? Can someone explain that to him? Will they never come back?

Maribel looks up at him with sad eyes that ask him where he is.

"Oh, I'm sorry," he says, tightening his arm on her shoulder. "I just wandered off thinking about Vera and Ollie." He sniffs. "I'm sure we'll never see them again."

"It's sad," she says, "seeing them go."

"It's a sad ending to such a happy party."

They linger on the veranda, not ready yet to go inside. Maribel bites her lower lip, not knowing how to begin, and then she says softly, apologetically, "I'm so sorry about the note."

"It's not your fault. You had no way of knowing. It was always hard to predict what Ashley was going to do." Maribel shivers and snuggles closer against him.

When they step back inside together, Marco tilts an ear to listen for the baby. Angelito sleeps.

18

THE VANISHING BUTTERFLY

Out on his deck, Ollie gazes at the foothills. Gray, overcast, cold. Typical weather for March, well, for Colorado, that is. There is a light dusting of snow over the foothills, demonstrating the continuing reluctance of spring to arrive, when what he was hoping for this morning was a bold burst of sunshine like they have in Mexico, which, to tell the truth, he misses more than he thought he would. He retreats into his study and sits down at the computer to compose an email to Marquito.

The computer has always had its special place in his study at a separate desk designed especially for a computer, and, in fact, over the years he and Vera often sat together in that room, he engrossed with his reading, and she engaged with her email correspondence with her friends and erstwhile colleagues. Yesterday, their son Peter was visiting with Katie, and he helped his father review once again the steps he needs to follow to bring up his email, to Compose, to Reply, to Send. Ollie told Peter that he used his email so infrequently that in between times he forgot what to do, and Peter suggested that he write it down someplace and when he got stuck to experiment or phone him. It was surely nice to have him visit and to see Katie again, although it bothered him tremendously when she looked up at him and asked, "Where's your mommy?" He reminds himself that it is not uncommon at that age for children to think that all women are mothers. Today, Ollie has promised himself that the sun will not set without his notifying Marquito.

Dear Marquito,

I hope I don't press any of the wrong keys and that this email will reach you alright. I apologize for not writing to you earlier and for not responding to the two emails you sent to Vera previously.

I am afraid that I have some bad news. Vera died in late February of a burst aneurism in the brain. If there is a weak spot in the wall of a blood vessel, a little sac forms around it, and if this breaks open, the blood gushes uncontrolled into tissue and the oxygen supply is disrupted. In the brain the result is often fatal, as it was in her case. The doctors told me that sometimes we have these small weak spots in our blood vessels and they are hard to detect. That's why we try to keep our blood pressure low. Our fragile bodies certainly make our lives precarious. In her case, she died almost immediately and without suffering. I miss her now tremendously; we were almost like one person after having lived so happily together in marriage for so many years.

Ollie answered all of the sympathy cards he received with handwritten notes. This is the first time he has written to someone through email to tell them the news himself first hand. Spelling out the words *Vera died* conveys a crushing finality. Although, it seems that each day brings its own insidious reminder of that finality through simple daily activities such as doing the dishes alone; there are too few now to even bother with the dishwasher. He wishes he could tell Marquito how miserable he feels and how sad he is, moping around the gloomy house by himself all day long. At night, too, which is the worst time of all for loneliness. Something in his temperament demands a positive account for Marquito, to reassure him that he is doing okay.

As often happens, the person who everyone thought would die first lives on, and the one predicted to outlive the other, instead, dies prematurely and instantly. It was a terrible shock, and I am only slowly recovering emotionally.

As he reads these words, he realizes that he is not recovering from Vera's death very well at all. He needs to begin a new life, as they say, without her. That's what survivors must do. How can he possibly explain to someone as young as Marquito what it is like to lose a lifetime companion? And who wants a new life when the old life was so good? He blinks back blurry tears and continues.

The doctors at Kaiser say that I am in good health, that the treatment I had done in Mexico was excellent, and that I could live for many years.

Ollie is not sure that he wants to live many years like this, but if he is honest with himself, he has to admit that there is nothing wrong with him but his persistent grief and intolerable loneliness. He tries to stay active—that's the most common advice he gets—but believing, as he does, that most activity is a mask for an essentially meaningless existence, he finds much that he does to be pointless. In retirement, he always got up early as if to go to work even when there was no work, but now he needs to push himself to get out of bed in the morning and probably wouldn't get up at all except that his aching bones and cramping muscles scream at him to arise.

It is very hard for me to write this to you, Marquito, but I know I must. I hope the news is not too upsetting to you because I know that Vera's compassion was very important in your life. Please let me hear from you when you have a moment. I am eager to know how you and Maribel and baby Angelito are doing.
Your friend from Colorado,
Oliver Webster.
P.S. How are all of our friends from Sunset Point? Please tell them about Vera for me. I can't write to them all.

Ollie becomes aware that he is having trouble recalling the names of those friends, having relied on Vera so frequently for remembering things he couldn't. He takes out a small pad of paper and starts to compose a list of the names of the people to whom he and Vera made the small grants. If he is to come back to earth to live another life, which he surely hopes he won't, he will ask for more hard drive memory the next time around. And that reminds him that the list of names and sums of money must surely be on this damn computer somewhere, maybe in the cloud. He starts to write his hand-written list of names, anyway. Surprisingly, he remembers the names of more people than he thought he would.

As he is finishing his list, a message saying, You Have Mail, appears on the screen. Ollie opens it successfully and reads it. Marquito has written back immediately.

Dear Ollie,
I am sure you are heartbroken as I am now, having learned of Vera's death. Really, I'm stunned. Certainly, you know how much both of you

have meant to our lives. Vera first spotted Maribel's liking for me and was the one who insisted on buying that beautiful ring that eventually ended up on Maribel's finger. It was Vera's concern that helped me find my way and discover my true self. I don't know what I would have done without her advice about the baby, and I am sure that it was because of her wisdom and encouragement that Maribel and I are married and have Angelito today.

You were both there for us at important times, and we miss seeing you. Please continue to write to us and send me interesting things to read. We are all fine, gracias a Dios, and we will think of you each day now. Of course, Maribel is praying for you.

With much love,
Marquito

Naturally Marquito's email sends Ollie into another paroxysm of sobbing, but when he recovers, he actually feels good for the first time in quite a while. What better memorial for one's life than to have helped another person? And not just one, but many. He feels like lifting up his head and telling the whole world what a wonderful person Vera Webster was. Perhaps he can begin to move on.

Ellen was wonderful to him through it all. She flew in from Dallas the very next day so he spent only one night alone. She helped him arrange for a simple memorial service at the Unitarian Universalist Church down the road past the brewery, and even though he and Vera had only attended a few times years ago, the minister remembered them. Arrangements for cremation had been made long ago. After Ellen returned to Dallas, she had phoned every day to check on him for a while, but her calls have started to taper off now. While Peter kept Katie, Amanda came down to help dispose of Vera's clothing and personal belongings, and she was very organized and efficient with that. He can see why Peter likes her and needs her. After Ollie took care of everything with the organized dispatch of a lawyer: the death certificate, the will, the bank accounts, and he didn't have anything left to do. Now he realizes that he is alone and that he needs something to fill up the emptiness.

One of the big surprises for Ollie has been the amount of interest the neighbors have taken in his wellbeing. At the time of the memorial service, they brought in food—covered dishes they called them back in Vermont—and every now and then Donald still rings the doorbell and holds out a casserole his wife has prepared, usually something with noodles or rice. Most surprising has been the soccer mom across the street, Tricia, the one married to the guy who wears the long shorts and shirts with big numbers. She seems to have made Ollie into one of her pet projects, suggesting to him a gluten free diet and pushing those pep drinks she sips all day long. It's as if she's training him for the Senior Olympics. Tricia stops by in the late morning after all of the kids have been shuttled to school and asks him if he would like her to take him to the park for a walk—apparently, she doesn't own a dog—and then she asks him if he has reconsidered the senior fitness class. He accepts the invitation to walk, but graciously declines the aerobics class, unable to picture himself in spandex, moving gracefully to blaring hard rock. Nothing quite arouses pity like a lonely old man.

The caring expressed by the neighbors has made him rethink his views of them. What does it matter whether they know their lives are pointless or not when they are so darn nice to him? So, they like sports or antique cars or collecting things. So what? If the crutch helps, use it, whatever helps a person to limp through life. Is it really so bad that the neighbors haven't read, and will never read, Kafka, Sartre and Camus? At least they appear to be relatively happy, and that's more than he has going for himself right now. He revisits that old idea, namely, that life is meaningless and asks himself: If an individual life is so meaningless, why is an individual death so significant?

Ollie is not very good yet at checking his email each day, so by the time he reads Marquito's next message, it is three days old.

Dear Ollie,

I hope that you are doing better and that by now there are more good days than bad. Be assured that many friends are in mourning for Vera here in Cabo San Lucas.

I know that you are a little nervous about traveling and that you may believe that it will be impossible for you to come to Mexico without Vera, but Maribel and I have been talking about this with each other and with her grandparents, and we would like to encourage you to come to visit us. You will have many memories, but look at it this way, all of those memories are good, and what could be better for you than to relive those good times you had together? Maribel, as you know, is my teacher when it comes to Mexican culture, and she tells me that our people don't think of life and death as two separate states, but as co-mingled, life with death and death with life, so that in coming here to walk in Vera's footsteps again you can be with her and not feel so terribly alone.

Besides, Angelito needs to see his great grandfather. You can be sure that we will provide the best Mexican hospitality for you while you are here. Please give this sincere invitation your thoughtful consideration.

Your friends,

Maribel and Marquito

P.S. Maribel wants to discuss with you an opportunity she has for a privately-owned art gallery in the mall.

Well, now, this is a new idea. Visiting them in Mexico? Something he certainly would not have thought up on his own. His first reaction always is to be cautious, especially now. What if he gets sick and dies in Mexico? Well, what if he does? He has to die somewhere so why be choosy? Something intrigues him about Marquito's suggestion. He must surely give it some consideration.

For two days he is not able to stop thinking about the invitation from Marquito and Maribel. Could this be exactly what he needs? He can't spend the rest of his life under a cloud of gloom. Perhaps he had grown too dependent on Vera, expecting her to be his administrative assistant, travel agent, and part time memory. It might be good for this old dog to learn some new tricks, take care of himself, be on his own. He has a sense that these young people have something to teach him, and of course, being Ollie, he will never miss an opportunity to learn.

This morning Ollie feels like he is moving toward a decision to go to Mexico. He smiles about how he and Vera made decisions. Actually, he never made decisions, he just moved toward them and then she would push him over the edge, something like El Greco falling over the railing that day at the resort. He thinks of asking Ellen to go with him, but decides that she might not be all that comfortable in Mexico. So why not go alone?

Ollie sends an email to Marquito to tell him that he has decided to come to Cabo and that he has asked Rosita to book two weeks in late April and early May. He asks Marquito to tell him more about Maribel's idea for a gallery. Marquito replies the next day.

Dear Ollie,

Maribel and I are really excited to see you and have you see Angelito again. I know you will love him. Each day he has a little more personality. They say he looks mostly like me, which is good, I guess, and so far, he is only manic.

You asked me to tell you more about Maribel's idea for the gallery. A space has come open in the Paraíso Mall, a small area facing along that wing beyond the escalators. She checked with Doña Conchita and Don Pedro about displaying some of their work there, and they have some other artists from Todos Santos who are also interested. Maribel has a sizable portfolio herself now and would like to try to sell some of her work as well. We would take things on consignment and sell what we can. We are hesitating because we don't know if we can sell enough to cover the rent in the beginning. Mainly, Maribel wants to know if you think it is a good business idea. We will discuss it when you get here.

With open arms to embrace you when you arrive,
Marquito

A good idea? Of course, it is a good idea, with all of the tourists that come through that town, with the new condominiums that need to be furnished, and the hotels that are constantly remodeling. If those kids wait, they will lose that space and someone else will take it. Every new business needs startup capital. He emails Marquito back directly.

Marquito,

It is a fantastic idea. You must know the expression we have in English from your background in running track: "He who hesitates is lost." Move ahead with plans to lease the space immediately. I will set up a fund that you can draw on to finance the first two years. Give me a few days to contact Scotia Bank, but please move ahead. U.S. dollars are on the way. Look in your bank account in a few days. Keep your jobs at the resort as long as possible.

Your friend and benefactor,
Ollie Webster

Good. This gives him something to do for the next few days. He will go to the broker tomorrow and instruct him to sell off another $50,000. He will put it in FirstBank in Golden and send a bank transfer to Mexico. How exciting! Now he can begin to think about what to pack for the trip.

Having successfully negotiated immigration and customs, Ollie finds himself unexpectedly filled with anticipation as he rides in the van from Los Cabos Airport to the resort. The guests sharing the ride are first-time visitors, a family of five, so he points out the native five-pronged desert cactus, the first glimpses of the sea along the way, and the new bridges and road. As the van passes through the cultivated pink and burgundy bougainvillea lining the gated driveway up to Sunset Point, he tells the children to order quesadillas and check out the parasailing. He steps from the van and the flurry of welcomes begins. Nothing is changed because Vera is not there, and if anything, there is more fuss than ever. "Bienvenido," says Sebastián.

"Welcome Señor Oily," says Óscar, as he unloads Ollie's solitary suitcase. "Just this?"

As Ollie signs the registration materials and picks up the cards – there is only one of each – Verónica tells him how sorry she was to hear about Vera. He nods and swallows hard. The concerned looks on the faces of the staff, the sudden dropping of eyes to the floor, tell him that she is missed even though everything proceeds exactly as if she were in their midst.

As if dropped from the dome in the lobby, Marquito and Maribel suddenly appear with little Angelito, who is really not so ito anymore. He's almost nine months now. Angelito reaches out his arms for Ollie, so Ollie scoops him up and curls a long arm around him. Angelito coos and smiles while Ollie and Maribel make arrangements for a visit to the gallery the next day.

"I'm sorry about Vera," Maribel says, touching his arm. "I know you have been suffering. We hope we can make you happy here."

"I'm happy just standing here holding this baby."

When he gets off of the elevator at the seventh floor, he pauses to take in the view of the swimming pools and the sea. When he is satisfied that he is once again in paradise, he sets off down the hallway following the pathway marked by the pattern of the more decorative little light blue and gray tiles set against the larger tiles of burnt orange. He remembers Carmelita sweeping all day long. When Óscar arrives with his suitcase, he tips him the usual, and Óscar shakes his head, as if to suggest too much. Ollie puts his shirts and trousers on hangers and his underwear and bathing suit in the chest of drawers. So far, so good. But then he remembers sipping the welcome wine on the balcony with Vera and decides he can't do that alone.

The next morning, Ollie goes down to breakfast at eight o'clock sharp, but neither Marquito nor Maribel is on duty because they are waiting for him at the gallery. Rather than explain his special breakfast order to a new waiter, Ollie opts for the buffet. He wanders from one serving area to the next to gather up a scoop of fried potatoes, a breakfast burrito, and a few crisp slices of bacon along with raisin-filled sweet rolls. When he returns to his table, the other settings of silverware and glasses have been removed, leaving only his. He places his mounded plate there and decides to stand at the rail and have a look at the ocean. The vendors, as always dressed in white jackets, pants and sneakers, are already moving silently along the beach like meandering ghosts, and the water taxis are idling just off shore looking for their first customers. Sunlight from a bright golden sphere still low in its arc, catches the tops of the waves, setting off a glint of sparkles jumping here and there at random, like little lights flashing on and off, as they bounce up from the sea. He turns, as if to comment on the magical splendor to Vera, and realizes that there is no Vera with whom to share it. He can't control his tears. Has he made a terrible mistake in coming here alone? Will he have two miserable weeks of unrelieved mourning? He needs to pull himself together.

Ollie makes it through breakfast and decides he'd better go back to the room to check his bloodshot eyes. With cupped hands, as if bending over a stream, he scoops cold water to his face. He changes into a patterned shirt, something a little happier with white and blue palm leaves. After a few deep breaths he descends to the lobby. "Buenos días," Señor Oily. "Buenos días, Verónica." Óscar asks if he needs anything, and Ollie says he would like to take a taxi to the Paraíso Mall. "No problema," he responds as he pushes the call button.

The attendant opens the door of the taxi as he arrives at the entrance to the mall, and soon he has pushed through the revolving door into the air-conditioned interior. He is eager to get a look at the gallery. When he finds it, Maribel and Marquito are both there to greet him. Ollie glances around to check out the location in the mall, the position of the gallery relative to the other shops, and the displays in the gallery windows. He steps inside and nods approvals. "You've done a lot of work in a short time."

"With your help and encouragement, Señor," Maribel says. "We wouldn't have done it otherwise."

Nothing makes Ollie happier than to see Marquito and Maribel prospering. "And where is Angelito this morning?" he asks.

"In the back with my mother," Maribel says. "You want to see him?"

"Can I hold him?"

"If he's not sleeping." She gives him one of her smiles with the dimples and it sends him back through what seems like eons of memories.

In no time she returns with Angelito and her mother. The little angel spots Ollie and holds out his arms again. Ollie has the little sack of sugar slung over his shoulder as Maribel begins to show the various works in the gallery, beginning with a nicely framed etching of butterflies by Doña Conchita. Next to that print are several new sketches with the butterfly motif, where the face comes out of a butterfly, or the butterfly comes out of a face. "Abuela discovered that some of the ancients believed that the human soul when freed of its body comes to rest briefly in the form of a butterfly," Maribel says.

Marco, who never leaves her side, says, "I just don't see how that could be."

To which Maribel replies firmly, "But we don't know that it can't be. Right? Remember our agreement?"

"Very interesting," Ollie nods, "like returning to the substance of the universe." Moving along to another area, they show him some small bronze castings and wood sculptures by Don Pedro. "And what is this?" Ollie asks, pointing to a large skeleton-like figure of polished tree branches carved into the shape of bones and cleverly assembled into a figure conveying a confident nonchalance.

"Oh, that's Abuelo's work, it's called 'Mocking Death.' There's a cultural tradition in Mexico of making fun of death, reminding us of our mortality. We have a celebration called 'The Day of the Dead,' and people dress up in costumes of skeletons, put on death masks, and decorate themselves with skulls. On that day, you can even go to the panadería and buy bread shaped in the form of bones." Suddenly Maribel is speechless. A look of dismay crosses her face as she looks up at Ollie and puts a hand over her mouth. "Oh, I am so sorry. This must be very painful for you. How thoughtless of me."

"No, not at all. I would like to learn more," Ollie replies. "Please continue."

"Seriously?" she squints. "Well, if you look closely at Don Pedro's work you will see one arm stretched out in front in a lively playful gesture clearing the way, but notice how the other elbow is held out, as if to invite us to latch on and go for a walk."

"Making death more familiar, less uncomfortable when it comes, as it will," Ollie says.

"Exactly. For us, death is not something to be hidden away. We pronounce the word death comfortably. We not only look at it and face it, we are fascinated with it."

Marco taps her arm. "Tell him about the ancients," he says.

"Yes, this is interesting. They didn't believe that their lives belonged to themselves, so how can you lose what isn't yours in the first place? The Aztecs, with their belief in cycles of continuous regeneration believed that death sparks the creative forces of new life. Abuelo is really into all of this, so here we are with his odd sculpture standing right here in our new gallery greeting our customers as they come through the door. But it has its beauty, too, don't you think?"

Angelito begins to fuss a little, so Maribel's mother takes him and returns to the back of the shop. Maribel points out the work of several artists from Todos Santos, including watercolors, ceramics, and very modern looking works of blown glass. To one side is a stack of hand-loomed rugs from a friend in Oaxaca. Ollie notices several nicely framed abstract blue and yellow watercolor and ink paintings with the shapes of fish. He notices the signature. "Why, these are yours, Maribel." Ollie points to them and says, "They are beautiful." She nods and smiles, saying thank-you, moving to another aisle. "And what is this over here?" he asks, pointing to a shelf of brightly-colored little dragon like figures.

"Oh, there's an artist in Mexico City who makes these highly decorated figures out of cardboard and papier-mâché. They are representations of ancient animal gods. His are over four meters high, and I have no budget or studio for such huge works, so I've adapted the idea to a much smaller scale."

"Dragonitos, I call them. They're cute, don't you think?" Marquito asks.

"Smaller gods are always better," Ollie quips with a twinkle in his eye directed toward Marquito. "I love the bright colors and those intricate patterns"

"Very Mexican, Señor, wouldn't you say?" Marquito asks.

"Yes, indeed, but I can't quite explain why."

After a brief silence, Marquito says, we want to thank you again for helping us get started. We wouldn't have done it without your encouragement."

"And how is it doing, if I may ask?"

"Well, our accountant here, "Maribel beams at Marquito, "tells me that it is not only paying the rent, but turning a profit already."

"You have many fine things here," Ollie says.

"But they sell," Marco points out, "because she describes everything so well. She opens the eyes of the customers, and when they see they buy."

As Ollie is drifting around examining everything more closely, Maribel comes up to him, takes his arm, pulls him aside, and speaks to him in a quiet serious voice, "Oh, Señor, we want to invite you to the Iglesia San Lucas on Saturday morning at eleven o'clock for a memorial service for Vera. You see, many of the staff at the hotel knew you both, like you were our honorary grandparents, part of our family, and they are also grieving now that Vera is gone. Everyone has been asking me and Marquito to hold a service so that we can remember and honor Vera properly. I know that you had a service in Colorado, but I hope you will join us. Abuelo and Abuela will be driving down from Todos Santos and they will pick you up at the resort and bring you back, if that works for you. Can we count on you?"

Ollie hesitates. If it is a Catholic church it will have a Catholic service, and he won't know what to do—when to stand, when to sit—and if he has to kneel, he's sure he will have trouble getting back up again. He remembers as a boy growing up in Vermont, he told his parents that he had a crush on an Irish girl, and they had a hissy-fit. They told him he would have to "turn Catholic," what, like he might have to "turn green" to become Irish? Such silly prejudices he has had to overcome. He swallows hard. "Of course, Maribel, what a thoughtful gesture," he says, even though he doesn't particularly want to sit through another service. What will he do without Vera to help him through it? Then he notices that his acceptance has put a smile on Maribel's face that doesn't fade. He won't tell her that he doesn't go to church.

Maribel's grandparents find a place to park the car not far from Iglesia San Lucas, and Ollie climbs up the steps leading past the high stone wall and passes through the iron gate. Arriving early, they have a choice of seats, but Ollie wants to be seated near the back on the aisle where he can watch the proceedings from a distance or escape if he starts sobbing and can't handle it. Marquito, Maribel, and her grandparents go to the front. The small church is in a cruciform with seating in each of the transepts as well as where he is seated at the back of the nave. As he looks forward, he notices two painted lifelike statues, one on the right which must surely be Mary, and another on the left, a bearded man holding up a scroll, as if to signify one of the Gospel writers. It dawns on him that it must be Saint Luke, of course, as in San Lucas. A small crucifix is attached to the unadorned wall behind the altar.

Ollie takes from his pocket the list of names he has composed and studies it so that he can greet Vera's friends—well, they are his friends, too—by name. As they arrive, they come up, one by one, to speak to Ollie, and he greets them. Rosita, and the boys, Fernando and Alfredo. Daniella and her daughters, Cena and Blanca. Lino, Ernesto, Óscar, Sebastián. Isabella and Solomón have driven over with Suzette. Carmelita hands him a paper flower. The church seems to be filling up with many other people as well, some familiar faces he has seen around the resort, but he fails to recognize others, simple people, humbly dressed. Did Vera know so many people? Did they know her or just know about her?

People chatter while they are filing in, but there is a hush when the priests come down the aisle, a younger man who looks handsome in his vestments, and an older priest with grey hair, followed by someone in a white surplice who appears to be too old for an altar boy, maybe some kind of assistant or just a supernumerary. As the church grows quiet, it also takes on the humble air of holiness, signaling that what takes place within its space is sacred. The young priest says some words that appear to be a welcome. Prayers are followed by music, a soft unfamiliar song sung meekly by the congregation. As the service progresses, Ollie notices an interesting phenomenon. The spoken words are in Spanish or Latin, neither of which he understands very well, and he can skip over the issues of belief that always entangle his skeptical mind. Now he can focus on the music, the movements and gestures of the clergy, and the mood created by the soft light streaming through the clear windows.

Three women are singing the "Dona, Nobis, Pacem" as a round, Verónica along with two others who work with her in the lobby at the resort. After more words from the younger priest, an older woman sings the "Ave Maria" very beautifully. This is a memorial service, but there is what appears to be a consecration of the bread and wine, and an invitation to Holy Communion to Catholics. After they come forward down the center aisle and return to their seats by the aisles at the side, the young priest invites Maribel to say something, so she comes forward. The priest looks like he knows her and he smiles at her tenderly.

She speaks rapidly in Spanish, and Ollie catches only a word here and there, but her face is so animated and expressive, and her gestures are so instructive, nearly a pantomime, that he knows she is speaking of Vera's simple acts of kindness, of her caring for each individual, her thoughtfulness and respect, and her gifts brought to Mexico in extra suitcases. Maribel seems to be thanking Vera, as if she were there. Ollie sees the backs of heads nodding agreement, and he thinks he hears some sobs and sniffling.

When Maribel has finished, she returns to her place beside Marquito and her grandparents. The older priest says some words now, and Ollie thinks he recognizes espíritu and cielo, something about spirit rising to heaven. The assistant helps light incense in a small gold container which the older priest waves about here and there across the steps leading up to the altar and the small carved wood crucifix. Soon the incense drifts back across those assembled. Ollie smells its sweet pungent odor and likes it. Then the young priest raises his arms up and outward and pronounces what must be a benediction.

People begin to whisper, stand up, and then step into the aisles. Ollie wants to hold on to these wonderful quiet moments in the church because of the sense of Vera's presence he had there. When Maribel spoke, it was as if she were speaking directly to Vera seated before her in the front row. When the light came through the windows, it felt like Vera's spirit riding in on a sunbeam through particles of dust. When the priest raised his arms toward the ceiling and looked up, it was as if he could see her up there somewhere. There was something quite mystical about it all, which Ollie had never experienced until now. Death in life, life in death, indeed.

Ollie stands up and greets people again as they leave the small oasis of holiness. Some offer their condolences in English, and of those who speak Spanish he hears over and over the words pésame and sentimiento. When Maribel and Marquito come back from the front of the church with her grandparents, they also bring the younger priest with them. "I want you to meet Padre Carlos," she says. "He married us in his church in Todos Santos. He has been a very special person in my life." They exchange greetings and condolences, and then Maribel says, "I'm sorry it was all in Spanish, but not many people speak good English. Did you understand?"

"Yes, Maribel, I understood. Not the words, but the sense of the sacred. It struck me that somehow church is better without words. Turning toward the priest he says, "Thank you for this beautiful service." Padre Carlos smiles.

Don Pedro tugs on his beard and says, "I've never thought that religion was about belief. More about this sense of the sacred you mention." Doña Conchita nods her agreement.

Ollie spends the afternoon beside the pool. He reads a little and catches a cat nap. Then he decides to get in the pool. He tests the temperature of the water with the toes of one foot as he holds the railing in the center of the broad descending steps. Not bad at all, amazingly warm, but he hasn't been swimming since he can't remember when. He eases into the pool and slides onto his back to see if he can still do the Resting Backstroke he learned as a kid on a lake in Vermont. It's odd how the body, actually the brain, never forgets how to swim or ride a bicycle. He reminds himself that the water supports the body if you let it. How pleasant it is gliding along looking up at the dark green palm leaves against the cloudless sky. He lets his feet down and turns around to check how far he has swum, not wanting to smack his noggin on the tiles at the end of the pool. He switches directions and makes his way back down the length of the pool. He does two more laps and decides that his creaky body has had enough swimming.

He grabs the handrail and climbs out. He dries off a little and then goes over to the hot tub. Funny thing, he hasn't been in the hot tub recently either. Why hasn't he been doing these things he enjoys so much? Vera never liked the water much—or was it wearing a bathing suit?—but that didn't mean he couldn't go in. Agua caliente. Hotter than he had remembered, but so soothing and relaxing with those hot jets and the bubbling sensation. A woman sitting on the edge of the tub with two young children gives him that poor-lonely-old-man look, but he doesn't feel alone.

Ever since the church service this morning, he has felt Vera close to him. He no longer finds it painful to remember her. In fact, it's quite enjoyable to think about her, his way of keeping her near to him. He marvels at how the mind can chop experience into little memories that can be stored and recalled, remembrances that can reach quite far back into the past, yet appear to be of the present moment. Vera buying the first timeshare. Marquito's intense anger. Maribel in her chef's hat cooking up special orders. Vera buying that ring. Ashley giving the little kids the Mayan Rain Dance itch. Poor Ashley, she's gone, too. What he likes to remember most is Vera encouraging him to make those gifts to their friends. Not much money really, but at least he and Vera were able to make a few people happy and secure. He gets out of the hot tub, dries off, and leaves his towel at the poolside desk. The attendant there is someone he doesn't recognize, but the two of them exchange friendly greetings anyway. Never too late to make a new friend.

He goes up to the room, and after a shower, he dresses in shorts and a polo shirt. He slides open the patio door and steps out onto the balcony. His wet bathing suit is arranged over the lounge chair to dry. Someone has published a book with the title The Meaning of Existence, and of course he couldn't pass that up. Intending to read—there is still time before the sun sets—he sits down in the chair at the table out there, but his mind is full of memories, more recent memories this time: Marquito and Maribel showing him through the gallery. The brilliant art of butterflies, fish, and bones. Baby Angelito at home in his arms. It's as if they have become part of his family, his son and daughter-in-law and his grandchild. Will they take care of him in his old age? He smiles to himself. They are taking care of him. He can't begin to measure their genuine affection or what he has learned from them today. They've already paid him back in happiness. How could he even think of not coming back to Mexico to visit them? Of course he will return.

He places his open book face down to hold his place and stares out into the open space above the swimming pools. What puzzles him about Mexico is the wealth of spiritual riches among the poverty. Bright colors decorating drab surroundings. Art full of ancient mysteries and modern styles. He takes a deep breath and listens for a moment to the waves. How can there be so much happiness among people who have known such suffering? Perpetual friendliness among those who have experienced so much rejection? People with so few belongings but a wealth of wisdom. And this morning, that sense of the sacred conveyed by traditional beliefs and practices. Even the delectable food is made from simple ingredients.

He is submerged in solitude, pleasantly lost in his thoughts. Maybe he has dozed off. Is he dreaming? On the back of the opposite chair a delicate yellow butterfly alights, flapping its wings gently up and down, as if to say, I'm here. How did the little creature get up so high, or did it just drop down from heaven? He stares at it. His mind says, that's impossible, but he remembers Maribel's words: we don't know that it can't be. Before he can decide what to think, the butterfly flutters its fragile yellow wings, lifts off from the chair, and continues meandering on its fleeting journey, vanishing before his eyes.

ACKNOWLEDGEMENTS

A fiction writer draws on many sources, but the most important of these is imagination, the capacity to turn important information, personal experiences, and ordinary events into an extraordinary story. Having spent many years as a professor and dean, I am very much aware of the need in non-fiction, academic writing to document sources. In fiction writing, custom discourages the use of footnotes, and the sources used by the author often go unacknowledged.

Three non-fiction works have been important as sources of information in the writing of this novel:

Amy S. Greenberg, *A Wicked War*. New York: Alfred A. Knopf, 2012.
Octavio Paz, *The Labyrinth of Solitude*. New York: Grove Press, 1961 and 1985.
Peter Eichstaedt, *The Dangerous Divide: Peril and Promise on the US-Mexico Border*. Chicago: Lawrence Books, 2014.

The following works are mentioned or alluded to in the novel:

Albert Camus, *The Stranger*. New York: Vintage Books, Random House, 1989. Originally published in France in 1947.
———, *The Plague*. New York: Vintage Books, Random House, 1991. Originally published in France in 1947.
Franz Kafka, "The Metamorphosis" in *Selected Stories of Franz Kafka*. New York: Random House, The Modern Library, 1952. Originally published in Prague in 1936.

The philosophical work quoted and alluded to is:

Jean-Paul Sartre, *Existentialism and Human Emotions.* New York: Kensington Publishing Corp., 1957. This book draws on sections of two other books written by Sartre, *Existentialism* and *Being and Nothingness*, published earlier in France and translated to English by Bernard Fechtman and Hazel E. Barnes, respectively.

In addition, I want to acknowledge the many people who have been important sources of information about Cabo San Lucas and Mexican culture, but here I need to be careful so as not to identify any real-life persons who might be confused with characters in the novel. Although I have borrowed some wonderful Mexican names, I have been careful to disguise identities, as if to drop the names in a big bowl, stir them up, and pull them out for the fictional characters. If any of you think you recognize yourselves or your friends, then my disguise has been incomplete, but please keep in mind that this is fiction and similarities are coincidental, not intentional. I want to thank my many Mexican amigos in a general way for their friendship, and as individuals for sharing their lives and in some cases showing me around town. I won't name names, but you know who you are, and I want to extend sincere thanks to you for being so open, friendly, and helpful.

Fiction writers often receive help in plot, character development, and the means of expression, including not only line editing but larger narrative issues. For this book I worked with Coralie Hunter, Editorial Consultant, formerly of New York City. Thanks to Cory for her patience, persistence, intelligent ideas, and concern for correct expression and accuracy.

For inspiration, I surely want to thank my wife, Adelaide Bouchardet Davis, not just for keeping me motivated to write this novel, but for her actual concrete suggestions for certain parts of the story that I never would have imagined on my own. I often turned to her to ask of my characters, as if they were real people: What will they do now? For the twists and turns and surprises in this story, we have Adelaide to thank. After this manuscript was completed and revised, and just a few months before it was published in its present form, Adelaide died of heart failure, having struggled for many years with a cardiac condition. Now I think I know how Ollie feels.

READERS GUIDE

1. Marco was the son of undocumented Mexican parents working in the US. He was raised in America, where he attended public schools and absorbed the culture, so it is natural that he was filled with dreams about an exciting future. Is the word *dreamer* useful for describing people like Marco? Is it a familiar concept?

2. Some "dreamers," for one reason or another, must return to Mexico from the US. What can that do to their life? Why?

3. Marco, sometimes referred to as Marquito, discovers that he is seriously disadvantaged in building a new life in Mexico. What is he facing? How does it make him feel to be a waiter at a stylish seaside resort? Is this his "last resort," so to speak? How does he become a hero?

4. Vera and Ollie, an older couple, financially secure in retirement, meet Marquito, where he works as a breakfast waiter at their time-share resort. They appear to have uncertainties and dreams of their own. What are they searching for?

5. Marco meets Ashley, the red-haired, run-away radical, who starts to lead him down a path that could get him into serious trouble. Can you remember a time when you fell in with the "wrong crowd" of so-called friends? If so, how do you look back on that now?

6. Vera and Ollie want to help people. Is giving people money helpful? Why do people sometimes refuse or resist assistance? Do Vera and Ollie also provide something more? What?

7. As Marco falls in love with Maribel and begins to discover the "real Mexico," through her grandparents, he receives some very shocking news from Ashley and turns to Vera for advice. What do you think of Vera's suggestions and Marco's decisions? Was this the best option?

8. Maribel also has some shocking news. Do things like this actually happen to young women? What do you think about the way the situation was handled? How has it affected Maribel?

9. Ollie worries that his life may have been pointless. He and Vera want to create a legacy. What are some of the things people do to make sure they leave a legacy?

10. The loss of a spouse, when lives have been positively intertwined as they were with Vera and Ollie, can often be very painful. How is grieving portrayed here? Will it help, or is there really no relief from grief?

www.ingramcontent.com/pod-product-compliance
Lightning Source LLC
Chambersburg PA
CBHW010746310726
48980CB00004B/378

* 9 7 8 1 6 3 2 9 3 6 3 8 7 *